Long Ago Memories

By

Judith Ann McDowell

World Castle Publishing
http://www.worldcastlepublishing.com

Judith Ann McDowell

This is a work of fiction. Names, characters, places, and incidents are products of the author's imagination or are used fictitiously and are not to be construed as real. Any resemblance to actual events, locations, organizations, or person, living or dead, is entirely coincidental.

World Castle Publishing
Pensacola, Florida

Copyright © Judith Ann McDowell 2010
ISBN: 9781937593407
First Edition 2010
Second Edition World Castle Publishing December 15, 2011
http://www.worldcastlepublishing.com

Cover Art: Karen Fuller
Editor: Beth Price

Dedication:

For Dale and Linda Curtiss my real life Eathen and Charlotte Thornton.

LONG AGO MEMORIES

A person dreams many dreams
But are they really dreams
Or...Long Ago Memories?

Chapter One
Cut Bank, Montana 1921

Low peals of thunder rumbled overhead as the Great Northern moved along the tracks at top speed, passing scattered ranch houses and open range in its haste. The sharp blast from the train's whistle echoed out over the desolate countryside, its incessant warning sending cattle, straying too close to the tracks, scurrying for cover.

Leaning forward in her seat, a young girl peered through the dirty window at the vast Montana prairie. Her almond-shaped brown eyes wide with alarm as she thought about all the trouble, perhaps, awaiting her in just a few short moments. She had been so sure her decision to wait until she had arrived at the train's depot before sending a wire to her grandmother advising her of her impending visit to Montana, had been the right thing to do. Now however as her long trip from Boston trickled down to a few short moments, she questioned the wisdom of such an impulsive move.

Brushing her long, dark-brown hair back from her face, she stared out at the land she had, thus far never seen before except in her dreams. Choosing not to dwell, right at that moment, on her night time illusions or the ever-present man who walked beside her in those nocturnal wanderings, she turned her attention away from the window to settle herself into a more comfortable position. Laying her head back against the seat cushion, she closed her eyes.

Unbidden, the faces of the two people she had always accepted as her mother and father pushed their way forward into her mind. They would be beside themselves when they learned she had gone against their wishes and taken it upon herself, at long last, to go to Montana, the one place in all her many travels, including Europe, she had always been forbidden to visit. Now, as a grown woman of seventeen, she felt it should be left to her choosing where she traveled. If closing her mind to the irrational fears of those around her meant she would finally know the truth, then so be it. If they truly loved her, as she knew deep in her heart they did, then she reasoned they would have to understand and forgive.

Too many questions had been left unanswered. Such as why, in all her years of growing up, she had never been invited to visit her grandmother in Montana. Instead, every summer, her grandmother had traveled the many miles to visit her in Boston. At first, this had not seemed strange, but as she grew older she found herself wondering why she had never been asked to visit the very house where her mother had been born and raised. Why she had never met her grandfather; had never even received a letter from him. And most important of all, why couldn't she ever get a straight answer to her questions about her father? As these thoughts skipped through her mind, she felt the train begin to lose speed. All too soon it braked to a complete stop in front of the Cut Bank depot.

With a resigned sigh she got to her feet. "There's no turning back now," she murmured, nodding to the woman across the aisle staring in open-mouth envy at her fashionable long, dark green woolen skirt, white silk blouse, and matching dark green woolen jacket. The rich color a striking contrast against her deep olive complexion. With a nervous smile she gathered her belongings.

Stepping down from the train she stood for a moment, trying to discern a familiar face among the curiously-dressed people moving at a fast pace all around her. To her surprise she noticed most of the men wore guns strapped to their hips.

"Tia, over here child," called out a well-known voice. Tia looked up to see her grandmother standing across the way waving her forward. With suitcase in hand, she began making her way across the busy street when the outraged shriek of a reined in horse grabbed her attention.

"You need to watch where the hell you're goin', squaw, fore you get run over!" the angry young man in the saddle yelled.

Before Tia could comment on the man's rude behavior, she saw him yanked from his horse to be sent sprawling into the muddy street. With a muttered curse and a loud, sour smelling belch the young man regained his footing but found his legs knocked out from beneath him once more. Not to be outdone, he tried pushing himself into a sitting position when he felt a hand grab the back of his neck, then jerk him to his feet. The cold green eyes of the man still holding him left no doubt in his mind as to the seriousness of his mistake.

"You owe this young lady an apology," the tall lean man breathed before releasing him.

"Yeah...I guess I do." the cowboy stammered, stooping to pick up his hat. Before replacing it on his head he muttered, "Sorry, ma'am. Guess I shoulda looked closer."

Nodding, Tia turned to the handsome, sable-haired man, watching her. "Thank you, but I'm all right now." A pleased smile touched his face as he placed her hand in the crook of his arm to escort her the rest of the way across the street.

"What brought all that on, Jed?" Charlotte asked, moving nearer to her granddaughter.

"It was my fault, Gram," Tia spoke up. "In my haste to get to you I almost caused that poor man to have an accident."

"From where I stood, it looked like he did anyway." Charlotte eyed her rugged foreman, then turned her gaze on Tia. "I can't say I didn't feel some unease when I received your wire tellin' me about your impending visit, but now that you're here we'll have to make the best of it."

In a trembling voice, Tia asked the question upper-most on her mind. "Is Grandfather Eathen angry about my coming?"

"He don't know anything about it," Charlotte laced their hands, turned them in the direction of a mud-spattered Buick parked up the street. "He's away on business at the state capitol, in Helena. With any luck we can have a nice little visit and you can be gone before he gets back." At the girl's sharp intake of breath, Charlotte stopped walking. "I know that sounds cold, Tia and I don't mean it to be, but it's for the best."

Before Tia could comment on what seemed to her, a less than ardent welcome, Jed arrived with the rest of her belongings.

"Get Tia's things loaded up, Jed, so we can go home." Charlotte pushed the front seat forward. "The two of you can sit up front. I'd appreciate it if you'd keep your voices down though, so I can get some sleep on the way back. I ain't as young as I used to be, and this little surprise, is probably gonna cost me the few good years I had left."

Seating herself as close to the car door as she could, Tia kept her face turned from the man sitting beside her as he turned the key then pushed the button, bringing the big car to life. She could feel his eyes on her as they pulled away from the curb. Instead of acknowledging his curious stare, she remained silent, thinking on the problems she had caused by being here. Her grandmother did not act happy to see her. She had made that quite clear. Could it be the workings of an over-tired mind or did she really glimpse fear in the small woman's blue eyes when she had mentioned her grandfather?

Focusing her mind on the countryside, Tia marveled at the vast foothills surrounded by huge snow-capped mountains. The rain-scented air flowing through the partially open window filled her with a sense of freedom. The smile she turned to Jed held the sheer pleasure she felt at the moment.

"It's a lot different out here ain't it?" he breathed, being sure to keep his voice low.

"It's lovely, and so open." She turned her attention back to the rural scene flashing past her window. "Back home the streets are always so crowded and noisy. I envy you, Jed. You must love it here."

With a slight nod, he stared straight ahead. "It suits me. I've lived here almost twenty-six- years, and I'll probably die here. Folks in this part of the country don't go in much for change. They marry early, start their families, and hope for lots of sons to help out on the ranch. That is, if they're lucky enough to have a ranch."

Before she thought, Tia replied, "Then there are those lucky enough to have the ranch, but not fortunate enough to have a son."

Glancing at her, he wondered why her arrival caused such unrest in the Thornton household. He had been at the house the night before, when Tia's telegram had arrived. After reading its contents, Charlotte had handed it to him. *"Jed, this ranch could be in for a storm the likes of which you've never seen. But I've weathered storms before. If our luck holds, Eathen'll stay in Helena the full two weeks like he planned, and that'll give me enough time to pack that little girl back to Boston where she belongs."*

His thoughts returned to the present as he felt Tia nudge him, her melodious voice commanding his complete attention.

"Jed, who is that odd-looking man out there?" she whispered pointing off to his left. Following her direction, Jed chuckled as he saw the man who had her so interested.

Dressed in his buckskins and wide brimmed hat, his long gray hair blowing in the wind as he rode across the prairie astride his black mount, he offered forth a sight to behold; especially to a young girl like Tia. As they passed, the man raised his hand in greeting. Jed smiled, returning the salute.

"Nobody knows for sure who he is, or where he comes from. Rumor has it his mother walked away from him and the Indians raised him. Everyone around here just calls him Wolfer, 'cause that's how he lives. Sometimes when the food gets scarce the wolves move down outta the hills and start attackin' the cattle, 'specially the newborns. The ranchers agreed to pay Wolfer two dollars a head for each one he brings in. He may look strange but he does a lotta good around this part of the country."

"It's all so new and exciting." Tia placed a slender hand on Jed's arm. "I feel as though I'm stepping into a whole new way of life. I can't wait to see the ranch. How much further is it?"

"Just up around the next bend," he replied, caught up in her eagerness.

Directly ahead, Tia saw a large wooden archway. The name "Thornton" had been burned into the wood in big, bold letters. Yellow Jonquils, still damp with the rains of the season, dotted the vast road leading up to a two-story log house. A short, stout black woman stood on the front porch watching them as they drove up.

"We're home, Miss Charlotte," Jed declared over his shoulder.

Leaning forward, Charlotte yawned then rubbed her eyes. "There's Hattie, and she's got her hands on her hips. A sure sign she ain't happy." Charlotte leaned toward the open window. "Hello, Hattie. We're back."

"'Bout time, too." Hattie mumbled, making her way down the porch steps.

Walking around the car Jed opened the door for Tia. As she stepped out, he pulled the seat forward, then stood back holding out his hand. "Let me help you there, Miss Charlotte."

"I can make it just fine on my own, Jed, if you'd get the hell outta my way and give me some room. If you really wanna help, you can start by takin' Tia's things inside."

Unable to contain herself any longer Hattie pulled a surprised Tia into her large arms. "Ah's been waitin' a lotta y'ars ter lays mah ole eyes on you, chile," she cried, holding her at arm's length to scan her small face. "You's jes' as pretty as yo' mama wuz." She pulled Tia against her mammoth bosom.

"All right, we can do our visitin' inside. No sense encouragin' that sky." Charlotte swung her head to the east where a smattering of ominous black clouds gathered. On the porch she turned to eye Jed as he walked towards her, his arms filled with luggage.

"Jed, put everything in the room farthest down the hall. That was your mother's room, Tia." She motioned the young girl forward. "I think you'll be most comfortable there." She pushed open the door, then stood back to let Jed go by.

Following Charlotte inside, Tia looked around the older house surprised to find it decorated in such good taste. Off to her left she could see a spacious parlor furnished in dove-gray leather. The much-polished hardwood floor, bordering a large Spanish-print rug, glistened with the reflection of the flames from a floor-to-ceiling fireplace. Its crackling warmth beckoned her. Without waiting to be asked, Tia stepped into the room.

High above the huge rock fireplace she saw a painting. The young girl smiling down at her seemed somewhat familiar. Walking nearer, Tia studied the striking features closer. The girl in the picture wore a gown of azure velvet. Her dark auburn hair swirled in wild disarray around her shoulders as though caught up by a strong wind. A slight hint of mischief showed in the large deep--set blue eyes and in the full pink mouth parted in laughter.

Stepping closer, Tia looked at the bottom of the painting to see an inscription, inlaid in gold and printed in small black letters. The inscription read, "Jessie Thornton, 1902". Now Tia knew why she looked so familiar.

Totally captivated, she could only stand in silence, staring at the beautiful vision before her. At the light touch on her arm, Tia turned to find Charlotte beside her. As her gaze fell once more on the painting, she whispered, "How beautiful she looked."

"Yes," Charlotte nodded, feeling again, that same dull ache each time she looked upon the portrait of her child, "my Jessie was a rare flower. Your grandfather tried to talk me into taking that paintin' down after her death, but he coulda saved his breath. It's hung in that exact spot for almost eighteen years. Far as I'm concerned it's gonna stay there."

Without warning, the long trip, and all she had had to endure to leave the safety of her sheltered life in Boston took its toll. Walking to the long sofa she slumped down, no longer able to contain the emotions spilling forth.

Motioning for Hattie to leave them alone, Charlotte sat down beside her. Pulling a white cotton handkerchief from her skirt pocket she handed it to Tia. "I know you gotta right to know 'bout your mama and I can understand you wantin' to come here. What I can't understand is John and Martha allowin' you to come. The day I signed the papers, givin' them the legal right to raise you John made me a promise. He promised he'd let you come if we sent for you but if we didn't then you would remain in Boston where you belong. I can't believe he went back on his word."

With both hands Tia pushed her long hair behind her ears, then dried her eyes. "He and Mother don't know anything about my coming here. I didn't tell them."

"Good god, girl!" Charlotte's head snapped around. "Where do they think you are?"

"I told them I would be spending a few weeks with a friend of mine from finishing school. Her name is Janet. Mother approves of her. She and her parents have been guests in our home."

"Which means her family must be quite wealthy." Charlotte settled herself more comfortably on the sofa.

A slight smile lifted the corners of Tia's mouth. "Her father is the president of The Bank of Maryland.

"And this... Janet," Charlotte threw up her hand, "has agreed to cover for you. Is that it?"

"Yes." she twisted the handkerchief in her hands.

"I'm glad to know I can still trust John. But, tell me, Tia," she glanced over at the small girl watching her, "where did you learn to be a liar?"

The dark eyes widened in alarm, then looked away. "I didn't want to lie," she said in a rush. "I felt I had no choice." Her voice became stronger in defense of her motives. "I'm seventeen- years-old. I think I'm old enough and mature enough to know about my mother."

"That's true you are, but you're goin' 'bout it the wrong way." Charlotte rose from the couch. "First thing tomorrow, I'll send Jed into Cut Bank to get a wire off to John and Martha, tellin' them you're here. That way I won't have to talk to her. Not yet anyway. Don't be surprised though if Martha's on the next train out here. God forbid!" She threw her hands into the air.

"Miss Charlotte," Hattie called out, "supper bes ready. Ah's fixin' ter puts it on de table effen y'all's ready."

"Yeah, go ahead, Hattie. We'll be right there." Charlotte ushered Tia to her feet. "We won't talk about this anymore tonight. You've had a long trip so after supper I want you to get to bed."

Tia slid her arm around Charlotte's small waist. "Are you very angry with me, Gram?"

Allowing the arm to stay where her granddaughter had placed it, she continued walking towards the dining room. "Let's just say right now, Tia, I'm not real happy with you."

***

Tia walked into the room that had belonged to her mother and knew at once everything in the room had been left the same. Walking over to the big four poster bed, with the over-sized feathered mattress, matching sheets, and homemade quilt, she sat down to look around her. A large oak dresser stood in one corner and over against the wall to the left of the door she saw a vanity table with an oval mirror inlaid in matching oak, and positioned at the back of the table. It had been hinged so it could be moved to any angle. Tia ran her hands over a heavy porcelain bowl, white with a large pink rose in its center, setting on the end of the table. A matching pitcher stood beside it. She kicked off her shoes running her feet over the wall to wall braided rug. Its pink and gray colors had faded and she could see the many worn spots, here and there, from its years of use.

Instead of walking to the bath down the hall, Tia poured cool water from the filled pitcher into the porcelain bowl, washing her face and hands just like she knew her mother had done before the house had been afforded the luxury of indoor plumbing. Walking over to the large dresser Tia pulled open all the drawers until she found what she sought. In the middle drawer a stack of different colored nightgowns had been neatly folded. Pulling one of the blue ones from the stack she laid it on the bed. The gown smelled musty but she didn't care.

She turned down the soft coverlet to sink into the fat featherbed. Her eyes felt heavy but as she lay there in the darkness, her tired mind refusing to relax, her thoughts turned backward. Back to a time when, even as a small child, she always felt pulled to find out exactly where she belonged.

The knowledge of her illegitimate birth to a mother she never knew and who, soon after Tia's birth, took her own life, led the young girl to wonder why she had been brought into this world in the first place. Raised by her Aunt Martha and Uncle John Sexton, Tia was like a Godsend to the barren couple. They never denied the little girl they adopted into their hearts in any way. But for some unknown reason, Tia always stood apart from the big house with its lavish furnishings, the fine Catholic education, and elite parties of which she had been the drawing attraction.

There was a wildness in the young girl that wouldn't allow her to conform to the easy life she had been handed. She found her questions, concerning her biological mother and father always put aside with one excuse after another, until finally she made up her mind to find out once and for all the truth surrounding the people who had been such an important part of her life.

As these thoughts wound down in her overtaxed mind, the dark eyes closed and before long she had drifted off, safe in the knowledge that here in this unspoiled land she would find the answers to her questions.

Walking through the quiet house early the next morning, Tia paused with her hand on the swinging kitchen door. She did not mean to eavesdrop, but the voices of her grandmother and Hattie, coming from beyond the door, held her unable to move.

"Ah wuz so happy 'bout Miss Tia's bein' hyah at las', ah doan think ah shut mah eyes fer one minute las night," Hattie laughed, flipping a hot-cake over in the skillet.

"I don't think I slept any better." Charlotte placed a heavy platter on the small bench beside the stove. "It kept runnin' through my mind 'bout Eathen comin' home early and findin' her here."

"Do you think Miss Tia's gwine ter wants eggs wid dese hotcakes?" She asked, her spatula suspended in midair.

"Go ahead and fry one. If she don't want it we'll throw it out."

"Miss Charlotte," Hattie tapped an egg against the skillet, "doan you think dat affer all des y'ars he jes' mout wants ter sees her?"

Taking a large jar of milk from the icebox Charlotte unscrewed the cap, poured the milk into a glass pitcher. "If I thought for one minute that could be the case I'd be on the phone gettin' him back here. No, he ain't changed the way he feels."

"Dat's too bad," Hattie flipped the egg over then slid it onto the platter beside the stack of hotcakes, "kase a body kin tells jes' by lookin' at her whut a fine young lady she tuhned out ter be. Our baby chile'd be so proud of her."

Before Charlotte could comment, Tia called out from the other room. "Gram, where are you?"

"I'm in the kitchen," Charlotte put a finger against her lips. "Go ahead and seat yourself at the table. I'll be out directly with your breakfast." Lifting the coffeepot off the stove she walked to the door. "You bring the platter. Maybe with you there, she won't be so apt to ask a lotta questions."

Seated at the big oak table, Tia tried to quiet her rising fears, but as Charlotte continued to sip her coffee Tia burst into tears.

Nodding for Hattie to finish her breakfast in the kitchen, Charlotte waited until the kitchen door swung shut. "Cryin' ain't gonna do a bitta good, so mop your face and tell me what's wrong."

"You know what's wrong, Gram." Tia pushed her plate out of the way. "You don't want me here. What have I done to make you turn against me? When you came to Boston, you always seemed so glad to see me. I thought you loved me. What has changed?"

Lifting her eyes, Charlotte took Tia's small hand in hers. "Nothin's changed, Tia. I love you with all my heart. It's just, that this little visit of yours has taken me by surprise."

Tia lowered her head drawing her wet face across Charlotte's knuckles. "Gram, I kept waiting for an invitation. You had to know that one day I would want to see where my mother had spent her life. I kept waiting, but you never asked. I want to know about my mother. What she liked. What made her happy."

"All right, Tia. I guess you gotta right to some answers. But before we go in the other room to talk I want you to know that I had Jed send a wire off to John and Martha. I'm sure one of them'll be callin'"

"At least this way," Tia lifted the linen napkin from her lap to lay it down on the table. "I'll have time to decide what to tell them."

"I suggest you tell them the truth." she advised, pushing her chair back away from the table.

Seating herself on the long sofa, Tia waited for Charlotte to take her place beside her. Instead Charlotte sat down in a chair across from her.

She can't even bare to be near me. Tia thought clutching her hands together in her lap.

"Tia, I know you've been told very little about your mother." Charlotte placed a cane she had been relying on of late, beside the chair. "I thought it best to wait until you got older and better able to handle the truth. I guess that time has come."

Tia could feel her excitement mounting. After seventeen years she was finally going to learn about her parents. She leaned forward in her chair.

"Tia, our Jessie meant everything to us. Comin', as she did, so late in our lives is probably the reason she grew up as spoiled as she did. I don't know." Charlotte pushed herself from her chair to walk over to the hearth. "One thing I do know, is of the two of us, she always favored Eathen. If she needed a spankin' or a scoldin' I had to do it." A slight frown passed over her face as she stood there allowing the scenes to come forward in her mind. "Eathen couldn't bring himself to raise his voice to her let alone a hand. I'll tell you somethin' though. I think those growin' up years had to be the happiest years of Eathen's and my life. The years before she met your father, and fell in love with him," she said, not bothering to hide the bitterness in her voice.

Charlotte pulled a small log from the walled-in log bin, tossed it onto the dying embers of the fire. As she waited for the wood to catch, she looked over at the girl watching her.

"Just a year younger than you when she met him. Still a baby." She blinked her eyes trying to halt the tears threatening to fall at the painful memory. "When I found out she'd gotten herself in trouble it almost broke my heart, and when your grandfather found out I thought he might break Jessie's neck."

"Even knowing she carried his child," coldness crept into Tia's voice, "you still tried to keep them apart?"

"That relationship couldn't work." Charlotte drew back her head to glower at her. "He couldn't even make a life for her." She slapped her hands back and forth, walked back to her chair.

"I can't believe you and Grandfather Eathen could be that judgmental." Her hand trembled against her mouth. "My father may not have been as wealthy as you, but you have to see that that didn't make him a bad person."

"We waited for Jessie all our married life." Charlotte beat her small fist on the arm of the chair. "We could not allow her to run off with that trash!"

"No, instead you turned your back on her." Tia rubbed at a dull ache beginning at the back of her neck. "You sent her away to have her illegitimate baby alone. She had no one." Her eyes locked onto the dancing blue eyes of her mother staring down at her from her portrait, then slid away. "Not even her baby's father to stand by her. No wonder she took her own life."

"Now you listen to me, girl." Charlotte moved to the sofa, jerked Tia around to face her. "We had no way of knowin' your mother planned on takin' her life. We did what we felt best at the time!"

"And my father?" Tia raised a questioning brow. "Where is he?"

An invisible wall slipped into place. "I've told you all I can 'bout your mother, Tia. As for your father, that's one subject I refuse to discuss in this house!" Charlotte ignored the pain in her granddaughter's eyes. When she felt sure her voice would not betray her own pain, she said. "I do have somethin' you may be interested in seein' though."

"What is that?" Tia pulled her hand away; disappointed at having her questions about her father still unanswered.

"Some pictures of your mother stored away in the attic."

Her curiosity piqued, Tia got to her feet, her grandmother's stubbornness, for the moment, pushed to the back of her mind. Within minutes the two climbed the stairs. Tia followed close behind as Charlotte led the way up the five steps leading to the attic. At the top of the stairs Charlotte hesitated for a brief moment before pushing open the attic door.

Walking into the large room with the steeped roof, Tia smelled a harsh musty odor. She shuddered as she heard the attics small inhabitants screeching and scurrying for cover across the cold bare floors.

Charlotte pulled on a chain hanging from a light socket. As the bare bulb lit up the chain swung back and forth casting eerie shadows over the room.

In the dim light Tia caught sight of a small rocking horse sitting off in a corner. She walked over to brush away the cobwebs. Covered in dust, with its life-like mane matted from years of neglect she took pity on its battered appearance. With the hem of her skirt she wiped off the little face and as she did the wooden horse rocked back and forth as though pleased someone had at last remembered it. She thought of her own rocking horse stored away back home, and wondered, if, in her mother's loneliness, she too had ridden to faraway places in search of another child to come and make the world a friendlier place.

Tia stood back looking at all the many toys and child-size furniture lining the wall. It reminded her of her own childhood. Anything and everything laid at her feet, but with no one to share it with. How alike their childhood had been.

"That was one of her favorite toys," Charlotte sighed, drawing Tia's attention away from her nostalgia.

"It looks sad sitting here without anyone to play with." Tia ran a loving hand down the matted mane.

"She rode many a mile on him and she always had a faraway look in her eyes. If I's less selfish, I'd box all this stuff up and give it to some needy kid who could use it." She swiped a quick hand across her eyes.

"But I just can't bring myself to let go of it. There are a lotta memories stored in this room, Tia. Some goin' back almost forty-nine years." Walking across the floor she knelt down in front of a large old trunk, and lifting the heavy lid, peered inside. At the sight of a long box, she declared, "God almighty. I ain't seen this in years." Lifting the box from the trunk, she laid it on the floor to remove the lid. Folding each side of the delicate tissue paper back over the sides, she withdrew its contents.

"Oh, Gram, it's beautiful!" Tia cried, as she spied the gown of off-white taffeta Charlotte held in her hands.

The neck of the gown wore a short vee and midway down the shoulders a mantle of the same material had been attached with three pleated rows of taffeta meeting in the middle of the fitted bodice. The skirt was floor-length and unadorned with a long train in the back.

"Somewhere in here's a bustle. Quite the fashion at the time. All it did is make the woman's backside look bigger. I hated it. I cheered when it went outta style. Here," she held the gown out to her, "shake it out and hold it up to you." At the sight of Tia standing there with the gown pressed against her, Charlotte shook her head.

"I wasn't much younger'n you are right now, when your grandfather and me got married." She sighed, reaching out to run a hand over the wrist-length sleeve. "It would've been your mother's when she got married." She brought the sleeve of the gown closer noticing a yellow smudge stained into the material, and dropped it from her hand. "Nothin' ever quite works out the way you plan."

"I'll wrap this back up, Gram."

At the bottom of the trunk Charlotte found what she wanted. She lifted the heavy album up and out of the trunk. Without opening it she handed it over to Tia. "I wish I could say you could keep this, but I can't. This, what's stored, and her portrait, are all I have left of her. It would break my heart to give them up. While you're here though," Charlotte grabbed hold of the trunk, pushing herself to her feet, "you can look through it any time you want. But it's not to leave this room."

"Don't you want to look at the pictures with me, Gram?" She seated herself on the floor, disappointment etching her face.

Charlotte remained where she stood for a moment staring down at the leather-bound album lying still unopened in Tia's lap. "No. You go ahead. When you're finished, be sure and put all this stuff back in the trunk and close the lid tight before you leave. I don't want the mice gettin' in there and destroyin' everything."

After Charlotte had gone, Tia opened the album scanning the pictures one by one, laughing aloud as she gazed at the photos of her mother. One in particular caught her eye. A plump little girl with dancing, bright blue eyes and ringlets of dark auburn smiled up at a big man holding her in a protective grip on his lap as one small hand caressed his cheek making him laugh into the camera.

"Grandfather Eathen," she whispered

Although she had never seen her grandfather, the love shining from the man's eyes for the little girl he held in his arms left no doubt in her mind as to his identity.

"It must have destroyed his world when my mother died." She clasped the picture to her chest. "I know I can't begin to fill the void she left in his life, but if he would only give me a chance, I know I can fill part of it."

Throughout the better part of the morning, she sat there in the quiet room, staring at memories from the past. Seeing her mother caught on camera as she grew from a cute, bubbly infant to a secure, if somewhat thin, adolescent, blossoming into the beautiful young woman Tia had seen in the portrait.

One thing stood out in Tia's mind as she viewed the pictures of her mother. Invariably, in each of the pictures, she could see a glow about her mother, an inner peace that couldn't fool the camera. The eyes staring out at her had been filled with happiness. All the pictures of her mother, happy, smiling, content, told her, none of these pictures had been taken after she met and fell in love with Tia's father. The eyes, in the pictures she held in her hands, looked to be alive with feeling. Not one of them mirrored the pain of a broken heart.

She had already put most of the pictures back in the album when something caught her eye. Withdrawing a thick piece of paper, she looked at it up close. It showed a drawing of a young Indian couple. The artist who drew the picture had been quite detailed, capturing the couple's likeness so well they almost looked real.

"I wonder why she looks so familiar?" she mused aloud, then realized her answer. "My god!" Tia breathed as the frightening picture slipped from her trembling fingers. "She looks just like me!"

In a rush to be gone from the cold, still room, Tia began shoving the pictures back inside the album, but as her eyes fell on the drawing, her breath caught in her throat. The handsome man standing beside her mirror image looked like the man in her dreams! The man who watched her from the shadows of her subconscious every night for as long as she could remember!

Without stopping to think, Tia put the album back inside the trunk, then reaching out she pulled the long box holding her grandmothers wedding gown over to her. Quickly she laid the box in the trunk and dropping the drawing on top slammed the lid down tight. Scrambling to her feet she ran for the attic door pulling on the handle and sobbing. For a few heart-stopping moments the door stuck, refusing to budge. Then, as if, of its own accord, it swung back, allowing her to leave. On shaking legs she climbed down the steep stairs. As her feet touched the landing, the door slammed shut behind her.

Without a backward glance, Tia ran down the long hall to her room. When she was safe inside with the door locked behind her, she tried to still her racing thoughts. "This can't be," she moaned, one hand covering her mouth while the other pressed tight against her heart, "it had to be my imagination playing tricks on me."

Stretched out across the bed she forced herself to relax. Clearing her mind, she tried to remember when the dreams had started. The dreams had always been a part of her. The man in her dreams had always watched her. At first he had stood in shadow, but as she grew older he seemed to step from the shadows, allowing her to at last see his face.

Now she had seen that face again. But this time she had been wide-awake. With every fiber of her being, Tia wanted to crawl into the comforting arms of her grandmother. And tell her what? She had seen a picture, up in the attic, of a man who has haunted her dreams for as long as she can remember? The woman would think her mad. She tried to stem the flow of "what ifs" but her frightened mind refused to cooperate. Maybe she was mad. Her mother died at her own hand. That certainly couldn't be explained as a sane act by any stretch of the imagination. Maybe insanity ran in her family. She had always heard it was inherent.

She knew one thing for certain. As much as she enjoyed looking at her mother's pictures, she would have to content herself with the portrait hanging in the parlor. The thought of going back up to the attic, filled her with such fear, she knew she never wanted to return.

Knowing her grandmother would be wondering about her, she sat up to swing her long legs off the bed. As she walked to the small vanity, she tried to smooth the wrinkles from her skirt and blouse. Picking up her brush she drew it through her long dark hair. After several brisk strokes, she laid the brush down on the table. At last, satisfied with her appearance, she turned to leave. As the door closed with a quiet click behind her, the sounds of low virile laughter echoed hauntingly throughout the empty room.

Chapter Two

Bright flashes of lightening zigzagged across the night sky spilling large pellets of angry rain to beat a demanding admittance against closed doors and shuttered windows.

Awaking with a start, Tia stared in the direction of the window, praying it would be strong enough to withstand the force against which it labored. She settled back beneath the covers, listening to the rain beating a hypnotic rhythm upon the roof. The even tempo seemed to lull her, at last, into a restful slumber.

Strong, dark brown fingers entwined themselves in her long, dark hair. The silken strands flowed with ease over his hands. She could feel his warm clean breath grazing her cheek before his mouth moved to capture hers.

Her love-dampened hands reached up skimming over his naked shoulders and down over his long black hair. The smell of pine and fresh-tanned leather filled her senses. Gazing into his midnight eyes, her breath caught at the love she saw reflected there.

"My beautiful Aakiiwa," he murmured, burying his face in the hollow of her throat, content to lie quiet for a moment before lowering his head to one passion-filled breast. Drawing an inflamed nipple between his teeth he flicked it with his tongue. Tiny flames licked at her already overheated womanhood, making her moan deep in her throat as his mouth burned a path down her sensitive skin. Tia cried out, her body begging him to end this torture consuming her.

In one swift move he pulled her beneath him, spreading her thighs with his strong firm legs. Suspended above her, he waited and watched...watched as the fire in her eyes burned out of control. With a low growl he lunged, stripping her forever of her innocence. A small scream tore from her throat as she locked her heels around his trim waist, holding him imprisoned within her softness until he had satisfied the agony pulsating throughout her hot young body. Her world exploded into a million burning pieces before jerking her from her slumber.

Sitting up, she looked around the dark room, surprised to find herself alone in the big four-poster bed, her body bathed in a cold sweat. As the dream replayed itself in vivid detail, she covered her face, trying to blot out the mental images. At seventeen, Tia remained a virgin to life. The mystery of what happened between a man and woman had always eluded the young girl, until a dream lover, with hair as black as the storm-filled night, came to teach her the answer to the mystery.

Of an instant the room lit up, banishing the shadows of night and bathing them in clarity. A small scream escaped Tia's dry throat as a loud clap of thunder echoed throughout the darkness. Throwing back the covers, she ran for the door, but just as her hand touched the knob unseen hands spun her around. Fighting in vain against terror and her unknown assailant, Tia lashed out only to find herself yanked against a naked chest. The strong arms surrounding her made fighting impossible.

"Who are you?" Tia whimpered. "What do you want from me?"

"Don't you know me, Tia?" came her shocking answer. "Have the years silenced your heart, made you forget the love we once shared?" murmured a deep male voice against her throat.

"I don't know you." Her voice shivered in her throat. "Please, let me go."

"No, Tia. The spirits have seen fit to return you to me after all this time. I have come to take you back. This night we will walk our path to the sun together."

A sharp rap sounded on the door, followed by Charlotte's sweet voice calling out for Tia to let her in. As fast as the strong arms had entrapped her, they disappeared. Forcing herself to react, Tia switched on the lamp, flooding the room with marvelous mind-soothing light.

Looking around, she could see no one else in the room. Swinging the door wide, she fell into the comforting arms of her grandmother. "Gram," Tia sobbed, "thank god you're here!"

Rocking the overwrought girl in a gentle sway, Charlotte soothed her. "There now. I knew you'd probably be frightened. You're safe. It's just a good ole Montana storm."

"You don't understand!" Tia wailed. "Someone came into my room! He told me he was going to take me with him!"

Wrapping a tight arm around Tia's waist, Charlotte stepped a cautious foot inside the room. Looking around, she assured herself no one waited to attack them. "Tia, child, you were dreamin'. It musta been a real heart-stopper, to upset you this much."

Glimpsing Tia's pale face, Charlotte tipped her chin towards hers. "Would you like me to stay with you tonight?"

"Oh, Gram, would you? I would be ever so grateful."

"Of course." Charlotte slipped off her bathrobe, revealing a long cotton nightgown, to lay it over the vanity chair. "It will be like when your mother woke up frightened of the night."

With her head snuggled on Charlotte's chest and surrounded by her comforting arms she listened to Charlotte as she tried to explain away the frightening incident. Finally, towards morning, Charlotte's theory of a bad dream began to make sense. *How silly*, she thought to herself before dozing off. *I actually thought he was real.*

Outside, the storm continued to rage. Drenching the rich land and cutting into the torn soil like a surgeon gone mad. For a split second the room glowed bright, showing the clear outline of a man. Then it was gone. Leaving the women shrouded once more in total darkness.

The early morning air felt cool to Tia as she walked out onto the neat, wide porch. Spying Charlotte sitting in a big swing, her lap covered with a large, green lap rug, she reached out pushing the cover to one side. "Mind if I join you, Gram?"

"Looks to me like you're already here," Charlotte teased her, a hint of mischief in her sparkling blue eyes. "You look mighty chipper this mornin'." No more ghosts tryin' to cart you off to the happy huntin' grounds?"

"Sitting here in the light of day, I know it had to have been a dream. But, Gram, last night it felt so real." Unable to control the bright blush staining her cheeks, Tia grew quiet.

"Don't let it worry you, child." Charlotte patted Tia's small hand. "I remember how the storms could raise the hairs on the back of my neck when I first came out here. I'd be surprised if you didn't feel a little uneasy."

"Are the storms always that bad in Montana?"

"Ever since I been here they have been, and that's been close to fifty years. Yeah, Montana can get pretty mean at times." She nodded. "But I wouldn't live anywhere else, that's for damn sure!"

At Charlotte's risqué language, Tia smiled. Then, not wishing to offend, she asked, "Have you always loved Montana, Gram?"

"Not like I do now, no. I was sixteen when Eathen first brought me out here from Boston in 1871. All I could see is open land. No house, no barn just a small tent Eathen lived in 'till we could start buildin'. I took one look and thought my life had ended."

Trying to imagine herself living under such conditions, Tia shuddered. "You must have been frightened to death."

"I was, but since I'd already married the man and I knew he would never live in Boston, all I could do is make the best of it." She drew a tight-woven shawl around her shoulders. "I told myself if I wanted to save my marriage, I better grow up fast and realize things aren't always as I want them to be."

"You had to have loved Grandfather Eathen very much."

"I did and I loved bein' a starry-eyed young bride." She laughed as she recalled the memory. "At that time the man I had just promised to love, honor, and obey could do no wrong." The smile disappeared from her face, replaced with a look of infinite sadness. "I know now it takes a lot more'n love to keep a marriage strong and enduring. Sometimes a woman has to close her eyes to the things her man does, then hope she made the right decision."

"Why are you afraid for Grandfather Eathen to find me here?" Tia turned sideways in the swing to gaze at her. "I'm all he has left of my mother. Don't you think, given the chance, he could learn to love me as he loved her?"

The question was so sudden, Charlotte found herself unable to answer. She knew she couldn't tell Tia why Eathen would never accept her. Tia could never understand how losing Jessie had changed him; almost from the moment he found out she carried her lover's child. Or how the very sight of that child would only make his pain that much sharper.

"Your Grandfather changed after Jessie's death, Tia." Her fingers plucked at the threads of her shawl. "I gave up years ago trying to talk him into comin' to see you, or to let you come out here."

The raw ache cutting into her heart at the unfairness of it all, almost made Tia leave the subject be, except she couldn't. "Why doesn't he want to know me? I didn't end my mother's life. She did that on her own."

"That's true, Tia, she did. The problem is, your grandfather just sees what he wants to see. Now," Charlotte slapped her hands down on her lap, "enough 'bout him. We were talkin' about when I first came out

26

here."

Satisfied, at least for the moment, with the easy camaraderie once more between them, Tia changed the subject.

Affecting a shocked manner Tia raised her dark brows to mimic Boston's upper-class citizens. "I can imagine what the proper people of Boston would have to say if they knew you had spent the first months of your marriage living in a tent."

"They would have had apoplexy!" Charlotte chuckled, relaxing. "I guess I didn't have it that bad. Especially after other families started puttin' down roots. I made a lotta friends." she drummed her fingers on the arm of the swing. "We used to have some high ole times. One of the reasons bein'," she gave Tia a conspiratorial wink, "Eathen always supplied the liquor. You see, back then, Montana wasn't a dry state like it is now. People would come from miles around to attend a Thornton dance or barbecue. And I enjoyed havin' people around, as long as they had a good time." The jaunty rhythm she had been tapping out with her foot stopped and a deep scowl covered her face. "The one person I never cared a hoot in hell for was Frank McKennah. His wife Sarah's one of my best friends." she hastened to tell her. "Why the good Lord ever paired her up with the likes of Frank's something I'll never understand."

In all her years of growing up, Tia had never known her grandmother to be so adamant in her dislike of another human being. "Would it be asking too much to know why you feel this way?"

"No. I don't mind tellin' you," Charlotte replied, as though speaking to herself. "Soon after we came here, we learned about a tribe of Indians camped less than an hour's ride from here. Accordin' to the white man's law, they were trespassin' on Thornton land, though I'm sure they didn't look at it that way. Eathen and me had no problem with them bein' there. But Frank McKennah did. Every time we had a get-together, all Frank could talk 'bout was drivin' the Indians out, That'n how Eathen and me went against our own by allowin' them to stay."

"Didn't it frighten you to have Indians living that near?" Tia shivered at the thought.

"Why?" Charlotte shrugged her shoulders. "They didn't bother anyone. I remember one mornin' in particular, I had some steaks roastin' over the campfire for breakfast, when I looked up to see a young girl standin' across the way watchin' me. She was such a pretty little thing, all dressed in deerskin with her long black hair hangin' in braids down her back. I motioned her to come forward, but just as she started to

Eathen and Mack, the man who helped us build this house, come walkin'
back from the creek and she ran away. The next time I saw her she had a
young man with her."

Tia could feel her stomach beginning to knot up as Charlotte,
unaware of the tension she caused, continued with her story.

"Eathen said they belonged to a tribe of Blackfoot camped down by
the lake. Come to think of it," she snapped her fingers, "I gotta picture of
them in the trunk in the attic. Mack drew it. Said he wanted to show his
grandbabies what a real Indian looked like. Guess he forgot it when he
left."

"I found the drawing while looking through the album," Tia
whispered, trying to keep her voice calm. "It's very life-like."

"I should get it out and hang it up, fore it gets ruined. Mack was
quite the artist; he also did the portrait of your mother."

Nodding, Tia tried to pay attention, but her mind kept returning to
the man in the picture.

"Did you ever see them again?"

"No, just that one time. Later, after the massacre, I found out, the
man she had with her was a war chief."

"Massacre!" Tia clutched Charlotte's arm. "Gram! You could have
been killed!"

"No, Tia, you don't understand." She patted her hand. "The whites
massacred the Blackfoot."

"What happened?"

"Near as we can tell it all started with a young man named Tom
Suiter." Charlotte settled herself to a more comfortable position in the
swing. "I think him and his family came from Arkansas. I just saw him
once or twice. Anyway," she waved her hand in dismissal, "what sticks
out in my mind, 'bout Tom has to be his ugliness." Charlotte spread the
palm of her hand to draw it down her face. "His features looked a lot like
the face of a horse. Long and thin with large protrudin' teeth, big flappin'
ears and thick lips. Course, needless to say, none of the young girls
'round the county'd have anything to do with him. One day, outta the
blue, he just up and disappeared." She hunched her shoulders, spread her
hands wide. "No one ever knew what happened. He rode out and never
returned. Somehow, Frank got it into his head the Blackfoot had to be
responsible."

At Tia's questioning look, Charlotte grinned. "In order to
understand Frank's way of thinkin' you'd first have to know Frank."

"He sounds like a very unusual man."

"That's one way to describe him. But to go on with my story," she crossed her legs at the ankles, drew them back beneath the swing, "we had the house pretty well finished by then and one evenin' after supper, Frank come callin'. Told Eathen he needed to talk with him in private. I didn't mind. I never had any great likin' for Frank even in the beginnin'. They went out on the front porch and I sat at the table finishin' my coffee. All of a sudden I heard this god-awful bellow."

I went to the screen door in time to see Eathen shove Frank away from him. As I stood there, I heard Eathen tellin' Frank he had to be crazy. He said, 'What you're purposin' here's out and out murder!' Frank's response proved Eathen's words when he roared, 'When you're talkin' 'bout animals, it ain't murder!'"

Tia sat listening, almost afraid to blink.

"Eathen saw me standin' there and told me to stay inside he'd handle it. As I walked away from the door, I heard Eathen tell him, "Frank, if this is what you got in mind, then you best count me out, 'cause I won't have any part of it."

A few minutes later, I heard Frank ride out. I looked up to see Eathen standin' in the doorway; I asked him what Frank had planned. He just stood there, shakin' his head. He said, "I always knew Frank to be a little crazy, but I never thought he'd go this far."

Then he told me, Frank planned on attackin' the Indian camp. I don't think he really believed Frank would do it. I don't guess I did either. But, we both guessed wrong." Her voice took on a pronounced coldness. "Early that next mornin', Frank and the men from the other families got together, and killed every man, woman, and child, in that camp. And you know, to this day, the anger I feel every time I look at Frank McKennah, is just as strong as if it happened yesterday."

As Charlotte's voice trailed off, Tia tried to shut out the picture forming in her mind. For a while, the creaking of the swing filled up the ensuing stillness as Charlotte continued to sway it back and forth as though reaching for the comforting motion of a rocked cradle.

The need to know about the men responsible for all those innocent lives pushed Tia to end the silence. "What happened to Frank and the men involved?"

"Nothin'. Not one of those men got brought up on charges." Charlotte closed her eyes as hot shame rolled over her. "Says a lot for the morals of the county at that time, don't it?"

"You find bad people everywhere, Gram. Is Frank still alive?"

"Oh yeah," she snorted a bitter laugh. "Ain't you ever heard that ole sayin' 'just the good die young'? That sure as hell leaves out Frank McKennah!" Charlotte edged her way forward. "Hold this swing steady, so I can get up."

Hiking her long dress high above her knees, Charlotte spread her legs wide, unmindful of the thick baggy stockings showing. With a firm hand planted on the arm of the swing she pushed herself up and out of her seat.

Tia grabbed hold of her arm to steady her. "Can you make it all right, Gram?"

"I guess so. I'm up!" Charlotte answered with a light chuckle, glancing over Tia's shoulder to see Jed coming around the side of the house.

"Mornin', Jed. What brings you here so early? No trouble with the ranch, I hope."

"No, Ma'am," Jed replied, walking up the porch steps. "I came to ask Tia if she'd like to take a little trip with me."

"Is that right? I wasn't aware you had time to take a trip in the middle of a workweek, Jed," Charlotte retorted, her blue eyes questioning.

"This ain't a pleasure trip, Miss Charlotte." He settled himself back against the porch-banister. "I told Hardiman we'd be there this mornin' to pick up them horses you bought off the reservation. We shoulda already been gone by now, but I thought Tia might like to ride along, so I waited." He rubbed a quick hand over his lightly stubbled chin, wishing now he'd taken the time to shave. "Would you like to go, Tia?"

"Sure she would. Give her a chance to see some of the land while she's here."

The idea of seeing a real trail drive, no matter how small, tempted her more than she could refuse. "Thank you, Jed. I'll go change."

Noting the gleam in his eye, as he watched Tia walk away, Charlotte stepped in front of him. "She might as well see all she can in the short time she's here. In the meantime, Jed, don't go gettin' attached to her. I meant what I said 'bout sendin' her back."

"Even if she don't wanna go?" He lifted a dark brow.

"She ain't got no choice. And as much as I hate to admit it, neither have I."

Chapter Three

As they rode, Jed told Tia about the Blackfoot and their difficulties in adapting to a new way of life, while at the same time fighting to keep their old ways alive as much as possible, so the young would not forget. Housed on the Browning Indian Reservation and presided over by the United States Government, he went on to explain how they could no longer roam at will in the land they had lived on for centuries.

With Jed's deep voice keeping her entertained Tia's mind touched on the warrior in the picture, and she turned her attention back to the man riding by her side.

"Jed, did you ever hear any stories about the tribe of Blackfoot killed down near the lake many years ago?"

"Sure. Anyone who's lived around these parts for any length of time's heard that story." He slowed his horse, glanced over at her. "From the way my granddad told it, the whole tribe, except for one warrior, got killed. I guess, as the story goes, the lone survivor of that hellish day had been in a Crow camp tryin' to talk the leaders into bannin' together with the Blackfoot to fight against the whites."

At Jed's words, Tia reined in her horse. "Are you saying the Blackfoot planned to harm Gram and Grandfather Eathen? Why? According to Gram, she and my grandfather helped the Indians. They allowed them to camp right on Thornton property."

After motioning the men to go on ahead, Jed turned his attention to the young girl waiting for him to explain a way of life she could never understand.

"Tia, before the white man came along, the Blackfoot roamed this land at will. The Indian never assumed, as the white man did, they owned the land. Different tribes occupied certain areas with the understanding that if another band came into this territory there'd be trouble. I doubt very much," he smiled over at her, "if the Blackfoot considered the land, which they had lived on for centuries, as belonging to Miss Charlotte and Mister Eathen. All they saw's the whites invadin' their territory. So they decided to do what they had always done. Kill the enemy and protect their domain."

Being born and raised in Boston and associating with the well-mannered elite, Tia found herself unable to accept Jed's reasoning.

"If that's how they settled their differences, then I'm glad they are on reservations where the government can keep an eye on them and teach them right from wrong. She kneed her horse forward once more.

The face of Jake Hardiman flashed through Jed's mind. "I wouldn't be too quick to assume the government's always in the right. You ain't met Jake Hardiman. The government appointed Jake as Indian Agent, which means, anything the Indians want or need they have to go through Jake to get it." The idea of anyone having to depend on Jake Hardiman for their needs called for more understanding than Jed could fathom.

"The best way to sum up Hardiman is to tell you what my ole grandma used to tell me. That is, keep your eyes and ears open and your mouth shut. You'll learn a lot." With that piece of advice Jed looked up to see Hardiman walking toward them.

"Hey, Stanford, 'bout time you showed up. Easy to see why you took your sweet time gettin' here though," the Indian Agent wheezed, leering with open interest at Tia.

"Hardiman, you got them horses ready?" Jed asked, in no mood to waste time.

"Yep." he gestured with a swing of his head. "They're in the south corral. Go ahead and send your men up there, then come on up to my office and I'll take care of the bill." Spitting a stream of tobacco juice off to the side he squinted up at Tia, drawing a dirty hand across his mouth. "Missy, you can come sit in my office while Stanford takes care of business. The smells a lot nicer."

"That's all right, Hardiman. Soon as I talk to the boys, we'll both come up to your office. Excuse me a moment, Tia. I'll be right back."

As Jed left to talk to the men, Hardiman took advantage of his absence by feasting his eyes on the young girl as she dismounted. His hungry stare glided upward from her leather boots to the long, straight blue skirt belted at her trim waist and stopping to linger on her full breasts hidden from view beneath a white cotton blouse.

Sure is a pretty bitch! But a might too prim for my taste, he thought to himself.

"You know, Missy. A person could almost mistake you for a breed, with that brown skin and long dark hair. What part of the country you from, anyway?" he looked around, being careful to keep his voice low.

Taken aback at the man's contemptible behavior, Tia felt at a loss for words. But the fire in her dark eyes as she glared at him, told Hardiman just how she felt.

"Got them hot injun eyes too," Hardiman breathed, skimming a moist tongue over lips gone dry at the thought of using her as he had used so many of the young girls on the reservation. The idea of being caught never entered his lecherous mind. He believed, without him, they could not survive.

The thought of being alone, one more second, with this vile creature called for more patience than Tia could summon. Without a backward glance, she set off to find Jed. She had gone but a short way when someone stepped in her path, leaving her no choice but to stop. The old Indian put his hands on her shoulders and drawing her close, peered into her face.

All the stories she had heard about Indians came rushing back to her. "What are you doing? Let me go," she whimpered, trying to pull away.

"No'ni'sa'ke'man," he whispered, trying to pull her against his sunken chest.

"What? I can't understand you," Tia said, still trying to loosen his hold on her.

"No'ni'sa'ke'man," he repeated, then sadly shook his white head releasing her.

With great relief, Tia looked up to see Jed riding toward her at a dead gallop. "What the hell's goin' on?!" he yelled, jumping from his horse. "What'd he say to you?" he pulled her into his arms, then held her at arm's length to scan her face.

"I don't know, Jed." She pushed her long hair over one shoulder with a nervous hand. "He seemed to think he knew me."

Keeping one hand secured on Tia, Jed reached out halting the other man as he began to walk away. "What were you tryin' to say to this girl, old man?"

Turning, the old warrior looked once more to Tia, his black eyes noting the fear in her tear-filled gaze. "No'ni'sa'ke'man," he whispered, then shrugging Jed's hand from his shoulder, walked away.

"What did he say, Jed?"

"I don't speak Blackfoot. We can go find out from Hardiman. He should know."

But Hardiman, yanking his baggy pants up higher on his hips, already wasted no time in walking their way. "What the hell'd that ole Indian want?" He rolled up the sleeves on his dirty red shirt. "If he told you the meat I give them is rotten, he's a damn liar!"

"I doubt if that's what he wanted to tell her, Hardiman," Jed drawled, removing his hat to run a hand over his damp hair. "My bet is the meat you give them probably ain't fit for the buzzards."

"Now just hold on, Stanford," he batted the straw hat off his head, pulled the large bead up the string to keep the hat from falling to the ground. "You ain't got no call to be accusin' me of any wrong doin'."

"If that's so, why'd you think the Indian had a complaint 'bout the meat?"

"Aw hell, you know injuns," he slapped Jed on his shoulder with a nervous laugh, "they'd bitch no matter what the hell's goin' on. Come on. Let's get the bill settled so you can be on your way."

"Hold up, Hardiman." Jed stopped him as he turned away. "What does,"No'ni'sa'ke'man" mean?"

Hardiman spun around to stare at him. "Now why'n the hell would you ask that?"

"I wanna know, because that's what the ole man said to Tia."

"Well," a satisfied smirk pulled at the corners of his stained mouth, "if that don't beat all. Guess it ain't just me who thinks you could pass for a breed, Missy."

"Just answer the question, Hardiman," Jed growled, taking a menacing step towards him.

At the cold anger in Jed's voice, Hardiman could feel his own anger boiling up in his throat, but he stifled the urge to give a heated response and turned his attention instead to Tia. "It'd be my pleasure to tell you what that ole Indian said, ma'am. No'ni'sa'ke'man means, 'wife of my brother'."

"Guess you're right, Tia," Jed told her, choosing to ignore Hardiman, "he mistook you for someone else."

"Gotta be more to it'n that," Hardiman spoke up, talking around the large plug of tobacco he had pushed far back in his jaw. "That ole man don't talk to no one. Now, outta the blue," his well-practiced tongue worked the chew behind his lower lip, "he comes up and starts a conversation with your lady friend here."

"Hardiman," Jed reached out, draping an arm around the man's bony shoulders, "I don't know where my manners are. I ain't even introduced you to this young lady. I'd like you to meet Eathen Thornton's granddaughter. His rough grip tightened on Hardiman's shoulders, as he heard him suck in air then hawk the plug of tobacco from his mouth, "You know the man I'm talkin' 'bout, he supplies the cattle to this reservation."

Hardiman stood as though frozen. "I beg your pardon young lady. Stanford should've introduced us sooner," he whined. "I certainly didn't mean to offend you."

"Next time you might try thinking before you speak, Mr. Hardiman," Tia advised him. "It could save you a lot of embarrassment."

"Yes, ma'am," Hardiman bobbed his head in agreement. "I'll certainly do that."

"Hardiman, if you're through grovelin', tell me who that ole Indian is."

"Name's Pehta," Jake said, glad to change the subject. "He's the sole survivor of that tribe wiped out all them years ago on Thornton's land."

"Oh yeah. He must be gettin' up in years by now."

"Yeah," he raked fingers through a head of dirty hair, "he must be pushin' seventy somethin'."

"Seems to me, my granddad mentioned something about his brother bein' a war chief."

"Yep," Hardiman replied, turning in the direction of his office, "that's who he is all right. Thinks it makes him somethin' special 'round here too." His steps quickened as the two fell in beside him. "Then hell, so do the rest of these heathens. His brother's name was Appearin' Wolf. Big Kainah war chief." A scowl of distaste etched his brow. "Didn't do him much good though; he's still just as dead."

White-hot pain ripped through her side as she fell to the ground, whimpering like a wounded animal. She tried to stand, but some force kept pulling her back. Without warning a shadow fell across her and she glimpsed the outline of a man before darkness spun her away.

When Tia came to, she could see Jed kneeling on the ground holding a cold cloth pressed to her forehead.

"Jed, what happened?"

"I guess that old Indian must of frightened you more than we thought, you passed out on us." He pushed the damp hair back from her forehead. "Don't you remember?"

"No." Tia tried to sit up. "The last thing I remember is talking with you and Mr. Hardiman."

Jed felt himself being pushed to the side. Before he could react, the old Indian had seated himself cross-legged beside Tia where he began to chant.

"What the hell do you think you're doin'?" Jed demanded, rising to his feet.

As though Jed had not spoken, Pehta continued his melodic chanting, all the while weaving back and forth. For some unknown reason Tia remained still, watching the old man whose black eyes never left her face.

The movement stopped. Reaching out he placed something around her neck. As Tia's fingers brushed the foreign object she felt an eerie coldness clutch her heart. As she made to remove it, the old man patted her hands, shaking his head.

By now, Jed had endured all he could stand of this strange ritual. He pulled the man to his feet. Then, without a word, he lifted a frightened Tia into his arms holding her close.

"What the hell's this?" he asked a gaping Hardiman, as he fingered the leather bag hanging from Tia's neck.

"It's a deerskin bag the injuns wear. Suppose' to be sacred to the wearer. I don't know why he'd be givin' it to Miss Tia though."

"Ask him!" Jed ordered.

Hardiman, turning his attention to the old warrior, spoke to him in Blackfoot. At Pehta's unblinking reply, the Indian agent shook his head in amazement.

"What'd he say?"

"It don't make no sense, but what he said, is he gave her that medicine bag because it belongs to her."

"You're right. It don't make no sense. Guess he still has Tia mixed up with his brother's wife."

"I sure hope not," Hardiman hastened to reply, "his brother's wife's long dead. I done told ya; ole Pehta here's the sole survivor in that whole tribe."

"Well it can't hurt. After we leave, I'll throw it away." Looking down at the small girl in his arms he asked her, "Tia, do you feel well enough to ride?"

"Yes, Jed," she lowered her eyes, leaned her dark head against his chest. "Please, get me out of here."

For a long while they rode in silence each lost in their own thoughts. The many miles, riding ahead of the herd as the ranch-hands tried to keep them bunched together, slid by without notice.

Jed didn't find it strange someone would try to get close to Tia. Her beauty could make anyone stop in their tracks, even an old Indian. He looked at her now noting the way she rode, straight and proud. He recalled the sleepless night he had spent thinking about this beautiful girl riding by his side. Tall and slender, Tia's body already showed promise of the heart-stopping woman she would become. The wind catching up her long hair blew wisps of brown satin across her face. With a slight toss of her head the silken strands fell once more down her slender back.

As Jed smiled over at her she returned his smile, her dark eyes alive with the innocence of youth. That certain light that those who have yet to experience the pain or sorrows of life, can have. The urge to reach out and pull her into his arms felt so strong it took every bit of willpower he possessed to stop himself from doing just that. At the same time he could see a fragile quality about her. A quality, that made him want to protect her from the baser side of life. To protect her, even from himself.

Tia couldn't explain why she had passed out. She couldn't remember ever doing so before, but maybe, as Jed explained, the Indian had frightened her more than she at first thought. In any event she told herself she wouldn't dwell on it. She would just blame what happened on the fantasies of an aged mind and put the entire episode behind her. As her spirits lifted, she glanced over at her handsome, rugged companion.

"Come on, Jed. I'll race you," she laughed, already pulling away from him.

"You're on!"

He didn't know what had put Tia in this good mood all of a sudden, but he didn't care, as he kneed his horse into a fast gallop ignoring the strange looks on the faces of his men as he passed them by on his way to catch the girl with the long flowing hair.

The warm wind caressing her skin and the thrill of the race seemed to be just what she needed to clear the cobwebs from her mind. Pulling up on the reins she turned to find Jed by her side.

"Getting a little slow in your old age, aren't you?" She smiled over at him.

"The next time you wanna race, you could give a guy a fightin' chance. Don't throw down a challenge when you're already fifty feet ahead of me!"

"Now, Jed," she gave him a coy glance, "a female always gets a head start. Don't you know that?"

"Yeah," he shot back, "them bein' the weaker of the sexes, they do need a little help."

"Weaker?" The flirting smile left her face. "Who told you girls are weaker?"

"No one had to tell me, Tia," Jed chuckled, enjoying the easy camaraderie between them. "It's a known fact."

"I'll show you who is weaker, Jed Stanford," she challenged, a look of determination knitting her brow. "We still have about a mile to go if I remember right. I'll race you back to the ranch."

"Without a head start..." he began, but she had already raced past him. "Damn," he muttered giving the big gray full rein, "she did it again!"

Charlotte stood at the front door watching as they rode up. When they drew even with the house she walked out onto the porch.

Tia jumped from her horse with a triumphant yell. "The winner!"

"Yeah, Tia, you beat me fair and square," he laughed, stepping from the saddle.

Charlotte watched this friendly exchange. "Looks like you two had a pleasant trip."

"Excitin' would be more like it!" Jed replied.

"Oh? I can't wait to hear about it, but right now supper's gettin' cold." She turned towards the door. "You can tell me all the excitin' details at the table. You're invited to join us, Jed."

"After you, Tia." Jed bowed, holding the door open for her.

"Thank you, Jed." She laughed at his dramatics as they followed behind Charlotte on their way to the dining room.

"Gram!" Tia squealed, stopping beside the over-laden table. "Hattie has made enough for an army!"

"Don't pay her any attention, Miss Charlotte." Jed moved to the side as Tia passed the table on her way through the propped-open kitchen door. "I'm so hungry I could eat my way through that'n more."

"In that case, why didn't you eat before leavin' the reservation?" Charlotte called after him.

"With Hardiman as Indian Agent?" he called back, lifting a teakettle off the stove as he walked toward the wash pan setting on the washstand.

Waiting while Tia dumped a ladle of cold water into the pan, Jed tipped the teakettle mixing hot water with cold until the temperature satisfied both of them. Finished with washing their face and hands, Jed dumped the dirty water into the sink. Snatching two towels from a peg above the washstand, he tossed one to Tia, smiling as she caught it in mid-air. "It woulda been safer doin' without!" he said walking back into the dining room.

"Why do you say that, Jed?" Charlotte looked up as he took a seat across from her.

"One of the Indians at the reservation thought he knew Tia and started talkin' to her in Blackfeet." He reached in front of Hattie for the platter of ham just as she sat a large pitcher of tea on the table. "Sorry, Hattie, I should of looked first."

Hattie looked at him then left to bring in more food.

"Anyway, Hardiman got all upset; Thought he wanted to complain 'bout the meat."

"A Blackfoot Indian thought he knew Tia?" Charlotte asked, overlooking the fact the cattle in question came from Thornton stock. "That's strange."

"Oh, Jed." Tia forked a piece of ham onto her plate. "Gram doesn't want to hear about all that."

"No, Tia. I want to hear this," Charlotte hushed her. "Did you find out who this man is?"

"Yeah," Jed put a dent in his mashed potatoes before spooning gravy over the top. "Hardiman said his name's Pehta, the sole survivor of that tribe wiped out down by the lake." He helped himself to the peas then handed the bowl to Tia. "Seems he's also the brother of that war chief, Appearing Wolf."

"Appearing Wolf? He's the Indian Mack drew that picture of. Well imagine that," Charlotte mused. "I wonder why an Indian of the Kainah Blackfoot would think he knew you, Tia?"

"I have no idea." She spooned a small amount of mashed potatoes onto her plate all the while trying to keep a straight face as she saw Jed mix potatoes with peas and handed the bowl to Charlotte, who shook her head in refusal. "Maybe he is just addlebrained." She set the bowl down on the table. "After all, he is quite old. No offense, Gram." she hastened to add.

"Thank you, Tia. " Charlotte gave her a sharp glance. "I'll try to keep my wits about me."

"I'm sorry, but everyone is making too much of this." Tia busied herself with cutting her ham into bite-size pieces. "The man mistook me for someone else." She laid her knife across the top of her plate. "End of discussion!"

But Hattie wouldn't let the subject drop. "Who'd he think you wuz, Miss Tia?" she asked, slicing a piece of bread from the still warm loaf

Before Tia could answer, Jed intervened.

"That's the really strange part," he poured himself a glass of tea, then noticing Tia held out her glass he filled it up to the brim. "He seemed to think Tia was his sister-in-law. How the hell... uh sorry, Miss Charlotte," he hastened to apologize. "But how he could mistake Tia for someone who would have to be in her seventies, don't make no sense to me."

"Don't make a whole hell-of-a-lotta sense to me," Charlotte agreed. "Maybe you're right, Tia. He's just an addlebrained ole Indian." Then she looked at Tia closer. "What's that you have around your neck, child?"

Tia had forgotten about the medicine bag. "Oh! It's something the Indian gave me."

"Let me see it." Charlotte held out her hand.

"No!" Tia yelped, jumping from her chair.

"Tia, what in the world's the matter with you?" Charlotte drew back.

"I don't want to know what is in it! I just want to throw it away!"

"Then throw the damn thing away. I don't care. But you needin' get all upset about it."

The carefree moments Tia had spent with Jed had come to a close, shadowed with frightening feelings. Leaning over Tia put her arm around her grandmother, hugging her close.

"I'm sorry, Gram. I guess I did get carried away. All this talk about Indians who died years ago is starting to frighten me."

"Well of course it would." Charlotte patted Tia's small hands. "I'm the one who should be apologizin'. I didn't think."

Jed had been sitting back, watching the closeness between the young girl who had his interest and Charlotte. Not wanting to add to her discomfort, he decided not to mention Tia's fainting spell. The less said about that, he reasoned, the better!

Chapter Four

A full moon shining through the open curtains cast a pale glow over the room. The young girl snuggled beneath the covers dreamed the dreams of the innocent, unaware of the dark eyes caressing her. Drawing nearer, he touched the face he loved beyond all else.

"My beautiful Aakiiwa," he whispered, "I have waited so long for you to come back to me. I cannot be content to hold you only in a dream. The time has come for you to awaken, little one."

Tia sat up and turned on the bedside lamp. Then her breath caught in her throat as she saw him. At the foot of her bed stood an Indian.

"Do not be frightened, Tia. He reached out his hand to her. "You know I could never hurt you."

"Oh god!" Tia moaned, pulling the blankets up to her chin. "Who are you?"

For an instant his ebony eyes reflected the pain her words had given him. Then it was gone. The strong warrior once more in command as he answered her.

"I am Appearing Wolf. I am your husband."

The storm-filled night and the arms that had imprisoned her came rushing back. "I didn't dream what happened before. Holy Mother, help me. I've got to get out of here!" she whimpered, trying in vain to untangle herself from the covers.

He moved across the floor. "No, Tia! There is nowhere for you to run!"

"Get away from me," her shrill voice rose. "You aren't real!"

"Quiet!" He jerked around as one large hand entwined itself in her tousled dark mane to press her against his chest. When at last he had her subdued, he talked to her in his deep voice.

"Do not fight me, Tia." He brushed the damp hair back from her forehead. "You are my Aakiiwa. My woman. You must think back to the times when your beautiful dark eyes would light up at the mere sight of me. Now they show fear." One large hand caressed the side of her face. "You do not know me. The pain I suffered at your death is nothing," his black eyes gazed deep into hers, "compared to the pain in my heart at your rejection of me and the love we shared."

Tia's heart pounded so hard she just knew it would burst right out of her chest. *How is this happening? I am going to be murdered right here in Gram's house.*

Trying to calm herself, she inhaled a trembling breath. The smell of pine and clean leather filled her senses. Some memory, imbedded deep in her mind, tugged at her but she couldn't grasp it. His warm breath brushed her face each time he spoke. She could feel the strength in his large arms as he held her. Then his words penetrated her fear-dazed mind. "The pain I suffered at your death. At your death."

As the shock of these words echoed through her brain, her mind slipped away, fleeing to that special place where fear and pain have no admittance. Laying her unconscious form on the bed, Appearing Wolf stood for a moment looking down at her. Then turning walked stealthily into the night. Facing the east and lifting his arms in prayer, he cried out in anguish.

"Grandfather, why have you returned her to me with the skin of my enemy? Eyes that looked at me with so much trust now show fear. How can my heart that is no longer of the flesh still bleed? My spirit has remained on this land searching for the one I lost. Now I have found her. Now I can return to my people. I can walk my path to the sun. Soon my heart will no longer bleed. For my woman will walk by my side!"

The moment she opened her eyes, early that next morning the memory of the Indian leapt into her mind. She had not been dreaming nor had she imagined him. But, how did he get into her room and why did he pretend to be Appearing Wolf? To even consider the man who had held her so close last night could really be Appearing Wolf made her pulse race.

"The whole tribe, except for one warrior, was destroyed," she recalled Jed telling her. That one warrior being Pehta, Appearing Wolf's brother.

An idea struck her, seeming to fit the pieces together. The man in her room last night could be Pehta's grandson, named after Appearing Wolf. But her theory soon dwindled into nothing as she remembered her late night visitor's words to her.

"I am Appearing Wolf. I am your husband!"

Something very strange had to be going on here. It is one thing for a stranger to invade her bedroom in the middle of the night, but to pretend he is someone long dead bordered on the insane!

As Tia dressed, she decided not to tell Charlotte about what happened during the night. To do so would just frighten her, not to mention Hattie. She knew the one to help her would have to be Jed. The no-nonsense foreman would be a match for anyone. Even a long-dead Kainah war chief.

Luck walked with her as she made her way down the stairs and out of the house. The sooner she found Jed and told him about the bizarre happenings going on in her grandmother's house, the better.

Jed had finished saddling his horse when he spied Tia walking towards him. *God! How can any female look as good as she does, first thing in the morning?*

"I sure hope I'm the one you're comin' out here to see," he called out to her. "Nothin' could start my day off any better."

"You may not feel that way, after you hear what I have to say."

After giving the cinch an extra pull Jed dropped the stirrup. "Whatever it is, I'm sure we can work it out."

"Jed, a man broke into my room last night, and last night isn't the first time it has happened." She looked around the area to be sure no one stood close by to overhear their conversation. "The first time it happened is the night of the bad storm, although that night Gram talked me into believing I had been dreaming. Last night I was not dreaming." She shivered as a cold chill passed over her. "I saw the man in my room!"

"What happened?! What did he look like?" Jed asked in quick succession.

"He looked like an Indian." Tia answered the second question, not sure how to reply to the first.

"An Indian?" He drew back, a doubtful look covering his face. "Are you sure?"

"Jed, I know an Indian when I see one!"

"Did he hurt you?" He griped her shoulders, his gray eyes alive with worry.

"No. He didn't harm me in any way. He did frighten me though, Jed. He said such crazy things."

"Like what?"

Stepping back, Tia rubbed her shoulders, massaging away the ache Jed's large hands had inflicted. "He called himself, Appearing Wolf."

"Appearing Wolf? That's the name of that Kainah war chief we talked about yesterday. Is this some kinda sick joke?"

"I don't know, Jed," she murmured turning away. "I don't know what to think anymore."

Placing a comforting arm around her slim shoulders, Jed led her over to a long bench outside of the bunkhouse.

"Sit down here. I want you to tell me all you know about this...Appearing Wolf!"

"I'm so frightened." Tia trembled. "I don't know where to begin."

"Just begin at the beginning," Jed told her seating himself beside her.

"The first time I can remember seeing him," she leaned her head back against the building and closed her eyes, "I had to be about fifteen-years-old. Until then, he always stood in shadow...." Tia's voice trailed off as she opened her eyes to see Jed watching her, a strange look on his face.

"You've seen this man before, in Boston?" Jed breathed.

"Not in person, no." Her dark gaze drifted away from his. "Although, for as long as I can remember, he has always been there in my dreams."

"But, last night you don't think you just had a dream? Tia, I'm not doubting you, but maybe, just maybe," he held his hands palm out in front of her, "you just thought you were awake. That episode at the reservation may have scared you more than you think."

"Jed, I did not dream this. I know it sounds strange, but it's the truth. If it isn't, then, the only logical answer is that I'm crazy and just imagined all of this."

"You're not crazy, Tia." He pulled her over against him. "Between the two of us we'll find out what's goin' on. In the meantime, I think it'd be a good idea if we keep this between us."

"Yes." She rubbed her head against his shoulder, then sat up. "If Gram finds out, she would send me back sooner. As it is, she's already taking a chance by letting me stay. If Grandfather Eathen should come home early and find me here she would never hear the end of it." She closed her eyes, massaging her temples. "There's no way I could add to her problems by telling her, I think I'm being haunted by the Indian in her picture."

"Picture?" he pulled her hand down from her face. "What are you talkin' about?"

"Gram has a picture of the Indian, Appearing Wolf. I saw it while looking at some pictures of my mother up in the attic."

"Would you show me the picture?"

The thought of going back to that cold, isolated room made Tia shudder.

"What is it, Tia?" He cupped her face in his hand. "Did something happen to you up there?"

"Yes," she nodded, "Jed, there's a girl in the picture with Appearing Wolf. In the dim light she looked just like me," she heard his sharp intake of breath, but finished what she had to tell him, "except, her hair is black and she's a lot darker."

Rising to his feet, Jed took her hand. "Come on, you're gonna show me this picture," he told her, placing his arm around her waist when she tried to pull back. "You don't have anything to be afraid of. I'll be with you."

With Jed close beside her, they made their way towards the house. As it was still quite early, the two walked inside and up the stairs to the attic.

"Where does Miss Charlotte keep the pictures?"

"There, inside that large trunk," Tia nodded. "The one we want should be right on top."

Trying to make as little noise as possible, he made his way across the room. Out of the corner of his eye he saw a large spider crawling up a web suspended from one of the rafters. He ignored the way his stomach recoiled and pushed his old fear to the back of his mind. Lifting the heavy trunk lid, Jed found what they sought. As he gazed at the young couple smiling back at him he drew in his breath. The girl's likeness to Tia was uncanny.

Placing the picture back in the trunk, he dropped the lid. "I'm not gonna lie to you, Tia, she could pass for your twin. What makes it even stranger, is you're not Indian. Did your father have dark skin?"

Without any hesitation, Tia replied, "I never knew my father, Jed. Or my mother either for that matter. Soon after my birth, she took her own life."

"I'm sorry, Tia." He pushed himself to his feet. "I had no way of knowin'."

"It's all right. They are the reason I came to Montana. I want to learn all I can of my mother, and I want to find out who my father is. I had thought when I started out that I'd have more time, but I guess that isn't to be, now."

"I don't think I can be of much help to you there, Tia. I'm not old enough to have known your folks." Jed placed the palms of his hands on the small of his back and stretched backward for a moment. "Most people around here are pretty closed mouthed when it comes to people's private affairs."

"Do you know if any of the hands worked on the ranch when my mother still lived here? If so, maybe one of them would know something."

"Tom might have been here then, but even if he knew anything, I doubt he'd say. Mister Eathen's well respected in this county; Especially by his ranch hands."

"There has to be somebody who knew my parents." She tapped a long nail against her front teeth. "A thing like that had to have caused talk."

"Just if people knew about it. Maybe your mother left before anyone knew about her bein' in trouble."

"Gram and Grandfather Eathen sent my mother away to Boston to have me and get her away from my father. I used to think I caused her to kill herself. I don't feel that way anymore. I need to find my father, Jed. Will you help me?"

"There could be someone who would know. Let me do some checkin' and as soon as I find out anything I'll let you know. Gettin' back to the problem of someone breaking into your room, I think we're dealin' with a flesh and blood man, not a phantom. Startin' tonight, I'll have some of the boys watchin' the house. If he shows up again, he'll be caught. You can put your mind at ease, Tia," he pulled her into his arms for a brief moment, "whoever this joker is he can't disappear into thin air."

After Tia's disclosure of a man breaking into her room and affecting to be the long-dead Kainah war chief, Appearing Wolf, Jed found any excuse he could to be near her. The thought of anyone trying to harm her seemed to instill an almost obsessive fear in the rugged foreman. Already admitting to himself the deep feelings he had for Tia Jed felt sure, given the chance, she would return those feelings.

As each day passed, with no sign of her late night visitor, Jed began to entertain a false sense of security. *Could* all this be in Tia's mind? He knew so little about her. Maybe she was given to flights of fancy. Or, just frightened of being in a new land surrounded by different people. Whatever the reason, Jed knew he would be there to protect her no matter what the circumstances turned out to be. And, if it turned out there really had been a man in her room that night Jed felt pretty sure he no longer posed a threat to Tia.

That night as he enjoyed dinner up at the main house, Jed broached a subject he felt anxious to discuss.

"You know, Miss Charlotte, this Saturday night's the big spring dance, and since Mister Eathen ain't here to escort you, I wondered if you've given any thought to who you're goin' with?"

Glancing to where Tia sat enjoying her meal, she declared, "I don't think I'll be goin' this year, Jed. Tia wouldn't enjoy goin' to a hoedown. She's used to concerts and the like."

"Oh but I would, Gram." She laid her fork down on her plate. "I think it would be a lot of fun." Tia laughed, then noting the stern look on her grandmother's face, grew quiet.

"Ah think Miss Tia'd fits in jes' fine," Hattie spoke up, pulling her feet beneath her chair as Charlotte's foot shot out in her direction.

"No, Hattie, Gram's right. It probably would be better if I stayed home. But you could still go, Gram. Besides, I have a book I want to finish. So, all of you go ahead."

As she sat there, Charlotte thought about all the trouble she could be inviting by allowing Tia to go to the dance. There would no longer be any way she could hide the fact of Tia's visit once her neighbors found out about her. Eathen would be sure to find out. Then, glancing across the table to where Hattie sat, a smug look on her face, she made her decision.

"I guess it'll be all right, Jed."

"Oh, Gram. Are you sure?" Tia jumped to her feet to run around the table. "I mean, I can read that old book any time." She leaned down putting her arms around Charlotte's neck giving her a big hug. "Thank you, Gram. I promise, you won't have any reason to be sorry."

"I hope you're right, Tia," Charlotte whispered returning Tia's affection.

Later that evening as she stepped out of her bath Tia wrapped a large towel around her slender body tucking the ends above her breasts. Bending forward she twisted another towel around her long hair. With that done, she padded barefoot into her room and sat down at the small vanity table. Her reflection in the mirror stared back at her as she uncapped a jar of her favorite body oil. A strong scent of Jasmine floated into the air as she dipped her fingers into the jar to apply the aromatic oil to her skin. When she finished rubbing the oil over her face, neck and arms she stood up unwrapping the towel to let it drop at her feet. Unashamed, she sat back down at the table to finish rubbing the oil over the rest of her body. The sensation of her own body heat mixed with the pungent smelling oil as it seeped into her skin began to have a very strange effect on her emotions. She smiled, as the face of the handsome foreman drifted into her thoughts. She wondered what it would be like to be held in his strong arms as they moved close together across a dance floor. She pulled the towel from her head letting her damp hair fall around her shoulders. Dipping her fingers, once more, into the jar of oil she touched them to one palm of her hand then rubbed both of her hands briskly together. Starting at her temples she moved her hands over her hair massaging her scalp and moving all the way to the very tips of her hair. Would Jed find her hair silky to the touch? She hoped he would. Running a scented fingertip over her full mouth she smiled once more as she fanaticized about their night together and what it might mean for the two of them.

From the shadows, a lone figure watched with anger as Tia ran scented hands over her body, guessing at the mental images running through her mind and of the man who inspired those thoughts.

Chapter Five

"You boys get them horses herded on in here," Jed yelled. "I gotta date with the prettiest girl in the county tonight and I wanna get finished fore dark!"

"Yeah, we heard you had a date with Miss Charlotte's granddaughter. Good thing for her, Miss Charlotte and Hattie's goin' along," Tom snickered. "Otherwise, we might be lookin' for a new foreman come mornin'."

"You can keep your smart-ass remarks to yourself, Tom," Jed told him, the corners of his full mouth lifting. "Now, let's get the lead out and get finished!"

"All right, Jed. We're movin'," Tom said, then added in a loud voice to the other riders. "You ever notice how downright nasty he turns when he ain't gettin' any?"

Billy, the youngest of the crew, joined in on the ribbing. "Yeah," he ran a hand through his thick, curly blond hair. "He can get pretty ornery all right. I just hope he ain't plannin' on bathin' in that strong smellin' shit he calls cologne again. Remember that?" His green eyes crinkled with dramatic mischief. "Took us three days to air out the bunkhouse! Smelled like the Miles City whorehouse!"

"I'll have you know, I paid two bucks for that cologne, you snot-nosed little turd!"

"Hell, Jed," Billy smirked. "I coulda put that two bucks to better use'n that."

"Billy," Jed rapped him across the backside with his gloves. "Ain't no woman, paid or otherwise, gonna waste her time with you. At your age you wouldn't even know where to stick it! Now," Jed shoved him out of the way, "unless you're all ready to have a foot up your ass, I suggest you start movin' these horses!"

The men worked throughout the day, getting the horses moved into the corrals, even choosing to forgo lunch so they could get done early and get ready for the big dance.

Jed jumped down off the fence and started toward the gate when he saw a movement out of the corner of his eye. Too late he tried stepping to the side. He felt himself lifted from the ground and slammed against the gate as a big Paint, his head down and moving fast, rammed into him. The next thing he knew he had landed flat on his back in the mud.

"What the hell happened?" Tom yelled, seeing the other hands gathered around Jed.

"Damnedest thing I ever saw," said Dusty, another of the hands. "That Paint was goin' in as smooth as anything when for no reason he spooked. He come at Jed so fast he didn't have a chance to get outta the way!"

"Well let's see what damage has been done." Tom dropped to one knee. "Can you stand, Jed?"

"Yeah I think so, if you can give me a hand."

"Get on the other side of him, Dusty, and help me get him up." Ignoring his curses they propelled Jed to an upright position. "Hold onto him while I do a quick check." Running gentle hands over Jed's ribs then up one side and down the other of his legs and arms, Tom stood back satisfied at least he hadn't been hurt too bad. "Don't feel like anything's broken, Jed, but just to be on the safe side, I think we best have the doc take a look at ya."

Knowing he had no choice, he allowed the two of them to carry him to the bunkhouse. "Yeah, go give him a call and for Christ's sake don't drop me."

"We got ya partner. Just be glad you didn't break a leg or worse, your neck!" Tom grunted.

"There might not be nothin' broken, but I sure feel like hell. Send one of the men up to the house to call the doc that way he can tell the women I won't be takin' them to the dance tonight. Of all the damn times for this to happen!"

After Doctor Prichard had examined Jed and found a lot of scrapes and bruises he stopped by the house to talk to Charlotte.

"He's gonna be pretty stoved up for a while, but he's young. He'll come out of it all right. The thing that's worryin' him the most right now's the fact he won't be escortin' you lovely ladies to the dance tonight." He tamped tobacco into his pipe.

"I'm just glad he's all right." Charlotte slid an ashtray towards him. "There'll be other dances."

"That's true, but why waste this one?" He struck a match holding the flame over the bowl of the pipe, puffing on the stem. "Granted now, I ain't as handsome as young Stanford, but I can still hold my own on a dance floor." A billow of smoke floated into the air. "If you ladies'll agree, I'd be honored to be your escort tonight."

Hattie spoke up, "Ah doan knows 'bout de rest of y'all, but ah shoh' wants ter go. It gits tiresome havin' ter eats mah own cookin' all de time."

"Then it's settled," Charlotte told him. "That is, if you think you can handle three women."

"I guess there's just one way to find out." He placed the pipe tobacco back in his pocket. "I'll be expectin' you to be ready when I get here at sundown."

As Prichard closed the door behind him, Charlotte headed for the stairs and her room. Going to her closet she started pulling out one dress then another until finally settling on a long dark brown cotton skirt with matching belt, a long-sleeved white cotton blouse with rust-colored buttons up the front, and a pale cinnamon-colored shawl to wear later in the evening. She had just stooped to pick out a pair of brown leather boots when someone tapped on her door.

"Come in," she called out.

"I hope I'm not disturbing you, Gram." Tia walked into the room.

"You're not disturbing me, Tia, I's just choosing what I'm gonna wear to the shindig tonight. What do you think?" Charlotte held up the outfit she had picked out.

"Very nice, but then anything you wear would look good on you."

"Thank you, Tia. Well I'm all set, so now all we gotta do is decide on what you're gonna wear."

"That's what I came to ask you. I brought some cotton dresses but I don't know which one would be suited for a hoedown," she laughed.

"Come on," Charlotte placed her arm around Tia's waist, "I'll help you pick out somethin'."

The long-sleeved, pink dress with the hem ending just below the ankles made the perfect outfit for a young girl to wear to a Harvest dance. Charlotte disappeared for a moment and when she returned she had a dark pink shawl made from the softest wool, draped over her arm. "Now all you need is your dancin' shoes and you're ready to go."

Tia twirled in front of the long mirror and the soft material of the dress swirled around her ankles. "What do you think, Gram?" Tia picked up a dark pink ribbon off the vanity table and tied her long hair back from her face.

"I think you look lovely, Tia. But we need to hurry so grab your shawl and let's go. With any luck, Hattie will already have on her best black satin and be ready to leave."

Although the night had lost most of its fascination for Tia now that Jed would not be accompanying them, she made up her mind she wouldn't let it show. She knew how anxious her grandmother was for her to make a good impression on their neighbors and she made up her mind she would not disappoint her.

"Poor Jed's gonna be sorry he missed this one," Charlotte laughed, looking around the decorated grange hall. "Everyone in the county's here tonight."

"Believe me," Prichard chanced a quick glance at Tia, "he's already more sorry than words can tell."

"Oh Lawd! Der went de evenin'," Hattie glanced over at Charlotte as a giant of a man, and a tall, gaunt woman, made their way across the floor towards them.

"'Bout time you folks showed up. Thought since that young pup you call a foreman went and got hisself busted up you'd stay close to the roost." The over-bearing man smirked.

"Hello, Sarah," Charlotte said, embracing the thin pale woman.

"Charlotte, it's so good to see you! I've been meanin' to get over your way, but it seems like every time I get a free moment, Frank comes up with somethin' that needs my attention." Sarah murmured fussing with the top button of her dark brown cotton dress, before tucking the straying wisps of brown hair streaked with gray back into a tight-clasped bun.

"Yes, I realize Frank's a man who needs a lotta help," Charlotte turned to draw Tia forward. "Sarah, I'd like you to meet my granddaughter, Tia. Tia, this lovely lady's my best friend, Sarah McKennah, and the man with her, is her husband, Frank."

The story Charlotte had told her about this man and the massacre of the Indian camp raced through Tia's mind as she looked into the beefy red face of Frank McKennah. As he reached out to clasp her hand, the thought of being touched by the man responsible for all those innocent lives was more than she could tolerate. Tia turned embracing a surprised

Sarah, then nodded a brief nod to Frank.

"Hattie, Doctor Prichard, why don't we go get something to drink while Gram visits with Mrs. McKennah?" Tia gave Charlotte's cheek a fond pat. "We'll bring you something, Gram, if you like."

"No, I'll be fine." Charlotte shooed them away. "You run along and enjoy yourselves."

"So, that's your granddaughter, huh?" Frank whistled through his teeth. "She sure is a looker. Plain to see she don't take after the Thornton side of the family." He winked at Charlotte. "What beats me though," he rolled one end of his long, bushy white mustache between thumb and forefinger, "is how Jessie met and married someone that dark in Massachusetts. She'd had better luck findin' that girl's daddy right here at home."

"Frank, please!" Sarah whispered, chancing a nervous glance at Charlotte.

"Oh hell, honey, Charlotte knows I don't mean nothin' by it. 'Sides, it's good for her to get a little riled now and then. Gets that adrenaline up. Ain't that right, Charlotte?"

"You know, Frank," Charlotte looked at him, "it just dawned on me where the good Lord went wrong when he made you. Bend down here a second."

When Frank did as she directed, Charlotte turned his head from side to side, then stood back, shaking her own head in bemusement. "Just as I thought, they ain't there."

"What ain't?" Frank boomed.

"The handles you need to pull your head outta your ass every time you open your mouth!" Charlotte delivered, before ushering a grinning Sarah ahead of her.

"Uppity Bitch!" Frank spat, drawing a small bottle from his suit-coat, unscrewing the lid, and taking a long drink. "One of these days," he drew a hand across his mouth, "she's gonna go too far! Wouldn't surprise me if her granddaughter is a half-breed wild as Jessie was." He recapped the bottle, sticking it back in his pocket.

As the women seated themselves at one of the many banquet tables set up around the crowded room, Sarah leaned forward. "I'm sorry, Charlotte. You know Frank. He always speaks before he thinks."

"No need to apologize, Sarah." Charlotte waved her apology away. "If he didn't open his mouth and say somethin' stupid, he wouldn't be Frank!"

"Tia's a beautiful girl. You must be very proud of her."

"Yes, she is. And she's a good girl, too." She glanced around, and lowered her voice. "I made the right decision in leaving her in John and Martha's care. They raised her up to be a fine young lady. I just hope her comin' out here don't undo everything we've all worked so hard to protect."

"Have you had any word from Eathen," Sarah leaned in close, "on when he plans to return?"

"Not yet, but I'm scared to death, he'll come home early and find her here. If that happens," she fanned herself with her hand, "I don't know what he'll do. Seein' her could reopen so many wounds, especially knowin' what he did."

Lowering her voice to just above a whisper, Sarah leaned in closer. "Has she asked you anything about her father?"

Nodding, Charlotte replied, "I told her I wouldn't discuss him. Perhaps I'm wrong, but if tellin' her the truth is gonna destroy everyone I hold dear, includin' her, then the truth is better left where it is. Buried in the past."

"God help us if Frank ever gets hold of the truth," Sarah declared.

"I doubt that'll ever happen, Sarah. I knew I could trust you to keep quiet about Jessie. If I couldn't, I'd never have told you."

"Our friendship means more to me than a bunch of malicious gossip." Sarah reached across the table to give Charlotte's hand a gentle shake. "But Frank's another matter. He thrives on trouble. I think Tia shows enough of her white side to fool him though."

"Thank god for that." Charlotte closed her eyes for a brief moment. "If Frank should ever get wind of Tia's parentage, the whole mess could blow right up in our faces."

Tia must have danced with every cowboy in the county that night. Each time a song ended another pair of arms encircled her, drawing her back onto the dance floor.

Although a proficient dancer, Tia found herself missing steps as her feet tried to keep up with the fast beat tempo of the fiddles and guitar. So different from the melodic pieces played on the family Steinway, and accompanied by the haunting strains of a mastered violin.

Shaking her head in refusal at the request of yet another hopeful cowboy, Tia glanced up to see Charlotte walking towards her.

"I was beginnin' to think you was gonna dance the night away. Can't wait to see Jed's face when these young swains start beatin' a path to my door."

"Now, Gram," Tia laughed, "everyone is just being nice to me because I'm a Thornton."

"You believe that if you want to. I know better," she chuckled, then drew in her breath at the sight of someone walking towards her. "Good god almighty!" She closed her eyes, turning away. "I've seen it all, now!"

Looking over Charlotte's shoulder Tia soon saw what had her so upset. A tall voluptuous woman with flaming red hair, and poured into a very low-cut, form-fitting, purple gown, swayed on the arm of a curly-haired young cowboy.

The young man, dressed in a western-cut dark brown suit, white silk shirt, and black string tie with the head of a horse made of turquoise, teetered back on his feet in a drunken stupor. "Evenin', Miss Charlotte." He waved a dark brown Stetson around the crowded room. This is one hell of a wing ding, ain't it?" As he brought his attention back to Charlotte, he grinned. "I'd like to introduce you to my lady-friend here." He turned to the woman standing almost on top of him. "Flossy, meet Mrs. Charlotte Thornton, richest broad in the county. Hell," he threw up his hands, "ten counties for that matter!"

With a nervous smile, Charlotte glanced at her granddaughter.

"My word! What we got here?" His young voice deepened. "Please, introduce me!"

Anxious to be rid of the boisterous intruder, Charlotte acquiesced. "Tia, this is Sarah's grandson, Jeremy, and his friend.... Flossy." Charlotte fluttered her hand in the woman's direction. "Tia's my granddaughter, Jeremy."

Tia couldn't be sure which of the two had her more perplexed. The tall, skinny man with his curly, light red hair and leering grin, or the green-eyed woman staring at her.

Taking Tia's small hand in his and snapping his dark brown, leather boots together, Jeremy placed a light kiss on her trembling fingers before releasing her. "I'm very pleased to make your acquaintance, Miss Tia."

At that moment, Charlotte felt someone bump against her. She turned her head in time to see Frank McKennah, stripped of his suit coat and tie, stagger past her.

"Where the hell you been, boy?" Frank spun the younger man around. "I's 'bout to give up on ya!"

"Just got back to town." Jeremy's hazel eyes lit up at the sight of his grandfather. "And none too soon by the looks of things." He shot an open leer at Tia. "You remember Flossy, don't you?" He drew back a hand, slapped the woman a smart rap across her rounded backside.

"Ain't a man breathin' could forget the best damn madam in all of Montana!" He undid the buttons on the cuffs of his white cotton shirt, rolled up the sleeves and threw his big arms open wide. "Come here you good lookin' heifer!" Amid squeals of bawdy laughter, McKennah swung the scantily dressed woman up in his arms.

With her full mouth open wide, Flossy placed both her hands on each side of Frank's face to yank him forward for a long passionate kiss. When she released him she arched her back, throwing her arms wide her ample breast all but swallowing Frank's face. "You always did have the longest tongue in captivity!" she laughed then squealed, pushing on his face and trying to squirm out of his embrace as Frank buried his face in her cleavage making sounds like a steam whistle.

"Let's get outta here, while their occupied!" Charlotte pulled a horrified Tia across the floor. "I can't believe he had the nerve to walk in here with that strumpet hangin' on his arm! Poor Sarah! Now," Charlotte huffed out a breath, looking around the packed hall, "where the hell's Hattie? After that fiasco, I'm ready to call it a night!"

"The last time I saw her she was over at the buffet tables. Yes," she nodded, as she caught sight of the big woman still seated at the table, "there she is."

"Then let's go gather up our wraps. By that time she should be finished and we can get outta here!"

"I want you to know, Gram," Tia told her, as they made their way through a throng of people. "I've had a very enjoyable evening."

"I'm glad you liked it, Tia. It's a lot different than what you're used to, but it keeps us country folk entertained."

"Do you think your neighbors will tell Grandfather Eathen about my being here?" She helped Charlotte on with her coat.

"I don't know." Charlotte shrugged her shoulders. "It's too late to worry about it now anyway. I couldn't disappoint Hattie. The Harvest dance is a time she gets to go somewhere that she can really enjoy herself and not haveta help with the clean up afterwards."

"Yes, but we both know you didn't have to bring me."

Stopping in mid-stride, Charlotte turned to stare up at her. "You're my granddaughter, Tia. I've never been ashamed of you. Why would I start now?" Charlotte slipped her arm around the girl's narrow waist as they walked toward Hattie.

"Ah kin sees you gots yo' pocketbook a-hangin' on yo' arm, so ah guess dat means we's a-fixin' ter leaves." Hattie hurried to spoon the last of her pumpkin pie, topped with a large spoonful of whip-cream, into her mouth.

"Just as soon as we find Doctor Prichard we are," Charlotte replied, then smiled as she saw the portly doctor hurrying towards them.

"I sure hope you ladies ain't been waitin' on me." He slipped his arms into the coat Charlotte held ready for him "I got tied up with Mrs. Flarady about her latest addition to the family," he apologized.

"Dat woman's gwine ter keeps on havin' youngin's 'til her po' husband ain' even gwine ter has a place ter sits down ter eats," Hattie laughed.

They had already walked to the door when for some reason Tia turned to find Jeremy McKennah watching her. Even from the long distance between them she could feel his cold eyes moving over her. Of all the people she had met since arriving in Montana, she knew Jeremy McKennah would be the last person she would ever wish to see again.

Chapter Six

"Tia," Charlotte tapped her knife against one of two soft-boiled eggs in her bowl, "the hands are gonna start brandin' this mornin'. You might wanna go along and watch how it's done." She scooped the eggs out of their shells, pulled the butter-dish across the table.

"You don't think Jed would mind?" She handed Charlotte the salt and pepper shakers.

"Are you kiddin'?" Charlotte picked up her bowl as she walked toward the dining room. "Jed would welcome the sight of you no matter what he had goin'."

"Miss Charlotte," Hattie raised her voice from the kitchen, "ah ain' sho dat's sech a good idea." She slid three fried eggs from the skillet onto a plate, already heaping with potatoes and bacon. "Brandin' time ain' no place fer a young girl lak Miss Tia." Her hands darted inside the hot oven for four pieces of dark toast to drop them on the table by the stove. "Ah knows it ain' any of mah bizness," she said, as she slathered butter over the toast followed by a large dollop of strawberry jelly on each piece, "but de smell of all dat buhnin' hide an de way dem po' lil babies cahy on? Lawd! You couldn' git me near dat place."

Taking a sip of her coffee, Charlotte turned, peering through the open kitchen door to see Hattie still busy fixing her breakfast "I had a call from Martha last night after we got home." She lowered her voice. "To say she's upset would not do her justice."

With real fear showing in her eyes, Tia placed a hand on Charlotte's arm. "Is she going to come out here to take me home?"

"She wanted to." Charlotte set her cup down on the saucer as she recalled the way her sister's screeching hysterics had continued long into the night. "I told her we have everything under control, and since Eathen's in Helena right now I could see no problem with your bein' here."

"Thank you, Gram." Tia lifted Charlotte's hand, placed a light kiss on the curled fingers. "I'm enjoying it here on the ranch so much; I really don't want to go back to Boston yet."

"I've enjoyed havin' you here, Tia. But I meant what I told you about your not bein' here when Eathen comes home, so enjoy the short time you have left. Jed would be more'n glad to show you all about the brandin. In fact..." she began, but a loud knocking on the back door interrupted anything further she had to say.

"Come in!" Charlotte yelled, before Hattie could pull open the door.

Upon seeing Jed, Charlotte directed. "Pull up a chair and help yourself to some coffee." She edged the coffeepot, setting on a thick potholder over towards him. "Gettin' kind of a late start this mornin' ain't ya?"

The usual bantering between the two was not forth coming this morning, as Jed poured himself a cup of coffee. "We got trouble, Miss Charlotte."

"What kinda trouble?" Charlotte pushed her cup away.

"The kind we don't need. Some fences in the south pasture's been cut and there's fresh blood on the ground." His hand shot out snatching a piece of jellied toast and a strip of bacon off Hattie's plate as she moved past his chair. "Looks like somebody had themselves a little butcherin' party last night."

"Effen you wants," Hattie glared at him before seating herself at the far end of the table, "ah'll be glad ter cooks you sum breakfast, Mist' Jed."

"Who the hell would rustle beef around here?" Charlotte put up a hand quieting Hattie. "I know times are hard right now, but folks know if they need beef all they gotta do is ask. I'd be more'n happy to let them have it. I know Eathen'd say the same."

"I don't think it's rustlers." He added cream and sugar to his coffee. "They wouldn't of skinned them out right there. In fact, there wasn't even a piece of hide left." He took a sip of coffee, reached for the sugarbowl. "Ain't but one kindda thief I know of that don't leave hide nor hair of their kill and that's Indians."

"Indians?" Charlotte glanced around the table; to be sure everyone else had heard the same thing she had.

"Yep'n less I miss my guess. Although with Hardiman as Indian Agent, I don't think I'm wrong." He sandwiched the slice of bacon into the jellied toast, dunking it in his coffee. "Could be a one night raid." He chewed, swallowed then, licked his fingers. "I'm gonna post some guards tonight just to be safe."

"Good idea, Jed. There's somethin' I don't understand though. We sell Hardiman top-of-the-line beef. If he ain't feedin' it to the Blackfeet, what the hell's he doin' with it?"

"Sellin' it to a slaughterhouse and makin' double his profit'd be my bet." He licked the last of the jelly off his fingers.

"That crooked bastard!" Charlotte got up from her chair to begin pacing the floor. "What are we plannin' on doin' 'bout this, Jed?"

"Like I said. I can go ahead and post guards tonight. Then if it's someone around here, it shouldn't be too hard to catch 'em. If it ain't, then it's a pretty safe bet it's like I thought. Some reservation Indians got tired of seein' their people doin' without and decided to do somethin' about it. We can't blame em. You'd do the same if one of your own had to do without."

"You know damn well I would. But all they had to do is ask! I don't begrudge anybody if I can help it. You know that."

"Yeah, Miss Charlotte, I know. 'Cept Indians know how the whites feel about them. This way they could be sure of the beef." He gave a slight laugh. "'Sides, it gave em a chance to feel like men again. Providin' for their people themselves without askin' the white man for a handout."

"If that's the case, yes," she nodded. "It's worth losin' a few headda beef. Jed, I want you to tell whoever you send out there tonight not to shoot unless it's white men." Charlotte's eyes narrowed with feeling. "If they ain't got enough balls to come ask me, by damn they deserve to be shot."

"Miss Charlotte, sech talk!" Hattie scolded, jabbing her fork into her fried potatoes. "Der bes a young lady hyah now you knows."

"Yes I do know, Hattie. I just get so damn mad sometimes I let fly with the first thing that pops into my head." She glanced at Tia. "You gotta overlook this ole lady sometimes, Tia. I ain't always the easiest person to be around."

Nodding, Tia dropped her eyes, a hot flush covering her cheeks.

At a quiet tapping on the back door Jed went out to see who could be calling at such an early hour.

"Miss Charlotte. I think you better come out here."

"Now what the hell's goin' on?" Charlotte grumbled, grabbing a dark shawl off the back of her chair and throwing it around her shoulders before going to the door followed by Tia and Hattie. At the sight of three Indians standing on her back porch, she whispered. "Who are they, Jed? Do you know?"

"I recognize the ole man in the middle. His name's Pehta." As Charlotte continued to stare at him, he reminded her. "The one who thought he knew Tia that day at the reservation?"

The name nagged at the back of her mind until she remembered him to also be an old friend of Eathen. "What in the world do you think they want?"

"Could be we're about to solve the mystery of your stolen beef."

Dressed in a well-worn red and white checkered shirt and faded Jeans, a man in his early thirties stepped forward. "Are you Mrs. Thornton?"

Charlotte answered, "I'm Charlotte Thornton,"

"My name is Black Elk." His dark eyes watched her.

"What can I do for you, Black Elk?"

"I have come to repay you for the beef some of my people took from you in the night. I have no money, or anything that would be of value to you, but we are willing to work until the debt has been paid."

"You admit the beef was stolen by your men?"

"The body must have food," he told her his dark eyes never wavering from hers, "our bellies are empty. Your name has always been spoken with much respect among my tribe. I am sorry some of my people could not wait any longer for the good beef the agent at the reservation has promised."

Cocking her head to one side, Charlotte stared at the man in disbelief. "Hardiman told you he was waitin' for beef to feed your people?"

"Yes. He kept telling us the meat would come soon."

"That lyin' bastard!" Charlotte jammed her hands into the pockets of her long skirt.

Black Elk had heard of the white woman who spoke like a man. The broad smile flashing across his handsome face was not missed by Charlotte.

"I see you feel the same way I do about Hardiman." Her brows lifted in amusement as she surveyed the tall well-built man, standing before her.

"The agent does not tell the truth." The man's eyes shifted to the other two men as they nodded in agreement. "The way you describe him is the same in any language."

"Yeah? Well I'll tell you what I'm gonna do, Black Elk." Charlotte pulled the dark shawl over her light blue cotton blouse. "You came here of your own free will and admitted to the theft of Thornton beef. To my way of thinkin' it takes a big man to do that. So you don't owe me anything. Hardiman promised you some beef? We'll chalk it up to an early delivery that'll come outta Hardiman's pocket, I can promise you that!" She elbowed Jed in the ribs as he stood beside her. "Go give Sheriff Wills a call."

"Miss Charlotte, I don't think this is a matter..." Jed began, then grew quiet as Charlotte raised her voice over his.

"I'm well aware this is a job for the government, Jed," she echoed his thoughts, "but I don't have time to put up with their bureaucratic bullshit! I want somethin' done now! Better yet, just tell him to meet us at the crossroads then go hitch up my buggy. Goin' cross country's a lot shorter'n takin' the road. I'm gonna tell Hardiman personally what I think of him!"

"You realize it's a pretty long ride goin' all the way out there and back." He tried to reason with her.

"Won't do no good tryin' to talk me out of it, Jed. My mind's made up." She shooed him away. "Now get goin' and do what I told ya!"

Muttering under his breath about the stubbornness of women, Jed stomped off to make the call.

Turning her attention back to the men standing in silence, Charlotte eyed their ragged clothing. Shirts worn clear through at the elbows, Jeans worn through at the knees and not a coat between the three of them. She made a mental note to have Hattie hunt up some of Eathen's old clothing to send back with them when they left. But two things stood out as she tried not to be too obvious in her perusal of them. Although their clothing may be threadbare and tattered they were clean and as her eyes traveled lower she smiled as she noted that instead of the white man's boots they chose to wear the comfortable footwear of the Indian moccasins. "Black Elk, you and your men come in the house and eat some breakfast." She motioned them forward, when they shook their heads. "I ain't takin' no for an answer, so you might just as well get your asses in here!"

In a low voice, the elder of the men spoke up. Throwing back his head, Black Elk laughed. "Pehta says you have much spirit for a white woman."

"He does, does he? Ain't he used to bein' around women with spirit?"

"No. Blackfeet women are very quiet."

"That must make their husbands happy." Charlotte grinned.

"Yes, at times it is very pleasant."

As Charlotte held open the door for them to enter, Pehta halted in front of her. His dark eyes warmed as he gazed at her. "You are not like most whites, Little Aakiiwa. Your heart does not turn away from your Indian brothers."

"Well...thank you, Pehta," Charlotte stammered.

Then Pehta's eyes fell upon Tia. "There was but one Blackfoot girl I knew who had your spirit, Miss Charlotte. The wife of my brother. I remember on their wedding night, she drew blood on her husband."

"What did your brother do with his wife?" Charlotte asked, her own eyes widening in surprise at Pehta's matter-of-fact-narrative.

"He kept her."

"Did he ever tame her?"

"Not her spirit." Pehta chuckled.

"That reminds me," she cocked her head to one side staring up at him; "I heard you mistook my granddaughter here," she nodded towards Tia, "for that girl you just spoke of. How in the world could you mistake someone as young as her for a body my age?"

For a long moment, the old man gazed over at Tia, then with a sad shake of his head, he answered, "In your granddaughter, I saw the beauty of my brother's wife. In her, I saw the spirit of Tia."

At Charlotte's astonished gasp, Tia spoke up, "Gram, I'm sure these men are hungry. Don't you think we should be giving them food instead of all this talk?"

"You're right, child." Charlotte motioned the men inside, but as Tia made to follow, Charlotte took hold of her arm. "Tia, I want you to stay away from him. As soon as they've eaten, I'll send them on their way. Until then, I don't want you near him!"

As Hattie set the steaming platter of hotcakes, eggs, and bacon on the table, the men looked on with longing.

"All right, we don't stand on ceremony around here. Just grab a plate and dig in," Charlotte declared, her eyes misting as she saw the men, who had to be all but starving, trying so hard not to gulp down their food. *Hardiman,* she thought to herself, *when I get through with you, there won't be a place in all of Montana where you'll be welcome.*

Later, as the men walked outside, Charlotte placed a bag in Black Elk's hand. "Take this with you. I'd rather see them put to good use 'stead of thrown away. It's just a little somethin' we don't need no more." She pushed the bag back to him when he tried to refuse. "Jed and me won't be far behind, but if Hardiman sees us come in together it'll tip him off. I want our visit to be a complete surprise."

"Thank you, Miss Charlotte." Black Elk covered both her hands with his. "My people and I will not forget your kindness."

"Don't worry." She patted his hands. "Your people won't go hungry again. Not as long as I have anything to say about it!"

Tia watched Pehta as he walked outside ahead of the others. On impulse he turned, his black eyes locking with hers. As she stood there, she felt some of the fear she had felt in his presence disappear. Without realizing it, she walked up to him. Taking his frail hand in hers, she told him, "Have a safe trip, Pehta."

Pehta's worn and weather-lined face clouded with emotion as he drew her against his chest for a brief moment. Looking over her shoulder, he whispered, "Good-bye, my brother."

As Charlotte, Jed, and the sheriff rode in, it was a nervous Hardiman who greeted them.

"Well, what in the world brings you folks all the way out here?"

"In your wildest dreams you couldn't guess, Hardiman!" Charlotte grasped Jed's hand getting down from the buggy.

"Why, whatta you mean, ma'am?" he clutched his stained hat in his hands. "I don't even know you."

"Don't ma'am me!" She slapped the dust from her dress. "And believe me, before I leave here today you're gonna know me. In more ways'n one."

"Stanford," Hardiman whipped his dirt-matted head around, "I don't know who this crazy bitch is," he jabbed a thumb in Charlotte's direction, "but for her own sake, you'd best get her the hell outta here." He hiked his baggy pants up higher around his waist.

Standing with a fistful of Charlotte's dress, Jed removed his hat to hold it in reverence against his chest. "There I go again! Forgettin' my manners! Hardiman," he released his grasp on Charlotte to hold the palm of one hand out straight, and wagging his fingers back and forth, motioned for the ill-kept man to step forward. Lowering his head, until it almost brushed against the man's stubbled cheek, Jed whispered in a loud voice, "Hardiman, I'd like to introduce you to Mrs. Eathen

Thornton."

With his watery eyes growing wide, Hardiman took a step backwards. Looking first to Jed then to Charlotte he tried to speak. Finally, in a voice much higher than his normal tone, he declared, "I'm sorry, Mrs. Thornton, for bein' so disrespectful." He reached out a dirty hand to her then thought better of it and shoved the hand, instead, into his pocket. "But I still got no idea why you're here."

"We're here, Hardiman, for a piece of your ass and we intend to get it!" She shook her small fist in his sweating face.

Hardiman drew himself up. "Now just you hold on there, ma'am."

"No! You hold on, Hardiman! We gotta little business of cattle stealin' to discuss!"

"What you talkin' 'bout?" Hardiman sputtered. "I ain't stole no cattle! I gotta bill of sale right in my office," he jabbed a finger in the direction of a small building, "sayin' Mister Eathen sold those cattle to this reservation and that they's paid for by the United States Government! Now," he puffed out his chest, "what do you have to say 'bout that?"

"Yeah, you gotta bill of sale sayin' my husband sold you cattle to feed the people on this reservation." Charlotte nodded. "On that, we agree. But," she stepped in front of him, poked a finger hard, against his chest, "that's where our agreein' ends! What the hell'd you do with the beef, Hardiman?"

"Why, I fed the people on this reservation, just like I was suppose' to!" He tried to bat her hand away.

"You're a damn liar!" Charlotte breathed, her small face mere inches from his.

"Now... you... just... hold... on... there, Missy!" He drew his head back, wiping collected spittle from the corners of his mouth. "Eathen Thornton's old lady or not, I don't haveta take that kinda talk!" He whipped a soiled bandanna from the back pocket of his pants.

"Hardiman," Sheriff Wilks snapped, dismounting. "You got some explainin' to do. You best start now!"

"I don't know where this woman gets off accusin' me of stealin'," he hurried to stand beside Wilks, "but I got the proof to show you!"

"Hardiman, the white woman speaks the truth."

The agent turned to find Pehta standing a short distance away, watching him. "Get on outta here, ole man! You ain't got nothin' in this!"

"Let him talk," Jed ordered.

"The Indian Agent starves our people while he sells the cattle you sold him, Miss Charlotte, to the whites."

"Why you lyin' ole bastard! I ain't done no such a thing! Stanford," Hardiman mopped his sweating face as he hastened toward Jed, "you ain't gonna believe the lies of a crazy ole Indian are ya?"

"You know my words are true," Pehta said. "Many of my people have died because we had no food."

"Is that true, Hardiman?" Sheriff Wilks asked.

"No it ain't true." Hardiman mimicked in a singsong nasal voice. "'Sides, what the hell you stickin' your nose into this for, Wilks?" He pushed the sleeves of his red shirt up higher on his arms. "You ain't got no jurisdiction out here. The one I have to answer to's the government, and that sure as hell ain't you! Now," Hardiman delivered, eyeing the angry crowd gathered around him, "I want every one of you off this reservation!"

"What are you plannin' on doin' 'bout this, Sheriff Wilks?" Charlotte asked.

"I'm afraid there ain't nothin' I can do." Wilks slapped his hat against his jeans. "Pehta can't prove the charges he just made and even if he could, it's like Hardiman said," his voice deepened with anger, "I got no jurisdiction here. I'm sorry, Miss Charlotte." Wilks stepped into the saddle.

"Not half as sorry as you're gonna be come next election," she predicted, grabbing hold of Jed's arm. "Come on, Jed. Let's go home. We may not be able to do anything now, but this ain't over by a long shot!"

After helping Charlotte into the buggy, Jed turned to find a smug Hardiman paring a plug of chewing tobacco, his short squat legs spread wide, watching him.

"'Case you got any ideas 'bout harmin' any of the people on this reservation for tellin' the truth, I'd think twice if I was you." His gray stare never wavered. "Even if somethin' happens by accident, I'm holdin' you," Jed stabbed a finger in his direction, "responsible."

"You talk mighty big with the sheriff here to back you up, Stanford." Hardiman drew back his thin lips, biting the plug of tobacco off the razor sharp edge of the knife. "Maybe you'd like to come on back when he ain't around." Hardiman grinned, a stream of tobacco juice escaping down his chin.

With lightning speed, Jed swung, dropping the little man where he stood. Without a word, Jed reached down jerking Hardiman to his feet before his fist connected once more with the man's already, bleeding face.

Placing a boot on each side of Hardiman's head, Jed stared down at him. "Do the job you're bein' paid to do, Hardiman, or I'll see to it the government gets another agent."

Smart enough to remain where Jed had left him, Hardiman lay on the hard ground, watching as the three rode out. Rolling to the side he pushed himself to his feet to see Pehta standing within hearing distance.

"You ever stick your nose in my business again, ole man, I'll slit your fuckin' throat," Hardiman wheezed limping away.

Chapter Seven

Walking into the kitchen Tia found Hattie bent over the stove, taking a pan of fresh baked cinnamon rolls out of the oven.

"Ef you'll gives me jes' a minute ter gits dese frosted," Hattie told her, setting the hot pan down on the stand beside the stove, "you kin enjoys sum wid yo' mawnin' coffee."

"They smell delicious." Tia bent over the pan to take a long sniff. "But I think I'll wait and have some with Gram."

"Dat case you's gwine ter be waitin' a long time." She poured a small amount of fresh milk followed by a few drops of vanilla over the powdered sugar and butter she had already stirred up in a bowl. "She bes awready up and gone."

"This early? Wherever to?"

"Tole me she wuz gwine ter spends de day wid Miss Sarah." Hattie held the large bowl against her ponderous belly, beating the sugar mixture with a wooden spoon. "W'en dem two gits tergither, you mout jes' as well not look fer her 'til suppertime," She set the frosting bowl down on the table. "A body'd think she'd want ter stays home an be wid you."

"I don't expect her to stop seeing her friends because I'm here, Hattie." Tia dipped up a finger-full of the stiffened frosting, being careful not to get any on her denim shirt. "It looks like it's going to be a beautiful day, maybe I'll go riding this afternoon. I'd like to see as much of the ranch as I can while I have the chance."

"Ah'd say git Mist' Jed ter gos wid you," she dropped the knife she had been using, to ice the rolls, into the bowl, "but he awready gots his hands full wid de brandin'."

"I don't want to bother Jed. I'll be fine." Tia held a plate ready, while Hattie lifted a frosted cinnamon roll out of the pan.

"Awright den," Hattie licked as much of the frosting, clinging to her fingers, as she could, wiping the rest off on her apron. "Mist' Tom's tekin' me inter town ter shop, so effen ah ain' hyah w'en you gits back dat's where ah'll bes. An doan you be gwine too far." She pumped cold water into the sticky bowl as it set in the sink filled with the knife and spatula. "You ain' all dat familiar wid de area round hyah."

"I'll be careful, Hattie. Don't worry," Tia told her, talking around the mouthful of gooey roll.

"Ah'll jes' goes ahead an' fix you up a basket of food ter teks wid you, Baby Chile." She said, already taking a platter of sliced ham from the icebox.

Riding with the sun on her back and a soft breeze blowing her hair, Tia felt free. Kneeing her horse into a run she laughed aloud, letting the wind take all the problems off her small shoulders.

Spying a large lake up ahead, she reined her horse to a walk. "That looks like a good place to stop. What do you think, boy?" she asked the big Paint, patting him on the side of his long neck. "Are you thirsty?" The horse, enjoying her gentle stroking, threw up his large head emitting a long whinny.

Dismounting, she walked through the tall bunch grass savoring her surroundings. She noticed how the wind made soft ripples in the grass, and swayed the tall aspens overhead.

She sensed the presence of someone nearby, and turned to see a man riding towards her. As he drew closer, she saw the man she and Jed had seen on her way to the ranch the day she arrived.

"Hello," she called out, throwing up her hand in greeting.

"Hello," he answered. "I hope I didn't frighten you. I saw you ride up. You're the Thornton's granddaughter, right?"

"Yes. I'm Tia Thornton. And what may I call you?" Tia smiled up at him.

"Folks round here just call me Wolfer." He wrapped the reins around the saddle horn, returning her smile.

"It's beautiful here, isn't it?"

"The Blackfoot thought so." He dismounted to stand beside her. "If you'd been here 'bout fifty years ago," he waved his hand, encompassing the area, "you'd been standin' smack dab in the middle of an Indian camp."

"Yes, Gram told me what happened here." She hooked her thumbs in the belt loops of her Jeans. "It's hard to believe, looking at it now," she murmured. "How terrible for them."

"Yep." He stooped down to pick a bright red flower. "Hatin' a person because he's of a different race never did set right with me."

"Do you come here often?" she asked, accepting the flower he held out to her and breathing in its fragrance.

"I stop when I'm in the area." He removed a rolled cigarette from the pocket of his long-fringed buckskin shirt to place it between his full lips. "The Kainah Blackfoot believe, since so many of their people died here, this place is, ka-ne-ma-ho." He flicked a match with his thumbnail, cupping a hand around the flame. "Means, filled with restless spirits," he explained at her questioning look.

"You mean haunted?" Tia breathed staring at him.

"Yep."

"You don't believe that do you?"

"Bein' raised by a Kainah Blackfoot myself, I gotta admit," he chuckled deep in his throat, "I've seen a lotta strange things over the years."

"If you don't mind my asking," she placed a tentative hand on his arm, "how did you come to be raised by an Indian?"

Pushing his wide brimmed hat further back on his head, he curled his fingers around hers as they continued to walk, "I's what's referred to, as a woods colt." He glanced down at her upturned face. "I had a mama, but no legal pa. Guess she got tired of raisin' a youngin' on her own. One day," he shrugged his massive shoulders, "she lit out, leavin' me behind. Few days later," a wide smile lit up his face, "an Indian by the name of Pehta came along and found me wonderin' alone out on the prairie. He raised me up as one of his own."

Tia remained silent watching him out of the corner of her eye. Taking in the contours of his wind-lined, high cheek-boned face, the straight nose with nostrils that flared when he breathed out, the deep set slate-gray eyes and full mouth that seemed to be set now in a tense line of concentration. Gathering up her courage, she said, "It would seem you and I have a lot in common, Wolfer. I'm a woods colt, too. Except, my mother killed herself right after my birth leaving me to be raised by relatives. Now I'm searching for my father."

"Have you talked to your grandmother 'bout this?" His gaze wondered out over the lake.

"I tried, but she refuses to discuss him." Dropping down on the grass skirting the bank of the lake, she removed her boots and socks, to push her feet into the crystal cool water.

"Maybe she has good reason." He seated himself beside her, grinning as he watched her shiver then pull her feet back from the lake's chilling touch. Stretching his booted feet out straight, he leaned back supporting his weight on his elbows. "Could be she's tryin' to keep you from bein' hurt."

"Whatever her reason," Tia withdrew a black kerchief from around her throat to begin drying her chilled feet, "I still want to know who he is. From what little Gram did tell me about him, it sounds like he had no choice about my mother and me. She and Grandfather Eathen sent her away as soon as they found out she was expecting me. Of course," a bitter smile settled over her lush mouth, "they told everyone here she met and married my father in Boston. So many lies," she whispered.

"No doubt about it, this is a cruel ole world. But sometimes what we think we want," he rolled to his feet, washing his face and hands in the cool water, "we're better off not findin' it," he told her, surprised at how relaxed he felt with her.

For some odd reason, Tia found she could be herself with this man seated beside her. Before long they were sharing the picnic lunch Hattie had packed for her and laughing over different things that had happened in their lives. To their surprise the afternoon passed quickly.

As they walked toward their tethered mounts, he advised her, "I think it's time you started for home. I'll ride along with you. I gotta meet a fellow out your way anyhow."

"I'd like that, Wolfer," Tia handed him the picnic basket to hold while she mounted. "From all we've told each other about ourselves, I feel as if I've known you a lot longer than just a few short hours."

"I feel the same, Tia," he said, helping her into the saddle.

They had ridden but a short way when without warning Tia's horse shied to the side of the path. It all happened so sudden. The Paint humped his broad back high in the air, before kicking his hind legs out behind him and throwing Tia from his back. Thankfully, she lost consciousness upon impact thus sparing herself extreme pain, as one large hoof gouged the side of her head.

Reining his horse, Wolfer drew his gun and taking careful aim, fired off two shots killing the deadly rattler as it curled, preparing to strike. Jumping from his horse he knelt beside the small, still form, wincing at the blood already staining the ground. Pulling his neck scarf from around his throat, he wadded it, then pressed it tight against the wound, tying it in place with a leather thong. Picking Tia up in his arms, he walked with her toward his skittish mount. The wild-eyed horse danced away just out of reach each time Wolfer tried to mount. With his pulse racing, the frightened man talked in a calm voice. His gentle words belying the cold hand of fear clutching his heart. When at last he had the horse under control, Wolfer remounted racing for the Thornton ranch, and praying all the while he would not be too late.

Wolfer yanked on the reins as the horse drew up in front of the Thornton's front porch. With an unconscious Tia cradled in his arms, he bounded up the porch steps and slammed against the door with the toe of his boot. When no one came forth, he drew back and with one vicious kick sent the door flying off its hinges.

"What the hell's goin' on!" roared an angry Eathen Thornton, coming down the stairs.

"Call Doc Prichard! Your granddaughter's had an accident!" Wolfer ordered, brushing past him to place Tia down on the sofa.

"My what?" Eathen breathed.

"You heard me, goddamn it! Tia's horse threw her! His back hoof caught her in the side of the head! Now get on the phone and get Doc Prichard's ass out here!"

As if in a daze, Eathen moved to the telephone.

Banging the swinging kitchen door back against the wall, Wolfer grabbed a clean towel off the rack to soak it beneath the large pump at the sink. Unmindful of the wet path trailing after him, he wrung the towel all but dry on his way back to Tia. Seating himself beside her on the couch and ignoring the bloodstains covering a good part of his buckskin pants, he pressed the cold cloth tight against the wound. Finally, the flow of blood stopped.

"Prichard's on his way," Thornton murmured, staring at the young girl lying on the couch.

"Good. I got the blood stopped," Wolfer glanced up at him, "but I don't think we oughta move her. I don't wanna do any more damage than's already been done."

"What in god's name is goin' on?" Charlotte cried, then stopped as she saw Eathen standing by the couch.

"Your granddaughter's had an accident," Wolfer spoke up. "She's hurt pretty bad. Eathen's already called Doc Prichard, he's on his way."

"Oh my word!" Charlotte whispered, walking to where Tia lay, still unconscious. When she saw blood covering her granddaughter's head, her own head snapped up. "What did you do to her, Eathen?"

"I didn't do anything to her!" Eathen yelled, unable to tear his gaze from the girl commanding his attention. "I didn't even know she was here 'til Wolfer kicked the goddamn door off the hinges and carried her in here!"

"All right, you two." Wolfer pushed himself up off the couch. "This ain't no time for a family feud! Your granddaughter's hurt! And hurt bad, less'n I miss my guess!"

"Miss Charlotte, whut happened to de door?" Hattie cried. Then spying Eathen let the groceries slip from her trembling hands. "Oh Lawd! He's home!"

"Yeah, I'm home!" Eathen growled. "And from the looks of things, I never shoulda left!"

Doctor Prichard arrived to move everyone out of the way. While he examined Tia, they waited in silence, each struggling with their own fears. After a while the doctor stood up.

"We need to keep her covered." Doctor Prichard advised, wiping his stained hands on the damp towel Wolfer had dropped on the end table. "She's in shock. I've stitched a pretty nasty gash on her head, but the thing that's worryin' me the most right now's that she's still unconscious." He shot a brief glance at Charlotte then pulled a stethoscope from around his neck dropping it in his bag. "We're gonna have to keep a real close eye on her." He snapped the bag shut. "You men get her upstairs while I go wash up. She'll be a lot more comfortable in her own bed."

"Hattie and Wolfer can take her," Eathen spoke up. "My wife and I have a few things to discuss."

Without a word Wolfer scooped Tia into his arms. A deep scowl covered his face as he brushed past Eathen on his way to the stairs followed by Hattie.

"De towels be in de drawer left of de sink, doctah," she called back over her shoulder. "You jes' he'p yoseff."

"You can rant and rave all you want, Eathen Thornton, but it ain't gonna do you a damn bitta good!" Charlotte railed, uncaring of her words or of how they must sound to the man washing up in the kitchen. "Tia came out here on her own, and the more I think about it I'm glad she did. If I'd known she planned to come, I woulda tried to stop her. As it is, she took the decision outta my hands." She reached out grabbing hold of his arm as he walked past her. "I've enjoyed havin' her here!

She's all I got left of her mother, and goddamn you, Eathen," she screamed the words at him as he yanked away from her; "you'll leave this house before she does!"

"In a pig's ass I will!" Eathen snarled, uncapping a decanter of brandy setting on a small portable bar. "I've been the bill payer in this house for almost fifty years." He pulled two glasses forward. At the slight shake of her head he shoved the one glass back and poured a hefty amount of liquor into the other. "I ain't heard no complaints. I told you," he lifted the glass to his lips taking a deep swallow, "damn near eighteen years ago, I'd never have anything to do with that little bastard and I meant it!"

The stinging slap Charlotte delivered across Eathen's face echoed throughout the quiet room.

"Don't you ever use that word, to describe my granddaughter again." Her white head trembled.

Slamming his glass down on the bar, Eathen walked from the room, brushing past a stunned Doctor Prichard as he stood staring at them. The resounding bang of the back door told them he had left.

"You're my husband, Eathen, and I love you with all my heart," Charlotte whispered, uncaring or unknowing of Prichard's presence, "but this is one battle you ain't gonna win," she promised him, as she made her way towards the stairs.

"Hattie," the doctor said as he and Charlotte walked into the room, "you can start gettin' her cleaned up. Be real careful not to get those stitches wet," he cautioned as he walked closer to Tia's bedside. "After that, if you could get a spare room ready for me, I'd appreciate it."

"Awright, Doctah, only stay wid me w'ile ah tends ter her. Ah's sceered ah jes' mout hu't her."

"Of course I will." He glanced across the room as Charlotte dropped into a nearby chair.

Appearing Wolf stood watching as the two tended to the girl he loved. In silence, he promised. Soon you will know why my spirit could not rest.

Throughout the long night someone stayed by Tia's side. In the morning she remained still unconscious. Flicking a small light once more across the unseeing eyes, Doctor Prichard stood back shaking his head. "She's slipped deeper into unconsciousness, Hattie, and that ain't good. The medical term for this unnatural sleep is coma." He laid the light back down on the nightstand. "I don't know much about it except the longer a person's in a coma the less chance they have of comin' out of it. I just don't know what to do!" He pounded a fist in his hand as a feeling of hopelessness washed over him. At the door he turned, his tired eyes sweeping over the girl lying unmoving in the bed. "If she stirs, Hattie, I'll be downstairs. I need a drink."

"You jes' he'p yoseff, Doctah. In de mean time ah's gwine ter keeps tryin' ter talks ter her." Hattie lowered her large girth down on the chair beside the bed.

"Might just as well save your breath, Hattie. She can't hear you. When a person's in this deep of a sleep, it's my understandin' they don't hear or feel anything. At least," he turned away, "wherever she is, she's outta pain."

Chapter Eight
Montana 1872

Tall pines with their long, low hanging branches casting dark shadows over the forest floor, made the surrounding area cool and inviting, offering some refuge against the sweltering heat already shimmering over the prairie. The air, strong with the scent of dried pine needles and wild flowers, mixed now with smoke from the many campfires being lit some distance away. In a small pool, surrounded by moss-covered banks, the happy laughter of two young Kainah Blackfoot girls rang out over the stillness.

"Keelah," Tia turned onto her side treading water, one arm stretched out straight. "I will race you to the other side."

Keelah leaned her head far back in the water to straighten her long hair, thinking about Tia's challenge, then smiled. "I will race you, but if I beat you, you will have to give me something."

Tia thought for a moment, then grinned over at her. "Would the right to choose the first dance tonight with the warrior of your choice be a worthy trophy?"

"That is nothing to win." she splashed a swoosh of water into Tia's face. "You already know the warrior I will choose. I will choose Konah, and you will choose Gray Dog."

"Do not be too sure." Tia gazed at her a wide smile playing at the corners of her full mouth. "Gray Dog is very handsome, but as your friend I should find out why you find Konah of such interest."

A look of anger flashed in Keelah's large black eyes, before giving way to a determined grin. "I accept your challenge." Bracing both feet against the bank, she shoved herself into an early lead, but not for long as Tia swam up beside her then ahead to reach the opposite bank first. As she reached down to help the other girl out of the water, Tia laughed. "It is a good thing for you I am such a kindhearted person. If not, I would be the one dancing in the strong arms of Konah this night."

"And," Keelah grasped the hand held out to her with one foot braced against the bank to haul herself up and out of the water. "I will not have to soothe my wounded heart in the arms of Gray Dog."

Unbeknown to the girls they held the attention of an admirer. Both girls were beautiful, but Tia is the one the black eyes kept returning to. At sixteen summers, her tall slender body already showed promise of the rare beauty she would become. Appearing Wolf had admired the young girl for a long time. He did not admire her for her beauty alone. Tia possessed a strong will. Taking her for a wife against her will, would not be an easy task, even more so, now that he knew she had eyes for another. But as war chief to their people Appearing Wolf knew his demand for her could not be denied.

As he looked at her now, standing tall and unashamed of her naked beauty, a smile spread across his handsome face. He noted the high firm breasts and tapered waist that looked even smaller as her hips flared out and curved. He had never seen her with her hair loose and flowing well past her hips. His hands ached to touch its shimmering softness. As he watched, he felt a tightening in his groin. The need to touch her and hold her to him felt almost overpowering. His mind made up he walked away determined to speak with her father without delay.

That night the two girls stood outside the lodge of the warrior society listening to the low chanting of Mahossa, the medicine man.

"Tia," Keelah said, "why are we coming to the dance so late? Mahossa does not like it when he is interrupted in his chanting."

"It is important for us to arrive after everyone else is seated. When we enter the lodge all eyes will turn to see who has dared to anger Mahossa by coming late. The warriors will watch to see where we sit."

Shaking her head at her friend's daring, Keelah bent to enter the lodge. As Tia made to follow she felt a small hand on her arm. She turned to see her younger brother, Tahelo. "Tia, he said in a quiet voice, "I have been sent by our father. You are to go to his lodge."

"Why does he wish to see me now, Tahelo?" she asked, not bothering to hide the irritation in her voice.

"He did not say," he told her, anxious to be away. "You must go, now."

"Oh! Keelah you go ahead. I will return as soon as I have spoken with my father."

What could her father wish to speak with her about that could not wait? Earlier, before she had left to meet Keelah at the dance, he had said nothing about talking to her.

Still trying to think what it could be she entered his lodge. She could see her father sitting on his couch talking with someone across the way. The young warrior, Appearing Wolf, looked at her then turned away.

"You wished to speak to me, father?"

"Yes, Tia." He motioned her to sit near him. "Tia, Appearing Wolf has come to speak with me on a matter of great importance."

Why did he look at her in such a strange manner? Fear crept into mind, but she did not know why. "Yes, father?" She waited for him to speak.

"Tia, Appearing Wolf has come to ask for you in marriage."

At the word "marriage", Tia's heart began to beat at a frantic pace. Without realizing it, she had risen to her feet. "No! Father, do not ask this of me! I do not wish to marry Appearing Wolf!"

Spotted Owl looked at his daughter, whom he loved beyond words. "Tia," he said his voice calm but stern, "Appearing Wolf is Chief Maheto's son. It is his right to choose a wife without her acceptance."

"Father, I have always been a good daughter! Please! Do not ask this of me!" Sheer will held her tears at bay.

Appearing Wolf watched Tia, watched as she fought to control her growing emotions. "Tia."

At the sound of her name on the warrior's lips she turned on him, her eyes flashing with anger. Appearing Wolf had begun to feel sorry for the young girl. But as he looked at her now, all thought of pity vanished. In its place was a need to have her. A need so strong, that with or without her acceptance, she would belong to him.

"Tia," he said again, a stronger tone in his voice, "I have not demanded your father give you to me, for I have deep respect for Spotted Owl. He is a fierce warrior and a good man amongst our people. Now, hear my words, Tia. I do not need Spotted Owl's permission to take you to my lodge. I do not need permission from any man to take you. As war chief to our people it is my right to choose the one who will be my wife. In five suns you will come to my lodge to be joined with me."

"Never!" she screamed the words at him. "I will never be your wife! The man I marry will be the man I love!"

Leaving the couch, he stood to tower over her. "After one night as my wife, I will be that man." In silence he turned and walked out of the lodge.

Afraid to even breathe, Tia looked to her father, waiting for him to tell her she did not have to do this thing that frightened her beyond all reason. Spotted Owl glanced at her then followed Appearing Wolf.

"This cannot be happening!" Tia raged, beginning to pace back and forth. "I will not do this! I will not!" Although in her heart she feared she had little choice.

With that thought burning through her mind, Tia left the lodge. The need to be alone, the need to be away from the laughter and gaiety drove her. She began to run. In her confused state, she paid no heed to where her feet carried her. Nor did she care, as long as she did not have to see anyone. She ran unaware of the tears streaming down her face or the wounded sounds coming from her throat. When at last she could run no more, she dropped down on the grassy bank of the lake.

"How could my father do this to me? How could I have not noticed when his love for me stopped? I have tried to be a good daughter. I have tried to quiet the wildness of my spirit, but I cannot! Now, he no longer wants me! He wants to give me to a man I do not love!"

Thinking herself alone, she spoke her words aloud. In the quiet, she sensed the presence of someone else. Looking up she found herself staring into the angry black eyes of Appearing Wolf!

He stood looking down at her. Then with a low growl his hand shot out jerking her to her feet. She tried to break free of him but his hands remained strong.

"Let go of me!" she screamed. "You have no right to touch me!"

"I have every right," he told her, the fire in his eyes making her tremble. Then the strong arms released her, causing her to stumble. As she hit the hard ground pain wiped all fear from her mind but taking root was cornered feline anger.

Jumping to her feet she leaped at him with no thought to the consequences. When he had pushed her away he'd turned to leave; so it was his naked back that took the full brunt of her long sharp nails. The sudden attack left him unprepared. But the quick reflexes of the warrior turned the odds to his favor. Upon feeling the trail of fire down his back, he turned and Tia soon found herself hitting the ground with such force she could not breathe. The hard fall and his added weight drained any remaining fight from her. She lay there looking up at the man straddling her.

"Get off of me," she whispered. "I cannot breathe." He stared at her for a moment longer then she felt the burden on her chest lift, as he released her. She remained on the ground, trying to get enough air into her lungs to move. Tia could feel his eyes watching her. When she looked up, a slow smile spread across his handsome face.

"My little she-cat," His deep voice caressed the words. "I will be more alert next time. You attack without warning. I will not allow my senses to be dulled a second time."

Reaching down he helped her to her feet. When she stood before him, he tipped her face up to his, holding her chin with a firm hand when she would have turned away from him.

"Is my touch that difficult for you to accept?"

"Yours is not the touch I long for." She met his eyes without flinching.

"Perhaps not, but mine is the only one you will ever know."

"Why does the mighty Appearing Wolf want a girl whose heart already belongs to another?"

"You think you want another, Tia. After you are my wife, you will know the difference." He slid his hand from beneath her chin and stepped back.

"I will never love you, Appearing Wolf! When Gray Dog learns of this, he will challenge you for the right to claim me!"

"I will answer that challenge. Gray Dog is one of my best warriors; his death will cause much sadness in our village."

"His death does not have to be!" Tia grabbed hold of Appearing Wolf's arm. "Gray Dog and I love each other! He planned to ask for me soon!"

Cocking his head to one side he gazed at her, a roguish smile pulling at the corners of his full mouth. "The first lesson a warrior learns is not to hesitate or all could be lost," he told her before walking away.

The next morning, sitting in front of her lodge, Tia thought upon the problems confronting her. She knew Gray Dog would challenge Appearing Wolf for her. Would he be a worthy opponent for the war chief of their people?

Tia caught her breath as someone stopped before her. Not wanting to look up lest it be Appearing Wolf, she felt great relief when she looked into the smiling face of Keelah.

"Tia, you did not return to the dance. Did you not return because of the talk with your father?"

"Come," Tia rose to her feet, "we cannot talk here. Walk with me to the lake."

Knowing well the strong will and wild spirit of her best friend, Keelah looked at her. "What have you done now, Tia?"

"It is not what I have done! It is what I am being forced to do!" Keelah waited for Tia to tell her what had her so upset. "Last night my father did not wait alone for me to come and talk with him." She dropped down onto the bank. "Appearing Wolf waited with him."

"Appearing Wolf?" Keelah sat down beside her. "Why would your father wish to speak with you in the presence of Appearing Wolf?" Tia gave her a brief glance, then burst into tears.

"Tia!" Keelah pulled her around to face her. "What is it?!"

"My father sent for me because of Appearing Wolf, Keelah." She gulped a sob trying to quiet the fear racing through her mind. "Appearing Wolf has asked for me!"

"Oh, Tia, no!" Keelah drew back, shocked at this new peril in her friend's life. "What are you going to do?"

"I must tell my father of my love for Gray Dog." Warming to her idea, she looked up. "Yes! If he knows my heart already belongs to another, he will not give me to Appearing Wolf."

"Tia, Spotted Owl has no choice but to give you to Appearing Wolf," Keelah tried to reason with her. "He is our war chief."

"Gray Dog will not let that happen. He will challenge Appearing Wolf for me." She nodded, smug in the ability of the one she loved to win her for his own. "The lodge of Maheto will be filled with much weeping when Appearing Wolf lies dead at Gray Dog's feet."

Appalled she would even consider pitting Gray Dog against the deadly prowess of Appearing Wolf, Keelah stared at her. "Tia, it has been less than a year since Gray Dog bore the tortures of the Sun Dance to become a warrior. He would be no match for Appearing Wolf! Would you want all he endured to become a man to be wasted? Would you want his life to be ended by the hand of one of our own people?"

Tia remained silent, unable to answer as her mind touched on the agony every young Blackfoot male must endure to become a warrior and earn his right to take a woman. In late summer, after the warriors and their women had returned from the buffalo grounds and the meat had been cured and put away for the winter, was the time of year when she and her people stopped in their everyday lives to give thanks to the Creator for all he has bestowed upon his children.

Days before the actual testing, each youth, who would participate in the ceremony of the Sun Dance, denied his body food and drink, making his body an empty vessel for the Holy Ones to dwell. When the drums called them to the giant lodge erected solely for the purpose of the Sun Dance, they came, proud in the knowledge that when the sun again rose in the east the days of their childhood would be over. They would be warriors able to fight and protect their people, earning their right to take a woman.

In the middle of the Sun Dance lodge, a huge fire burned bright. As the youths stood, waiting, Mahossa walked to the fire and in its blaze cleansed his knife. When it was ready he turned to the young boys. One by one they stepped forward to be prepared for the ceremony.

With steady hands Mahossa made two deep cuts on each side of the boy's breast. Under each deep gash he ran a thong pulling the skin up tight. As the boys stood in silence with the thongs sewed into their chests, Mahossa attached the thongs to longer ones hanging from the Sun Dance Pole. As the drums beat louder the boys danced around the pole. Round and round they went faster and faster, the sweat glistening on their young bodies to mix with the blood running down their chests as they strained against the thongs holding them secure, until, at last, they pulled themselves free. From that day forward they would bare the ragged scars for all to see.

Yes, Tia thought as she recalled the day she had watched Gray Dog earn his right to claim her, he will be a worthy opponent for Appearing Wolf. Had he not been the first to break free of the Sun Dance Pole? Did that not prove how much the Holy Ones looked upon him with favor? Gray dog would fight for her and he would win, she felt sure of it!

"I believe in Gray Dog's abilities as a warrior," she told Keelah, a flood of excitement rushing over her. "If my father will not listen when I tell him of my love for another, then Appearing Wolf will die!"

Knowing anything further she could offer would go unheard, Keelah remained silent.

Jumping to her feet, Tia walked with quick strides back to camp. "I will talk with my father," she called back over her shoulder. "I will make him see I could never be the wife of Appearing Wolf."

After leaving Keelah, Tia continued walking through the village searching for Spotted Owl when she caught sight of Gray Dog coming out of his lodge. Her pulse quickened as she watched him coming towards her. A scant year older than Tia herself, his boyish good looks hinted at the handsome man he would someday become. Tall and lean he walked with an unhurried natural gate. Gray dog, like most Blackfeet men, wore his waist-length black hair straight down his back, instead of in tight braids. At the sight of Tia, his face lit up.

"I was coming to ask you to ride with me." He smiled, taking her small hands in his.

"I would like that, Gray Dog, but right now I must speak with my father. Have you seen him?" Her young voice sounded breathless even to her as she looked into his midnight eyes.

"No." His eyes lingered on her full lush mouth, his own mouth becoming dry as his mind filled with titillating thoughts. "I do not think he is in camp," he heard himself telling her, his voice deepening with the fires sweeping over his young loins. "So, now you can spend your time with me." He forced a laugh. Tia returned his laugh, allowing him to hold her close for just a moment.

She felt herself jerked around to stare into the angry black eyes of Appearing Wolf. "You take your father's word lightly!" he hissed, his dark gaze shifting to the young man standing by her side. "You will never touch this girl again! She has been promised to me! Soon, she will come to my lodge as my wife!"

"How dare you!" Tia squealed, jerking her arm away. "My father has not given his word yet! He would have told me!"

"Spotted Owl gave me his word. That is enough," Appearing Wolf told her, walking away.

"Gray Dog will never allow you to take me without a challenge!" she called out, directing a smug smile at the young warrior standing by her side.

Stopping in mid-stride Appearing Wolf turned, eyeing the handsome youth standing a short distance away from him. "You have earned the right as a protector of our people to challenge me for this girl. But know this, Gray Dog. Tia will bring no warmth to your couch."

"Tia is mine!" Gray Dog beat a closed fist against his chest. "You will never take her from me!"

"The daughter of Spotted Owl needs a strong hand to guide her," Appearing Wolf kept his voice calm controlling the anger fighting to spew forth. "When she is in my lodge with her belly swollen with my son she will behave as a good wife should." His eyes never wavered from those of Gray Dog.

"When the sun rises in the east Tia will belong to me, and the lodge of Maheto, our chief, will be filled with mourning!" Gray Dog shouted unable to leash his own anger.

In the heat of the moment, Appearing Wolf allowed his own smoldering rage to overshadow his wisdom. "I accept your challenge, Gray Dog." His voice gave no hint as to the fury he kept at bay as Tia smiled a loving smile at the boy whose life he would be forced to end at first light.

Appearing Wolf had already passed his twenty-fifth summer. As war chief to the Kainah, every move he made, he made with the welfare of his people in mind. They respected his word, trusted his decisions. As their leader he had fought and counted coup on their enemies the Snake and the Crow many times, making his name well-known among those who would challenge him. Now, as he sat alone in his lodge, his fingers brushed the scars of his youth. The scars he bore with pride from the Sun Dance.

Throughout the long night the wailing of Gray Dog's mother could be heard crying out to the spirits to protect her only son when he took up the lance against their leader.

With a low growl Appearing Wolf rose to his feet. "How could I have allowed this to happen?" he snarled. "Gray Dog is but a boy!"

"Whose vision has been clouded, because of his lust for your chosen one."

"I do not know what to do, Pehta."

Walking the rest of the way inside the lodge, Pehta sat down in front of the fire pit, "Gray Dog is the one who challenged you, my brother. Why do you torture yourself with what must be done?"

"Gray Dog is no match for me," Appearing Wolf growled, beginning to pace back and forth in long determined strides. "There will be no honor when I end his life!" His steps ceased their frantic pacing and the dark scowl relaxed on his broad face as he whirled to glare into the face of the man watching him. "My mind will be filled with bitter shame for allowing anger to speak instead of wisdom."

"Does it show wisdom to allow one of your own warriors to try to take what has been promised to you?" Pehta asked, his deep voice revealing none of the unease he felt at the pain showing plain upon his brother's face.

"Gray Dog is young, he spoke from his loins. I am our leader." His eyes closed in self-admonishment. "I should have thought before accepting his challenge."

"What stopped you?" Pehta touched a lit piece of kindling to a filled pipe he held in his hands.

"Tia thinks what she feels in her heart for Gray Dog is love," he answered without hesitation. "The light shining from her eyes as she looked at him drove all reason from my mind."

"Could it be what you saw in her eyes is real?" Pehta leaned forward, tossed the kindling back into the fire. "If her heart already belongs to another, why not allow the one she wants to have her? Then you would not have to kill him."

"No! The daughter of Spotted Owl is mine!" The fire in Appearing Wolf's tormented eyes leaped to new life. "She will never accept the touch of another!"

As the first rays of dawn crept into the lodge Pehta uncrossed his legs rising in one smooth movement to his feet, "The time has come, my brother. Do not allow your feelings for one of our own to dull your senses," he cautioned, then walked from the lodge.

The early morning silence surrounded him. The wailing of Gray Dog's mother had ceased its awful begging. It felt as though all of Mother Earth waited to see what would happen next. Walking across the lodge Appearing Wolf began preparing himself to face the young rival whose life Tia had placed in his unwilling hands.

Chapter Nine

Hearing his master's step and anxious to be gone, Shadow Dancer pawed the ground. His silky black mane shimmered in the early morning sunlight as he threw up his head, emitting a loud whinny. Stroking the big, black and white Paint with fondness, Appearing Wolf mounted. Together they made their way out upon the prairie where a crowd already waited.

Ignoring the loud cries and waving hands, Shadow Dancer moved between the lines of shouting onlookers until, with a tightening of his strong legs, Appearing Wolf signaled him to stop. Sitting proud astride his war pony, the fierce leader of the Kainah looked straight ahead. A gentle wind blowing down from the mountains stirred the two ideally matched Eagle feathers interwoven in the back of his tight braids. Dressed in a brief loincloth, with his face and body unadorned of the black and red paint he always wore when meeting another warrior in mortal combat, Appearing Wolf watched and waited.

As the cheering grew louder, Appearing Wolf saw the warrior who had challenged him riding through the crowd. He noted how the bright red paint dotted with white covering the left side of Gray Dog's face made him look older than his seventeen summers. His hair no longer hung in wild disarray down his lean back but had been woven into two tight braids. He too chose the brief covering of a loin cloth, but his raven black hair did not hold the adornment of the Eagle feather. Such an honor must be earned and thus far, Gray Dog had not achieved that honor. Stopping a short distance away Gray Dog sat waiting.

Tia reached out to grasp Keelah's hand. "If either one is killed it will be because of me," she moaned.

"You did not make the challenge to Appearing Wolf, Gray Dog did." Keelah glanced over at her trying to ease Tia's needless fear.

Unable to meet the searching gaze of her best friend, Tia remained silent.

"Gray Dog!" Appearing Wolf called out. "This does not have to be. The daughter of Spotted Owl has already been promised to me. Accept her loss and all will be forgotten."

Sitting proud astride a dark buckskin, whose sides and hindquarters matched the same colors of paint and design as his master, the arrogant warrior replied with like self-assuredness. "The spirits have given Tia's heart to me! All will see this when the mighty Appearing Wolf lies dead at my feet!"

"Gray Dog!" Chief Maheto called out to him, walking toward the mounted warriors. "You are not acting like a warrior of the Kainah Blackfoot. Your reasons are selfish. Your thoughts linger on your own needs. If you follow through with this you will be taking a life. Only the Holy Ones can choose when a life is to be ended!"

"Does the great Maheto come to beg for the life of his son?" Gray Dog taunted.

"The life you take is your own, Gray Dog," Maheto told him, steeling his heart against the boy who lay hidden beneath the strong words and fierce-looking war paint. "I do not doubt the abilities of Appearing Wolf. My son is offering you your life. Take it and go!"

For a long moment Gray Dog sat his horse in silence. Some of the arrogance seemed to leave his young face as his eyes searched the watching crowd. As his gaze locked with those of the girl he loved, he raised his hand. Then, before anyone knew what he was about, he kicked his horse into an all-out run. With a high pitched death cry screaming from his lips he charged in a direct path at Appearing Wolf.

Shadow Dancer shied to the side showing his unease as the other horse rushed at him. Talking in a calm voice, Appearing Wolf sought to quiet his prancing mount. When he realized, at the last possible moment, the horse and its rider had no intention of veering off, Appearing Wolf yanked on Shadow Dancer's rein trying to back him up out of the way. But to his dismay the frightened horse reared up almost unseating him.

"What is Shadow Dancer doing?" Keelah screamed.

"He did not expect Gray Dog to ride straight at him." Konah pulled Keelah to his side. "Appearing Wolf is trying to get him under control."

Leaping from the now, out of control horse, Appearing Wolf rolled out of the way just in time to keep from being trampled by Gray Dog's charging mount. Before Gray Dog could turn his horse, Appearing Wolf had already jumped to his feet to reach for his knife. His hand come away empty. In the excitement of trying to control his frightened mount, his knife and all his weapons had been lost.

Through the dust Appearing Wolf watched as Gray Dog rode towards him at a slow pace then stopped a few feet away. Appearing Wolf could smell the sweat from his prancing, anxiously snorting mount.

"You think because you are our leader it is your right to take by force what is not given. Before this day, the name of Appearing Wolf had always been spoken with much gladness in my heart. I respected the war chief of our people. I do not feel this way any longer." His proud head came up higher as he squinted into the sun. "If this is to be the day of my death, I will walk my path to our ancestors with pride."

Then to Appearing Wolf's surprise Gray Dog threw a knife point down at his feet. Dismounting and drawing his own knife, Gray Dog crouched low commencing to circle his opponent. Knowing any further words would be useless, Appearing Wolf hardened his heart against the young warrior trying to end his life.

Gray Dog lunged, the point of his knife drawing first blood. "So! The mighty Appearing Wolf bleeds like any other man."

In silence Appearing Wolf continued to circle, his watchful eyes never leaving those of his assailant's. Gray Dog attacked again, and again his knife found its mark, leaving a trail of blood down the war-chief's chest.

The harsh breathing of the fighting men grew louder. The watching crowd murmured their disbelief at their leader's inability to best the young brave laughing and taunting him each time his knife found its mark.

"Your mother will not be abandoned in the village of her people," Appearing Wolf breathed the words. "I will see to it, that she has enough fresh meat for her cooking fire."

"You think to anger me with words of my mother, but it will be I and your chosen one who will see to her safety," he grunted, lunging once more. This time his arm was stilled in the fierce grip of his leader. With one quick move Appearing Wolf's own knife flashed across Gray Dog's throat, ending the life of his opponent.

As Gray Dog's blood spewed out to cover the ground his body slumped forward to the loud cheering of the watching crowd. Appearing Wolf walked to his horse and without a backward glance, mounted. Turning Shadow Dancer in the direction of the mountains, he rode away with the wailing of Gray Dog's mother echoing in his ears.

With a pounding heart, Tia drug her feet towards the fallen warrior. His mother's mournful cries almost made her stumble, but she forced herself to continue until she stood over the body of the boy she loved. Dropping to her knees she lifted her arms upwards and in a rocking motion keened the high pitched wailing for the dead. Others joined her, adding their own voices until the prairie abounded with the eerie wailing. In her anguish, Tia caught up a handful of her long black hair, but as she reached for the knife all Blackfeet women carried, someone grabbed her hand. Confused, she looked up into the angry face of Pehta.

"What are you doing?" she whimpered, trying to pull away from him. "I must morn Gray Dog's passing!"

"You will not cut off your hair or mutilate your flesh for someone who had no right to you. Appearing Wolf is your chosen one!"

"I will! You cannot stop me, Pehta!" She stumbled to her feet.

Yanking her towards him, Pehta commenced walking with her toward the village, grabbing her by the back of her neck when she would have jerked away.

Jolisha, Tia's mother, walked out of her lodge just as Pehta halted an angry Tia at the door. "Pehta, she looked from one to the other, "what are you doing?"

"She thought to cut off her hair and mutilate her body because of Gray Dog's death. Appearing Wolf would not want this." He shoved Tia forward. "I will leave her with you to make sure she does not harm herself."

Nodding, Jolisha guided her sobbing daughter into their lodge dropping the flap into place. When she felt sure Pehta no longer waited outside, she turned to her stricken daughter.

"Tia, why would you do this?"

"Gray Dog and I loved each other. It is my right to mourn for him." She threw herself down on her couch. "Pehta had no right to stop me!"

"Tia, in three days you are to go to Appearing Wolf." Jolisha glanced over at her, her stomach tightening as she glimpsed the tear-stained face so filled with pain. Her heart ached for her, but she knew she had to remain strong and be stern with her or Tia would give into the pain threatening to overpower her. "Do you think he would want a bride who is marked and bleeding from mourning another?"

"Please, my mother, do not remind me how my father sold me to a man I hate."

"Your father is doing what he thinks is best for you, Tia."

When Tia did not answer, her mother walked across the lodge to sit beside her. "I am not so old I cannot remember how it feels when love first touches the heart. How the sight of that special one can make the heart leap to new life."

"Did my father bring these new feelings," Tia lifted her head to peer at her mother through her long black hair, "or had you, too, been forced to accept someone you did not want?" Tia watched her.

"For me there could never be anyone but Spotted Owl." A slight smile touched Jolisha's face as she recalled her memory. "We grew up together in this village, but for some reason I never really saw him until one night he choose me at the warrior society to dance with. It was the celebration after the Sun Dance."

At the mention of the Sun Dance Tia felt her heart quicken. After a deep swallow, she asked. "What happened?"

"As soon as he took me in his arms I knew I would never want another." Her face flushed broadening the smile already present. "Soon after that night, we joined."

"I am happy for you, my mother." Sniffing, she wiped at the tears staining her face. "Your father did not give you to a man you did not love. Your life stayed filled with happiness. I envy you."

"I am glad I could join with the man I love." Her voice lowered as she peered over at Tia. "But my days have not always been filled with happiness."

As Tia looked at her, her dark brows raised in question, Jolisha replied, "In the early days of our marriage your father and I lived as one. But, soon after your birth my happiness came to an end."

"Are you saying my father did not want me?" Tia breathed, rising up on her elbows.

"Oh no, Tia." Jolisha ruffled her hair. "Your father wanted you very much. He has always held much love in his heart for his daughter."

"Then why did your life change?" She gazed at her mother in doubt of what she told her.

"Spotted Owl is a warrior." Jolisha lifted her proud head. "He needed sons. A man does not feel he is complete without a son. Many times I tried to give him what he wanted, but each time I failed. His seed would no longer grow inside my body. Then," her voice caught making it difficult for Tia to understand her words, "the day came when he told me he had found another. Although he said his new wife's place in his lodge would not lessen his love for me, I thought myself a failure, unworthy of his love."

Reaching out, Tia took her mother's small hand in hers. "I am sorry I could not be the son he wanted," she whispered.

A look of contentment touched her face as Jolisha pushed herself from the couch. "I am not. I do not know what I would have done without you in my life, Tia. But, perhaps now you can understand why your father wants you to be the wife of Appearing Wolf. I could not give your father the son he wished for, but the daughter I did bare him can give him a chief."

"Is that what you want, my mother?" A slight tremble sounded in her voice.

"Every mother wants the best for her child." Jolisha busied herself with putting the dirty clothes she had nearby into a large basket. Later when the sun cooled she would take them to the lake to wash them. "Appearing Wolf will always be a good provider." She placed the filled basket beside the door. "Our people will look upon you with great respect, Tia. The boy you gave your heart to is no longer here."

"No," she sighed, turning onto her stomach, "and I could not even mourn for him."

"Mourn for him in your heart, Tia." Jolisha picked up a long wooden spoon she used to stir the stew simmering in a big kettle hanging over the cooking fire. "But, do not mourn for him too long. Your father and I will not always be here to look out for you." She tapped the spoon against the kettle, loosening the slivers of meat sticking to its edges to make it drop back into the broth. "You must look at tomorrow."

Jolisha's heart went out to her daughter as she watched her out of the corner of her eye. The urge to take her into her arms and comfort her tugged at her, but she did not. The life of an Indian woman was hard. To survive she could not be weak in spirit or endurance.

"Tia, the life you have known, in the lodge of your father, will soon be over," she told her, dropping the wild onions she had chopped into the pot. "You will have a husband to care for. His needs must come first. You will no longer be able to go to the lake with Keelah in the early morning dawn, or ride in the mountains when the sun is high overhead. Your work will take longer now, for I will not be there to help you." She looked toward the couch to make sure her daughter listened to her words. "You must be a good wife, Tia, and when Appearing Wolf calls you to his couch, you must not refuse him."

The thought of any man, except Gray Dog, touching her filled her with loathing. The anger she felt at that moment showed upon her face.

"No, anger will do you no good." Jolisha glanced at her over the cooking pot. "You must keep an open mind, and above all try to keep a silent tongue." She laid the spoon down beside the pot. "This will be very hard for you, Tia. If you anger your husband he has the right to beat you. Neither your father nor I can interfere. I tell you these things to help you."

With the quickness of the cat Tia sprang to her feet. "No man will beat me! Husband or not! No man will ever beat me and live to tell about it!"

"Tia!" Jolisha cried. "You will only bring yourself trouble thinking this way."

"You have not seen trouble until Appearing Wolf raises his hand to me!"

"Oh Tia," her mother wailed wringing her hands in a worried manner. "You could have such a good life as Appearing Wolf's wife, but the way you are talking he will send you back to us. Only by then it will be too late." She came across the lodge, and taking Tia by the shoulders she shook her. "You will no longer be untouched. No man in the village will want you. How will you survive?"

"I will survive, my mother. I can promise you that! Which is more than I can say for the war chief of our people if he dares to play warrior with me!"

Judith Ann McDowell

Chapter Ten

It was the time of the Crow moon. The time of year when the wind howled and rain washed the earth clean. The elements beat a steady rhythm upon the lodge skins and inside it remained warm but this night the soft glow from the fire burning in the fire pit brought little comfort. Sitting cross-legged before its warmth, Appearing Wolf talked with his father, Maheto.

"Has Tia accepted her father's decision to send her to your lodge, Appearing Wolf?"

"Spotted Owl has told her I am to be her husband," Appearing Wolf stared into the flames.

"How does she feel about this?"

The hatred burning in Tia's dark eyes each time she looked at him left little doubt in his mind as to how she felt about him and their approaching marriage. "It is not important how she feels; she will do as she is told."

"Why do I hear anger in your voice, my son?" the deep voice of Maheto questioned. "Is this anger directed at me or the girl who does not wish to be the wife of Appearing Wolf?"

"My anger is not directed at my father," Appearing Wolf breathed, trying to still the bitterness welling up inside of him. "My anger is directed at me for allowing myself to lose control of a situation that should never have been.

"Gray Dog was the taker of life this day, Appearing Wolf, not you."

He fought the urge to reach out to his son. Instead he picked up his pipe and tobacco pouch. Pinching a small amount of the tobacco between his thumb and forefinger he tamped it into the bowl of the pipe.

"Letta, his mother, would still have a protector and hunter in her lodge. He would be here to take care of her in her old age." Appearing

Wolf tossed a chunk of wood on the fire with such force sparks flew into the air. "Now she has no one. Her wailing continues deep into the night." He shook his head in a vain attempt to quiet the disheartening sound. "I can hear it even now. It carries over the howling wind."

"Gray Dog left you no choice but to end his life." Maheto reached a thin piece of kindling toward the flames. "It is not easy to be a leader, Appearing Wolf. Many times you are called upon to make decisions that do not meet with the approval of others." He held the burning wood against the tobacco drawing on the stem of the pipe until the tobacco caught fire. Smoke curling from the bowl sent an aromatic scent of burning leaves wafting throughout the lodge. "A leader must be strong. He cannot worry about what others will think." His steely gaze fastened on that of his son's. "Do you think it has always been easy for me to be chief of the Kainah?"

"No." Appearing Wolf answered on a long drawn out breath.

"Letta will always be cared for." Maheto's long legs stretched out straight. "Our people do not turn their back on those in need. Appearing Wolf," The older man leaned forward on his couch. "Why does your mind dwell on the pain of a woman who has already tasted of life, when you should be thinking of your chosen one?"

"I am thinking of her." Appearing Wolf glanced across the flames to where Maheto sat staring at him. "She wanted to mourn Gray Dog's death as though they had already been joined." He shook his head in refusal of the pipe Maheto held out to him. "Pehta stopped her." Anger and pity warred within him for the girl who remained uppermost on both their minds. "How she must hate me."

"Tia is young." Maheto cocked his graying head to one side, nodding over the dilemma facing them. "Gray Dog had been the first boy she saw in her newly awakened womanhood. She has not learned the passion that comes with these new feelings. As her husband you must teach her the difference. However," he held up his hand, "you must do this with gentleness, Appearing Wolf. Do not allow the anger you feel now over an innocent moment of youth to destroy what can be."

"Tia will be the wife of a chief. I am not a boy who yearns to hold her hand and whisper silly words of love." Appearing Wolf hastened to explain his feelings on the matter. "I need sons in my lodge. Sons she will provide!"

For a while neither man spoke, each lost in his own thoughts as the storm continued to rage, beating a stronger rhythm against the primitive dwelling. It was Maheto who broke the silence.

"Appearing Wolf, I will speak to you from my heart. This night I will reopen old wounds and cleanse them with words I should have said to you, long ago."

Appearing Wolf remained silent.

"From my vision quest, in the days of my youth, the Holy Ones showed me how I would someday become a leader of our people. I took great pride in this, knowing the power I would have as chief of the Kainah. But," he fought against the pain already welling up inside of him, "with power comes responsibility. As chief of our people I hold each life in the palm of my hand." He spread his hands wide in front of him staring at them as though they held the answer, he searched for. "So much power in one man can be very dangerous," he whispered.

As Appearing Wolf continued to sit staring into the fire, Maheto released a long shuddering breath.

"As a young man I fought and counted many coups against our enemies, and like you, I thought my youth would never end," He glanced down at the aged hand holding the pipe. "The days of youth are fleeting."

"Why do you suffer these thoughts, my father?" Appearing Wolf chided him, rising to his feet and, taking the water pouch down from the hook, drank long and deep of its coolness. "The life of a warrior is now." He replaced the pouch on the hook then returned to take his place beside the fire. "He cannot allow his mind to dwell on what is yet to come."

"You are so wrong," Maheto told him, ignoring his son's light scolding. "If the Holy Ones see the winters of your life, then you must prepare for them now." His tone of voice, usually so gentle when he spoke with his son, took on a sternness Appearing Wolf had never heard before. "You must think ahead to that time when your strength and virility will be but a memory. You must choose that someone now who can still warm you in those golden years."

Leaning forward, Appearing Wolf stared at his father. "I have never heard you speak like this. What has happened to bring this sadness to your heart?"

"The story I will tell you cuts deep into my very soul." Maheto waved Appearing Wolf's concern away. "Listen close, for I will not repeat it."

"I am here, my father."

"Of my five wives, I really loved but one." His voice lost its sharpness, taking on the gentleness of tone Appearing Wolf knew well.

"She was but fifteen summers when I stole her from the Crows." The calm admission shot a look of utter astonishment across Appearing Wolf's otherwise, smooth features. "So beautiful, so small… like… like a flower that had yet to open, but you knew when it did, it would be the most beautiful the eyes have ever looked upon. I could not bring myself to use her and then trade her to another. She had to belong to me." He smiled bringing a smoothness to his stern features. "I made her my third wife."

"You took a captive woman into your lodge?" Appearing Wolf asked him, unable to believe what his father told him.

"Yes," Maheto admitted; "I kept myself from her. I kept her clean so I could join with her as if she had been born Blackfeet."

"You had to be very sure of your leadership," Appearing Wolf grinned, "to brave the council's acceptance of such a move."

"A very bold move when I had been chief for a short time." Maheto nodded in agreement; a slight smile broadening his full mouth.

Reaching out, Appearing Wolf threw more branches on the dying fire. As the flames bit into the pitch, a loud hissing sound filled the lodge then grew quiet as though waiting for Maheto to continue. Pulling a well-worn buffalo robe higher upon his shoulders, Maheto reached once more into the past.

"By now the jealousy in my lodge made my life unbearable. Always they blamed her. When I asked why she could not get along, all she would say is she would try harder. Sometimes when she came to my couch I would find bruises on her body." A deep groove between his brows deepened somewhat as he recalled how she would try to hide herself from him, "When I asked how she got them, all she would say is she was a clumsy girl." He snorted, as though it all happened now instead of many years ago. "I knew this could not be true her grace would not allow it. The more my other wives complained, the quieter she became. Before long, I wanted to be with her alone. I moved my other wives into a lodge of their own. Alone with her, my life took on new meaning. When she smiled it felt like seeing the sun after the long night."

Appearing Wolf sat watching the deep feelings play across his father's face in confusion. This man who, up until now, had always kept his thoughts and feelings to himself, now shared his emotions as easily as though the sharing had always been a part of their relationship.

"We began spending more and more time together. I remember

when she told me she carried my child." He puffed on the still lit pipe, drawing the smoke deep into his lungs then exhaled. "I felt as though the Holy Ones had blessed me beyond my deepest hopes. I made my other wives do her share of the work. When she gave me a strong healthy son, my life felt complete."

"I am glad for your good fortune," Appearing Wolf told him then drew back at the pain covering his father's face. "My father...." he began, then stopped as Maheto raised his hand for silence.

"No." Maheto shook his head. "What you are hearing is not joy, Appearing Wolf. What you are hearing is pain! But you must hear these words. I cannot hide from the pain of that time. I will not allow you to turn from the memory. When my son passed his second summer," he continued, with renewed strength, "I led a raid against the Crow. We stayed gone many days. I remember how my heart missed her. All I wanted to do is get back to her, hold her close and know in my heart she remained safe. When I returned, I searched out her face amongst our people." His dark eyes glazed over as he sought to call forth every detail. "I found her in our lodge holding my son to her breast. The smile on her face as she looked at him made my heart leap." He reached out as though he could still feel her warmth then let his hands drop heavily back to his side. "I knelt down kissing the side of her face, then, sat watching the two of them no longer tired from my long journey."

Rising to his feet, Maheto walked on unsteady legs to the lodge opening. Pulling back the flap he stood in silence looking out upon the rain-drenched earth. With a resigned sigh, he turned a haunting look on his face as he gazed at his son.

"I heard my first wife, Eneuhahkeea call out to enter our lodge. I went to the opening intending to send her away, but she said I needed to hear her words. I told her to speak." He closed his eyes as the pain of that time washed over him as strong as though it happened now. "I should have cut out her tongue instead, for she told me the woman I loved with all my heart had been with another while I had been gone." The groove between his brows grew longer and more pronounced. "I grabbed her and shook her, telling her she lied, that she said this only to hurt me! But she said she had proof! She took me to her sister who swore she too had seen my wife with a Sioux warrior who had visited our camp. Two witnesses stood against her." His voice pleaded for understanding. "My wife said they lied, that they said this in hate! But she could not prove they lied." Instinctively his hands curled into fists. "I could not disprove their lies."

"What happened?" Appearing Wolf asked unable to look away.

"The people demanded her punishment," he breathed, his strong voice laboring to speak the dreaded words. "They chose the punishment of disfigurement."

Maheto's breath caught as he struggled to speak. "She did not even cry out as I raised the knife to defile her beauty. She only looked at me. Her black eyes filled with so much pain and fear I wanted to plunge the knife into my own heart." The closed fist beat an angry tempo against his breast as hot tears ran, unheeded, down his lined and weathered face. "As I stared down into that beautiful face filled with so much trust, I knew I could never let her go through the rest of her life scarred with the mark of an unfaithful wife. I did the only thing I could" His dark eyes closed against the memory searing through his mind. "I ended the life of the one woman I ever loved."

"What was her name?" Appearing Wolf asked, his discomfort, at witnessing his father's show of weakness, sounding in his voice.

"Night Snow," Maheto answered, his dark gaze refusing to waver. "She was your mother."

Total silence ensued as Appearing Wolf, his dark face drained of color, sat looking at the man he thought he knew until now. Finally he spoke and the pain in his voice sounded so unlike the strong young warrior, Maheto had to look away.

"You ended the life of my mother on the word of a woman filled with hate? Why, my father? You, as chief of our people, could have refused. You could have protected her. But you didn't. Answer me!"

"As chief of our people I had no choice! Do you think I wanted to end her life? Holy Ones," he lifted his arms in supplication, "give me your strength!" The wound, closed for so long, was now fresh and bleeding.

"Why did you tell me this?" Appearing Wolf demanded. "What demons have touched you that you would take the love I have for you and defile it?"

The hate in Appearing Wolf's voice descended on him like a slap across his face. Fighting to keep his voice even, he tried as best he could to explain. "I tell you this for I see you making the same mistake. Go to Tia, my son. Tell her what is in your heart. The death of Gray Dog will pale in time. Ask her to be your wife. Do not let the power you will have as chief of our people blind you. The love I shared with your mother is a rare thing." His gray head trembled. "Do not throw it away as I did. If I must endure your hatred, then learn from this. I beg of you, Appearing Wolf. Do not let the bleeding of my soul this night be wasted."

Appearing Wolf looked at the man he had loved more than his own life, and before his eyes he seemed to age. Rising to his feet he stood unable to move, clenching and unclenching his fists as he fought for control.

"If this is what it means to be a leader of our people, I walk away." He turned and left the lodge. Knowing he sat alone in the cold gray dawn, Maheto allowed the tears to flow from his shattered heart.

Judith Ann McDowell

Chapter Eleven

The day of Tia's and Appearing Wolf's wedding dawned with the dark skies of an approaching storm. Huge black clouds moved to swallow up the last patches of blue.

"Even the heavens will be crying over what I will be forced to do this night." Tia said, standing at the lodge opening, looking out over the village.

Jolisha stared at her daughter, then smiled. "Tia. The heavens do not lament because you will be the wife of Appearing Wolf. Their tears are tears of joy because you will be the wife of a chief."

"My mother, I do not wish to be the wife of a chief. I would be happy if time could stand still. Then tonight would not have to come."

"Time stands still for no one." Jolisha busied herself around the lodge. "Tonight will come and you will go to Appearing Wolf. This you must accept for you cannot change it."

"Tonight is not here, yet," Tia spoke her thoughts aloud.

"Tia," her mother dropped hunks of meat into a large cooking pot. "You remind me of a horse your father once traded for from the Flat Heads. He did not behave like other horses." She stopped what she had been doing to better tell her story. "He had very long ears and when he called to the other horses it sounded like someone who had run a long way and could not catch his breath. Spotted Owl gave him to me for a packhorse. He proved to be very strong, but also very stubborn." She laughed at the memory. "I could hit him over and over with a switch, but still he would not move until he felt ready. "You," she wagged a wooden spoon in Tia's direction, "you are like that horse. You know tonight will come and you will go to Appearing Wolf, but still you fight what will be."

"Please, my mother," Tia turned away from the opening, "do not compare me to a stupid horse. I am a girl who is being forced to join with a man I do not like, let alone love."

"You could learn to love him if you would give yourself a chance." Jolisha chanced a quick glance at her daughter.

"Appearing Wolf is a killer of young warriors. All I want from him is to be left alone." Tia crossed her arms across her chest rubbing her hands over her lower shoulders in an attempt to dispel the coldness creeping over her.

"He will not do this, Tia." Jolisha's voice took on a warning tone. "If you do not fight him perhaps your life with him will be easier." At her daughter's look of disbelief, Jolisha turned away.

"Tia." Keelah called out. Turning back to the door, Tia motioned her friend inside. "I have come to see how I can help you prepare for tonight." Keelah said.

"No one can help me."

Keelah looked at her, surprised at the anger in her face. "You have not accepted this night."

"Is there not one person who does not wish me to destroy my life?" Tia whirled to glare at her. "Even my best friend is against me!"

"I am not against you, Tia," Keelah whispered, wounded by the coldness in Tia's voice. "Only," Keelah spread her hands wide, hunched her shoulders, "I do not see how you are going to stop your marriage to a man who can come here and drag you to the medicine lodge if he wants to. You cannot hide from him. Appearing Wolf is not one to play games with. As our war-chief, he is a man to fear."

"Tia," Jolisha spoke up, "listen to her." She tapped the spoon hard against the rim of the pot. "She is trying to keep you from needless pain. She is telling you this to keep you from bringing shame on yourself and your father's lodge."

Tia forced herself to relax, pushing the fear and anger deep inside where it lay hidden. When she turned all bitterness had left her voice. "You are both right. To fight would be useless."

"Oh Tia!" Jolisha breathed, dropping the broth-stained spoon in a wooden cup setting beside the pot. "I am so happy to hear you talk like this. Appearing Wolf is a good man! He will make you happy! Goodness! There is so much to do before tonight, I must hurry!" She laughed as she rushed around the lodge, snatching up items of clothing she would need to get ready for the ceremony. At the door she turned. "Everything will be all right, Tia. You will see!" Then she closed the flap, leaving the two girls alone to prepare for the coming night.

"Tia," Keelah cast a sideways glance at the girl she had known since childhood, "what are you up to?"

"What do you mean? I said I will not fight." She affected an innocent look. "Why are you not pleased?"

"I know you. You do not give in this easy."

Going to the door, Tia peeked out. Satisfied that no one lingered nearby, she turned back to her friend. "Keelah, can I speak with you?"

"You know I will always listen."

"Then I will trust you. This night Appearing Wolf will be at the wedding ceremony alone, for I will not be there."

"Tia!" Keelah took the girl's cold hands in hers. "What are you saying?"

"I am telling you I cannot be joined with Appearing Wolf."

"But," Keelah drew back staring at her, "you have already been promised!"

"Then I can get un-promised!" She jerked her hands away. "I will not marry the man who killed Gray Dog!"

"Oh Tia. You are going to cause yourself so much trouble and you know Appearing Wolf will come and take you to the ceremony."

"No, Keelah, he won't, for I will not be here."

"Where will you be? There is nowhere in the village for you to hide."

"I will not be in the village. I am not wanted here. My family does not love me!" Tia's full mouth curled into a childish pout. "If they did they would not give me to a man I hate!"

"You are so wrong, Tia," Keelah told her, her mind racing for some way to talk her out of going ahead with such a dangerous plan. "Your family loves you very much."

"They do not show it, Keelah."

Knowing it would do no good to argue, Keelah tried another way around the problem. "Where can you go that Appearing Wolf will not find you?"

"I have planned everything out. I will ride to the village of the Flat Heads. They have always been a friend of the Blackfeet."

"Tia. The Flat Heads live very far from here. How will you find your way?"

"I do not know, Keelah!" The gaping holes in her well-thought-out plans balled her stomach into hard knots all over again. "All I know, is I will not stay here and be given to a man who will beat me!"

"Why would Appearing Wolf beat you if you do not give him a reason?"

"He would beat me, Keelah. You know I could not keep a silent tongue!"

Her mind made up, as to what she must do, Tia readied what little she would need for her trip. When she had finished she turned to a nervous Keelah.

"Come, we must go now. If we see my mother I will tell her we are going riding so I can calm myself for tonight. I do not like lying to her, but I must go!" She took Keelah's arm. "Will you help me?"

"I do not know what to do," Keelah whispered, looking around as if waiting for the fierce war chief to leap out at her for even thinking of betraying him.

"Keelah! Will you help me?"

For a long moment, Keelah looked at her, then nodded. "Yes, Tia. I will help you."

***

"Father, may I speak with you?"

At the sound of Appearing Wolf's voice, Maheto hastened to greet him. "You are always welcome in my lodge, Appearing Wolf." Pride in the old chief's eyes as he looked upon his son showed strong upon his face. "Have you spoken with Tia yet?"

"No," came the quiet answer. "She knows the ceremony is at sundown."

"You did not hear my words." Maheto shook his head.

"I heard your words, my father, and I am sorry for my words to you."

"Why do you feel the need to apologize? Did you not speak your words from your heart?

"Yes, but I spoke words filled with pain. I did not need to add to your suffering."

"Have your feelings changed?"

"No. I still do not understand why you did not protect my mother. No, wait my father." Appearing Wolf said as Maheto began to speak. "I will not talk with you about what is so close to both our hearts. This night I will take Tia as my wife. There will be time enough later for us to talk."

"I know the feelings you hold in your heart for this girl. I will be silent."

"The feelings you think I hold for her are not here." He touched his chest. "She will give me sons. That is all I want from her. I am not without mercy my father. I will be gentle when I teach her to be my woman. You can trust there is no longer any anger in my heart for this girl who, after tonight, will be mine."

***

For the third time that day, Jolisha walked outside, her worried eyes scanning the horizon for any sign of Tia's return. Each time her searching gaze saw only the prairie. She had been so sure Tia had had a change of heart. Now she knew it had all been a ploy. Her strong willed daughter had no intentions of marrying a man she did not love. Jolisha had never known Tia to tell a deliberate lie. Her fear of what tonight would bring must have weighed heavy upon her heart.

As she stood there in the hot sun, another more frightening thought occurred to her. Could Tia have changed enough to put her best friend's life in danger? If Keelah knew of Tia's plan to run away, Appearing Wolf would not hesitate to extract the truth from her in any way needed. The young war chief's pride could not allow him to do any less.

Jolisha knew that in Tia's running away she had brought shame on all of them. When Spotted Owl discovered her gone he might go after her. He would allow no man to follow him in this search for his wayward daughter. A warrior never put another's life in danger because of one of his own. Alone upon the prairie he could fall prey to many dangers.

With a sinking heart she spied Spotted Owl walking towards her. Lest he read the fear showing upon her face, Jolisha retraced her steps.

Spotted Owl gave his wife but a brief glance before going to his couch. Thoughts of what this night held for his eldest daughter weighed heavy upon his heart. Lying there in the quiet, his thoughts flew back to the night of her birth.

Snow had fallen during the day and the wet flakes gave his black hair a premature gray look, as he continued to pace back and forth in front of his lodge. His feet ceased their frantic pacing and his eyes turned in the direction of the birthing teepee as a high pitched scream rant the frigid air. With rapid steps he moved towards the dwelling in preparation to greet his son.

Kneeling beside the still panting woman he brushed the damp hair back from her forehead. She smiled up at him. As he watched, her face became flushed as she bore down with all her might. Then, giving a final

107

push, she brought the mewling baby the rest of the way into the world. Mahossa cut the life-sustaining link between mother and child, proclaiming its first moments as a free entity.

Placing a kiss on her moist brow, Spotted Owl gazed on the woman he cherished. "You have done well, my woman," he whispered, drawing back as the medicine man placed the new-born in his arms. The child he held was not the son he had wanted, but as he looked down on the small round face it didn't matter. He brushed a finger down one chubby cheek. She moved her mouth against the foreign object, emitting loud sucking noises.

"I think she is in need of her mother," he chuckled.

Jolisha placed the babe to her breast, a sad look covering her face. "I am sorry I did not give you the son you wished for. I will try harder next time," she vowed, only to watch other women fulfill her empty promise.

Now as he sat thinking on the pain this child of his heart was enduring, he reached out to the woman whose strength had always been there for him. "Jolisha, where is Tia?" I must speak with her. I must make her understand I want her happiness. Appearing Wolf will make her a good husband, Aakiiwa." In silence he offered up a prayer to the Creator, for his words to be true.

When she did not respond, Spotted Owl sat up. "Jolisha, what is it?"

"It is Tia, my husband," she whispered.

"What about Tia? Is she ill?" He rose from his couch.

"No she is not ill. She is gone."

"To visit with Keelah?"

"No! Tia has disappeared!"

"What are you saying, woman?"

"I am saying our daughter has run away!"

"That cannot be! She is to marry Appearing Wolf! The time for the ceremony is soon!"

"She is gone my husband. She went riding this morning with Keelah. She has not returned!" Jolisha stood before him wringing her hands. "What are we going to do?!"

The fear in Jolisha's voice was something Spotted Owl had not heard in a long time. She had always been so strong. "We must find her!"

"I do not know where she has gone."

"Keelah will know." He walked to the door.

Every few minutes Jolisha would go to the opening, peering out over the village hoping to catch a glimpse of her wayward daughter.

"Where could she have gone? What could she have been thinking?" she moaned aloud, pacing back and forth. At the sounds of footsteps outside she lifted the flap. The sight of Maheto standing before her made her heart leap in her chest.

"Jolisha. I have come to speak with Tia." At her stricken look he demanded. "What has happened? Where is she?" Jolisha knew she could not lie. With her head bowed in shame she told him what had happened.

"This will cause much trouble for your daughter. My son will be very angry."

"Oh, my chief. I beg you," Jolisha clung to his arm, "do not let him hurt her!"

"Jolisha, I can do nothing." Maheto removed her hands. "My son walks his own path. Your daughter is promised to Appearing Wolf. She has brought shame on the word of Spotted Owl.

Spotted Owl and Keelah had just entered the lodge as Maheto spoke.

"What you say is true, Maheto. My daughter has not shown wisdom."

With her heart pounding in her ears, Keelah stood just inside the door, her mind racing for a means to save Tia from her latest predicament. As the three waited for her to tell them what they wanted to hear, Keelah could feel her body tremble.

"Keelah. Do you know where Tia has gone?" Maheto asked.

Unable to speak she nodded. Her terror at lying to her chief mounting.

"Tell me where my daughter is! Now!" Spotted Owl demanded moving in anger towards the frightened girl.

Stepping between the two, Jolisha spoke in a quiet voice. "Keelah, please. Tell us where she has gone."

"Tia ran away," she whispered.

Knowing the frightened girl could say no more at the moment, Jolisha turned a pleading face to Spotted Owl. "My husband, cannot someone go after her?"

"Someone is going after her!" breathed a deep male voice.

At these words all eyes turned to the lodge opening. The leashed anger in Appearing Wolf's ebony eyes made Jolisha's breath catch in her throat.

"I beg of you..." she began, but the frigid words of Appearing Wolf stopped her.

"Silence, woman!" With a quickness, he jerked Keelah to him. White-hot fire shot down her arm as his fingers dug into her skin. "Where is she, Keelah?" The anger in his eyes made any words she might have spoken impossible. "Answer me!" To her shame hot tears ran down her face. "Answer me!" he hissed. "If your tongue is useless then I will cut it out!" Throwing the terrified girl to the floor he drew his knife.

"Appearing Wolf!" Maheto growled. "Keelah cannot tell you what you want to know. Her fear is too great!"

"Then I will end her fear, my father!" He raised the knife but his hand was stilled.

"No, my son! I will not let you do this!"

Jolisha gathered the frightened girl into her arms. "Keelah, tell us where Tia has gone. You cannot help her now. All you can do is bring yourself more pain."

Like a cowed animal, the girl leaned deeper into the comforting arms of Jolisha. "Tia has ridden to the land of the Flat Heads. She does not want this marriage. Her heart still belongs to Gray Dog."

Upon hearing these words Appearing Wolf turned and left the lodge.

"Holy Ones," Jolisha prayed, "don't let him hurt her."

Chapter Twelve

After leaving Keelah, Tia rode hard and fast, trying to put as much distance between herself and Appearing Wolf as she could. She knew that by leaving the village, alone, she put herself in extreme danger. Her need to run from this marriage she did not want drove her ever further from her land, this land that had always felt so safe. The chances of Appearing Wolf finding her never entered her mind. She would not let herself think of that possibility; she could not.

Tia continued on her journey; stopping long enough to rest herself and her horse. As evening neared she began to feel uneasy. She did not like traveling alone after sundown. Stories she had heard as a child came back to haunt her. The cries of wild animals coming down out of the hills in search of food made her blood run cold but still she went on. Appearing Wolf must not find her.

Beginning to feel the strain of such a rigorous journey, Tia at last had to stop. Sliding to the ground she pulled the blanket from her horse's back, leading him the rest of the way into the forest. With the evening light dwindling she began a thorough rubdown of her lathered mount, knowing his well-being had to come first if she hoped to continue.

Stroking the big horse with large handfuls of grass, she scoffed aloud. "Let Appearing Wolf be shamed before his warriors for choosing a girl who would rather risk being captured by a murderous Crow or eaten alive by a wild animal than to belong to him. I told him I did not want him, now he knows I do not lie. In time he will choose another for his woman. He would not dare come after a girl who ran away rather than be joined with him."

She laughed thinking on the teasing he could be receiving right at this moment. The happy thoughts helped to drive away some of the fear she had begun to feel over the lengthening shadows. As she thought of the anger her father would be feeling, some of the happiness left her and a deep sense of foreboding filled her mind. Appearing Wolf might not come after her but Spotted Owl would. He did not go back on his word.

Another more frightening idea occurred to her. What if Appearing Wolf finds out Keelah helped her in deceiving him?" Fear of what he might do to her friend clutched her heart. "Oh Night Star, what have I done?" she whispered. With a sinking heart she curled up in the thin blanket willing her mind to relax, but each time she heard the snapping of a twig as an animal ran across the forest floor her heart leapt in her chest. Finally, toward dawn, she at last fell into a fitful sleep.

When she woke hours later, the sun was straight overhead. Jumping to her feet she started walking toward Night Star when she stopped, and placing both hands, palm down, against the small of her back stretched her taut muscles until she felt the soreness starting to disappear. Angry at herself for sleeping so long she bent down to grab the blanket from the ground when she heard the sounds of many voices nearby. Swiftly Tia straightened and reaching out covered the horse's nose to insure his silence. Crouching low, she waited to see who threatened her safety.

"Crow!" she whispered her heart in her throat at the sight of her most dreaded enemy. All the stories she had ever heard over the years, about the cruelty her people had suffered at their hands flooded her mind, as she crouched in the tall foliage. From her hiding place she watched as five hideously painted Crow moved towards her, stopping so close to where she crouched, she felt_sure they would see her. They looked terrifying with black paint covering their faces and the way some had their heads shaven with a swath of painted hair sticking straight up on their heads. Tia could hear their laughter as they stood nearby. Almost all of the men looked to be young, their hard, taut bodies bared except for loincloths in defense of the sweltering heat.

Afraid to breathe lest they hear her, she waited. Never had she felt so frightened. She could feel the cold sweat sliding down her back, its icy touch making her shiver.

The horse, smelling her fear, pawed the ground inpatient to be gone. Trying in vain to calm him, Tia put her mouth close to his ear talking in a soothing voice, but the fear in her voice added to his discomfort. Throwing back his head he emitted a loud snort.

Without a second thought Tia jumped on his back to send him racing from their hiding place. At first she had hopes they would be safe. She had glimpsed the total surprise on her enemy's faces as she tore past them on her way to freedom. Giving the frightened animal full rein they raced over the prairie. She could hear the bloodcurdling screams of the angry Crow coming closer.

"Run, Night Star! Run! They must not catch us!" she urged, kneeing him in her frantic need to escape. Chancing a quick glance over her shoulder she saw they had gained on her. Her heart pounded so hard she found it difficult to breathe.

Within moments they rode all around her. To her horror she watched as one would ride at her then veer off at the last possible moment. They toyed with her, making the sport last longer until they became bored with the game and moved in for the kill. At this thought, Tia lost her fear and replaced it with cold, hard fury.

Pulling Night Star to an abrupt halt, she sat astride his lathered back watching them. As though she had all the time she needed, Tia told them in sign language what she thought of them.

"You do not frighten me, sons of a she-dog!" She smiled. "I am Blackfeet! We do not cower before our enemies!"

Taken aback at the strength of this small Blackfoot girl sitting proud astride her horse telling them of her hatred, they laughed, glancing from one to the other in disbelief.

Of the five, one did not find her daring amusing. Urging his horse forward he watched her, a deep scowl covering his face. He signed back.

"Do you think to trick us? You are but a girl. I am Young Buffalo of the mighty Crow nation. Does the great Appearing Wolf fear us so much he would send a female dog to draw us into his trap?"

At this thought, Tia laughed aloud. "Our war chief has no fear of cowards. Just as I do not! Move out of my way! I have no time to waste sitting in the hot sun listening to you whine your fear over a mere girl."

"Where are your warriors, woman? They will come soon enough when they hear your screams of pain," the Crow declared, drawing his knife, unable to believe she could be here alone.

"No one will ride to my defense, evil one! Even the women of the mighty Blackfeet are unafraid of you!" she taunted turning to leave.

He spurred his horse forward to block her path. Undaunted, she backed Night Star out of his way, looking for an opening of escape. The other warriors sat watching this duel of wits between one of their own and the small Blackfeet girl whose beautiful face never betrayed the fear she had to be feeling.

Too late, she saw Young Buffalo's fist draw back to deliver a stunning blow to the side of her head. She heard their chilling cries before darkness settled over her.

Young Buffalo placed Tia over her horse himself being careful to make sure her bindings would not come undone. With deliberate cunning he moved to the side blocking the view of the other warriors as he proceeded to fondle her lush body, running his hands over her ripe curves and marveling at her fresh beauty. He wished for the time to take her here and now but knew they had already delayed leaving this area long enough. In real pain he mounted, and grabbing the reins of the girl's horse, signaled his braves to ride out.

When Tia came to, she found herself lying face down across her horse. Not wanting the men riding on both sides of her to know she had awakened, she kept her eyes closed, allowing her head to continue bobbing of its own free will. Would any of her people ever find her? She knew what trouble she would bring about should the warriors of her village learn of her being held hostage in a Crow camp. Her father would have to fight for her, if he ever found her at all. Would she be the instrument of his death? As these thoughts wound down in her tortured mind the horses picked up speed. Thankful at least, they had had the presence of mind to tie her onto her horse, she felt herself being spun once more into darkness.

When she finally woke darkness surrounded her and water dripped down her face from the thick branches overhead. They had bound her, sitting up against a tall pine, with her hands and feet secured and a long strip of leather looped around her waist, attaching her to the tree. Since the Crow had not had the decency to cover her with a robe, her dress had been soaked through to the skin. "Brainless dogs," she murmured. "Can they not see I will be useless to them dead?"

All through the long night Tia remained awake. She watched the Crow sleeping on the wet ground rolled up in their blankets. She smiled as she saw them twitch and shiver as the dampness crept inside chilling them without mercy.

"I hope they all get the sickness in their chests and die!" She tried moving her bound hands and feet once more to no avail. Her tight bindings left her limbs numb and useless. Her chilled body yearned for a fire to dispel the cold but the Crow knew the danger of having a fire at night. Its glow and smoke could be seen from a long way off and they already feared approaching Blackfeet.

Tia tried to stay calm. The knowledge of her captivity warred on her mind. She did her best to push the thought away breathing deep against the panic threatening to overpower her. She would not admit, even to herself, she dwelled in the midst of her greatest weakness. She closed her eyes shutting out her surroundings and forced herself to breathe in slow breaths in an effort to shut out her fear. Long hours passed as she continued to work on bringing herself under control.

In the early dawn, someone stirred. As though coming out of a fog Tia opened her eyes to see the one she had goaded earlier walking towards her. Her fear at being bound, unable to move left her mind as another more imminent danger reared its ugly head. Tia watched him approach, noting how the paint covering his face earlier and now washed away by the rain, allowed her to see his features. She guessed his age to be close to that of her father noting the many lines crisscrossing his broad and deep-pocked face. The bridge of his nose bore a prominent hump and his wide lips drawn back in a deep scowl, showed rotten uneven teeth. She shivered as he stopped in front of her. She closed her eyes unable to look at him.

Young Buffalo dropped to his knees his breath already rushing from his lungs. He reached out, running a callused hand over her face, watching her young body tense, then recoil at his touch. His breath became labored as one hand moved to squeeze her firm breast. Drawing a thick bladed knife from its sheath he ran the edge beneath the strips of leather holding her secure. Tia rubbed her numbed wrists, moved her feet back and forth to try and bring feeling back into her limbs. Young Buffalo watched her running a moist tongue over his dry lips. With the point of his knife he lifted the hem of her dress.

His hands started to shake as they always did when he had a young female at his mercy. His lust for the smell and taste of blood, that always tasted stronger when it pumped through the body with fear, made it difficult to slow down and enjoy himself. He felt the onrush of power as she cowered on the ground begging him with her eyes not to hurt her. It always felt the same as the first time. But with that time the terrified eyes had been those of a trapped doe. The memory rushed through his mind calling forth images of himself as a young boy on his first kill. He remembered how his heart had pumped with excitement as he watched the deer stumble with the arrow imbedded deep in her neck. He ran up to where she had fallen, and as he drew his knife to slit her throat, he saw her eyes bulging with fear. She knew she would die and the power he felt right at that moment was not like anything he had ever felt before. When he drew the blade across her throat, her blood had gushed out, spraying his face and running into his mouth. The blood had been thick and had a wild taste to it. But most of all the blood tasted of strength. He had been a young boy and yet he held the power of life and death in his hands. His young heart had soared with strange feelings as the image of the doe replayed itself over and over in his mind. When he grew older and went on raids he found the same feelings could be had with the female captives they brought back to camp. Young Buffalo did not find it strange that taking them against their will did not equal the thrill of seeing their fear just before he plunged the knife into their hearts proving once again the power he held in his hands. Now as he looked down at the young girl lying on the ground he prepared himself to feel that power again.

Tia felt surprised he had waited this long. Determined he would not take her without a fight she kicked out panting what she thought of him.

"Get away from me! I would rather die here and now than let you enter my body!" Rolling away she scrambled to her feet, only to fall back to the hard ground. In an instant he covered her body, laughing an obscene laugh as he secured both arms above her head with one large hand. She could feel him fumbling with his clothing trying to rid himself of their covering.

Sheer panic seized her as she felt his heavy weight fall upon her. Bucking and screaming like a savage animal, Tia would not allow him to take her. His anger at last out of control, the Crow reached for his knife, determined to still her wild thrashings.

Seeing his intent, the terrified girl grabbed his hair and jerked his throat to her mouth. Without stopping to think she sank her teeth deep into his flesh. As her mouth filled with his blood, and his painful shrieks filled the air around them she felt his weight lift from her. She leaped for the knife lying on the ground beside her.

The injured warrior, intent on stopping the flow of blood pouring from his neck, did not see her grab the knife. With a scream rivaling that of her male protectors, she plunged the knife into his heart.

Hearing the screams the roused Crow leapt to their feet, reaching for their weapons, ready to do battle against their enemies. Then they spied their leader lying on the ground with the Blackfeet captive hovered over him. Amazement showed upon their faces as they stood, as if in a daze, glancing from one to the other.

Like a crazed animal Tia crouched on the ground watching them, the dead warrior's blood still dripping from her mouth. Her frozen mind tried to make sense of what had happened. She closed her eyes for a moment trying to bring the watching men into focus, but as hard as she tried they continued to weave in and out of her vision, shimmering, as though surrounded by intense heat. Without being aware of her movements Tia pushed herself to her feet to walk with unsteady steps to her horse. Her actions seemed to snap the watching men out of their stupor. One of the men reached out grabbing her by her hair and slinging her to the ground. Tia could feel their angry fists raining blows over her unprotected body but she could do nothing to stop them. At last, bored with their torture of her, one of the men retrieved the long strip of leather that had been used before to tie her to the tree, and bound her once more.

As the sun broke through the clouds, she found herself led away to a fate that only the passing of time could reveal.

***

Riding alone across the rolling prairie Appearing Wolf could not believe Tia had dared to challenge him! The anger he felt right at this moment chilled him to his heart. If the spirits were with her, he would not find her right away. Right now even he could not be sure what he would do if he had her standing before him.

As a leader of their people, he could not allow himself to be lenient with her in any way. She must learn his word is law. So far she had tried to make him a fool at every turn. At this thought the coldness in his heart grew stronger, pushing any feeling he had for her ever deeper.

With his mind filled with heated thoughts, his senses did not pick up on the presence of another close by. Reining his horse, he waited back among the trees. Presently the one trailing him appeared. With a low growl the rugged war chief spied his younger brother, Pehta, riding towards him.

"It is a good thing for you, my brother, I am not Crow." Pehta chuckled with good humor, eyeing the stern-faced man before him.

Unamused, Appearing Wolf told him, "Go back, Pehta. I do not want you with me."

"The fire in your eyes tells me your heart could not be tempered with mercy should it be needed."

"Now is not the time for mercy." Appearing Wolf glared at him. "I have been too tolerant of this girl's actions already. She has made me a fool before our people." His eyes flashed with the anger boiling inside him. "Soon she will learn I am not one to be played with."

"No," Pehta agreed. "The girl has not acted in a wise manner. But, Appearing Wolf, you must see the strongness of spirit here. Would you want a woman who would always do your bidding? I think not." The handsome warrior smiled.

"There is a big difference in doing as she is told and open defiance."

"The daughter of Spotted Owl is a fighter; she needs a strong hand to guide her."

With no warning the memory of Tia the night she learned she would belong to him flashed through his mind. She had attacked without weighing the outcome. The feel of her soft body pressed tight against him made him shutter in his need for her. Even now, the very reminder brought an ache to his strong young loins. If she had not run from him he would be enjoying her on his couch right at this moment, instead of riding across the prairie in search of her. Cold hard fury, coupled with his unsatisfied lust, doused his wayward thoughts making him more determined than ever to find her.

Kicking his horse forward, he replied in a cold voice. "The daughter of Spotted Owl has found a strong hand. One she will not want to challenge ever again."

In silence, Pehta fell in beside his angry brother. As the horses picked up speed he felt an ominous foreboding clutch his heart. He too, had entertained thoughts of the beautiful young girl they pursued. Her laughing black eyes slipped into his thoughts calling to mind her fearless antics amongst the people. While other women of the village found pleasure in the decorating of a well-tanned shirt or their quickness in erecting a lodge, Tia kept finding herself being reproached for her daring feats of bravery.

Pehta recalled a long-ago day when she had been but nine-summers old. She had listened with growing admiration of the young brave's tales of the vision quest. They had talked of how, when it came their time to seek the spirits, the old ones would bestow upon them great knowledge to help their people. They practiced denying their bodies needed food and drink, and purging their spirits of impurities in the sweat lodge. The dangers of this inner testing had always been spoken of in hushed tones, making the event even more exciting and longed for.

Neither Jolisha nor Spotted Owl had noticed Tia's own forsaking of food and drink. Three days later the warriors had been summoned to the council-house to begin a search for the missing girl. They had found her late the next day lying unconscious in the forest. To his father and the other leaders, she was thought of as a rebellious young girl. In the eyes of the upcoming warriors Tia deserved much admiration and respect.

Another memory came unbidden to his mind of a small girl, her long black hair flying back from her face, riding through the village astride a half-broke stallion, all because of a bet. That challenge had cost her the beautiful spotted pony given to her by Keelah's father for Tia's tending to his wife in a time of illness. When told of her loss of the animal, Tia herself brought him to the council-house to hand him over. With her head held high she walked through the village, her black eyes daring anyone to make sport of her.

Now once again, Tia had defied the laws of her people. Fear of what Appearing Wolf might do when he found her prompted Pehta's accompaniment of the volatile warrior.

Numerous times the pair had to dismount in order to look closer for any sign of Tia's passing. Admiration for her skills at hiding her tracks made Pehta's heart swell with pride. To Appearing Wolf, her ability to stay hidden filled him with rage.

"Where did she learn these tricks?" he breathed, rising to his feet. "She is a girl, not a warrior."

"Your woman is a fast learner," Pehta laughed, removing two small rawhide bags of pemmican, a mixture of dried meat, melted fat, and berries from his supplies. "She has always been a warrior at heart."

"When she is in my lodge with my sons to care for, she will have no time to get into trouble." He took one of the bags, Pehta offered him.

"Perhaps she will not give you only sons." Pehta stuffed a handful of the dried mixture into his mouth. "A daughter with the same wild spirit as her mother," he talked around the food, "could make life even more hectic. Maybe another could give you the peace of mind you need." He swallowed, then reached for the water pouch. "One who would not fight the strong hand of her husband."

"Tia is mine! She will learn to behave as a woman should!" He yanked the leather ties shut on the bag. "When I am through with her," he tossed the bag back with a sharp flick of his wrist, "she will never wish to defy me again!"

Knowing any advice he could offer at that time would be ignored, Pehta remained silent. His brother had a lot to learn about this woman he refused to give up. With her, his life would never be peaceful. Pehta knew, at that moment, he had lost all chance to win her for himself, but it didn't quiet the love he felt for her in his heart. He would be there when

Appearing Wolf caught up to her. If need be, he would defend her with his life.

Far off in the distance the low rumblings of thunder echoed out over the early morning stillness. Dark and fast moving clouds overhead, warned of an impending storm. Seeking cover, they rode towards the tree.

In Appearing Wolf's heart, the fierce anger burned brighter. The storm would wipe out any tracks Tia had left. This would make his finding her more difficult. He could not believe she had eluded him this long. When he thought of all the dangers she could encounter, his anger faltered. He hardened his heart against this weakness. Tia had chosen to put herself in this danger, he could not allow himself to forget this. Without warning, his eyes fell on something that made his heart leap. Dismounting, he picked up a soiled blanket. With haste his dark gaze scanned the surrounding area. Spying the trampled grass, his heart thudded at a sickening pace.

"The tracks of many ponies there, by that tall pine," Pehta nodded, "does not bode well for your woman, my brother," Then, seeing the blanket Appearing Wolf held in his hands, he breathed. "They have taken her!"

As the brothers ran for their horses, the heavens opened up soaking them to the skin. Uncaring, they raced toward the land of their enemies.

Chapter Thirteen

For three long exhausting days and nights, the Crow and their captive rode almost without stopping. Unused to such rigorous traveling Tia winced in pain with each step Night Star took. Without anything between her and his lathered back the sweat stinging her chafed legs made it all but impossible to stay sitting upright as the torturous journey continued. Finally, on the fourth day as darkness gave way to dawn, it was almost with relief Tia saw in the valley below, the many lodges of her enemies

One of her captors snatched Night Star's reins from her hands. With a high-pitched yell, alerting the camp of their arrival, she and her captors started down the steep hill leading into the valley. Determined not to show any fear in the face of this new threat to her young life, Tia held her head high, refusing to cower before her enemies.

A piercing scream tore from the throat of one of the watching women. Before anyone could stop her she ran forward to clutch the lifeless hand dangling from beneath the worn buffalo robe. The woman, fat with long stringy hair in much need of washing, ran alongside the moving horses. When she, at last, ceased her loud shrieking, everyone grew quiet so they could hear what had befallen one of their bravest leaders.

In great detail one of Tia's captors related how Young Buffalo had been lured by the beauty of the evil Blackfeet captive and how, when he had given into her charms, she had stabbed him in the heart with his own knife. When he had finished all eyes turned toward Tia.

With a grief-stricken wail the bereaved woman drew her knife, advancing on the young girl still sitting astride her horse. Waiting until the angry woman came within reach, Tia kicked out knocking the weapon from her hand.

At her daring the crowd moved back out of reach. With her hair falling in wild disarray down her back and her face and arms still covered with blood and bruises Tia looked very frightening. Reading the disdain in the faces staring up at her Tia felt her anger rising, knowing they had not been told the truth of Young Buffalo's death or the reason she had been forced to end his life. Without any thought as to the consequences, she called out for their attention. Satisfied when they all grew quiet, she began signing the true story of their fallen warrior.

"Crows! Hear the wailing of Young Buffalo's woman." Her hostile eyes caught and held the other woman's chilling gaze. "She mourns the death of her man whose life was taken when he tried to enter the body of a Blackfeet girl." Disgust showed plain upon her face as her eyes raked the face of the one trembling in her anger. "Remove the robe! See his wounds! If a mere Blackfeet girl can do this, think what our warriors can do, if you seek revenge. If you wish to save yourselves, release me and I will be gone!"

"Blackfeet woman! What is your name?" a voice called out in her language. Staring straight ahead she saw a tall man walking towards her with an unhurried step, through the throng of people. The man looked no older than her father. His long black hair, parted in the middle and falling well below his shoulders, was streaked with gray. Halting beside her horse, he stared up at her, waiting for her to tell him her name.

"I am Tia. Daughter of Spotted Owl," she told him, her dark head rising with pride. "Your warriors captured me. I am on my way to visit the land of the Flat Heads."

"Why is the daughter of Spotted Owl riding alone and not with the protection of many warriors?"

"I have no fear of meeting Crows!" she laughed derisively. "I am Blackfeet. Look beneath the buffalo robe!" She swung her head in the direction of the dead Crow lying across his horse. "See what happens when I am defied!"

Without hesitation he walked to the slain warrior's horse, peeled back the weather-beaten robe. He stepped back, at the sight that met his eyes. A deep moan came from the woman of Young Buffalo. Tia knew, of all the enemies she had in this camp, this woman would be her worst.

The man spoke in quiet to two warriors standing nearby. They pulled Tia from her horse, shoving her between the rows of people. Tia ducked her head to protect her face from being spit upon. Women reached out yanking on her long hair, and children, caught up in the anger picked up rocks and clods of dirt to sling at her.

After following their leader inside a large dwelling, the men threw Tia to the floor. There they left her alone with the one person who could understand her heated words.

"My people will kill you for this," she told him, rubbing her bound and chafed wrists. "Their anger will not be avenged until everyone in this camp lies dead and rotting in the hot sun!"

Waiting until all of the wrathful words had been spoken, the man seated across from her remained silent. Finally when she at last looked away, he spoke.

"You do not speak the truth, Little One. Spotted Owl does not know where his wandering daughter is at this moment. What has driven you from the land of your people?"

Surprised at his insight, she once again turned to face him. "Where did you learn the language of my people?"

"It is always good to know the words spoken by one's enemy. As a leader of my people I must learn all I can of those who would take my life," he said, his dark gaze unwavering. "Captive Blackfeet can be persuaded to do many things."

"Who are you?"

"I am Chief Yellow Calf," he told her in a calm voice.

"If you value the safety of your people, you will let me go," she warned, her eyes meeting his in a direct stare. "If you do not, their blood will be on your hands."

"Are you asking to be returned to your camp?" he appraised her with a sideways glance.

Stepping blindly into his trap she replied. "No. I wish to be set free to continue on my journey."

Getting to his feet, Yellow Calf stood for a moment, looking down at her, then chuckling left her alone. As soon as he had gone, the same two warriors entered to remove her from his lodge. Shoving her ahead of them down a winding twisting path, they halted beside a small, secluded lake, then signed for her to bath.

She shook her head holding out her bound wrists. "Do you expect me to bath with my hands tied?" Uncaring of her dilemma one man picked her up to throw her into the clear water, laughing at her valiant attempts to stay afloat.

Sputtering and choking Tia cried out to the spirits to free her, to grant her the means with which to end their worthless lives. Time and again she made her way to the bank, but each time she tried to leave the water one of the Crows would place a foot on her shoulder to shove her back in.

Just when she thought she could endure no more, they dragged her from the water to deposit her on the grassy bank. Turning onto her stomach, Tia lay where they had dropped her, coughing up water from her tortured lungs. Unable to verbally attack her tormentors, she glared at them, her black eyes screaming of the deep hatred smoldering within.

Sure now, no one in the camp of her enemies knew where Tia was, Yellow Calf sat pondering what to do with her. Never had he seen a girl with such bravery as this one. Tradition dictated she be given to Padrah, Young Buffalo's widow. Tia had been the one to take the warrior's life; therefore, she must pay for that life with her own. He could not envision this girl living out the rest of her days as a mere slave. Besides, the slain warrior's woman would be no match for this fierce Blackfeet girl whose spirit demanded she escape such a humble existence.

Rising to his feet he walked outside in time to see his warriors leading a sodden Tia back to camp. With great interest he stood watching her, noting the proud, upright way she walked. Even bound and surrounded by her enemies she refused to acknowledge their strength. At that moment, Yellow Calf felt a great respect for this captive girl whose fate lay in his hands.

She would be placed in a lodge set apart from the rest of the village until he decided what to do with her. Knowing well the hatred of his people for any captive, especially one who had ended the life of one of their warriors, Yellow Calf knew she would have to be guarded against their wrath at all times.

Tia sat alone in the secluded teepee. Running her fingers through her tangled hair, she looked around taking in at a glance the worn skins that would allow rain to seep through with little effort. Because of the constant moving in search of the buffalo and seasonal camp changes, the skins had to be replaced often. The lodge poles rubbed against the skins in transit, causing thinning. Ignored, the lodge and its inhabitants would be left to the mercy of the elements. This lodge had been sadly neglected, with little thought to the comfort of those inside. Stripped of any essentials, even a worn buffalo robe, Tia knew she could look forward to an uncomfortable night.

A young girl entered. Turning, Tia looked at her watching her wary steps, glad to see the stark fear in the girl's eyes as she moved around the dwelling. As soon as she could the girl scurried back outside.

Walking over, Tia peered down at the steaming bowl of food, its aroma making her empty stomach grumble with hunger. Beside the bowl sat a full water pouch. Lifting the small opening to her bruised lips, she drank long and deep of the sweet liquid. After satisfying her body's hunger she looked to see what else had been brought for her use.

Wrapped within a small worn buffalo robe she found a deerskin dress. She felt surprised to find no holes or patches. Then her eyes fell on an ill-constructed comb. She picked it up, drawing the teeth through her snarled hair being careful not to break the long strands in her haste. Without a thong to secure her braids, she had to leave her long hair hanging free. Her beaded headband kept the shiny locks back away from her face.

Tia decided she would accept food and water but she refused to dress as a Crow. Her own dress, clean now from her sojourn at the lake earlier. The moccasins she had made with her own hands remained in good repair. She had all she needed to survive.

Of an instant her senses alerted her to someone approaching from outside. As she watched, the flap lifted and Yellow Calf stooped to enter. She heard his sharp intake of breath as he looked at her.

He had known she would have much beauty, as most young Blackfeet girls. The one sitting before him now took his breath away. Moving closer he held out his hand. When she got to her feet he enjoyed the fact she held her head erect, refusing to cower in his presence. What a magnificent mate she would be for his eldest son, Spirit Walker. The pride in his eyes as he thought upon this match brought a cold hand of fear to Tia's heart.

Why did he look at her this way? The idea that this man, who treated her unlike a captive, might want her for himself made Tia want to back away, but she forced herself to remain. Had she escaped the clutches of one man to be entrapped by another?

Leading her from the lodge, he began walking towards the council-house when the sounds of many horses riding into camp stopped him in mid-stride. A wide grin crossing his face, as he turned to watch the approaching riders, made Tia turn to follow his gaze.

Seated astride a snow-white horse rode one of the most handsome men she had ever seen. Almost as breathtaking as Appearing Wolf, she allowed the thought. His flowing, waist-length black hair caught by the sun, glistened in the afternoon light. The people gathered around him smiling and laughing.

Spying his father up ahead, the young warrior kneed his horse around the crowd of people reaching out for him. As his keen eye caught sight of the small girl standing by his side, his black gaze never left her face. When he drew even with them he dismounted, clasping his father's forearms in a firm grip. His full lips parted showing strong, even white teeth. As his attention turned once more to the young girl standing in silence beside his father, he smiled.

She ignored his smile with a proud lift of her head. At her arrogant refusal to acknowledge him, Spirit Walker threw back his head, laughing.

After motioning a brave standing nearby to take Tia to her lodge, Chief Yellow Calf began talking in earnest with his roguish son. As Tia walked away, she could hear their bold laughter echoing out over the happy village.

Soon after sundown the drums called the people from their lodges. They would celebrate the safe return of the warriors. Tia could hear the laughter and gaiety continuing long into the night. Afraid to close her eyes she watched the lodge opening, her senses alert to any danger that might be awaiting her.

***

Appearing Wolf and Pehta rode over the prairie at a fast pace, each lost in his own thoughts. They would have been surprised to know how their thoughts paralleled.

***

The storm had grown in its intensity. Strong gusts of wind blew rain back into their faces, making it all but impossible to see. Finally they had to seek shelter. Guiding the sodden horses into a grove of pines, they dismounted. Beneath the overhanging branches Appearing Wolf, spread a large buffalo robe over the damp pine needles. Throwing another less heavy robe over the stronger limbs he constructed a make-shift dwelling to protect them from the elements.

Seated now within the small area, Appearing Wolf's thoughts turned once again to the one upper-most on his mind. What torture might she be enduring at the hands of their enemies at this moment? If she had been violated would he still want her for his wife? Trying to still the ugly questions running rampant through his mind, he turned his attention to the young warrior seated beside him.

"Why did you choose to follow me, my brother?"

"I did not know if the anger in your heart could be stilled long enough to listen," Pehta answered without bothering to soften his words.

At the younger man's tone, Appearing Wolf grew angry. "Should I allow this girl to shame me before my warriors and do nothing?"

"Is your shame worth her life?" Pehta responded without the heat of anger. "If this is the reason you search for her, why not take another?"

"I am a leader! I would not allow an enemy to shame me, why would I let a girl of our village?"

"Tia is more than a girl of our village. She is the one you have chosen to bear your sons. Let her tell you why she took such drastic means to get away from you!"

At the heat in the other man's voice, Appearing Wolf drew back. "Could it be, Pehta, you want this girl for your own?"

"I would never try to steal my brother's woman," Pehta told him, "But hear my words, Appearing Wolf. I would never touch your woman with lust in my heart, but neither would I stand by while you harm her."

For a long moment their black eyes locked. Appearing Wolf spoke first.

"What I plan to do with this girl is of no concern of yours, Pehta. I will allow no interference. If this is how you feel, then you should return to camp."

"I will not interfere unless I see you cannot control the anger this girl brings to your heart."

Knowing of Pehta's nature to be a go-between, Appearing Wolf turned away. Stretching his long legs out straight, he allowed his body the rest it needed for the hard journey yet to come.

Rest did not come that easy for Pehta. His thoughts kept returning to the harsh words of his brother. Could this girl with the strong spirit be worth losing one of his own blood? What would he do if Appearing Wolf could not still his wrath? With these thoughts still churning in his mind he fell at last into a fitful sleep.

They woke to a star-lit sky. The storm had lost its fury, leaving but a mild wind to stir the branches overhead. Leaving their make-shift shelter, Appearing Wolf walked to where the horses stood, his mind still troubled over the insight he had gained into Pehta's heart. He had been unaware of the young warrior's feelings for his woman. Now, as he thought upon this new problem confronting him, he felt the anger inside his heart begin to grow. The fact that Tia could not hold blame for the feelings of another did not seem to matter. Once again she stood at the root of his problems.

Appearing Wolf dropped a closed bag of dried meat into the yet, unmoving warrior's lap. "It is time to leave. Already the night is half-over."

In silence the horses moved from amongst the trees, their unshod hoofs making little noise as they stepped light over the thick carpet of fallen pine needles. Like phantoms, the warriors rode over the prairie in search of the girl who had stolen both their hearts.

They had ridden for some distance when Appearing Wolf caught sight of a lone rider. Reining his horse he pointed toward the horizon. "Crow! He will warn Chief Yellow Calf we are near!"

The brothers knew they had lost the element of surprise. Lone warriors could ride into the camp of their enemies to challenge the warriors of their choice without fear of reprisal from others. Now this would no-longer be possible. On the open prairie they would be fair game.

They turned their ponies toward the mountains. Only a fool would stay to fight when he would soon be outnumbered. Higher and higher they climbed until they could be in a position to look out over the prairie below. Satisfied they had not yet been followed, the two men talked about how they could go about getting into the Crow camp undetected.

"He had to be a scout. If he belonged to a war party they would have been looking for us by now. The Crow chief is not stupid. He knows someone from Tia's village will be looking for her," Appearing Wolf declared.

"If he has harmed her, I will cut out his heart myself!" Pehta breathed.

"You forget, my brother, this is my woman we speak of. The right of his death belongs to me!"

At the fire in the war chief's eyes, Pehta grew quiet. How could he argue against such logic? The small girl who laughed and teased him in his dreams each night was lost to him forever. All he could do now is be there for her should she ever need him.

As Pehta left to see to the horses, Appearing Wolf sat thinking about their new dilemma. If they did not meet the Crow upon the plains, he could challenge the leader to a fight for Tia. If not the leader, then the one who had claimed her for his own. At this thought he felt his fury rising. He knew the spirited girl he had chosen for his woman would do everything in her power before she would allow herself to be taken by their enemy. She belonged to him! He must be the first to enter her! How could he ever accept a woman who had been soiled by another?

Again white-hot anger filled him. The daughter of Spotted Owl would pay a dear price for placing herself in this danger. Knowing the peril of staying in one place too long, Appearing Wolf and Pehta plotted their strategy. The Crow would be expecting them to stay in the mountains until they thought it safe to travel. They would not be looking for them right near the Crow village.

"Chief Yellow Calf's camp is still another hard day's ride from here. The scout we saw will not rest until he reaches his village. While the evil ones search for us here, we will have their people at our mercy," Appearing Wolf vowed.

"Do not take their war chief for a fool," Pehta cautioned him. "He can be a very dangerous foe."

Appearing Wolf had ridden into battle against the Crow war chief many times. He had to admit, even to himself, Spirit Walker would be a worthy opponent.

Without warning a story he had heard long ago came stealing into his mind. The tale concerned the capture of an Arapaho woman by the rugged Crow war chief. The story told of how she had been carried, kicking and screaming, to his lodge. After three days the virile warrior had tired of the woman and out of the goodness of his heart offered to return her to her husband. Whereupon the desire-crazed woman, begged him to keep her. Returning her but a short distance from her village he released her, only to find her back in his camp a few days later. Finally in order to be rid of her he had been forced to sell her to a band of Crow who lived further to the north. As the tale spread to the other tribes it became a warning to be joked about among the warriors. 'Do not let your woman be captured by the handsome war chief, Spirit Walker, for she will never wish to be returned!'

He could not help but wonder what had happened when Spirit Walker laid eyes on Tia. How could any man let her go once he had seen her? His heart filled with tortuous thoughts. What if the stories he had heard of the Crow leader been true? Would his woman choose to stay in the camp of their enemy, just to be near him like the Arapaho captive?

In a fury he began striding toward his horse. At Pehta's surprised look, Appearing Wolf stopped to glare at him. "Do you wish to wait for our enemies to come to us? Stay if you will! I am going for my woman!"

Drawing his mount even with the fleet-footed war-horse, Pehta chanced a hurried glance at his somber-faced brother. He had a good idea what had put the angry warrior in such a volatile mood. The mere mention of the name, Spirit Walker, was enough to spur any male into action. Especially, one whose woman could be, as they spoke, at the mercy of the legendary warrior.

Chapter Fourteen

Her tired body relaxed. Steeling her thoughts against her immediate problems, Tia at last fell into a deep sleep. Haunting dreams took her back in time. Once again she found herself running for her life. Trying to escape the fierce war chief who blocked her path every which way she turned. His black eyes filled with fire as he reached out for her, drawing her unyielding body against him. As his hot mouth came down on hers, she felt herself losing consciousness. She could not breathe. Her lungs pleaded for air as she fought to get away from his smothering desire.

In an instant the dream changed. The handsome warrior no longer held her in his tight grip. Someone pushed her face beneath the water to take her breath. The more she struggled the deeper she sank into a black void. With a scream she woke, to someone holding a thick buffalo robe over her face.

Tia started to fight in earnest, knowing her very life depended on beating her unknown assailant. Heaving her body upward she finally knocked her attacker off her body. Leaping to her feet she stood ready to confront her would-be killer. Shaking her head to clear the loud buzzing sound echoing in her ears, she at last saw the one who had come to do her harm.

At the sight of Young Buffalo's woman, Tia felt her anger surge through her body, giving her the added strength she needed to defeat her foe.

Crouching low, she advanced on the other female. Then she stopped as she saw the woman remove a knife from a sheath hanging from a leather thong tied around her waist.

With a scream of fury, Tia leaped on her driving the surprised woman to the floor of the lodge. Over and over they tumbled as Tia tried to wrest the weapon from her grip. Grabbing the other's wrist with both hands, Tia slammed it over her own knee. With a sickening snap the knife dropped from her hand. The beaten woman rocked her body back and forth, moaning with pain as she cradled her broken wrist against her heaving chest.

Weary Tia picked up the knife, placing it in her own sheath. Then hauling the still, sobbing woman to her feet, shoved her out of the lodge. After securing the flap, she lay back down falling into a sound sleep.

Waking much later, Tia sat up stretching her relaxed limbs, her dark gaze roaming over the quiet lodge. As her eyes fell on the still, closed flap, a smile lit up her small face as she recalled her earlier battle with the dead Crow's vindictive woman. Knowing she would have to answer for yet another wrong done her captors, Tia got up moving with purpose towards the opening. Undoing the laces she peered out, surprised to find propped against the lodge poles a full water pouch, dried meat, wood for a fire, and a clean buffalo robe. After dragging her treasures inside, she once again secured the door. Dropping her dress to the floor she took a long and unhurried bath.

With the flap closed the dwelling grew hot and stuffy in the early morning heat. Without thought, Tia walked outside, unmindful of the hostile stares coming her way. A small boy playing nearby spied her standing within his reach. Still young enough to view the world through eyes yet innocent of the hatred, the different tribes fostered for one another, he toddled over to her. Laughing at his childish antics, Tia picked him up hugging his small body close.

Across the way a man stood watching this odd display of affection. From all the stories he had been told of this beautiful captive's fierce spirit, he would have thought her to be cold of heart too. Seeing her now he knew this not to be true.

"The Blackfeet woman is most unusual do you not agree, my son?" a deep voice questioned nearby.

With a start, Spirit Walker turned to see his father walking towards him. "It has been my belief when a woman is beautiful of face and body these gifts take away from the spirit. I do not see this in the Blackfeet captive. What are your plans for her now that Padrah refuses to have her in her lodge?"

Recalling the older woman's screeching relinquishment of the one who had ended her husband's life and almost her own, Chief Yellow Calf chuckled. "A woman such as this one needs a strong husband to keep her out of mischief. She has too much boldness for an older man. It would take a fierce young warrior to tame her. One who is not afraid to risk his life against such a worthy opponent. I will call a meeting of the council to see if such a man exists," he watched his son out of the corner of his eye.

"Perhaps that will not be necessary," Spirit Walker mused. "Our people have enough enemies. We do not need to fight amongst ourselves. This one," he gestured toward the unsuspecting girl, "stirs the blood of any male with eyes to see. Out of the goodness of my heart I will take her, my father." The roguish warrior laughed a hearty laugh.

"What of Neuaki, your promised one? She will not take kindly to your wanting another. Especially one of our enemies."

In the presence of the Blackfeet captive, he had forgotten the lovely Neuaki, the tall slender girl with eyes like the fawn. He had wanted this girl for as long as he could remember. Now she had reached an age that he could ask for her. Her father had accepted the many fine ponies and gifts the young warrior had offered for his beautiful daughter. Now in three days she would be his.

With a racing heart he recalled the night he had told her she would be his wife. Although shy, she had allowed him to hold her. Her young body trembling at his nearness. He knew his love to be returned by the one he held close. In his joy, Spirit Walker had wanted to shout his happiness to grandfather he had felt so blessed. Now his loins desired another. One who could bring much sadness, to the heart of his beloved. Under the laws of his people he would be within his rights to take another. Many times he had eased his basic need on the unwilling body of a captured female enemy. But he had a feeling that, if he touched the one before his eyes now, once would not be enough.

Sensing the struggle going on in Spirit Walker's heart, Chief Yellow Calf in his wisdom, walked away. His son must make his own decisions. A warrior can take many wives, however, when a man loves but one, desires of the flesh can have dire consequences.

Almost against his will, Spirit Walker moved towards the Blackfeet girl whose beauty held him captivated. Once Neuaki moved to his lodge she would be under his command. He did not wish to hurt her, but hurt her he would, rather than give up the prize standing before him now.

Noting the handsome warrior's approach, Tia put the small child back down, swatting his little bottom as he scampered away.

"Little Coyote warms the heart of every one he touches. Even," he smiled, "the fierce heart of a Blackfeet maiden."

"If he led his people, you would have no enemies," Tia returned. Then realizing he had spoken his words in her own language, her voice tuned cold. "I see you too made use of Blackfeet captives."

For a moment, her meaning escaped him. Then he understood. "My father saw the wisdom in learning the language of our enemies. As war chief to my people, I could do no less."

"You are Chief Yellow Calf's son?"

With a slight nod, he replied. "I am Spirit Walker." He could feel his breath becoming ragged in his lungs as he gazed down at her. "My father says you have the heart of a warrior. This is great praise for a captive."

Tia felt a warning move forward from the back of her mind. Not stopping to weigh her words, she said. "What do you think, Crow?"

"I think it is time you had someone teach you your place, woman." He moved nearer, a slight smile pulling at the corners of his full mouth. "I think that someone is me."

"Think again, Crow dog!" she panted backing out of his reach. "I have already killed one of you who dared to put his hands on me. I will not hesitate to kill another."

With a steady advance on the girl whose mere presence heated his blood, he laughed deep in his throat. "You have met your match, Blackfeet Woman. This time, you will be taken."

Picking her thrashing body up in his arms, he moved at a fast towards her lodge when his fevered eyes caught sight of someone standing across the way. Neuaki stood, her small hand pressed to her throat, her astonished eyes filled with so much pain, at the ugly sight confronting her, she could not move.

As though in a daze Spirit Walker lowered Tia to her feet. Without stopping to find out why, she ran inside the lodge securing the flap behind her. Tia's heart pounded so hard she could not think. Hugging her tense body close, she paced back and forth. She had to get away from here! But how?! "Grandfather," she moaned aloud to the spirits. Never had she felt so trapped.

At the sound of many voices filling the air, Tia walked to the lodge opening and pulled back the flap enough to see out. The camp teamed with mounted warriors. At the front, rode Spirit Walker. As if he sensed her watching him, his ebony eyes stared in the direction of her dwelling. With a high pitched yell he brandished his war lance high above his head. As their shrill cries joined with those of their leader, Spirit Walker led his warriors from the Crow camp.

Turning away, Tia started to lie down when she heard someone outside. Moving with quiet steps she listened. Soon a female voice called out. Unloosing the ties, Tia stood back expecting to see the girl who always brought her food. To her surprise another girl stood before her, empty handed. Tia waited for the girl to tell her why she had come.

The young girl, standing just inside the lodge, was very beautiful. Her luminous black eyes kept darting to the opening as if afraid someone would discover her there. Trying to put her at ease, Tia motioned her to be seated. When the girl did as directed, Tia asked her in sign why she had come.

"My name is Neuaki. In three days I will be the wife of Spirit Walker. My heart is sad, for now I see the hunger in his eyes for you, a captured enemy of my people. Many times the women of my village have tried to steal his heart. I would be filled with fear each time. I have loved Spirit Walker since I have been a very small girl. Always I would watch him. Each night I would pray to the spirits to help me grow up fast before he chose another. When he came to my father to ask for me my heart soared with happy feelings. Now I wish he had never noticed me. Each time I see him look at you, I feel the knife go deeper into my wounded heart."

At last Neuaki's hands were stilled. Tia felt her anger at the uncaring actions of the Crow war chief leap to new life. With rapid speed she signed her thoughts to the unhappy girl sitting beside her.

"I am Tia of the Blackfeet nation. I feel only hatred for the man who tried to invade my body this day. I am captive of your people. I do not wish to be here. Tell me how to leave and I will be gone."

Neuaki looked at Tia, unable to believe any girl would not want the handsome warrior as much as she did. When she read the truth in the open gaze staring back at her, her small hands moved quickly. The girl told her, Spirit Walker and his braves had left camp because two Blackfoot warriors had been seen nearby.

This news brought Tia to her feet! "Please!" she signed. "You must help me to leave here! I ran away from my village, on the night of my joining, to a man I do not love. He must not find me!"

Neuaki's eyes grew large with alarm. "I cannot help you!" she signed.

"You must! The one who searches for me might be my father! If he rides into your camp to challenge for me your warriors will kill him!"

Tia told her, uncaring of the insult she had just directed at Neuaki's people.

"Do not worry," the girl signed back, "the scout saw the one who comes. It is your war chief, Appearing Wolf, and another."

"Appearing Wolf?!" Tia yelped, startling the Crow girl to her feet. As Neuaki edged her way towards the opening, Tia remembered the girl could not understand her words. Forcing a calmness she did not feel, Tia signed her fears. "Appearing Wolf is the one I am being forced to marry. If he finds me in your camp, all is lost. He will take me back! You must help me!"

Staring at the wild-eyed girl pleading for her help, Neuaki felt torn. She knew the danger awaiting her if it became known she had helped an enemy of her people to escape. Then in her mind's eye she saw the man she loved holding this girl in his arms. The fear in her heart became silent. Her mind made up, as to what she must do, Neuaki told Tia that as soon as it grew dark, she would come for her.

Tia had never known time to move so slowly. She had been so sure Appearing Wolf would not come after her. Pacing the quiet lodge, her mind whirled with frightening questions. Who would ride with Appearing Wolf? Spotted Owl would be easy to recognize to a Crow scout. How had he known where to begin searching for her? As these thoughts turned over and over in her tortured mind, Tia watched and waited throughout the long day, for the small girl who would risk her own life to save the life of her enemy.

Chapter Fifteen

So far they had been able to remain unseen. Darkness drifted towards the prairie, and as yet there had been no sighting of Spirit Walker and his warriors.

"You are right, my brother," Pehta said. "They search for us in the mountains. We will be in the Crow camp with the people at our mercy while the mighty Spirit Walker follows a cold trail."

"Chief Yellow Calf's people will not know we are near. My woman is all I will take this day," Appearing Wolf breathed.

"Have you thought about what you will do if it is learned Tia has already been taken by another?"

Halting his horse, Appearing Wolf glared over at his brother, his anger, at having his own thoughts voiced aloud, almost sparking a confrontation. "Do not look for trouble before it is time, Pehta! Tia is my promised one! She would die at her own hand before she would let that happen!"

"I believe she would do all in her power to save herself from such a fate, my brother. But if she could not, would you still want her for your wife?" Pehta persisted.

Unable to answer honestly, Appearing Wolf kneed his horse forward once more. The question burning in his mind would not allow him to be silent. "I am a leader of our people. The sons born in my lodge must come from my seed."

"If Tia has been made unclean through no fault of her own, you could still join with her after it is known she does not carry the seed of another in her body."

"And if she does, what would become of the child? He would be the son of our enemy. Our people would never accept him."

"If she carries a child of the Crow, Mahossa could give her herbs to

137

make her lose him. I have heard this can be done." Pehta said.

With an unwavering quickness, the story Maheto told him of his mother flashed through his mind. He had lived all of his life in the village of his father without anyone telling him that his own mother had been a Crow captive. If his mother had taken herbs to flush him from her body, he would not be here today to lead the Kainah.

"The Creator is the giver of life. He is the one who says when a life should be ended."

"You are right, Appearing Wolf."

"We will hope my woman has remained safe in the hands of our enemies. Should I learn that she has not, then the one who has harmed her will die by my hand."

Pehta knew he should not dwell on what he would do if Tia had been violated, but he could not help himself. The thought of this small girl who had stolen his heart being punished for something not of her choosing, filled him with fury. If the time came when Appearing Wolf no longer wanted her, he would take her for his woman.

Knowing they would have little chance of getting into the Crow camp undetected by taking the trail leading into the valley, the two began making their way with added caution down the treacherous mountain trail. The full moon rising overhead cast a pale light out over the surrounding area, aiding them in their slow decent. When at last they reached the bottom, they could see smoke from the many lodges hanging over the valley.

The pungent odor of the horse herds warned them to get downwind before their presence could be detected. Leaving their mounts tethered back among the trees, they crept towards the busy camp. Sounds of laughter and the crying of small children floated out to them. They could see women preparing the evening meal on a campfire outside their lodges, visiting and enjoying the warm wind blowing down from the mountains. From their hiding place, they observed the familiar sights and sounds of an Indian village.

As the unsuspecting Crow went about their normal lives, Appearing Wolf felt a cold shiver pass over him. He knew how easy death could strike.

His arm shot out, pointing to a single lodge set apart from the others. As they watched, Chief Yellow Calf walked from the dwelling with Tia by his side. His heart leapt as he saw the gentle way in which the old chief treated her.

"What is this? She is a captive! Why does he smile and laugh with her?!"

"I do not know, my brother. It is very strange."

"She is very friendly with the enemy of her people!" Appearing Wolf observed hotly.

"The father of Spirit Walker seems to find your woman very interesting."

As soon as the dreaded name had left his lips, Pehta knew he had made a mistake.

"If he has touched her, I will kill them both!" Appearing Wolf hissed already drawing his knife.

"Perhaps she seeks to make her stay in his camp easier," Pehta offered, his theory, sounding weak even to him.

Turning an angry face to the one standing beside him, Appearing Wolf growled. "We have had Crow captives at our mercy many times! We did not laugh and play games with them! We treated them as our enemy."

Unable to argue, Pehta nodded. With a sinking heart, he wondered if, like the Arapaho woman, Tia too had found the war chief too hard to resist. If that is what had happened, Pehta knew Appearing Wolf's hand could not be stayed. Lost now to their view the brothers, unable to move from where they stood in the shadows, could only surmise what could be happening with Tia and her captor.

***

Walking through the camp with Yellow Calf beside her, Tia could feel the angry stares coming from the women who busied themselves with preparing the evening meal. As Yellow Calf pointed out certain things about his village, Tia found herself peering about the camp searching for any sign of Neuaki. The lengthening shadows of night had already gathered. What if Neuaki already waited for her? Dragging her mind back to the man walking beside her, she realized Yellow Calf had stopped talking. Turning to look at him, she found him staring at her with a knowing look on his face.

"What is it?" Tia murmured.

"Who is it that you search for, Tia?"

"I search for no one. No one else understands my language."

"No, Tia. There is another in my camp who can understand your words. Do you watch for him?"

Stalling, she replied. "Is your son here?"

"No. Spirit Walker is with his warriors."

"Oh," she whispered, casting her eyes to the ground. "Chief Yellow Calf," she touched his arm, "please take me back to my lodge. I do not wish to walk any longer."

"Yes, Tia," he patted her shoulder, "I will take you back."

After seeing Tia safely to her dwelling, Yellow Calf walked away, sure in the belief Spirit Walker had captured yet another heart.

Alone, Tia paced with worry. Every few moments she would go to the opening to peer out, searching for any sign of the girl who had promised to help her. At last, she heard someone approaching.

Neuaki ducked into the lodge, dropping the flap. For a long moment she stood, unable to move. Never had she been so frightened. If anyone in the Crow camp found her helping a captured enemy to escape, her life would be worthless. After forcing herself to take several deep breaths in an attempt to quell her unease, she asked Tia in sign if she still wanted to leave.

Holding up her hand for Neuaki to wait, Tia went to retrieve the knife she had taken from Padra, then nodded. In silence, they left the lodge. Keeping low the girls ran for the forest. Up ahead, Tia saw a sight that made her heart leap for joy as she approached.

"Night Star," she whispered, running loving hands over the big horse's soft muzzle. At her familiar touch, he rubbed his head against her snorting a loud welcome. She felt so happy to be leaving. Tia reached out drawing the young girl close. "Good-bye, Neuaki." She signed, releasing her. "I will always remember you with gladness in my heart."

"As I will you, Tia," she signed back. "May the spirits keep you safe upon your journey."

With a wave of her hand, Tia guided Night Star through the forest on their way to freedom.

Tia rode as if all the spirits of darkness chased after her. She had changed her mind about trying to reach the village of the Flat Heads, choosing instead to take her chances in her own village.

She knew Appearing Wolf would be angry when he found her back in camp, but now that he knew she did not want him, and he had seen the extreme lengths she had been willing to go to avoid being joined with him he would let her go. But it had to be her choice. He must not find her before she reached the camp and told him of all she had endured rather than belong to him.

Knowing she ran the risk of meeting Appearing Wolf on the prairie or worse, Spirit Walker and his warriors, she would not allow herself to think about what else could be awaiting her as she rode alone through the night. Realizing she could not keep up such a fast pace, Tia finally reined her horse to a walk.

Somewhere up ahead a cougar screamed, the eerie sound making Night Star shy to the side. "Quiet," she told him running a loving hand down the side of his neck. The big horse nudged her, then throwing up his head, gave out with a loud whinny. "He is making you nervous. He must be getting closer."

Night Star bolted. His movement so sudden, Tia felt herself slipping from his lathered back. When she looked up from where she lay on the hard ground, she saw Night Star running across the prairie. Then her breath froze in her throat as she saw the reason for Night Star's hasty departure. Crouched on a ledge above her sat the cougar. The cat screamed once more, its chilling cry echoing through the pre-dawn stillness.

Trying to remain as still as possible, Tia watched in terror as the large cat prepared to spring. Out of the corner of her eye, she saw a movement. Unable to even scream, she lay transfixed as a shot rang out, the bullet slamming into the cat as he flew through the air.

Scrambling to her feet she could not believe her eyes as she saw Appearing Wolf walking towards her.

"How did you find me?" He watched her, his hot-eyed stare never leaving her face. "What are you going to do?" she whispered, backing away. Still, he did not answer.

All at once, the fatigue of an all-night ride and the fear she had endured with the cougar, came together in one thoughtless show of spirit. "You do not frighten me, Appearing Wolf. I told you I would not accept a man I did not love; now you know I speak the truth. Before Pehta could stop him, Appearing Wolf's hand shot out to deliver a stinging slap across Tia's face.

She felt herself hit the hard ground and felt fire burn a trail down the side of her face. Bringing her hand to her mouth, she saw the blood that covered her fingers. Red-hot fury possessed her as she leaped to her feet.

The one thought in her mind centered on the death of the man who had dared to strike her. In an instant the knife she had taken from Young Buffalo's woman filled her hand, and a scream, that rivaled that of the cougar, tore from her throat as she leaped at him.

This time Appearing Wolf stood ready for her.

Tia's last conscious thought before the hard ground drove all else from her mind was, "This is the day of my death."

As she struggled toward consciousness, the first sensation she felt was pain. It felt as if a thousand drums beat a repetitive rhythm inside her head.

She had been tied and slung across the front of Appearing Wolf's horse. Each step the animal took brought new agony. I will die before I ask him to stop, she thought. As the horses picked up speed and the pain in her head grew in its intensity, all she could think of is how much she would enjoy ending the war chief's life. He will never live to be the chief of our people, she vowed. At this thought, a cold chill passed over her.

As darkness gave way to light, Appearing Wolf led them into a grove of trees. Dismounting, he pulled Tia to the ground. Crouched on a blanket of pine needles, she watched him pull a blanket and rolled up robes from Shadow Dancer's back. Springing to her feet, she backed away. Appearing Wolf spread the robes upon the ground then turned to find her staring at him with anger. As he walked towards her, she shook her head in refusal.

"No! I will not do this! You will not put your hands on me!"

Striding to where she stood, he caught up a handful of her long black hair to send her sprawling upon the make-shift bed of soft buffalo robes. Before she could roll away, he crouched beside her to secure one of her wrists with a long strip of leather. In disbelief, she watched as he tied the other end of the strip to his own wrist.

Without a word, he lay down, exercising a contented stretch before turning his back to her. Within moments, she could hear his even breathing, telling her he slept.

In the days it took them to return to their camp, Appearing Wolf never spoke to her. Even the good-natured Pehta ignored her, although she would catch him looking at her from time to time when he knew Appearing Wolf could not see him. Tia told herself she did not care; as long as Appearing Wolf did not touch her, she could endure anything.

The low throbbing of the drums greeted them as they halted in front of Spotted Owl's lodge. Before dismounting, Appearing Wolf dropped a bound and gagged Tia to the ground. As she tried to roll away from him, he reached down, jerking her to her feet. With a firm hand on the back of her neck, he threw back the lodge flap to shove her inside. Then he spoke for the first time since he had found her.

"Prepare her for the ceremony. It will take place after sundown."

Without another word, he walked away, leaving a stunned Spotted Owl and Jolisha staring after him.

When Jolisha had freed her, Tia threw herself down upon her couch. She knew her parents waited for her to tell them what had happened, but she felt too exhausted. Flipping onto her side, she lay quiet.

Nodding for Spotted Owl to leave them alone, Jolisha sat down beside her angry daughter. "Where have you been?"

"I have been in the camp of Chief Yellow Calf!" Tia said her voice cold at having to explain herself.

"Tia!" Jolisha breathed. "Did they…?"

"No!" She hastened to alleviate her mother's fears. "I was treated better in the camp of our enemies than I am in my own village!"

"Why do you say that?"

Turning onto her back, Tia told her mother all that had happened in the Crow camp. When she had finished, Jolisha looked at her in amazement.

"This is very interesting. Chief Yellow Calf wanted you for his son? What did Appearing Wolf say when you told him?"

"Appearing Wolf did not give me a chance to explain. He is a cruel man, and I hate him!"

"You should not have run away, Tia. You have caused much trouble for all of us," Jolisha whispered.

"Is that all you care about?" she squealed sitting up. "What of me? I could have been killed!"

"You brought everything on yourself, Tia." Jolisha's voice took on an angry tone. "You knew the ceremony, for your joining, would be on that night. You have brought much shame on the lodge of your father."

Stunned by her soft-spoken mother's wrath Tia lay back when the thought of her best friend brought her all the way to her feet. "Keelah!"

"Yes, Keelah." Jolisha nodded. "She almost died at the hand of Appearing Wolf that night when he learned she had helped you to run away. If Chief Maheto had not stayed his hand, Keelah would be dead."

"I must go to her," Tia said.

As she walked through the village in search of her best friend, Tia could feel the stares of her people. What must they be thinking? Everyone knew how Appearing Wolf had returned her. Would her friend even want to see her after all the trouble she had caused her?

"Tia."

Turning, Tia saw Keelah walking towards her. Hurrying forward

Tia embraced her. "I came looking for you."

"I am so glad you are safe."

"Come, we will walk to the lake. After we have bathed, you can help me prepare for the joining ceremony. Everything I did has been for nothing. I almost caused your death, and my own, and tonight I will be joined to a man I do not love anyway."

As they continued walking toward the lake, Keelah gave her friend a gentle nudge. Bringing a finger to her lips, she pointed to the edge of the forest. There, emerging from beneath the low hanging branches of a tall pine they saw a young doe. As they watched, she lifted her proud head to sniff the air. Satisfied, she made her way to the lake followed by two small fawns. As the little ones lowered their heads to drink, the watchful mother kept a keen eye on the surrounding area. A fish jumped out of the water, startling the deer. Within moments, they had bounded back into the forest to disappear among the tall foliage.

"If I could be that young again," Tia whispered, "then tonight would not bring the destruction of my soul."

"Tia, I am so sorry, I betrayed your trust," Keelah told her, her eyes filling with tears.

"No. Do not apologize." Tia took her hand in hers. "It was thoughtless of me to put your life in danger. All I wanted is to escape from Appearing Wolf. I did not think he might harm you."

"Before you ran away, I thought being the wife of our war chief would be a good thing for you. Now, I am not so sure. Appearing Wolf's anger knows no bounds. He is a cruel and heartless man. No wonder he is a leader of our warriors. He would have killed me if Maheto had not stopped him." She shivered at the thought.

"I am the one who is sorry, Keelah."

The cold water felt good to Tia's aching body, and the soreness on the side of her face where Appearing Wolf had hit her had finally gone away. Climbing to the grassy bank, she lay there letting the hot sun calm her troubled mind. Unbidden, the days she had spent as a captive in the Crow camp came stealing into her thoughts.

"Appearing Wolf does not know the Crows captured me."

In an instant, Keelah moved over beside her. "Tia! Did they harm you?"

"In the beginning they treated me without feeling, but no, they did not treat me as a captive. The Crow people are much like us. I do not know why there must be so much hatred between us. Are we not all Our

Father's children?" she whispered.

"Why would you say this?" Keelah drew back in astonishment. "The Crows are our fiercest enemies!"

Turning onto her stomach, Tia tried to explain something she did not fully understand herself. "In the Crow camp, I learned we are all the same; all trying to survive. There are good people amongst the Crow."

At Keelah's startled look, she smiled. "I know my words must sound strange to you."

"You and I have been as close as sisters for as long as I can remember. Yet, I do not know you."

"Sometimes I do not know myself."

"Are you afraid of what tonight will bring?" Keelah asked of her friend in a subtle change of the subject.

"Yes. Appearing Wolf has already shown me I can expect no gentleness when he takes me for the first time."

"My heart is sad for you, Tia."

"Appearing Wolf will not know my pain. No matter what he does, he will not know my pain!"

Chapter Sixteen

Jolisha handed her a dress made of doeskin, bleached white and made from the softest leather she had ever felt. Long fringe hung from the elbow-length sleeves and around the calf-length hem to fall over the high-top moccasins of the same white leather. Below the scooped neckline, blue beads had been sown in the shape of a star.

"This is my wedding dress," Jolisha told her daughter. "The moccasins are new, as your feet are smaller than mine."

"They are beautiful, my mother. I will wear them with pride."

She saw Jolisha's eyes mist as she looked at her.

"We must hurry now," Jolisha wiped her eyes, then reached out to help Tia off with her dress.

The years slipped away as Jolisha recalled her own wedding ceremony, dressed in the same finery as Tia wore now. In her innocence, she believed in her love, then she learned how that love could be clouded with shadows so strong that even the most promising of lights can be doused. Shaking her head to rid herself of her own failed life she brought her attention back to her daughter.

Tia braided her long black hair. Above the thong securing the ebony tresses, she placed a soft white plume. The long pendants, she placed in her ears, made from the teeth of a bear and highly polished flashed now with the light from the lodge fire. In all her life, Jolisha had never seen anyone as beautiful as Tia. Not because of Tia being a child of her body, but because Tia had a rare beauty few women could equal.

"I wish you happiness, my daughter," Jolisha whispered holding Tia to her.

"I do not want this marriage, my mother. But I will try not to bring more shame to the lodge of my father."

The Blackfeet People gathered to witness the joining of their war chief to the strong-spirited daughter of Spotted Owl. Confusion ran rampant as to why any girl would not wish to be the wife of the handsome Appearing Wolf.

The story of Tia's running away and of Appearing Wolf bringing her back bound, gagged, and thrown over the front of his horse laid on everyone's tongue. Mothers looked at Tia as if she had been touched by the spirits. Fathers looked at their own daughters with regret it would not be one of them being joined this night with the future chief of their people.

Appearing Wolf, dressed in a tanned, long fringed shirt of elk skin, with double rows of red and black beadwork running down each sleeve, stood watching as Tia walked towards him. All around him could be heard the low murmurs of praise. Her beauty took one's breath away. The knowledge that tonight she would belong to him seemed almost overwhelming. Why had she felt the need to run from him? Had her love for the slain warrior, Gray Dog, really been that strong? What would he do if he found she had already been with another? Wiping his sweaty palms down the sides of his elk skin pants, he forced these unwanted thoughts to the back of his mind, as he waited for the girl walking with slow steps towards him.

She stood in silence by his side, and although the ceremony would soon begin, she refused to look at him. All I feel is loathing for this man, she thought with bitterness. He has caused me shame before our people. My father cannot look at me without turning away. How can I live the rest of my days with a man I do not love?

Mahossa lifted his arms as a signal the ceremony would now begin. Silence surrounded them so the voice of the medicine man could be heard.

"Hear me, oh Great Father, as I ask for your blessing in the joining of Appearing Wolf, war chief of the Kainah, and Tia, daughter of Spotted Owl."

Removing a sharp knife from its leather sheath, he offered it to the four winds, chanting in a faint voice. Turning to the young couple, Mahossa reached for the right arm of Appearing Wolf. After making a small cut on the side of his wrist, he then repeated the ritual on the wrist of Tia. Taking both their arms, he joined their wounds binding them with a leather thong.

As their blood mixed, Appearing Wolf looked down at the small girl standing by his side, his piercing gaze forcing her to look at him. In a quiet voice, he whispered, "Now you are mine, Tia. In body and in spirit."

At his words, Tia felt a hot flush covering her cheeks. She dropped her eyes as Mahossa said the words that bound her forever to a man she did not love.

"Now your life circles are joined, each giving strength to the other. Now the golden years of your life on Mother Earth will never find you alone, for she has clothed you in the robes of unity."

Taking the thong from off their wrists, he said. "May the Holy Ones smile upon your joining and the path you walk lead back to him." Mahossa then handed Appearing Wolf the thong stained with their blood. Appearing Wolf raised the thong high into the air to signify the feasting, in honor of the joined couple, could begin.

Tia felt a hand on her arm. Turning she looked into the kind eyes of Maheto.

"I am happy to welcome you as my daughter," he said as he embraced her.

"I am proud to call you my father," she smiled, returning the old chief's warmth.

Appearing Wolf, watching this exchange between his new wife and his father, felt surprised to see tears touching the old man's face. "I will remember the words you spoke in my lodge, my son," Maheto breathed, before turning to walk away, leaving no doubt in Appearing Wolf's mind as to his meaning.

Before Tia could comment on this odd behavior, Keelah took hold of her arm. "Tia, Appearing Wolf, I wish you much happiness in your new life," she whispered, but her eyes only looked upon Tia.

"Thank you, Keelah," Tia answered. "I would be happy if you would sit with us when the feasting begins."

"I would be honored."

The wedding feast continued with much dancing and merrymaking far into the night. Tia tried not to think about later that night. She could feel Appearing Wolf watching her, almost as though he knew what dwelled in her mind. In an effort to calm her mounting fears she stared out over the dancing couples. She caught sight of Keelah and Kona, a blanket wrapped around them, as their bodies swayed to the music of the flute and the drums.

"They look very happy together, do you not agree?" Appearing Wolf leaned close to whisper in Tia's ear.

The smell of his fresh-washed hair so close to her face made her move away. With an angry glare, she focused her attention once more on the dancers.

"If you would like we could share a blanket. It is our wedding feast." He handed her a piece of fried bread filled with wild berries and honey. As he placed a spoon into her hand, his own hand lingered for a brief moment on her skin. His touch sent a warm tingle up her arm. Without thinking, she jerked her hand away almost upending the bowl he had handed to her. With rapid ease, Appearing Wolf reached out balancing the bowl in place.

Pehta sat watching the couple as they shared their first meal, as husband and wife. He tried not to think about the coming hours. Part of him almost wished for Tia to be found impure on the wedding couch but another part, the part he demanded of himself, hoped his brother would not find any fault with his new bride. He knew her to be lost to him forever, and no matter how deep the knowledge of that loss stabbed into his heart he must accept what he could not change. With resigned determination he stood up, letting his gaze wander out over the circle of laughing maidens who teased and beckoned in the warm night for a warrior to come and join them beneath their colorful blankets. Spying a girl who had been thrown away by her husband, Pehta walked over to her and taking one side of her blanket, wrapped them inside.

At last Appearing Wolf stood and pulling Tia to her feet, walked to the edge of the ceremonial fire. Upon lifting his arms, everyone grew quiet.

Standing with his new wife by his side, he said in a voice all could hear, "My people. My new bride and I are honored at your presence on this night of our joining."

At his words, someone led two horses towards them. They would take them to their wedding lodge set apart from the rest of the village. Upon seeing the horses, Tia trembled. She could no longer delay what would be. With shaking hands, she prepared to mount, but Appearing Wolf stopped her. With gentle hands, he lifted her into his arms, to place her on his horse. Mounting behind her, he whispered. "You will not shame me again, my wife. This night you will belong to me." Then growing silent, he led them from the village.

Cold paralyzing fear gripped her mind as they rode. She could feel Appearing Wolf's strong arm imprisoning her. Ahead, she saw smoke curling from the top of a lodge setting back among the tall pines.

Dismounting, Appearing Wolf lifted Tia to her feet. "I will attend to the horses," he declared without looking at her.

Entering the dwelling, she stood just inside the door, her feet refusing to move. Looking around, she saw all her belongings had been brought from her father's lodge. Among them, the wedding gifts from family and friends. Cast iron skillets and pots, spoons of wood and some of tin, assorted weapons for Appearing Wolf with the leatherwork all elaborately quilled and beaded. She knew the beaded backrest came from Keelah. Then her eyes fell upon the couch she would be forced to share with her new husband.

"No! I will not do this! I will not!"

You have no choice," Appearing Wolf told her, his moccasined tread making no sound as he walked up behind her.

Tia jumped at the sound of his deep voice, then, like a trapped animal, she moved with wary steps around the lodge. Appearing Wolf stood in silence watching her. She stopped, her frightened eyes going to the closed flap, betraying her thoughts.

In an instant, he moved to stand before her barring any escape. For a long moment, their dark eyes locked, then he smiled. "No, my little she cat. You will not escape this night that easy. It is time to disrobe, Tia. The dress you wear holds special meaning for your mother. She would not wish it to be returned in shreds."

The heat in Tia's black eyes, as she looked at him, would have deterred a lesser man, but at her look of defiance a low sound much like that of a laugh, could be heard coming from the throat of Appearing Wolf. Of an instant, all she had endured at the hands of this man who stood smiling at her became too much. Her hand moved to her side, withdrawing her knife then crouching low, she waited for him to move.

"Tia," he said in a soft voice, pulling his shirt over his head, "it is time you learned you are a woman not a warrior."

Tia watched as he walked closer, her eyes never leaving his. As a war chief, the thought of this mere girl pulling a knife on him filled him with humor. But Tia entered into this fight with no thought of stopping, her instinct for survival giving her added courage. Before he could judge her desperation, Tia lashed out, drawing a trail of blood down the arm of her husband.

Complete surprise at her daring made him draw back. At the sight of blood dripping from his arm, he turned to stare at her. She refused to drop her gaze, her black eyes daring him to come closer.

The woman he had taken for his wife would not cower before anyone, not even her husband. This knowledge filled his heart with new respect. At the same time it filled his body with a desire stronger than ever to make her his.

He reached out and without any effort, knocked the weapon from her hand. As she turned to retrieve it, he picked her up to carry her kicking to his couch. Before she could move, he had removed the wedding dress from her body.

Lying naked, except for her moccasins, Tia tried to cover herself, but he stayed her hands. "No, Tia. Your beauty will not be hidden from me. I do not wish to bring you pain as I teach you to be my woman. Do not fight me."

She knew to refuse him would be useless. "I will not fight you, Appearing Wolf, but neither will I give in to you. You cannot teach me of love between a man and woman, for we feel no love for each other." Then with a pretentious smile, she added, "Tell me, Appearing Wolf, after you take me, where will your victory be in the taking of a woman whose heart still mourns another?"

Undaunted, he answered her. "Gray Dog was a young boy, Tia. I am a man. And, I am your husband." His eyes moved over her. Unable to stop himself he reached out running one large hand over her soft skin. As he felt her body grow rigid beneath his touch, he pushed the spark of anger far back in his mind. "I will teach your body to know the feel of my touch." His voice grew huskier and labored. "To hunger for the fulfillment I alone can give you. For now, that is enough." Then he began to instruct her as to the wisdom of his words.

Pulling her to a sitting position on the side of the couch, he knelt before her. Taking her bound hair into his hands, he undid the thongs holding it secure. With gentleness, he shook the braids until they came undone. Like a dark waterfall, the silken masses tumbled down her back and over her small breasts to hide them from his hungry eyes. Burying his face in its loveliness, he inhaled a deep breath.

The urge to take her grew strong. He had denied himself the pleasure of venting his basic needs with another, for he knew no woman could satisfy him like this small girl sitting before him now. Understanding her fear of this night, he talked to her in a soft voice.

"Do not turn away from this moment, Tia." He reclined her back on his couch. "Accept what must be." He stood, removing his moccasins, rolling his elk skin pants down his legs and over his feet to toss them in a careless heap. "Do not struggle and bring yourself needless pain." The corners of his mouth lifted somewhat as she glanced at him, her eyes widening in alarm, as a deep flush crept over her face before her eyes darted away.

She had never seen a naked man before, but in her imaginings, had though them to be disgusting. She had been wrong. How can he have the heart of a man without feeling and yet possess such a beautiful body? Her face flushed with her wayward thoughts.

Lowering himself beside her, he ran one hand up and down her arm. "Let me show you what our life can be like if you will but trust me." Tia remained silent, her body stiff and unyielding, her frightened eyes refusing to look at him.

Taking her small face between his hands, Appearing Wolf kissed her long and deep, trying to halt the anger building within him at her refusal to meet him in this.

Tia felt a strange warmth move up her body as Appearing Wolf's hot mouth covered hers. The feeling felt so different from the few times she had allowed Gray Dog to press his lips to hers. With Gray Dog, she had felt no different than when her mother had pressed her lips against her forehead in times of illness. With Appearing Wolf, it felt as though she stood too close to a fire. The odd sensation felt exciting and at the same time frightening.

Appearing Wolf moved a gentle hand down her body spreading her legs wide enough to accommodate his searching hand, smiling when he felt her warm moistness. With great care, he found the small nub hidden within the folds of her womanhood. With tenderness, he caressed it waiting for Tia to open her legs wider.

Tia could not believe the feelings he brought forth within her innocent young body. She knew she should be fighting him, but her swirling mind refused to listen, choosing instead to lay quiet and unmoving.

"The choice was yours, little one," he whispered in a husky voice, pushing her long legs wide and entering her with one sharp thrust of his hips. As he felt the protective sheath, like a valiant sentinel, step aside, he heard her shrill cry of pain. At once he stopped, giving her time to master her body. Raining light kisses over her face and throat he, at last, felt her begin to relax. Then he continued. It took all the self-discipline in his powerful young body not to end this agony and leave her unfulfilled. Just when he thought he could endure no more, he felt the first spasms rack her body. He drew back as he watched the wonder on her face at this unknown feeling. Finally, he allowed his body total release.

When his harsh breathing had quieted somewhat, Appearing Wolf left his couch, going to where their belongings had been left to search out a small bowl Mahossa had given him after the ceremony.

Tia lay quiet, trying to understand what had happened between them. Her sated body still pulsed with the curious feelings she had experienced while wrapped in his arms. She watched him now as he moved across the lodge. Almost against her will, her eyes moved over his naked back and firm buttocks, noting how his body lost none of its muscle tone as he hunkered down searching among their possessions. He reminded her of a sleek young cougar the way he moved on the balls of his feet. As this thought crept into her mind she turned away remembering the harshness she had suffered at his hand.

Walking back to where Tia lay, as far to the side of the couch as room would permit, he sat down, and reaching out, gathered her small body over close to him.

"Mahossa gave us a wedding present." He smiled, dipping his fingers into the bowl. "It is a special ointment to take away your soreness on the first night of your joining." With her eyes shut tight, she allowed him to rub the soothing salve between her legs, then, to her mortification, within the soft folds of her aching womanhood.

When he finished, he set the bowl to the side then leaned back drawing Tia into his arms. "Sleep, my woman," he told her, "your body needs to heal."

Tia lay beside her husband willing herself not to move away. She knew if she did, he would tighten his hold or worse make love to her again. Although the burning sensation, between her legs, had lessened somewhat , the thought of experiencing again so soon, the emotions she seemed to have no control over left her fighting a silent war against giving in and standing strong. She turned onto her side glowering into the firelight as he pulled her up against him throwing one long leg over her hip. To her chagrin, she felt his manhood pulse against her skin.

"No," she whispered, trying to squirm away.

"Sleep, Tia," he told her, a satisfied smile covering his face as his own eyes closed in slumber.

Chapter Seventeen

Tia woke in the early morn with her head pillowed on Appearing Wolf's chest, his strong arms holding her close. Lying very quiet, she looked around the lodge trying to see where her clothes had been placed. Then her eyes fell on her wedding dress, the only piece of clothing available. Being careful not to disturb the man sleeping beside her, she removed his arms from around her, to leave the couch. Snatching up her dress, she slipped it over her head. Without a backward glance, she left the lodge.

Going to the lake, she walked to the highest bank, letting the dress fall at her feet to jump into the crystal clear water. Tia drew in her breath as the cold water engulfed her. In quick strokes, she swam to the opposite bank. Leaving the water, she walked up and down the shore, uncaring of her nakedness. The one thing on her mind being her behavior of the night before.

"How could I have welcomed his touch when my love for Gray Dog is still fresh in my heart?" she scolded herself. "The things I let him do, and I enjoyed all of it! What is wrong with me?" Thinking herself alone, she spoke her anguished thoughts aloud.

"You behaved as a woman should in the arms of her husband," said the quiet voice of Appearing Wolf.

Whirling, Tia stared into his smiling face. Then remembering her nakedness, turned to jump back into the water.

"No, Tia! Do not run from me!"

"I do as I please, Appearing Wolf!" she said, diving beneath the water, showing him the truth of her words as she swum towards the opposite shore. Of a sudden, she felt herself being dragged downward. In a frenzy she tried to fight, the hand holding her secured, but her need for air quailed her struggles. When she felt as though she could stand no more, she found herself being lifted from the water.

On the bank, Appearing Wolf dropped her to the ground. Tia lay where she had landed trying to catch her breath.

"You animal!" she gasped. "You are no better than the Crow!"

"Why do you say this, Tia?" he hunkered down on one knee beside her.

"Chief Yellow Calf's warriors captured me while I rode to get away from you. Two of his braves threw me into the water with my hands bound. I almost drowned!"

"If you had stayed in our camp," he said in a stern voice, "that would not have happened."

"I did not think about putting myself in danger, Appearing Wolf." She wrung the water from her hair glaring at him. "I thought about getting away from you!"

"How did they treat you in the camp of our enemies?" Appearing Wolf patted her on the back, as she started to cough.

The night Young Buffalo's woman tried to smother her and how she conquered the woman, flashed through her mind bringing a smile to her lips. "At times my stay in the Crow camp felt very rewarding."

For an instant his ebony eyes flashed fire, but when he spoke, his voice sounded calm. "I am hungry. You will go to our lodge and prepare my food." He stood up reaching out a hand to help her to her feet.

"I need my dress." She refused the hand he held out to her.

"No, Tia." Appearing Wolf hauled her to her feet.

"You can't expect me to walk naked," she squealed, yanking away from him.

"If you touch that dress, I will cut it to shreds!" His hand touched the sodden knife sheath.

"You can't mean that!" She stared at him in disbelief. "That is my mother's dress! You know this!"

"Then do not cause me to ruin it."

For a long moment, Tia stood glaring at him. Then turned away.

Suppressing a grin, Appearing Wolf stood watching, as Tia, her head held high, stomped off down the trail, her angry tread giving him an enticing view of her rounded backside as her firm buttocks bounced to the rhythm of her step. When she disappeared from his view he reached down, picking up her dress to sling it over his shoulder, then followed a furious Tia back to their dwelling. Upon entering, he found her fully dressed preparing the morning meal.

"Something smells very good. What are you cooking, my wife?" He removed the wet moccasins from his feet, setting them outside the lodge to dry.

"Your horse," she replied, sparing him a brief glance.

"I hope you are joking, Tia. I need my horse." He pulled his shirt up and over his head then stripped his pants down his legs to kick them from his feet.

"You could get another one," she advised in a cool voice, keeping her eyes lowered as she filled his bowl with the venison stew someone had left outside their door.

"Not already trained as this one is." Appearing Wolf pulled on a dry pair of buckskin pants, but as he reached for a shirt, he pulled his hand back, deciding to go without one. "I have worked many long hours teaching him to obey me."

"Do you plan to spend many long hours trying to teach me to obey you as well?" She filled a bowl of the stew for herself.

"No," he shook his head. "You will be much easier to teach than my horse, Tia."

"Do you believe that?" She glanced at him.

With a slight smile, he nodded.

"Why? Because you will beat me if I do not obey?"

"I will not have to beat you." His voice deepened with feeling, as he accepted the bowl of food she held out to him. "In a short time all I will need do is touch you."

Tia sat trying to eat but she felt too nervous. Giving up, she pushed her bowl away.

In time, Appearing Wolf set his own bowl aside, and rising to his feet held out his hand to her. "Come Tia. You have satisfied my physical hunger. Now, you will satisfy my animal hunger.

"No!" she shook her dark head in refusal. "Mahossa's salve has not healed all of my soreness yet."

"We have more."

Still, she did not move. Shaking his head in amazement, he jerked her to her feet. Then without a word, slung her with ease over his shoulder to walk to his couch. Dropping her down on the soft robes, he whispered. "You do try a man's patience, my woman. He removed the dress she had earlier donned, to throw it across the lodge. Pulling her into his arms, he smiled down at her. "Why do you continue to fight me, when you know you cannot win?"

"Someday I will win, Appearing Wolf." She batted his hands from her breasts. "The day will come when you will waken to find me gone."

"No, Tia," he caught both her hands in one of his, "soon you will come to me with your own animal hunger."

Arching her back, she tried to squirm away from him. "Do not wait for that day, Appearing Wolf, for you will never see it. You killed the one man I will ever love."

With a low growl, he silenced her. "I will see it, Tia!" He promised in his husky voice.

Sliding a practiced hand down her slender body, he moaned as he saw the small nipples begin to rise and harden. Lowering his head, he drew one dusky bud into his eager mouth, circling it with his warm tongue. At her sharp intake of breath, he released her hands to cup the breast closer to his waiting mouth. Unwilling to let him see how much pleasure his suckling tongue brought to her, she grabbed hold of his thick dark hair and with a determined yank, pulled his mouth from her breast. To her shocked surprise, his head moved lower trailing a hot path down the satin skin to invoke shivers up and down her body.

Placing his hands beneath her hips, he lifted her moistness to his waiting mouth, tasting at last the sweetness for which he hungered. Unable to halt the cry of passion building within her heated body Tia moaned aloud.

As he felt the tiny nub, sheathed within its pedal-soft cover, begin to throb, he pulled her beneath him. In one swift move, he entered her. At the same time, she arched her back in an attempt to draw him deeper. Never had he felt the heat of his blood burn out of control like he did with this small writhing girl beneath him now. At the same moment he felt his body explode within hers, she cried out her passions. Turning her in his arms, he pulled a robe up and over their sweating bodies. Wrapping his large arms around her he pulled her in close, his body still joined with hers.

Lying within his strong arms, Tia wondered at these feelings she had no control over. How could someone she had no love for bring about such total abandonment? Could she be like the women of her people who would take any man to her couch? The thought of accepting another, the way she accepted her husband, made her recoil with distaste. No, no one else could make her heart race and give her body such complete satisfaction. She might not love him, but the feelings he brought to her young body no longer felt that difficult to accept.

During the night, Appearing Wolf reached for her many times, and each time she met him in her lust. When at last their bodies had been sated, they fell into a deep sleep.

In her dreams, the sad face of Gray Dog watched her, his blood still fresh and flowing from Appearing Wolf's knife. When the first light of dawn peered through the smoke hole, Appearing Wolf reached down and kissed the tears from her dampened cheeks. Not yet awake she whispered the slain warrior's name.

In a rage, Appearing Wolf threw back the cumbersome robe to leave their couch. Pulling on a brief loincloth, he left her alone with the images of the warrior who still claimed her heart.

Walking towards the lake, he welcomed the cool touch of the morning air. Dropping his loincloth to the ground, he dove into the clear water. Again and again, he plunged beneath the surface, trying to wash away her scent. Gray Dog still remained. In her thoughts! In her dreams! Did she pretend it was Gray Dog who held her when they made love? "She is mine! She will never know the touch of another!" he vowed, pushing the wet hair back from his face.

But he knew he could not control her dreams. In her dreams, Gray Dog still called to her. In her dreams, Appearing Wolf knew he had no part of her.

With the lodge flap pulled back and secured to let in the fresh air, Jolisha stood inside the door watching as her daughter and Appearing Wolf rode into the village. At the sight of Tia sitting so straight and proud, her heart beat with pride.

"She is the wife of our war chief. I am proud to see she does not hang her head before our people," she murmured aloud.

She watched as the couple reined their horses in front of Appearing Wolf's lodge. Tia dismounted, and without a backward glance entered her new home. After tethering his horse, he too entered the lodge to lower the flap and ward off any well-meaning intruders.

"This does not bode well. When will she learn that to fight him will bring her more pain?"

The fear in her heart for her daughter grew strong. Appearing Wolf was a fierce warrior. He would not allow Tia to defy him. For a long while, she stood thinking on this child of her heart and the unhappiness she must be enduring. Jolisha had started to turn away, when she saw Appearing Wolf walk outside. Waiting until she knew he would not be coming back anytime soon, she closed the distance between the two lodges.

"Tia," she called out.

"Enter, my mother." Tia answered her in a soft voice.

"I do not wish to intrude." She secured the lacings. "I saw Appearing Wolf leaving. Is everything well with you?"

"No." Tia sighed.

"Tell me what is wrong, my daughter." Jolisha seated herself beside Tia on the couch. "I can see your heart is troubled."

Without realizing it, Tia's gaze wondered over Appearing Wolf's couch, still in wild disarray from their recent lovemaking. Then, recalling who sat beside her, she looked away. Drawing a deep breath in an attempt to calm her wayward thoughts, she declared in a nervous rush. "I do not understand what is happening to me."

"What don't you understand, Tia?" Jolisha ran a light hand down Tia's face.

"I feel no love in my heart for my husband." She caught her mother's hand to hold it still against her cheek. "Yet, when he takes me in his arms, I find myself responding to his touch." Her face flushed with discomfort.

"Tia," Jolisha tried to still the grin spreading across her face. "You are a young woman now. Your body is ready for a man's touch."

"Why would I want the touch of a man I hate? Appearing Wolf killed the one man I will ever love!" She tried to fill her mind with the carefree days she had spent with Gray Dog, but all she could think about now is the feelings she had been experiencing of late in the arms of her husband. "When I am in Appearing Wolf's arms, I act like a female dog that cannot wait to be mounted!" The shame and guilt she felt at that moment almost made her physically ill.

"Appearing Wolf is a man. I am sure he has been with many women. He knows how to make your body respond to him. Be glad you can take pleasure in mating with him."

"The only thing I would be glad about, is if I never had to see him again." She moved off the couch.

"Where is your husband now?"

"He has gone to speak with Mahossa."

"Why?"

"I do not know. Perhaps he seeks to find why he wants a girl who cannot stand the sight of him."

"I do not think that is the reason for his visit, Tia."

A thought crossed her mind that made her heart race with happiness. "Perhaps he has gone to ask Mahossa to undo the wedding ceremony," she whirled to face her mother.

"Would that please you, Tia?" Jolisha asked, watching her.

"I could not think of anything that would make me happier," Tia hugged her body close.

"All right," Jolisha stood, facing her headstrong daughter, "let us say, this is the reason for Appearing Wolf's visit to Mahossa. But think, if Appearing Wolf throws you away, how will you survive? Who will hunt for you?" She spread her hands wide in front of her. "Where will you live? Do you think your father will welcome you back into his lodge after Appearing Wolf has thrown you away? I can tell you now, Tia. He will not. You would be a source of shame for him. Let us hope Appearing Wolf seeks Mahossa's advice on another matter!" Jolisha said, then turning, she walked away leaving a confused Tia to stare after her.

***

Mahossa sat listening and watched as Appearing Wolf paced his lodge, all the while describing the upheaval his young life had taken.

"The spirit of Gray Dog calls to her in her sleep. This morning, while still on my couch, she cried out his name. I am her husband!" He pounded a clutched fist to his chest. "It should be my name she whispers!"

"You could send her back to her father," Mahossa declared, all the while spooning the rich stew he had made for himself into his mouth.

"No! She is mine! I will never let her go!"

"The shame would be hers not yours, Appearing Wolf."

"Tia is my wife. She will stay with me!"

"Is the love you hold in your heart for her this strong?" At Appearing Wolf's silence Mahossa ideally stirred the food in his bowl. "Had you not been aware of your love for this girl?"

"I knew I wanted her," he whispered.

"But you did not know you love her," Mahossa looked up at him, surprised at his blindness in matters of the heart.

"Not until now." Appearing Wolf stopped his frantic pacing to stare at the man continuing to eat his food.

"When you took her to your couch for the first time, did she come willingly?"

"No. She drew a knife on me," he admitted a sheepish look covering his face. "She cut me before I could stop her."

The spoon Mahossa had been holding fell with a clang against his bowl. "And still you do not wish to return her to Spotted Owl?"

"No!" Appearing Wolf shook his head. "I will not let her go!"

"You must love her very much!" the old man said, unable to halt the laughter in his voice. At the warrior's stern look, Mahossa cleared his throat.

"When you take her to your couch now, does she respond to you?" His white brows lifted.

Unaware of how the memory of holding Tia in his arms softened his stern features, he breathed. "Yes, she is like a different woman when she is on my couch."

"Appearing Wolf," Mahossa set his bowl to the side to take out his pipe, "she is young. The relationship between a man and woman is all very new to Tia. I think in time," he tamped the tobacco down tight, "the memory of Gray Dog will be less painful for her."

Long after Appearing Wolf had left his lodge, Mahossa sat in thought staring at the dying embers of the lodge fire. "This girl will cause you much pain, my young war chief. For with her, not even death will silence your heart."

That night, sitting in the quiet of their lodge, Tia turned to her husband. "Is Mahossa well?"

"Mahossa never changes," he told her, a far off look in his eyes.

Tia noticed how distracted he seemed but thought better than to mention it. "Are you ready to eat?"

At his slight nod, Tia walked over to the cooking-fire to withdraw the wide strips of venison she had hung above the fire to place them in a large bowl. Returning to where he sat, waiting for her, she handed him the food she had prepared.

Without even tasting it, he set it aside, then reached for her. Taking her small face in his hands he admonished her, "Tia, look at me."

When she did, he kissed her, then pulled her into his arms. "I do not wish to fight with you, Aakiiwa," he whispered, rubbing his chin on the top of her head.

Holding her body stiff, she refused to look at him. "I do not wish to fight with you either, Appearing Wolf," she answered him in a cold voice.

Trying to quell the anger already beginning to build at her refusal to yield herself to him, he replied. "If you do not wish to fight, perhaps you would rather go to my couch."

Disentangling herself from his arms, she got to her feet. "I do not wish to do anything with you!" She ran for the door. "Can you not understand? I hate you!"

In an instant, he stood before her. "You are my wife! You will behave as a woman should in the lodge of her husband!"

"And if I do not?" Tia asked, in a smug tone.

The words had scarce left her throat when she found herself in his arms. But this time he showed her no mercy.

"Put me down!"

"I intend to, my woman." He dropped her onto his couch.

"No!" she squealed. "I do not want this!"

"Oh, but you do, Tia," he breathed, pulling her dress over her head to throw it out of her reach. "The one time you behave like a good and dutiful wife is when you are on my couch."

Trying to burrow beneath the thick buffalo robes, she felt all but the one she laid upon, snatched from her hands. Then to her horror, she stared as Appearing Wolf began to disrobe. Firelight danced upon his golden body, his black hair shimmered in its glow. He was the most beautiful man she had ever seen.

She could feel the fire's heat spreading across the lodge to envelop her. She could not take her eyes from him. As she watched, he came to her, lowering himself beside her on the soft robes. Almost against her will she found herself reaching for him, drawing him into her arms.

With a low moan, Tia covered his hot mouth with her own, savoring the taste of him. Moving her body in a seductive plea, she begged him to take her.

Appearing Wolf removed himself from her arms to leave their couch. In silence, he pulled on his leggings. At the door he turned. "If Gray Dog is the one you cry for why does your body beg for me?" Then he left her alone to think on his words.

He had been gone but a short while when someone called out to enter. Sitting up, Tia wiped her eyes, smoothing her hair as best she could. As she made her way to the door, she scooped up her dress to pull it over her head. When she drew back the flap, she felt surprised to find Gray Dog's mother waiting for her.

The older woman smiled when Tia motioned her inside. She had been near the lodge and heard the angry words the war chief had spoken to his new wife before leaving her alone.

"I hope I am not intruding." She stood just inside the lodge. "I wanted to come earlier, but it is so hard for me to see the happiness of others when my own heart is filled with such stabbing pain," she whispered.

"Letta, my heart aches for Gray Dog, too," Tia gathered the saddened woman into her arms.

"I knew such happiness when my son told me of his love for you. I was ready to welcome you into our lodge as my daughter. Now," she cried, pulling away, "that will never be. Appearing Wolf killed my son. His body lies rotting in the burial grounds, while he enjoys life with my son's woman."

The bitterness in Letta's voice brought an icy chill to Tia's heart. "It is all my fault. If Appearing Wolf had not wanted me for his wife, Gray Dog would still be alive." She bowed her head hugging her body close.

Yes, Tia! And the days will come and go many times before I allow you to forget it! Letta vowed in silence. The killing anger, filling her heart for this girl she held responsible for her son's death, the one emotion her cold heart could feel.

"How are you surviving? Do you have fresh meat for your cooking-fire?" Tia looked over at her.

"When the spirit is already dead, it takes very little to sustain the body," she said, with as much sadness in her voice as she could call forth, knowing all the while Appearing Wolf made sure she had fresh meat, and anything else she needed to make her life easier.

"Letta, you are always welcome to come to Appearing Wolf's lodge to share our food," Tia offered." Her voice cheerful.

"I could never share food with a man whose hands are stained with my son's blood."

Tia felt the sting of guilt becoming sharper with each word Gray Dog's mother uttered.

"Does the slayer of my son treat you well? I feel such sadness in my heart for you, Tia. How I wish…" shaking her head, Letta turned away.

Tia moved to stand beside her, taking the older woman once more into her arms. "Letta, my heart cries for your pain. What can I do to help you?"

Sniffing, Letta remained in the arms of the one she loathed a moment longer, then in a quiet voice she replied, "You can tell Appearing Wolf, you want out of your marriage. Then you can come live with me, where you belong."

"Letta, Appearing Wolf knows I hold no love in my heart for him, but it does not seem to matter. He will not let me go."

"You must make him want to let you go!" She glared at Tia, unable to mask the rage she felt for her. "When he takes you to his couch, you must fight him! Fill his lodge with bitterness! You owe this to the memory of my son!" She shook an angry fist in front of Tia's face. "You owe this to me! I have no one to take care of me now!"

At the sounds of footsteps outside the women drew apart, as Appearing Wolf entered. With a look of pure hatred, Letta brushed past the man staring at her. When she had gone, Appearing Wolf secured the flap.

"Why did the mother of Gray Dog feel the need to come to our lodge?"

"She came to make sure I am well."

"Why wouldn't you be, Tia?" he asked, looking at her in his calm manner.

She is the mother of the man I love. She worries for my safety."

"The boy… you thought you loved no longer exists. His mother has no need to come to our lodge."

"Are you forbidding me to have visitors now? Am I also to tell my own mother she is no longer welcome?"

"Do not mock my words, Tia! The mother of Gray Dog is filled with bitterness. She will seek to cause trouble between us."

"There is already trouble between us! I do not love you! I do not want you!"

In one quick stride, Appearing Wolf moved across their dwelling to jerk her against him. "You may not love me, Tia," his deep voice shook with emotion, "but even you cannot deny your need for me!" He picked her up in his arms to carry her once more to his couch. This time, he did not leave.

Judith Ann McDowell

Chapter Eighteen

Standing across the way, Letta all but shook with anger as she listened to the cries of passion coming from Appearing Wolf's lodge.

"She enjoys the touch of my son's killer!" she hissed, walking in quick strides from the inner circle of teepees. Her husband had never gained the status of a leader; therefore, his lodge had always stood outside the circle of the high chiefs. Gray Dog had been her last hope of achieving that coveted place. Now, that too, had been taken from her.

Seated alone, within the empty dwelling Appearing Wolf had given her after her own lodge had been burned out of mourning for Gray Dog, she felt consumed with the hatred festering within her for Appearing Wolf and the woman he had stolen from her son. All around her, she could see the different objects that had belonged to Gray Dog. What had not been placed upon the burial scaffold with the dead warrior's body, she had taken with her to her new dwelling for she had been unable to bring herself to destroy them.

Rising to her feet, she walked outside, her eyes staring in the direction of the burial grounds. With slow and labored steps she made her way out of the village. A strong breeze blew her short chopped hair into her face, but she didn't care as she continued on to cross the logs lashed together across the edge of the lake. At last, she could see the place where the dead rested high above the ground. The full moon shown upon their faces and the wind moaning through the trees moved the weapons placed beside them back and forth. Standing beneath his burial platform, she cried out her pain.

"The day will come when they will be made to answer for what they have done to you, my son. Your woman thinks to fool me with her talk of hatred for her husband. But I have heard her cries of hunger when she thinks no one can hear. You are no longer in her thoughts. The one whose hands are covered with your blood makes her forget the name of Gray Dog. She will come to regret the day she turned her evil eyes towards you, for I will not rest until her body lies beside you where it belongs."

Spotted Owl had ridden into camp when he saw someone leaving the burial grounds. Reining his horse, he sat watching as the shadowy figure walked to the outer lodges. Nudging his horse forward, he stayed far enough back so as not to be seen, following the late night visitor, until he recognized the one who walked ahead of him.

"Letta." he breathed, unable to fathom why the woman would be in the burial grounds well after sundown. Even the fearless Kainah warriors avoided the place where the dead rested when the shadows of night covered the earth. Turning his horse in the direction of his dwelling, Spotted Owl felt an icy chill pass over him as he thought upon the woman's strange actions. The loss of her son had left her troubled. But wondering alone at night could not be wise. He would speak to Chief Maheto about her. Perhaps he could ask one of the women in the village to stay with her until enough time had passed and she could accept her grief.

Dismounting in front of his lodge, he hastened inside, anxious for the peaceful surroundings of a loving home. One look into the troubled face of Jolisha told him this would not be. "What is it, my woman?"

"I went to speak with Tia earlier. She is still very unhappy. Although some of the things she said lead me to believe her life with Appearing Wolf may be changing."

"What has happened?" He seated himself on his couch.

With a slight smile, Jolisha told him of the awakening feeling their daughter experienced in the arms of her new husband. When Spotted Owl did not respond, Jolisha frowned. "Do you not care our daughter may be changing toward her husband?"

"I care very much," he replied, "but I have seen something that has made my heart uneasy."

"What is it, my husband?" She took a seat beside him.

"When I rode into camp I saw Letta coming from the burial grounds."

Jolisha felt her heart leap. "It is not good to disturb the dead," she whispered, one small hand going to her throat.

"She goes to visit with Gray Dog. It is not safe for her to be walking the grounds alone at night. I will speak with Chief Maheto in the morning. He will know what to do to help her."

She leaned her head against her husband's shoulder, taking strength in his nearness. "My heart aches for her loss. Our daughter may not be happy right now, but at least she is alive and well. Letta has no one. I will ask Tia to go with me to visit with her."

Her words made him turn to put her from him. "No! Tia is to stay away from her!"

"My husband," she drew back to stare at him, "what is wrong?"

"The mother of Gray Dog is filled with grief. I do not want our daughter near her!"

"Letta would never harm Tia," she told him as though speaking to a child. "She always welcomed her with gladness."

"Yes," he cocked his head to one side nodding at her, "when her son still lived. Now, she looks at life through the eyes of pain. Do not ignore my words, Aakiiwa. The girlish feelings Tia still holds for Gray Dog will dim in time. Appearing Wolf will see to this."

"I hear your words, Spotted Owl and I heed them."

Drawing the woman he loved close once more, he held her, glad in his heart for the strong love and contentment in his lodge.

Long after Spotted Owl had fallen asleep in her arms, Jolisha lay awake thinking on the problems filling her child's heart. Could Tia be changing towards her husband? Appearing Wolf was a man of strength. He ruled his lodge with a strong hand and would allow no one to defy him. If Letta had anger in her heart towards Tia as Spotted Owl believed, she would never try to harm Tia with Appearing Wolf close by. Jolisha could understand the woman's hatred toward him, but she had to see Tia had no choice but to marry Appearing Wolf. As these thoughts began to fall naturally into place, her dark eyes closed and before long she fell asleep, content with the seeming order of her world.

The next morning Tia walked to the lake with Keelah. She felt anxious to tell someone about the strange visit she had had with Letta. Knowing she could not share the bitter woman's words with Appearing Wolf, she knew the one to confide in would be Keelah.

"I think you should tell your husband what Letta said to you. A man and his wife should have no secrets from each other," Keelah cautioned her.

"Gray Dog's mother has enough grief without Appearing Wolf giving her more. I will make her understand it is not possible for me to get out of my marriage. She will have to accept."

"Do you still want to get out of your marriage to Appearing Wolf?"

"I still feel no love for the man who killed Gray Dog." She spoke her words with anger and a hint of the pain Gray Dog's name always invoked in her.

"Is the hate you held in your heart still as strong?"

For a long moment, Tia found she could not answer Keelah's question, then she replied. "I cannot really explain the feelings I have for my husband now. They are not the feelings I had in my heart for Gray Dog. Yet when I am on Appearing Wolf's couch his touch is not all that hard for me to accept."

"Are you saying it is no more than the desires of the flesh drawing you to Appearing Wolf?" Keelah gave her a shy glance.

With a slight nod, she whispered. "Yes. It is almost like I am not complete when he is away from me. He has bound me to him in some strange way."

"Does he ever beat you?"

"No," Tia shook her head. "Appearing Wolf has not raised his hand to me since our joining. It is like a change has come over him. One night he pulled me to him and his voice held such gentleness," her eyes warmed at the memory, "it made me feel strange. It frightened me for some reason. I felt like I wanted to meet him in his gentleness, but I did not. When he took me to his couch, I held myself from him as long as I could. But, I did not want to. I am so confused," she murmured.

"Your husband is a very handsome man. Few women would be able to deny him once he decided they would be his."

"No woman would dare touch Appearing Wolf!" Tia snapped. Her luminous dark eyes flashing fire. "Except one whose heart is unclean!"

At the anger in her friend's voice, Keelah halted. Could it be Tia found herself falling in love with Appearing Wolf? Perhaps she could find out. "Tia," she said, with as straight a face as she could manage, "if another woman found favor in your husband's eyes he would be in his lodge a lot less. Would that not please you?"

At the look of pure rage covering Tia's face, Keelah burst out laughing. But her laughter died as she stared straight ahead.

Following Keelah's stunned gaze Tia soon saw the reason for her friend's discomfort. Even from this distance, the interest in the handsome warrior's eyes for the beautiful young girl laughing up at him could not be missed.

"My little sister is very brave when our father is gone from the village. I will put a stop to her daring behavior before she shames his good name before the whole camp," Tia breathed, already on her feet and walking away.

"Tawna, I have need of you in my lodge." She took her sister by the hand. "I am sure Konah has more important things to do than standing in the hot sun playing games with a maiden."

At Konah's sheepish grin, the young girl gave him a seductive smile, as she followed an angry Tia to her dwelling. Once inside Tia lowered the flap, deterring anyone from interrupting what she had to say to her defiant young sister.

"Tell me, Tawna," Tia cocked her head to one side, a balled fist on each hip, "since when have your days become so idle you can afford to waste them?"

"How I fill my days is of no concern of yours, Tia." Tawna tossed her dark head, refusing to be cowed by her older sister. "You are angry because you saw me talking with Konah."

"You know the feelings Keelah has for him. Why do you set your sights on a man who will not have you?"

"You say he will not have me, Tia, but I have seen the way he looks at me." She licked her full pink lips. "Why would he desire me if it is Keelah he loves?"

The stinging slap Tia delivered across Tawna's face echoed throughout the quiet lodge. "It is not desire you saw in his eyes, you little fool. Konah is a man. It is his pride you stoked not his passion."

At these harsh words, Tawna's head snapped up in disbelieve. Then before Tia's eyes, she changed. Within moments, the tempting seductress had vanished, and in her place stood the little girl Tia loved. With a gentle hand, Tia brushed the back of her hand over the angry welts covering her sister's cheek. "You are a beautiful girl, Tawna. The day is fast approaching when you will fire passion in a man's heart, but Konah's heart belongs to Keelah."

As the girls walked outside, Tia saw Appearing Wolf rein in his horse. "He is back," she whispered.

"I envy you, my sister." Tawna watched as the handsome man dismounted. "He is the most beautiful man I have ever seen."

At Tia's stern glare, Tawna turned away.

"Little sister, tell your mother she will have fresh meat for her cooking fire this night," Appearing Wolf called out, his smoldering gaze sliding over Tia. "I have missed you my woman," he whispered, drawing her into his strong, naked arms. He smelled of sweat, fresh blood, and pine. Tia tried to push away from him to no avail.

Pulling her in closer, he nuzzled her neck, emitting a soft growl. "My hunger is strong, Aakiiwa."

Tia could feel her sister's dark eyes watching them. With her face flaming she turned in his arms, murmuring, "Tawna, tell your mother Appearing Wolf has fresh meat for her. He will bring it to her lodge soon."

"I will tell her, Tia," she giggled, walking away.

When Tawna no longer stood within hearing distance, Tia turned on her husband in anger. "Why do you have to behave like a rutting animal in front of my sister? Do you think because she is untouched, she does not have eyes to see?"

Appearing Wolf smiled into her fiery eyes. "You are my woman. My feelings for you will not be hidden."

"Oh!" Tia said, stamping her small foot. "I am only someone you bought! I will not be treated like the unclean women of our village!"

Jerking her against him, Appearing Wolf growled, "You are the woman I have joined with. I have not made you unclean! Do not mock what we have together."

Unable to argue against his words, Tia stared at him. Did she see pain in the black eyes gazing back at her?

"Appearing Wolf."

Looking up, Appearing Wolf saw Letta standing a short distance away. Keeping a firm arm around Tia's waist, he acknowledged her. "What is it, Letta?"

Moving closer she whined in a pitiful voice. "I have no food. I do not have a hunter in my lodge to provide for my needs." She stretched her large hands out before her. "What am I to do?" At the sight of Gray Dog's mother standing near them, Appearing Wolf could feel Tia's body stiffen. Keeping his voice calm he eyed the woman standing in a smug stance before him.

"Have I not provided you with a warm dwelling, Letta?" At her slight nod, he ventured further. "Have you been deprived of fresh meat or wood for your cooking fire?"

"No," she admitted in a cold voice.

"Then tell me, Letta, why are you standing in front of my lodge begging like a woman who has no place in the village of her people?"

"I have no place amongst our people, Appearing Wolf. I am all-alone." She swiped at the tears running in dirty streaks down her face. "I need someone to share my life!"

"I will speak to my father. I am sure he can find a man in our camp who is in need of another wife to help with the keeping of his lodge."

Shaking a greasy fist in Appearing Wolf's direction, Letta stomped off muttering to herself.

Giving her husband a stern look, Tia walked into their lodge, but not before Appearing Wolf caught the slight smile lifting the corners of her full mouth. Chuckling, he turned his attention to his packhorse and the task at hand.

Unnoticed by the man busy skinning out the fresh killed elk, Letta stood a short distance away, her hate-filled eyes glaring with rage. "You think to make a fool of me in front of my son's woman! Your lodge will soon be filled with mourning, for the time is near when she will be gone!"

Chapter Nineteen

Something was wrong. Her woman's time should have been here by now. She had never been this late. Always before her body had been filled with the awful belly pain that kept her on her couch for days. Perhaps Mahossa could give her something to bring on the normal flow of blood her young body had thus far failed to produce.

She had been so intent on finding Mahossa she did not hear her mother calling out to her until Jolisha caught up with her.

"Tia, could you not hear me call you?"

"No." She turned around. "I am looking for Mahossa, have you seen him?"

"Not this morning, why?"

"I have need of him, I am not feeling well."

"Is it your woman's time?" Jolisha asked her voice low and gentle.

"No, and it should be." Tia chewed on one of her long nails. "I thought perhaps he could give me something to bring it on."

At Jolisha's look of amusement, Tia dropped her hand to her side. "What is it? Why are you looking at me like that?"

"Come, Tia." Jolisha slipped an arm around her daughter's waist. "I will go with you to see Mahossa."

Sitting in silence in the lodge of Mahossa, with the strong smell of herbs permeating the air around her, Tia again felt the same awe as she always did when in the presence of this ancient man. Looking at him now, she could see the many years of living etched upon his face.

Mahossa took her small hand in his. He did not speak, but sat in perfect stillness as his piercing eyes watched her. A slow smile crossed his face as he patted her hand. "The son of Appearing Wolf grows strong within your body."

Although she had known how children were conceived since she

175

had been a young girl, the fact that she herself could be with child had never entered her mind.

"No! That cannot be!" she whispered. "Appearing Wolf and I have been joined but a short time."

Ignoring her, Mahossa gathered the different herbs hanging out of the way across the lodge.

Jolisha, who had not spoken since entering the dwelling, could be silent no longer. "Mahossa, you said Appearing Wolf's son. Are you sure the child she carries is a boy?"

Mahossa continued mixing the herbs as if she had not spoken. Building a fire beneath a large kettle, he waited for the wood to catch. As the flames began to rise, he dropped crushed herbs into the water-filled pot. Satisfied his odd smelling concoction would be all right, he turned his attention to the woman waiting for him to speak.

"The wife of Spotted Owl need no longer feel she is a failure," he said, softening his usual gruff tone. At his words, Tia's mother turned away. "Jolisha, did you think I did not know of your shame? I have watched you bow your head in sorrow each time one of Spotted Owl's other wives bore him a son."

"Mahossa," she met his strong gaze, "I did not wish ill-will for my husband's sons!"

"I know this also, Jolisha," he nodded. "The burden you carried for so long was not yours to carry. The Creator determines who will be given life. Because you did not give Spotted Owl a son, you thought yourself a failure as a wife. The Creator chose to give Tia life. It was her time to live. Now this child of your body has given you a son who may someday be chief of all the Kainah. Hold your head high, wife of Spotted Owl; you have no need for shame."

After Tia had drank the herbal mixture Mahossa had prepared for her, telling her it would eliminate the sickness that unusually plagued women upon arising, she and her mother walked outside to the sight of the warriors riding into camp.

Appearing Wolf, seeing the women standing in front of Mahossa's lodge, dismounted in haste.

"Appearing Wolf, what is it? What has happened?" Tia asked.

"Both of you go back inside!" he ordered them. "You do not need to see this."

"See what?" She peered around him. She caught site of her father and what he carried in his arms. Even from a distance, Tia recognized the small body of Tawna. Before Appearing Wolf could stop her, she ran forward. Reaching out, she touched the still face of her sister.

"She is so cold." Tia drew her hand back. "My father," her stricken gaze met his, "what happened? Did the Crows do this to Tawna?"

"No, Tia, not Crows" He sat his horse, staring down at the daughter he held in his arms. "This was done by a white man," The suffering on Spotted Owl's face and in his voice, robbed Tia of any grasp she held on her emotions.

At the strong hands gripping her shoulders, Tia leaned back against her husband. Anguished cries filled the air surrounding the shocked crowd, and a cold hand clutched her heart as Jolisha led Tawna's mother to her lodge.

Staring straight ahead, Tia saw the first white man she had ever seen. His long face looked even more repulsive smeared with blood. His light blue shirt had been ripped and his pants covered with mud. The warriors had bound his hands, tying them around his white-man's saddle-horn. The fear showing in his bulging eyes brought a moment of pleasure to her revengeful heart. Drawing her knife, she took a step towards him.

"No, Tia!" Appearing Wolf's hand shot out, halting her. "The right of his death belongs to Spotted Owl! This night, the white one will know what he has done!"

Sheathing her knife, Tia walked over to look closer at the one who had ended the life of her beloved sister. His hair reminded her of dead prairie grass, and his eyes, the coat of the buffalo in winter. The thick hair covering his pale arms made Tia turn away with distaste.

"Appearing Wolf, I will go now to help my mother prepare Tawna's body," she told him, her voice filled with her pain. His sad gaze followed her until she disappeared from his sight.

***

That night the low throbbing of many drums could be heard echoing throughout the village. Everyone in camp left their lodges to witness the death of the white man who had taken the life of Tawna.

In the center of the village an area had been cleared and four stakes driven into the ground. The white man lay on his back, his arms and legs attached to the stakes, his body bared for all to see. The drums grew silent, and a hush fell over the crowd as Spotted Owl walked to the feet of his prisoner.

The white man's name was Tom Suiter. Although he had lived just twenty-one years on this earth, he knew as sure as he lay there, he would not live to see twenty-two. He had not meant to kill the Indian girl. He just wanted to spy on her as she swam. But as he watched her, the throbbing in his loins grew worse leaving him unable to turn away. Then she spotted him. Tom knew she would scream, alerting the camp to his presence. His one thought was to silence her. He never meant to use the knife, but she had left him no choice. Holding her naked body in his arms, he kept thinking how lovely she looked, and how long it had been since he had been with a woman. What did it matter that she was already dead? She didn't look dead and she sure didn't feel dead. He would take her and be gone before anyone even knew he had been there.

He had finished closing his pants and turned to leave, when his heart jumped into his throat. Two braves stood before him. Although Tom knew he did not stand a chance, he still had to try. But his reactions started too late. Now here he lay, spread-eagled in the middle of an Indian camp, about to die. The warrior spoke to him now, although Tom couldn't understand his words. But then, he didn't need to. The hate in the Indian's eyes spoke clear the words he wanted to say.

Spotted Owl walked to the head of the white man, and bending down, made two deep slashes just below each collarbone. Taking the strips of flesh in his hands, he began to pull in a slow and downward motion.

The Indian's intentions became very clear now and the last rational thought to go through Tom's mind before pain drove all else away, was the punishment his daddy always threatened him with, when he said, 'boy, I'm gonna skin you alive.'

In the days that followed, Tia saw more and more whites. A young man and his wife worked on building their home a mere hour's ride from the village. When she could break away from her busy day she would go, and keeping well hidden, spy on the two men and one woman.

One morning as Tia stood watching them, the white woman saw her. Motioning her to come forward, Tia ventured a few feet from her hiding place amongst the trees. The woman looked small and very pretty dressed in her long, dark green dress. But her hair is what caught Tia's attention. Never had she seen anyone with hair the color of a fiery sunset. The urge to see it up close became too strong for the strong-willed Indian girl to resist. With her hand on the knife she always wore, Tia decided she would find out more about this strange new person. She had been within speaking distance when she spied the two men, walk out of the forest. Without a backward glance, Tia fled. One white person she could handle, but not three.

That night Tia approached her husband as he sat talking with Pehta.

"Appearing Wolf, I almost touched a white woman today. She has hair the color of the sun." At his sharp intake of breath, she looked at him. "What is it?"

"Tia, you must stay away from the whites. They will harm you if they get the chance."

"The white woman does not look like a bad person." She brought the woman's image into her mind, smiling as she did so.

"You do not know this! As your husband, you will obey me!"

As though he had not spoken, she continued mashing the wild blue berries she had picked earlier, "If you would go with me some morning to watch them as I do, you would see they mean us no harm."

"Tia, sometimes I think the spirits should have made you a warrior," Pehta chuckled. "You have no fear."

"Pehta, will you go with me?" She left her task to move towards him. "I promise to protect you in case of danger," she bantered.

Gazing with fondness at his brother's wife, the handsome warrior shook his head. "No, Tia. I will leave that task to our fearless leader. He is the only one in the village who can control the wildness of your spirit when you get something into your head."

Without thinking, she came up behind her husband, laying both hands on his shoulders to lean over and peer into his face. "Appearing Wolf, it would seem we have a timid coyote for a brother. Since he will not go with me, will you?"

At her gentle touch, Appearing Wolf turned his face towards her, dropping a tender kiss on her forehead. "Yes, Tia. I will go with you." Then with a gentle chiding he added, "So I can have peace in my lodge, I will go with you to see these whites you speak of."

Pehta watched the way Tia leaned into his brother's arms receiving his touch. He watched her eyes lock with Appearing Wolf's piercing gaze a moment longer before hastening away. Snatching up a pile of clothes she had ready to be washed, she hurried from the lodge.

"Do my eyes deceive me, my brother, or is your woman beginning to return your feelings for her?"

"I think the child growing beneath her heart has quieted her longing to be away from me," Appearing Wolf smiled, his ebony eyes filled with happiness.

"It would appear so."

Bright and early the next morning Tia and Appearing Wolf watched from a distance, as the whites went about their day.

"See, my husband, they build a wooden lodge."

"Yes. That means they do not plan to leave."

"If they mean us no harm, would it be so bad having them near?"

"Do not be so quick to trust, Tia. We do not know they mean us no harm."

As they watched, one of the men walked to a nearby wagon. Within moments, he returned carrying a large bundle to sit cross-legged against a tree.

"Appearing Wolf, why does the white one not work with the others?"

"May be he is lazy," Appearing Wolf replied, without taking his eyes from the man in question.

"No, he looks to where we stand, then he scratches on something with a big stick."

"Perhaps he draws a picture of the Indian couple who came early one morning to watch the whites."

"That could be what he is doing, my husband. Come, let us go and see!"

Tia had already moved away when Appearing Wolf pulled her back. "No, Tia! You will not go to them! They might try to kill you! When will you stop and think before you do something?" Taking her by the arm, Appearing Wolf whispered. "Come, we will go back now, I do not want you to come here again. It is not safe."

But Tia knew she would return, just as she knew Appearing Wolf would be with her, if only to keep her out of mischief. There was so much more she wanted to know. So much she needed to understand about these whites that had invaded her life.

Chapter Twenty
Cut Bank, Montana 1920

Coming to the point, Doctor Prichard summed up Tia's condition. Afraid they may have already waited too long, he approached Charlotte on the idea of consulting with another doctor.

"Without help from a person trained to treat the type of injury Tia has, she ain't gonna make it."

"You're referrin' to this Doctor Rayford from back east," Charlotte murmured.

"Yes." Prichard nodded. "I've checked around and from what I can gather he's the best in his field. All I need is permission to bring him in on the case."

"Eathen?" Charlotte eyed the somber-faced man sitting across from her.

"Whatever you wanna do," Eathen replied.

The anger, leaping to life in Charlotte's blue eyes at her husband's cold indifference, did not go unnoticed by the watching doctor.

"Yes, well... I'll give you both some time to decide what you wanna do. When you're ready, I'll be in the kitchen with Hattie."

"I realize Tia's welfare is of no concern to you, Eathen," Charlotte told her husband as soon as the doctor walked out of hearing distance. "But it wouldn't hurt you to at least help me decide what's the best course to take right now!"

Pushing himself out of his chair, Eathen slammed the half glass of whiskey he had been drinking down on the mantel. "How many times do I have to tell you, woman, that girl, layin' in that bed up there," he gestured with his head toward the stairs, "don't mean a goddamn thing to me! For all I care you can bury her! Hell, she's as good as dead anyway!"

181

"Lower… your… voice!" Charlotte hissed each word through lips gone dry with anger. "I'm well aware of what an unfeelin' bastard you are, but you don't have to tell the whole county!"

"I've lived in this county for damn near sixty eight years!" he threw his arms wide. "If they don't know what I am by now, they never will!"

"All right!" she declared, sitting forward in her chair. "I'll tell Doc. Prichard to go ahead and bring this Doctor Rayford out here, and we'll cover all his expenses! You want me to handle everything! I'll do just that. All you gotta do is sign the checks!"

"Then get Prichard's ass back in here and get it done! The sooner I'm through with this mess, the better!"

"The best I can do," Doctor Prichard said after hearing Charlotte's decision, "is get a wire off to Philadelphia and see what he wants to do. He may want us to bring Tia to the hospital there."

"You can't be serious. There's no way we could do that! She'd never last the trip!" Charlotte whispered.

"Oh, bull shit!" Eathen thundered, sloshing more whiskey into his glass. "Get a sleepin' compartment on the train! She'll be fine!"

"We may not have a choice, Miss Charlotte." Prichard shot a brief glance across the room, trying to cover his disgust at Thornton's callus attitude.

"Well, find out as soon as you can, and we'll just have to go from there." Charlotte rubbed her hand over a small broach pinned beneath her collar.

"I'll send the wire off as soon as I get back to town." He stood, waiting for Eathen to escort him to the door. When he remained seated, Prichard declared. "No need to see me out, I know the way."

"You sure as hell should by now," Eathen growled.

Charlotte sat looking at the man she had been married to for almost fifty years, and for the first time she saw a stranger.

"I don't know you anymore, Eathen. What's more, I don't think I care to." She left her chair to walk toward the stairs.

"You haven't known me for years, Charlotte." His blue eyes stayed riveted on Jessie's portrait. "We both know it."

With her hand on the banister, she stopped, and a small tremor shook the white head as she looked straight ahead, "There's no need to tell me how far we've grown apart, Eathen. In a county as small as this one, people like to talk."

Unwilling right at that moment, to hear his worse fears confirmed he set the empty glass down on the end table. Then, without a word, he walked out of the house.

Without looking back, Charlotte continued on her way up the stairs, stopping when she stood outside her granddaughter's room. Turning the knob, she pushed open the door.

The shock of seeing Tia lying so still never failed to make her breath catch. Forcing herself to move forward, she eased her body down in the chair beside the bed.

"It's time to wake up, Tia." She smoothed the dark brown hair back from the damp forehead. "I need you, child. I can't face this burden in my life alone any longer."

When her pleading continued to go unheard, Charlotte laid her head beside the young girl so far removed from her. Only then did she allow the tears she had fought so hard to control earlier, fall unchecked down her face. All the fear she felt for Tia and the anger she felt for Eathen and the whole unjust world came pouring out, as she lay there sobbing as if her heart would break.

When Hattie walked into the room some time later, she found Charlotte still slumped in her chair. Trying to be as quiet as possible, she went about taking care of the girl who refused to wake up.

At last the white head moved as Charlotte sat up to find Hattie watching her. Wiping her face on the blanket, she whispered hoarsely. "How long have I been asleep?"

"Jes' a lil w'ile. Ah's glad ter sees you gittin' sum rest. Lawd knows you needs it."

"Is Eathen still gone?" Charlotte withdrew a handkerchief from her skirt pocket to blow her nose.

"Yas'm. An ah's glad ter sees dat too." Hattie removed the covers and top sheet from Tia's bed, then positioned Tia onto her side, rolling the bottom sheet up against her back as far as she could to place a fresh sheet in its place. As she returned the girl to her back, she reached across her pulling the soiled linen off the mattress, "De doctah done called. Said he sen' de wire awready."

Charlotte held Tia steady as Hattie finished getting the clean sheet beneath her. That done, Hattie flipped a fresh sheet over the girl lying motionless in the bed. "Guess we'll knows sumpin' in a few days."

"If she would just wake up!" Charlotte whispered.

"Ah knows dis ain' any of mah bizness," she lifted Tia's head to remove her pillow, then slipped a pillow with a fresh pillowcase into its place, "but right now de way things is, it jes' mout bes fer de best. Effen she wuz awake, Mist' Eathen'd jes' bes makin' her life sorry too."

"No he won't, Hattie." Charlotte slapped one hand down forcefully on the arm of the chair. "I'm gonna take Tia to Boston. She'll get just as good care there as she would in Philadelphia" she said, as she saw Hattie's look of disapproval. "There's no way I can put up with Eathen any longer. He's made my life miserable for years, and I'll be damned if I'll allow him to do the same to Tia!"

"Ah'll hates ter sees you go," she smoothed out the fresh blanket, pulling Tia's arms from beneath the covers to position them close to her side. "But ah sho kain' blames you fer gwine."

"I want you to know," She got to her feet. "I appreciate the good care you're givin' Tia. God knows I couldn't take care of her."

"Ah doan mine tekin' care of Miss Jessie's baby."

"Thank you, Hattie," she whispered opening the door.

Sitting there in the quiet parlor, Charlotte could hear the monotonous ticking of the old grandfather clock. Its dull rhythm made her all too aware of how fast time was running out for them. Glancing across the room, her eyes fell on Jessie's painting.

"Not doin' too good, am I?"

As the cold blue eyes stared back at her, Charlotte looked away. Leaving her chair, she walked to the hearth to throw a small log on the already crackling fire.

"Seems like every year this old house gets harder and harder to heat." She turned her back to the beckoning warmth.

"I feel that way myself," Eathen breathed.

Thinking herself alone, she jumped. "I thought you'd gone."

"I came back." He walked over to stand beside her. "Figured you might need me."

"For what?" Charlotte glanced over at him.

At her cold tone, Eathen took down his pipe from its wooden holder atop the mantelpiece.

"I've decided to take Tia to Boston." Charlotte left him standing by the hearth. "They got fine doctors there, and this way she'll be nearer to John and Martha." She pushed an Ottoman closer to her chair, then seating herself, stretched her legs out straight. "I'll drive into Cut Bank tomorrow, and see 'bout getting' a sleeper for us." She positioned a pair of reading glasses into place, picked up a pad and pencil.

"What about me?" Eathen drew a match across the bricks of the hearth.

"What about you, Eathen?" She gazed at him over her glasses. "You don't need me. I've finally realized that."

"You're wrong, Charlotte," Eathen told her, touching the lit match to the bowl of the pipe, "I do need you."

"Then so much the worse for you. I don't figure I got a lotta years left in this world. What time I do have, I'd like to spend with someone who loves me." She pushed the glasses back in place, went back to planning her trip to Boston.

"I sure never thought it'd come to this. And all because of Jessie's kid."

"She's my granddaughter, Eathen. I love her," she said without looking up. "I'll have her out of your house as soon as I can arrange it."

Unknown to the two people busy destroying each other's lives, they were being watched by an angry Appearing Wolf. "You will not move my woman from this dwelling!" he swore. "If her body dies before her spirit is returned, she will walk in darkness for all eternity." Then he was gone. Back to a distant past where a happy Tia lived and loved with a man who could damn her soul forever.

Chapter Twenty-One
Montana 1872

The large fire in the middle of the council-house burned bright, casting eerie shadows over the faces of the seated men. Rising to his feet, Chief Maheto walked to the head of his warriors. For a moment he stood, waiting until everyone in the room gave him their full attention.

"My heart is heavy with the words I must speak this night." A slight tremor in his voice made him swallow, trying to push the dreaded words past his lips. "The whites come in larger numbers to the land of the Kainah. Their numbers mark the end of life, as we know it, for the Blackfeet People."

"No!" Appearing Wolf shouted, jumping to his feet. "It must not be! If we kill the white dogs, their numbers will grow smaller!"

"We do not have the weapons with which to wage war, Appearing Wolf," Maheto tried to reason with his hotheaded son. "They have many guns! We have but a few."

"Then we will get them!" Appearing Wolf growled, unwilling to be deterred from what he thought best for his people.

"Yes!" said another, standing to make his voice heard. "With guns we can destroy those who have stolen our land." He looked around him, his confidence in his words growing as he saw the others nodding in agreement. "But we must strike now while they are still few in numbers!"

"No." With just that one word spoken so softly, a hush fell over the angry men. "I wish I could say that by fighting the whites they would leave us in peace, but I know this cannot be. I am your chief. I will not lie to you."

"If we will not fight, my father, what will we do?" Appearing Wolf asked, trying to keep the bitterness from his voice.

"Talk." Maheto breathed.

"The whites will not listen to talk," Appearing Wolf snarled, all thought of control gone now from his voice. "We must band together." His voice grew louder. "Our enemies can no longer be the Crow and the Snake. The time has come for us to choose between the Indian people and the whites!" he cried, in hopes Maheto would stand beside him in a joint effort to bring all the people together.

"The soldiers from the fort will come with their big guns," Maheto shouted, trying to make himself heard over the ear-piercing war cries of the frenzied warriors. "They will destroy our lodges! They will kill our people! You must listen, Appearing Wolf!"

"No, my father. I will not listen! I would rather die than cower before the whites!"

As the shouting men stood and shook their arms in respect, Appearing Wolf silenced them with a lift of his hand.

Waiting until they had been seated once more with low murmurs filtering throughout the room, Maheto looked at his son. "You believe with the heart of the young our people will live forever."

"No!" Appearing Wolf replied the anger still strong in his voice. "As war chief to the Kainah, I believe in the strength of our warriors to protect our land!"

"The strength of our warriors is only as strong as the man who leads them, my son."

"The name of Chief Maheto is well respected amongst our enemies. Soon," his black eyes flashed with the heat of his anger, "the whites will learn to respect my name!"

"As a leader of our people you hold their fate in your hands. Remember, Appearing Wolf, I speak from experience." he told him, his gaze never wavering. "Do not let your hatred overshadow your wisdom."

"Does it show wisdom to do nothing and allow the whites to take our land?" he shouted, ignoring his father's double meaning. "The white couple has been allowed to stay. Because of this, others have come. We are being pushed further and further from the way of life we have always known. The days of fighting amongst ourselves is over! The day has come when we must call the Crows our brothers and fight side by side!"

"The Crows will not fight beside the Blackfeet!" shouted Konah, staring at the shocked faces around him.

"We do not know this until we speak with them," Appearing Wolf replied.

"There is too much hatred between us to be brothers!" said another.

"If that is true, then the words of my father are also true. If we cannot stand side by side, then our days of freedom are numbered."

For awhile total silence filled the lodge as each man thought upon the words of Appearing Wolf.

The silence was broken by Konah. "I agree with the words of our war chief. We will talk with the Crow. We will see if the Blackfeet and Crow will remain as enemies or stand together as brothers against the whites."

"My Father," Pehta spoke up, "the Crow will not trust our sign of peace. They will see only our warriors. Let me go alone into their land. I will speak with Chief Yellow Calf about our council's decision on the whites. Even the Crow must respect a man riding alone and unarmed amid their people," he said, his eyes alive with challenge.

Maheto agreed. "Chief Yellow Calf is our enemy but he is not without honor. Riding alone into his land you will be one against many."

"I am not afraid. The spirits will guide my step. Do not fear for me, my father."

Pride for his younger son showed upon Maheto's face. He looked so much like Appearing Wolf. Each tall and handsome of body and of spirit. He felt his pride in his sons soar.

"Ho, my brother," Appearing Wolf laughed, clasping the other's forearms in a strong grip. "Be careful your long shiny locks do not decorate a Crow's lodge pole."

"I will return swiftly to ride by your side against the whites," Pehta grinned, his strong teeth showing stark white against his dark skin. Then, as an afterthought, he added. "I will be safer in the land of our enemies than you were in your own lodge on the night of your joining."

"Yes, but the Crow would be offended, if you tried taming them as I did my woman." Appearing Wolf returned with great humor.

As Maheto raised his arms for silence, the lodge grew quiet. "After my son has fasted and cleansed his spirit, he will ride alone to the camp of Chief Yellow Calf. We will see if the Indian People will stand together to make our enemies the whites."

Leaving the council-house, the brothers spied Tia waiting for them across the way. As she walked up to them, Pehta gave her a gentle embrace. Without warning, great fear clutched his heart as he held her small body close. Before releasing her, he placed a light kiss on her forehead. "You will always remain very close to me, Little Sister," he told her, before walking away. At Pehta's odd behavior, Tia and Appearing Wolf looked at one another, both at a loss as to what could have brought on this sudden sadness.

For a fleeting moment Appearing Wolf wondered if Pehta had received a warning against his going alone to the Crow camp, then put it from his mind as Tia touched his arm.

"I hope whatever is troubling our brother has a swift passing," she whispered, as she watched Pehta walk away. "I hold much love in my heart for him."

"Pehta is a good man. The spirits will return him safely."

Upon hearing this, Tia turned to her husband waiting for him to explain. When he did not, she continued walking with him toward their lodge. She knew that words discussed in the tribal meetings could not always be shared.

Far off in the distance the high-pitched wail of the timber wolf echoed out over the quieting village. Its mournful cry seemed almost like a warning.

Unable to sleep, Pehta left his couch. Walking to the opening, he lifted the flap then secured it back to let in the cool night air. As he stood there breathing in the night's freshness, he noted a slight movement out of the corner of his eye. As he watched, a fine white mist swirled before him ultimately taking the shape of a small white owl. Like a brave warrior it sat very still, showing no fear as Pehta watched him. Then it turned, staring in the direction of Appearing Wolf's dwelling. As it brought its gaze back to the watchful man, it began to fade. Blending into the night as if it had never been.

With a heavy heart, Pehta lowered the flap, no longer able to deny what he knew in his heart to be true. Taker of Life would be coming soon for the spirit of his beloved sister. Wearing but a brief loincloth, Pehta walked out into the cold night air. The cool winds blowing down from the mountains made him tremble, but he welcomed their chilling touch.

As he walked on, he thought he heard someone call his name. Turning, he saw Mahossa, his long white hair whipping about his face, signing over the howling winds for him to come back. He retraced his steps until he came to Mahossa's lodge. Mahossa held open the flap for him to enter.

Seated cross-legged before the roaring fire, Pehta looked up as the old man handed him a strong smelling brew, nodding for him to drink it down. As he did so, he felt the chill beginning to leave his body and a strange sense of peace envelope him. The fear gone now from his mind, he stretched his lean body out straight on the soft buffalo robe.

"The little white warrior did not come to wish you harm. He is but a messenger," Pehta heard Mahossa saying, his voice sounding as if it came from a long way off.

"The message he came to give you concerns the wife of your brother. Two times her life will be in mortal danger. The first time will come soon, through the twisted hatred of another. The second time bodes ill for all our people. The spirits will not show me when or why, but this much I know. Tia's *life* will be taken but not her spirit. You will see her again in your lifetime, but you will be a stranger to her. The Creator know why this must be. We are not to question them in their wisdom. You are a good and caring man, Pehta, but your journey to the Crow camp will be in vain."

Dazed and weakened from his trance-like revelations, Mahossa rose to his feet. Walking with unsteady steps to where Pehta lay beside the fire, he leaned down placing a warm robe over his shoulders.

"Now sleep," he told him, "and when the sun rises in the east your mind will no longer be troubled."

Seated beside the sleeping warrior, Mahossa's thoughts flew back to a time many years ago when he had sat listening to the vision quest of a young Appearing Wolf.

Chief Maheto's elder son had been but sixteen-summers-old when he had first sought the powers of the spirits. For three days he had denied his body of food and drink and cleansed his spirit of impurities. On the last day of his fast, she came to him. Standing in silence, she watched him from across the waters. She was a young maiden dressed in the robes of his people. Calling his name, she motioned for him to join her, but some force held him still, unable to move. When he turned she stood beside him. Before his eyes, her Indian robe fell to her feet to be replaced with a manner of clothing he had never seen before. Reaching out, he tried to draw her near, but she backed away out of his reach. A terrible sadness filled his heart as he watched her disappear into the early morning mist.

Now, as Mahossa sat pondering this long-ago memory, he knew Appearing Wolf's vision would soon be fulfilled.

Chapter Twenty-Two

Snuggled deep within the plush robes of her bedding, Tia groped for the familiar warmth of her husband. Finding herself alone she threw off the warm cover shivering as the early morning air touched her. Snatching up a fresh dress, she pulled it over her head to walk outside. The village remained quiet, the cooking fires yet unlit, as she walked toward the council house in search of Appearing Wolf. Her step faltered as her gaze fell on Pehta's lodge.

"Caquay is not tethered in front of Pehta's door," she breathed, knowing the war-horse would never be far away from his owner. "That means Pehta is not in camp."

Recalling the unusual behavior of her husband's brother the night before, Tia felt a deep sadness. With a heavy heart, she looked up to see Appearing Wolf walking towards her.

"Tia, why are you about the village so early?" He placed both hands on her slim shoulders. "Is something wrong?"

"I reached for you in my sleep." Without thinking, she brought her hands up placing them palm down against his chest. "When I could not find you I became worried."

At her words, Appearing Wolf's ebony eyes lit up. She had been turning to him more and more of late. Could it be because of the child growing within her body that made her need him, or was she at last beginning to return his love?

Stepping back she looked up into midnight eyes filled with love for her. "Appearing Wolf, where is Pehta?"

For a long moment, he did not respond. Draping a strong arm about her shoulders, he walked with her back to their lodge. As they walked, Tia placed her own arm around his waist.

Smiling down at her, he replied. "Pehta has ridden to the land of the

Crow to speak with Chief Yellow Calf. Do not worry, he will have a safe return."

Letta, on her way to the lake, spied the couple walking towards their dwelling. Noting the closeness between them she felt her anger leap to new heights. When they had gone from her sight, she threw the water pouches into the dirt.

"She walks and laughs in the morning light," her body shook with her anger, "while my son's body lies in shadow. Her belly will grow large with new life, but Gray Dog's life is over! I cannot allow this to happen!" Then, as quickly as her anger had erupted, it disappeared. Staring in the direction of Appearing Wolf's lodge she laughed, and reaching down picked up the dirty water pouches to continue on her way.

Turning onto her side, Tia could feel Appearing Wolf pressed against her. Brushing her long hair back away from her face he leaned forward kissing the side of her throat. "What is it, Aakiiwa? Tell me why you are so sad."

"I am so confused in my heart." She tilted her head back gazing up at him.

"Why do you say this?" He moved her to a more comfortable position.

Trying to still her pounding heart, she touched his face, marveling at its smoothness. "After all that has happened between us I feel I should hate you," her long slender fingers splayed out to touch his full mouth, "but I do not."

Afraid to hope he pursued further. "What are your feelings for me, Tia? No, don't hide your face. Look at me and tell me what your heart feels for your husband."

"The feelings I had in my heart for Gray Dog have gone, no matter how hard I try to hold on to them."

Taking a deep breath, he asked the question that could wound him to his very soul. "And your feelings for me?"

"My feelings for you have also changed. I no longer wish to be away from you. When you are out of my sight, I feel so empty."

"I find that hard to believe, Aakiiwa." He emitted a gentle laugh, running a warm hand over her flat stomach.

Joining him in his playful mood, she turned onto her back, pulling his face closer she kissed him long and deep. "I love you, my husband," she whispered.

The light in his eyes could not be hidden. Without taking his gaze from hers, he replied in a voice filled with feeling. "I love you, my strong-spirited woman."

For the first time in their marriage, Tia went to Appearing Wolf's arms of her own free will and shared in the wonder that love given is the most beautiful love of all.

A deep closeness grew between them. Appearing Wolf shared thoughts and feelings with her he would not have voiced before. When he told her about Pehta's going to speak with Chief Yellow Calf, she surprised him by telling him about her stay in the Crow camp, and the gentle way she had been treated by the old chief.

"Chief Yellow Calf is a caring man," she murmured. "He has much love for his people. Appearing Wolf," she gazed up at him, "we are all Grandfather's children. Why must there be so much hatred between us?"

"I do not know, Tia. Perhaps the whites coming into our land is the Creator's way of healing the bad feelings between the Indian people. They are telling us we must band together, or all is lost."

"The spirits have always looked with much favor upon Pehta. They have allowed him to see what others cannot. Perhaps this is why it is Pehta going to speak for the Blackfeet instead of you."

With a slight nod, Appearing Wolf lay silent, staring through the smoke hole as the lengthening shadows of night filled the lodge. He could not shake the feeling that all was not right somehow. All through the day with Tia beside him, he had talked, listened, and shared feelings with her he had thought beyond his reach. He should have been happy, but instead his heart filled with a suffocating fear that would not be silenced.

"My husband, what is it?" she shifted in his arms to stare into his face.

Rising to his feet, he left their couch. "I must speak with my father, Tia. Something is wrong, but I do not know what it is."

As he left the lodge, Tia lay back her heart beating in fear. She had been raised to accept the inner warnings of impending danger.

"Tia," a voice called from outside the lodge.

Tia scrambled from beneath the cumbersome robe. When she had dressed, she went to the opening to see who called her name. She felt surprised to see Letta standing before her.

"I do not mean to intrude, Tia, but I have need of you in my lodge. Will you come?" Letta whined.

Looking at Gray Dog's mother standing just inside, Tia took pity on the older woman. She herself had so much, a husband whom she loved and who loved her, and now a child of that love growing strong within her body. The large woman, with her beautiful, black hair chopped short from her grieving and hanging in greasy unwashed clumps about her face, touched Tia's heart.

"Of course I will go with you, Letta." Tia took the woman's strong hand in hers. "On our way to your lodge, we will stop by Maheto's dwelling. I will tell Appearing Wolf I am with you, so he will not worry."

At Letta's look of alarm, she stopped. "What is it, Letta?"

"Appearing Wolf hates me. He will not allow you to go with me. Before your husband took Gray Dog from me, you loved and trusted me. Now, you do not want to be with me." She wiped a filthy hand across her eyes.

"Letta, that is not true." Tia wrapped the big woman in her arms. "Come, we will not tell Appearing Wolf where we are going. I am sure we will not be gone long."

"No, Tia," Letta whispered, stepping from the comforting arms, "this will not take long at all."

Seated within the large dwelling of Maheto, Appearing Wolf told his father of his unease. "I feel I should leave for the land of the Crow."

"No, my son. If you follow Pehta, the Crow will not trust our sign of peace. You could be putting your brother's life in great danger. You must have faith he will return to us."

"I feel death is going to touch someone very near to me this night," Appearing Wolf breathed.

Leaving his couch, Maheto walked to the door of the lodge as the first rumbles of thunder echoed overhead. "A storm is coming." He watched the trees shake as the wind blew through their branches. "Perhaps you should return to your dwelling before it is here," he cautioned him, dropping the flap into place.

"I will not allow Tia to see me quaking with fear like an old woman." He breathed a deep breath trying to rid himself of his unease. "I am a leader! What is it that clutches my heart with such unspeakable evil?!"

The scream had no beginning and no end. It cut through the still night bringing terror to the hearts of both father and son as they stood staring at one another unable to move. Then, in an instant, Appearing Wolf knew whose life the evil had come for.

"Tia!" he yelled, jumping to his feet, as the agonizing scream tore through the night again and again. As he rushed from Maheto's lodge, the first drops of rain began to fall

***

Tia felt herself being dragged over the muddy ground. But why? She should be safe in her lodge with her husband where she belonged. Then it all came rushing back to her. She remembered walking with Letta toward her lodge when everything went dark.

Without warning lightning flashed, turning night into day for a split second, allowing Tia to see her surroundings. "I am in the burial grounds," she moaned.

In a daze, she tried getting to her feet, but someone kicked her in the side of her face. Unable to fight her attacker, she remained on the wet ground trying to see who caused her so much pain.

Once more, the heavens lit up, and she drew in her breath as she found herself staring into the face of madness. Letta stood over her, laughing shrilly as she raised a large skinning knife over her head.

"The time has come for you to join the one whose life you took from me!" Letta screamed, as she brought the knife down again and again into Tia's body.

She tried to crawl away, but the awful knife followed cutting and slashing her without mercy.

Someone screamed, the sound coming from a long way off. She could feel the tears of Mother Earth washing over her as she lay on the soft ground. Who moaned so sadly? She must go to them. But her body refused to move.

Appearing Wolf found her lying in the rain. As he knelt down to gather her in his arms, he saw a movement out of the corner of his eye. A cold chill passed over him as the silence erupted with eerie laughter. Drawing his knife and crouching low, he ran forward.

The sight meeting his shocked eyes filled him with disbelief. In the bright flashes of lightning, he could see Letta and the body she held in her arms. Pulled from his burial scaffold the decaying body of Gray Dog was being rocked back and forth, as his mother sang to him in a high unnatural voice.

The singing stopped as she spied Appearing Wolf watching her. Lowering her son's body to the ground she stood, and raising the same knife she had used on Tia, ran towards him screaming out her hatred.

Waiting until she had almost reached him, Appearing Wolf reached out and with one quick jerk, snapped her neck. As her lifeless body slid to the ground, Appearing Wolf rushed to gather the woman he loved into his arms.

He could not see the full extent of the damage Letta's madness had wrought until he carried her into their dwelling. After placing her unconscious body upon his couch, he went to build up the lodge fire. Then he saw the damage that had been done.

Tia's beautiful face was swollen beyond recognition. Blood poured in steady streams from her nose and mouth and from the many stab wounds covering her body. With his breath, catching on a sob he turned to find Jolisha standing just inside, her small hand clutched to her throat.

"Stay with her," he told her, already on his way out of the lodge to summon Mahossa.

Time seemed to crawl as Jolisha sat on the sodden couch holding the hand of her wounded daughter. Who could have done such an evil thing? she wondered again and again. The light from the lodge fire glistened, its orange glow merging with the dark red blood covering Tia's body. As she saw Mahossa, she moved out of the way across the lodge.

The moment he entered Appearing Wolf's dwelling, his senses became alert to another's presence hovering nearby. He could feel its evil eyes watching and waiting for Tia's spirit to leave her body. The anxious presence filled his heart with unspeakable terror. "Carry her to my lodge! Now!" he ordered, shoving Appearing Wolf ahead of him. "It is not only her life that is in danger, but her spirit!"

When Appearing Wolf placed Tia's still body upon the couch nearest the lodge fire, he stood back watching Mahossa as he moved with quick steps around his lodge gathering the different herbs he would need to save Tia's young life. When he felt satisfied with everything, he turned to Appearing Wolf.

"Leave us!"

"I can't," he stood as though frozen in place. "She might..." he could not get the dreaded words past his fear. Mahossa grabbed his arm shoving him towards the door. With tears streaming unashamed, down his face, Appearing Wolf turned and left the lodge.

Mahossa laced the opening. He could feel the evil in his dwelling growing stronger. He dropped the herbs he had set aside into boiling water. As steam wafted from the roiling pot, a strong pungent odor filled the air.

Mahossa began to chant. His voice rising higher and higher until his eerie keening could be heard throughout the village. Stripping Tia of her muddy dress, he washed the still flowing blood from her body. Giving no heed to how the scalding water burned his hands, he plunged the cloth into the pot then shook it out to cool before rubbing it over her tender skin. When he knew the wounds to be free of any objects, he covered her with an odd smelling salve.

Satisfied, at last, he watched as the profuse bleeding slowed then stopped altogether. Kneeling behind her, he placed both hands on each side of her head. His hands trembled as he felt the struggle going on inside her body.

Many times, he watched as a dark spirit would leave her body then reenter it moments later. Mahossa's chanting grew louder, filling the lodge with his eerie wailing.

"Tia, Wife of Appearing Wolf, you must fight the one who dwells within your body!" he told her. "Turn away from him! His strength is evil! Your heart has always been pure! You can come back from the darkness in which you walk! Hear me, Tia! Walk towards me! Reach out and take my hand. Join your spirit with mine! It is time to reenter the body lying cold and empty without the spirit to give it warmth and life."

All through the long night Mahossa stayed, kneeling and chanting as he joined his spirit with hers. As the first rays of dawn touched the lodge skins, he felt her body regain its natural warmth. Only then did he leave her. Exhausted, he walked to the door. Unlacing the flap, he threw it open to motion an anxious Appearing Wolf inside.

"The evil has left her body. In time her wounds will heal." As Appearing Wolf continued to stare at him, he told him what he wanted to hear. "Your son remains safe. She will rest here until she is stronger," he said, before leaving the concerned warrior alone with the woman he loved.

Mahossa walked alone out upon the prairie. He kept seeing the images he had seen while his soul linked with Tia's. He had known, from Appearing Wolf's quest to become a warrior, her spirit would not walk her path to the sun in this life. Now he knew why. Her soul had been touched by one whose mind dwelt in the land of darkness. Because of this, her life must begin a new circle. Her spirit would be reborn into a new life. One altogether different from the life she had always known. Appearing Wolf would be her link to the Creator. He had to be the one to lead her on her path to the sun. If she could not find him in her new life, she would repeat her rebirth until she did.

Chapter Twenty-Three

The first one Tia thought of, when she finally woke, was her unborn child. Her frightened eyes beseeched Appearing Wolf to tell her the child still lived safe within her body.

Placing his strong hand over her small one, as it lay upon her flat stomach, he whispered. "Our son yet lives. Do not worry, Aakiiwa."

Turning her face to the side, she allowed the tears she had been holding back to flow. When her husband reached out to wipe them away, she caught his hand to her lips.

"I should have listened to you," she sobbed. "You tried to tell me she was too filled with anger for me to trust her. I could have lost our child!"

"It is over, Tia. You must allow your body to heal. Put the bad thoughts from your mind. Trust that I will be here to care for you."

"You are not angry with me?" she whispered, staring at him through her tears.

"No," he leaned forward to place a gentle kiss on her swollen lips, "you did not choose to ignore my warnings. You trusted a woman sick with grief. In her madness, she thought to destroy you. Try not to remember her with anger. She could not accept Gray Dog's death. She was to be pitied."

Bringing her hand up to her swollen face, she tried to turn away from him. "How can you bare to look at me?"

"Your face will not remain as it is now. You will heal, Aakiiwa." Appearing Wolf rubbed his thumb lightly down her cheekbone.

"Did the people give Letta a decent burial?"

"Yes." he nodded. "Her scaffold is right next to her son's."

"All of this trouble because I thought I loved Gray Dog," she gulped a sob.

"You did love Gray Dog, Tia." With a gentle hand, he tipped her face up so she had no choice but to look at him. "But your love is that of the innocent. Not the love of a woman. You could not have known the difference."

"Any other man would have returned me to my father. You have much patience, my husband."

"This is why I am the war chief of our people." He smiled into her eyes, dropping a light kiss on the tip of her nose.

Reaching up, she touched his face with loving fingers. "Would you do something for me?"

"You need but to ask, Aakiiwa."

"Would you bring my father to see me? I must speak with him."

Gathering her into his arms, Appearing Wolf pulled her against him for just a moment, then without a word, he left her, to do as she asked.

Within moments, Spotted Owl knelt by his daughter's side. When he saw the love in her eyes for him, his own eyes misted. "I am here, my daughter."

With a half-sob, Tia threw her arms around Spotted Owl's neck holding him as close as she dared. "I am so sorry for all the trouble I have caused you, my father. Can you find it in your heart to forgive me?"

"All I ever wanted is your happiness, Tia. Appearing Wolf is a good man, who loves you very much."

"I feel so blessed. Thank you for your wisdom in seeing what I could not."

For seven days Tia remained under the sharp eye of Mahossa. He would allow no one else to attend to her healing. When Tia did not want to do something he told her to do, the old medicine man would become stern with her. He determined she would become whole again, in body and in spirit.

On the eight day, he carried her outside. "It is time to receive the healing of Mother Earth," he told her. "Feel the air and sun upon your face, Tia. Your wounds are healing."

"How are you feeling?" Keelah asked, walking over when she saw Tia being carried outside, giving thanks in her heart she did not have to visit her friend in the Medicine Lodge.

"I am better," Tia said.

"I will be glad when you can walk to the lake with me again." Keelah laughed, dropping down beside her on the blanket.

"Yes," Tia emitted a deep sigh, "but I fear that will not be soon."

"After you have finished with your work tomorrow, Keelah, come to my lodge. Tia will walk with you," Mahossa said, before going back inside his dwelling.

"I will not be able to walk that soon! I am still too weak!"

"I will help you, Aakiiwa," Appearing Wolf walked over to her scooping her up in his arms.

At his closeness, Tia trembled. It had been too long since he had held her. When she looked at him, her smoldering eyes told him of her need.

Nuzzling her neck, he uttered a soft growl. "My hunger grows too, little one. You must do everything Mahossa tells you, so you will grow strong."

Tia could feel Keelah watching them. Squirming she replied, "I think I need to lay down again, my husband."

Propping her against the beaded backrest Keelah had given them for a wedding present, he turned to leave when she caught hold of his hand. "Do not stay away long, my love. I miss you when you are not near."

Kneeling, he kissed her long and deep. When he drew away, they both felt shaken. With real pain showing in his eyes, he left her to visit with Keelah.

"He loves you very much," Keelah murmured.

"Appearing Wolf is my life." Tia watched him leave. "I wasted so much time trying to hold on to a feeling that should have never been."

"You had much fear of your husband in the beginning. I felt afraid for you. Now, I can see you are happy in your marriage."

"The spirits have blessed us both," Tia gazed with fondness at her friend.

When Keelah did not respond, she touched her hand. "Keelah, what is it? Has something happened between you and Konah?"

Keelah remained silent, her slender fingers covering her mouth. Then on a shuddering breath, she replied. "Konah does not return my love. He has already spoken for another."

"I am sorry. Who is the one he will join with?"

"The daughter of Little Dog."

"Summer Rain?" Shock showed upon her face, "She is but thirteen-summers. Why would Little Dog accept Konah's offer for her?"

"If he does not, she will shame his name before the whole village." Keelah's lips curled with bitterness. "Summer Rain is carrying Konah's child!"

Recalling the day she had seen the young warrior laughing and talking with her own sister, Tawna, Tia felt her anger rising. "It would seem Konah thought he could play with a young girl's affections and not have to pay for it."

"Little Dog has taught him otherwise. They are to be joined in two days."

"I know you have much love for Konah, but it is better to find out now what kind of person he is instead of after he is your husband."

"When you told me of your being forced to marry Appearing Wolf my heart filled with pain for you." She turned, looking at her friend. "At the same time I felt glad that it was you and not me who had to join with a man you did not have love in your heart for. I felt secure in the feelings Konah said he shared with me. Now you are happy with your husband while the man I love will join with another."

"Yes, Keelah, I am happy with Appearing Wolf." Tia told her, unwilling to allow Keelah's suffering to dim her happiness. "When the winter snows blanket the ground, we will be safe and warm inside our lodge with our son. I feared Letta's attack would take him from my body. I thank the Creator, he remains safe and strong."

"I envy you, Tia." She looked away.

"When I found I loved Appearing Wolf, I felt so much happiness it frightened me. I feared something would go wrong and all my happy feelings would be gone."

"You should not dwell on these thoughts, Tia. Appearing Wolf will protect you. He will see that your life is filled with happiness from now on."

"I know what you are saying is true, Keelah. But after what happened with Letta, I see how swiftly death can strike."

Keelah nodded. "Death seeks more than the body, death also seeks the soul."

At her sadness, Tia touched her arm. "If your love for Konah is this strong, why not become his second wife?"

Keelah drew a sharp breath. "Would you choose to put your life in the hands of Letta's madness again?"

"No, Keelah." She withdrew her hand. "Of course I would not."

"Then why do you ask me to put my life in Konah's hands?"

"I am sorry, Keelah. I did not see our situations as being the same."

"Death is death, Tia," she rose to her feet as she spoke, "no matter what form it takes."

***

Swimming in the cool clear water Tia felt a slight touch on her leg and tried to kick what swam beneath her. Her squeals of laughter rang out in the early morning stillness as Appearing Wolf splashed to the top to grab her.

"It seems I have captured a creature of the water. Let me see if she tastes as good as she looks," he growled, nipping on Tia's rounded shoulder.

"You should beware, my handsome warrior, for you do not know what powers the creature of the water has." Tia wiggled her brows at him. "She could put a spell on you making you her slave for the rest of your days."

"Little does she know," he returned her mischievous dark look with one of his own, "I am already enslaved by her beauty." The teasing grin vanished from her face, Staring at her, he turned her so she would have to look at him. "What is it, Aakiiwa?"

"My body is scarred and bruised, how can you find beauty in that?"

Lifting her in his arms, he carried her to the bank. As he stood her in front of him, he saw the way she tried to lean into him in an attempt to shield her nakedness from his gaze.

"Your wounds will heal, Tia. I do not find your body hard to look upon. I am the one who will see any scars that may remain. If I still find your body beautiful, what does it matter?"

"It matters to me, Appearing Wolf. If I am not pleasing to you, the day will come when your eyes will seek another."

"What has happened to make you distrust my love for you?" He tipped her face, making her look at him.

At the love shining from his sincere gaze, she whispered. "Keelah told me of Konah's joining with Summer Rain. I am afraid of losing you to another, too."

"Konah did not show wisdom in taking a mere girl to his couch. Now he must pay for that mistake with his freedom. Do not judge me by what another does."

Putting her arms around his trim waist, she leaned her dark head against his chest. "Do not scold, my husband. Now that I have found you, I never want to lose you."

"Put your mind at ease, little one. I already have the woman who stirs the fire in my blood."

Tilting her head back, she stared up at him. "And what of later, my husband, if I cannot fill our lodge with sons? Will another share your couch who can?"

"My son already grows strong within your body, Aakiiwa. If he is to be the only one the Creator blesses us with, then we will be satisfied".

"I can feel your heart beating with such love for me." She rubbed her cheek against him.

"Although I did not know it, my heart filled with love for you the first time I saw you."

"When was that, my husband?"

"During my vision quest. You came to me early one morning. I am the reason the Creator placed you upon Mother Earth, Tia. It is not by chance you that I found you."

"If we had known, Letta and Gray Dog would still be alive."

"No, Tia," Appearing Wolf corrected her, "The Creator decides when our time here is over. You cannot blame yourself for what is not your fault."

"I know what you say is true, but I cannot help feeling somehow responsible."

"Tia, could it be the spirits worked through you to call their feet upon the wolf trail?"

For a long moment, she stared at him in disbelief. Then she nodded.

"Accept what you cannot change, Tia. Now is not the time to think of death. New life grows strong within your body. Be glad for the blessings you have been given."

"My body held on to the life of our son even though Letta's knife would have taken him from where he rests safe and secure within me. How can that be, my husband?"

"I do not know. You suffered many wounds. I, too, feared for his life. We will not think about what could have been. We will give thanks in our hearts it is over."

Snuggling closer into the arms of her husband, she could feel all the doubts she had been feeling slipping away. Her body had not healed enough to receive him physically, but as she stood wrapped within his arms with the glow of their love surrounding her, she knew it did not matter.

"What are you thinking, Aakiiwa?" He kissed the top of her head.

"I am not thinking of anything, my husband. I am enjoying the closeness of the man I love. My fears are gone, Appearing Wolf. My father's taking of other wives to fill his lodge with the sons my mother could not give him, and Konah's joining with someone other than Keelah, are of no concern to me anymore. I have been blessed with the love of the one man I could ever be happy with. I could not wish for more."

"Nor will I, Aakiiwa." He pulled her in closer. "If the spirits call our names right at this moment I will be ready to walk my path to them. Giving thanks in my heart with each step of my journey."

Drawing away from him, Tia looked up into eyes filled with love for her. "Then I will be the greedy one, my husband, for I want to live to see our son enjoy the same love we have found. I want to see our grandchildren laughing and playing in a safe world. When I see this, then I, too will be ready to walk my path to the spirit world."

For a fleeting moment, his ebony eyes became shadowed with fear. He believed it unwise to dictate the number of one's days on Mother Earth. When the spirits called your name, you must not hesitate.

"If the spirits are kind we will walk our path together, little one," he murmured.

Fully dressed they made their way back to the village. They had reached their dwelling and prepared to enter when Tia heard a loud explosion. She felt herself knocked to the ground with the full weight of Appearing Wolf falling upon her. With her heart in her throat, she managed to pull herself from beneath his still body. At the sight of a reddish brown stain spreading across his shirt Tia screamed, then drew her knife.

Jumping to her feet, she turned to face the horror closing in on her. She found the scene meeting her eyes unbelievable. White rode at a fast pace through the village shooting anything that moved. Tia saw her brother Tahelo fall, the whole side of his face gone.

A sound tore from her throat as she started to go to him. She had taken but a few steps when she felt a burning pain rip through her side. Sobbing she tried to move, but some force kept pulling her down.

From her position on the ground she could see the terror swirling around her. Being unable to move, she was forced to witness the mindless slaughter of her people.

"Grandfather," she cried out, "why have you allowed this to happen?"

Once more, she tried to stand, but her body no longer obeyed her commands. The smoke from the many burning lodges made it all but impossible to see, while from all sides could be heard the angry voices of the white men. Tia could not understand their words, only their hatred.

Amid a world gone mad, she thought of Appearing Wolf and their life together. "How I wish I had not fought against belonging to you, my husband, but how could I know I would come to love you more than my own life?"

At this thought, Tia remembered their unborn child and covered her stomach, trying in vain to protect him from a fate already out of her hands.

"Please, Grandfather, do not let me walk my path to the sun without Appearing Wolf. Let me look upon his beloved face one more time."

Then from out of the mists, he was there holding her close. While the pain in her side continued to throb.

"I am here, Aakiiwa. I am here. This day we will walk our path to the sun together." Rising with ease to his feet, he waited for her to join him.

Steeling herself against the pain, she reached out for his hand. A shadow crossed her face and she looked up into the smiling face of a white man. She saw, as if in slow motion, as he raised a gun toward someone beyond her. Following his aim she watched in chilling horror as Jolisha, her knife raised and screaming, ran towards them.

"Noooo....!" she screamed, trying to crawl towards the woman who had given her life, but before she could move, a loud explosion echoed through the madness. As her mother's lifeless body fell beside her, Tia slumped back to the ground as darkness descended over her. Tia never heard the second shot.

Chapter Twenty-Four
Cut Bank, Montana 1921

Large drops of rain tapping against the shuttered window pulled the weary mind back to reality. Lifting her head from the edge of the mattress, Charlotte looked around, at a loss as to her surroundings. As her tired eyes fell on the still figure on the bed beside her chair, it all came rushing back. Breathing a deep breath, she brushed the damp hair back from the flushed forehead.

"It's time to wake up, child. Life's too short to just sleep it away." When her mild chiding drew no response, Charlotte shook her head. Pushing herself from her chair, she stood for a moment, willing her cramped muscles to respond. Upon hearing the slight creaking of the bedroom door, she straightened up.

"Miss Charlotte, ah's hyah now so why doan you gos an gits sum sleep?" Hattie placed a large wash pan, filled with warm water, on the nightstand.

"I'm goin' to, Hattie. Doctor Prichard say what time he planned on bringin' hisself out here?"

"Said he'd bes hyah fust thing dis mawnin," She lifted Tia's gown over her head.

"All right," she turned towards the door. "I'm gonna go lay down for a little while. Soon as he gets here though, you call me."

"Ah kin do dat," Hattie soaked a washrag in the wash pan before applying more soap. Wringing the soft cloth all but dry, she bent over, washing Tia's face, being careful not to get soap in the closed eyes. Clicking her tongue in sympathy she declared, "You po lil chile." She turned to dunk the cooled rag back into the water. "Effen yo' ma could sees you a-layin' hyah in dis bed lak dis," Hattie rinsed the soap from Tia's face, "she'd bes tuhnin' over in her grabe." With a soft towel, she dried Tia's face, picked up the nightgown she had ready on the chair, and opening the neck as wide as possible, placed it over Tia's head. "Ah swear you's jes' lak a lil rag dol." She lifted the limp arms one at a time into the long sleeves then pulled the gown into place, being careful to smooth out all the wrinkles.

Hattie brushed Tia's long hair until it crackled, laid the brush back down on the small nightstand. Satisfied she had done all she could do to make Tia as clean and comfortable as possible, she pulled the sheet up to her waist, to fold it neatly into place.

"How's our girl this morning?" Doctor Prichard pushed open the bedroom door.

"Ah sho kain sees no diffunce, doctah." Hattie removed any hair, clinging to the brush, to drop it into the small wastebasket.

"Pull those curtains, would you Hattie? We'll have a look anyway." Bending over the still form on the bed, he flicked a light across the unseeing eyes of his patient. As he saw a slight contracting of the pupils, he flicked the light again. "Tia, can you hear me?"

Tia...Tia...Tia... hear me...hear me...hear me..." The words vibrated through her skull, pulling her closer and closer towards the light. She spiraled through the darkness faster and faster, and the throbbing pain inside her head grew sharper with every beat of her heart. With a scream, torn from the very depths of her soul, Tia opened her eyes to the smiling face of a white man.

"Hattie! Help me hold her! She's got to come all the way out of it!" Prichard ordered, pinning a wild-eyed Tia to the bed.

"Gawdlmighty!" Hattie cried, leaning over and pressing down on Tia's thrashing legs. "Whut bes de matter wid her? She actin' lak she bes possessed or sumpin'!"

"She'll be all right as soon as she calms down enough to see her surroundin's. Tia. Tia, it's all right. You're safe. Ain't nobody gonna hurt ya."

"I am here, Aakiiwa. I will protect you from all harm," Appearing Wolf told her.

At the familiar sound of Appearing Wolf's deep voice, the terror left Tia's eyes, the wild thrashing ceased. Curling into a ball Tia placed her hand on her now empty stomach and allowed herself to give into her grief.

Unable to see the handsome warrior, standing by the bed, Doctor Prichard straightened up, rubbing the back of his neck.

"She's gonna be all right. Her pupils are dilated and there don't seem to be any paralysis of the limbs. I'd say she's a mighty lucky young miss. 'Course we don't know if her memory's been affected. That sometimes happens in cases like this. Time will tell about that. Right now, I think it'd be best, if we give her time to collect herself and get some rest."

"Rest!" Hattie's eyes widened in amazement. "Effen she had any mo' of dat, she'd bes Daid!"

"I mean normal rest. Healthy rest, so the body can begin to heal itself. In the meantime," he laid a hand on Tia's forehead, smiling as he felt the coolness touch his skin, "I think there's someone who'd be hard put to forgive us, if we don't wake her with this news."

"Amens, ter dat!" Hattie grinned, shaking her linen-wrapped head in agreement.

As the door closed behind Hattie and the doctor, Appearing Wolf pulled a sobbing Tia into his arms. "Now you know why my spirit could not rest. You are my woman, my bridge to the spirit world. I will never lose you."

"All our people, gone...our son...why? How could anyone hate that much, to destroy so...so..."

"The pain of that time is still fresh in your mind, little one. You must not allow this to grow. The Creator knows why you have been returned with the skin of our enemy. You must not fight against his wisdom. Your spirit is Blackfeet. This will give you the strength you will need to live as they have intended." He put her away from him and getting to his feet, stood for a moment looking down at her. "I must leave you now, Aakiiwa," he told her his voice filled with sorrow.

"No, Appearing Wolf." She reached out for him. "You cannot leave me now!" She struggled to reach him as hot tears streamed down her face.

"I cannot stay with you, my woman. The spirits are calling me. When they call your name, I will be the one who will come for you," he promised her.

At the sound of footsteps coming down the hall, Tia drew in her breath, trying to calm the fear threatening to overpower her. Looking to the tall warrior standing by her side, she watched in awe as he faded from her sight.

Within moments, the door flew open as Charlotte, followed by an excited Hattie, came rushing inside.

"Tia, child, you are awake. I wouldn't believe it until I saw it for myself," Charlotte chuckled, seating herself on the side of the bed.

"How long have I been asleep?" Tia asked, her cold voice little more than a whisper.

Something was wrong. Her granddaughter acted as though she feared her. Leaning forward, Charlotte made to gather the frightened girl into her arms then, drew back, as she saw her visibly recoil. A slight tremor shook the white head and the frail shoulders seemed to fall.

"Miss Charlotte", Hattie said hesitantly, "maybes Miss Tia'd lak sum of mah homemade vegetable soup. She wuz right partial ter it befo' she tuck sick."

"I think that would do nicely, Hattie," Charlotte replied, her worried gaze refusing to leave Tia's stricken face even for a moment. "Just some broth though. We want her to keep it down."

"Ah woan bes but a minute. Does you wants me ter brings you sum too?" Hattie asked standing by the door.

"No, you go ahead. I want to sit here a spell. I'll be all right." She shooed her away. "Go... on...and get the soup!"

Scooting off the bed Charlotte walked over to the closed window, and reaching down pulled up on the handle. A soft breeze flowed through the stuffy room, filling it with the scent of recent rain.

Tia watched her as she stood there looking out over the yard, taking in the neat trim figure, the full head of snow white hair braided down her back. A sweet memory filled her mind as she thought back to the beautiful young girl with the fiery red hair. That girl had never wished her harm in any way. Just as this woman, who tried so hard to hide her pain, had shown nothing but love. Of a sudden, the need to be cradled in those loving arms overpowered the dark fears and bitter memories.

"Gram!" Tia cried.

Afraid to hope, Charlotte turned around. The sight meeting her eyes left no doubt in her mind she was needed.

***

The loud honking of the car horn drew Jed's attention. Glancing out the window, he saw Doctor Prichard seated behind the wheel, waiting for him to come outside.

"Be right with ya!" he yelled, sloshing water over any remaining soap still lingering on his face. Grabbing a towel off the hook, he dried his face then picked up the wash pan to dispose of the dirty water. As he cocked back his hand, he spied a bar of soap, already turning to mush, lying in the middle of the pan. With a muttered curse, he plucked out the soap, dropped it on the windowsill, and tossed the dirty water out the door.

"What the hell could he want this hour of the mornin'?" Tom grumbled, pulling on his boots.

"Ain't no tellin." Jed grabbed his shirt off the back of a chair and headed out the door.

"Mornin', Jed," Prichard leaned his head out of the car window. "Glad to see you're up and about."

"'Bout half-assed. What's so all fired important?" He finished stuffing his shirttail into his jeans.

"Oh nothin' really." Prichard drummed ideal fingers against the car. "Just thought you'd like to know Tia regained consciousness earlier this mornin'."

Without waiting to comment, Jed took off for the ranch house at a dead run.

"Thought that'd put him in a better mood." Prichard laughed, as the old car came to life.

Tapping a light knock on Tia's bedroom door, Jed tried to hold on to his patience. Wanting to look his best for the girl who had captured his heart, he began shining the toe of his boots on the pant leg of his jeans when he noticed the cockeyed way his shirt hung. Jerking the shirt from the waistband, he righted the sloppy buttoning, then turned to the wall to undo his jeans. As his nervous fingers busied themselves with closing the last two buttons, Hattie pulled open the door. Thinking fast, Jed laced his fingers over the gap.

When she saw who stood waiting in the hallway, her broad face broke into a wide grin. "You waits right der, Mist' Jed," She pointed a finger at the floor, "an' ah'll go sees effen it bes awright fer you ter comes in." With an eager bob of his head, he finished closing his pants. Within moments Hattie came back to usher Jed inside. As he stepped into the room Jed knew, he had never seen a more beautiful sight than the one that greeted him now.

"Well look at you." He grinned over at her.

"Hello, Jed," Tia cast a bright smile as the young cowboy came forward.

"Girl, you sure have great timin." He dropped a light kiss on her rosy cheek. "They's all set to ship you back east."

"Jed," Charlotte spoke up from the chair beside the bed, "Tia don't need to be bothered with all that. She's all right now, that's all that matters."

"She's more'n all right," Jed delivered with a roguish grin.

"Yes, well, don't go tirin' her out with a lotta foolish nonsense. If you're gonna be here for a little while, Hattie'n me'll go get some breakfast."

"I couldn't think of anything more important than sittin' right here." He filled the chair Charlotte had vacated.

"I could," Charlotte grumbled, walking to the door, "and runnin' a ranch is just one of em."

Alone with Jed, Tia found she could still enjoy their former closeness. This good-natured man, with his teasing grin and warm heart, could never be like the ones who had destroyed her world.

"All right, Jed. Tell me all that has happened around here since I've been ill."

"There really ain't much to tell. Everyone's been so worried about you they ain't had time to do anything worth talkin' about."

"It's nice to know I have so many friends"

"I'll tell you one that should go right to the top of your list, and that's Wolfer. He's the one brought you back to the ranch after your horse threw you. I don't think he let more'n three days go by that he didn't ride over to check on you."

As she recalled the odd-dressed man, she had shared so many of her inner feelings with, a soft smile touched her lips. "Wolfer is a good man. I hope to see a lot of him before I leave."

"That case, you should get to know him pretty good. Doc. says you'll be here for a spell so he can keep an eye on you."

A thought crossed her mind that made her sit straight up in bed. "Has Grandfather Eathen returned yet?"

With unease, Jed confirmed her worst fears. "Eathen had just come back to the ranch when Wolfer brought you in."

"Oh no!" Tia caught her bottom lip between her teeth worrying it back and forth. "Is he very angry that I'm here?"

Leaning forward in the chair, Jed tried to make light of the serious problems going on in the Thornton household since Eathen's early return. "Eathen's your grandfather, Tia. He wants you to get well just like the rest of us."

Tia slumped back against the pillows. "Poor Gram. I've caused her so much trouble."

Jed had never been a convincing liar, and as he stared down at the pale girl lying before him, he knew better than to even try.

"I best be goin' now, Tia." He stood up from his chair. "The Thorntons don't pay me to sit around. You take care, you hear?" He patted her shoulder. "Maybe, if it wouldn't be too much trouble, I'll stop by after work to see how you're doin'."

"I would like that, Jed." She smiled up at him.

Closing the door with a quiet click, he stood for a moment trying to quell his anger before going downstairs. If he should run into his boss right at this moment, he couldn't be sure what would happen. Miss Charlotte already had enough problems. His beating the hell out of Eathen Thornton would just add one more.

***

Days slipped into weeks and still her grandfather had not come to visit her. Her strength returned much faster than the doctor had hoped, but he still refused to release her from his care. Seated before the open window Tia looked out over the yard, noting how the wind swayed the big oaks towering above the roof, their full green leaves seeming to mutter as they moved in the breeze.

At a slight tapping on the bedroom door, she turned to find her grandmother and Hattie watching her.

"Come in," she motioned them both forward. "I'm just sitting here enjoying the fresh air."

"It's such a nice day, I'm gonna let you go outside for a while. Do you feel up to gettin' dressed?" Charlotte grinned as she saw the bright smile lighting up Tia's dark eyes.

"I'd go with just a blanket wrapped around me if I had to," Tia told her.

"We kin do better'n dat." Hattie opened Tia's closet to take out one of her many dresses. "How's 'bout dis'n, Miss Tia?" she held up a light yellow dress of soft cotton. "You'll put de sun ter shame for sho effen you goes outside a-wearin' dis."

Laughing, partly at Hattie and partly because she felt so happy to be getting out of her room, Tia nodded her agreement on Hattie's choice of what she should wear. When fully dressed, Tia began making her way with slow steps down the wide staircase with Hattie walking behind her holding onto her waist and Charlotte walking beside her with Tia's arm held snug in her hand. Her legs felt a little shaky and she tried not to lean too much of her weight on Charlotte.

"Just a little further," Charlotte prompted. "We gotta chair already waitin' on the porch. I thought if you sat in the swing, the swayin' might make you sick."

"Thank you, Gram," Tia replied somewhat out of breath. The moment the fresh air and sunshine touched her, she felt her spirits lift. Seated in one of Charlotte's best, overstuffed chairs, a light blanket covering her legs, with her feet propped up on the porch banister, she breathed the fresh air into her lungs.

"There now," Charlotte stepped back to observe her granddaughter. "That's a lot better'n sittin' up in that stuffy bedroom, ain't it?"

"A lot better," Tia smiled. "I feel stronger already."

"Good. Hattie and I got some things we need to get finished, so I'll trust you to stay seated. If you should need anything just holler." She turned away, then stopped. "I almost forgot. Martha called earlier. I told her you was restin' so she said she'd call back tonight. Just thought I better warn you." She walked into the house.

Alone with the sweet smell of Charlotte's flower garden filling the air around her, Tia looked out over the well-tended grounds. So much had changed since her spirit had returned to the past. Even though in reality she had been back in the past less than a week, Appearing Wolf had been able to show her all the days of their life together. To her it had seemed like a lifetime.

Early summer had always been one of her favorite times of the year. The grass was lush and green and the sounds of honeybees buzzing around the many blossoms filled her with a sense of ease. The urge to walk around the ranch, to see all the changes not within her view, felt strong but she knew her strength had not returned enough for that yet. The weeks she had spent confined to her bed had weakened her considerably. Content with being out in the open, she leaned back in the chair allowing her body to relax.

She sat forward as the sounds of men's voices, raised in anger, floated to her on the breeze. One she recognized as being Jed's, the other sounded unfamiliar.

"I'm not oversteppin' anything!" Jed growled. "All I said, is it wouldn't hurt you to at least be civil to her while she's here!"

"You got enough to worry about with keepin' this ranch runnin', don't concern yourself with me and mine, Stanford!" the deep voice ordered.

"Somebody needs to goddamn it! You got Miss Charlotte almost crazy with worry, and she sure as hell don't need that, with the way she's been feelin' lately!"

"I'll take care of my wife! You just do the job you're bein' paid to do. If you can't do that, then by god I'll get someone who can!"

"Is that a threat, Eathen?"

"You take it any goddamn way you want! This is my spread and I'll run it the way I see fit! If that ain't to your likin', then pack your shit and get the hell off my property!"

For a moment, all turned silent. Then Jed's voice filled the air again. "It's damn lucky for you I have so much respect for Miss Charlotte. Otherwise you'd be lookin' for a new foreman."

As Tia sat listening to the hateful words filling the air she could feel her heart beginning to pound, knowing she was the reason for their contention.

Before she could move, she saw a man coming around the side of the house. When he saw her sitting there, he stopped, glaring up at her.

"I hope you enjoy all the trouble you're causin' 'round here!" Eathen growled.

Unable to speak Tia sat looking at the man she had waited all her life to meet. All she could do is gaze back at the cold hard eyes watching her.

"You just couldn't stay away, could you?" he snarled, walking up the porch steps towards her. "You hadda come out here and let everyone know whose whelp you are." He threw his hands up in the air. "Didn't matter how it would affect the rest of us."

"I don't understand your words," Tia whispered, one small hand going to her throat.

"No," he snorted a look of disgust covering his face, "I guess you wouldn't. They didn't teach you those kindda words at that fancy girl's school did they?"

"If you're referring to my parentage...," she began, then stopped as Eathen scoffed.

"Your parentage? Girl, you ain't got no parentage!" He spat the word at her his lips curled with distaste. "Because of you, your mother killed herself and your pa was just a filthy..."

"Eathen, that's enough!" Charlotte cried, stepping out onto the porch.

"No, Gram," Tia braced tight hands on the banister. "Let him finish."

"I'm warnin' you, Eathen." Charlotte grabbed hold of his arm.

"My father was a filthy what, Grandfather Eathen?"

"She's gotta right to know, Charlotte!" He shrugged her hand from his arm, "You been protectin' her from the truth for seventeen goddamn years!"

"All right, Eathen, go ahead," she told him, her soft voice taking on a steely edge, "tell her about her pa. While you're at it, you can also tell her where he is."

Eathen stood looking at the woman daring him to destroy her granddaughter's world. Then without a word, he turned away.

"Why did you stop him?" Tia slumped into her chair. "I want to know about my father."

"When I think the time's right," she watched Eathen slam into the house. "I'll tell you about your father, Tia."

"All this secrecy." Her hands twisted the light blanket in her lap: "What is the terrible wrong that everyone keeps hinting at?"

Charlotte seated herself on the porch banister. "I guess some would say he didn't do anything. But then, their daughter ain't the one he got in trouble."

"Is that why you and Grandfather Eathen hate him so much? Because he got my mother pregnant?" Tia's normally soft and quiet voice rose in its anger, "Do you really think they were the first couple to ever make love before being married?"

"No, that ain't why I think of him like I do." Charlotte tucked a straying wisp of hair back into place. "Desires of the flesh may not be an excuse, but it's a human weakness that can't always be stopped. I don't fault Jessie for givin' into him." She shook her head, the adamant motion giving conviction to her belief. "He knew he shouldn't touch a young girl too innocent to know better."

"I realize my being here is causing you a lot of trouble, Gram. As soon as Doctor Prichard releases me, I'll leave. There is one thing I will ask of you, and that is, before I go, I want to meet my father. Please, if you have any love in your heart for me at all, you won't begrudge me that one favor!"

"Sometimes, no matter how much we love someone, there are things that can't be helped. Trust me, Tia, you're better off not knowin' 'bout the man."

"Then you won't help me find him." She eased herself to her feet.

"I can't, Tia. I'm sorry, I just can't."

Later, up in her room, Tia thought about the vicious words her grandfather had said to her. He blamed her for her mother's death. Why? She hadn't asked to be brought into this world. How could a man who had amassed so much in his lifetime, be so illogical when it came to his family?

How can I stay in a house filled with so much bitterness? she wondered. *Grandfather Eathen has no love in his heart for me, and all because of something that could not be my fault. His heart is bitter at losing my mother, but I lost her too.* She beat her small fists on the bed. *Why can't he understand that? I should leave here, but who would be here to take care of Gram if I go? She needs me! I know she does. Besides,* she sat up in bed, wiping a hand across her face, *I can't leave until I find out about my father. Why do they keep hiding the truth from me?*

Words Appearing Wolf once said came back to her.

'The whites do not think like the Indian, Tia. They try to protect those they love by keeping silent. They do not know, that by keeping the words inside, they will gain more power until one day, they will rise to destroy them."

Chapter Twenty-Five

A sharp rapping on the front door brought Eathen to his feet. Flipping on the porch light, he opened the door to see who could be calling at such a late hour. When he saw who waited, he breathed a sigh of relief that he'd been the one to answer the door instead of Hattie. Within moments, the two men had shut themselves away in Eathen's den.

"What have you been able to find out, Simmons?" Eathen pushed a glass of his best whisky across the desk.

"It's just as you suspected," Simmons nodded, lifting the glass to his lips, "Hardiman's rakin' in quite a tidy little sum."

"That crooked son-of-a-bitch," Thornton leaned his chair back, propped his boots up on the desk.

"He ain't the only one at fault here, Eathen." He set the glass down on the desk. "The ones buyin' the beef are just as guilty. Guess this has been goin' on for some time." Simmons scratched his bald head, then reached again for his glass. "If you hadn't become suspicious, Hardiman would continue to work the government for all he can."

"So now what happens?" Eathen replenished his drink, holding the bottle uncapped for Simmons.

"Since we have to catch him in the act," he pushed his glass forward, "we're gonna need your help."

"The government sure as hell ain't gonna take the word of anyone on the reservation," Eathen snorted a deprecatory laugh. "I can guaran-goddamn-tee you that!"

"They can't, Eathen. It ain't been that long since we went to war against the Blackfeet."

"Some of us still are." Eathen swallowed the last of his drink.

The government-man glanced at the big rancher seated across from him, observing the anger glittering in his cold blue eyes. His ill feelings towards the Blackfeet came as no surprise to Simmons, although he could never pinpoint why he felt the way he did. He knew that as determined as Eathen was to catch the Indian Agent in the act of stealing from the government, that determination paled dramatically, compared to his malice towards the very people being starved because of Hardiman's thievery.

"We realize you don't have anything to lose by not helpin' us, Eathen. You already got your money."

"That's right, I do." Eathen drug his boots to the floor. "But Hardiman involved me when he started sellin' my cattle off the reservation. I'll do my part."

"Even if it means pretendin' to be friends with the Blackfeet?" He took a large swallow of his drink watching Eathen over the rim of his glass.

"My personal feelin's are nobody else's business, Simmons." Eathen eyed the other man, his voice taking on a razor-sharp edge. "You asked for my help on this and I told you I'd give it. If that ain't good enough for you," the chair squawked as he leaned forward, "then you're on your own."

"Just makin' sure I understand you, Eathen," Simmons stammered, pushing a pair of horn-rimmed glasses further back on his nose.

"Who the hell's the one that's been feedin' you all the information?" Eathen pulled his cigars from his vest pocket.

"An old man by the name of Pehta," Simmons told him, eager to take a cigar from the pack Eathen handed him, knowing the man only smoked the best. "Do you know him?"

"Yeah," Eathen withdrew one of the rum-soaked cigars, "I know him. I didn't know the old fart's still strong enough to travel all the way to Helena though."

"He ain't." Simmons sniffed the cigar with appreciation, then alternated the ends between his lips to dampen them. "He's workin' through a man called Wolfer."

"I shoulda guessed that son-of-a-bitch'd be involved," Eathen laughed, propping his feet back on the desk.

"Why's that?" Simmons started to bite the end off the cigar, then changed his mind his face flushed with embarrassment as Eathen pushed a Cigar Cutter across the desk.

"Old Pehta's the one who raised Wolfer." Eathen retrieved the Cigar

Cutter. "Found him wonderin' alone out on the prairie when he was just a snot-nosed kid." He dropped the end of the clipped cigar into the ashtray. "They're real close. If Wolfer says Hardiman's involved, that's good enough for me."

"What we got planned, is to send a couple of our men to Keyl, which as you know is in Teton County and outta Sheriff Wilk's jurisdiction, so he can't be of any help when things start gettin' heavy." He squinted at Eathen through the smoke. "We'll give them enough time to get pretty well-known around town, then they can put the word out they're lookin' for work." Simmons smiled, pleased with the plan he and his men had come up with. "Since they'll be stayin' at the local flop house, everyone'll figure they'll be willin' to settle for just about anything."

"Could work." Eathen tapped his ash into the ashtray, before settling back in his chair. "But, these men got one hellava business goin' here. They ain't apt to let just anybody in." He talked around the cigar clamped between his teeth. "The men you send up there are gonna have to look like the dregs of the earth."

"Not only are they gonna appear to be the dregs of the earth, they're gonna let it be known the one thing they hate worse'n starvin', is Indians."

"Where do I come in?"

"From what I understand, Wolfer's pretty well-known throughout the Northwest. It'd get too many tongues waggin' if he started makin' a lotta trips to the capital. He's already been seen there too many times of late as it is. What we're purposin', is for him to go to Keyl and gather as much information as he can, then pass it on to you."

"Now ain't a good time for me to be away." He dropped his feet to the floor. "Looks like you'll haveta get someone else."

"There is no one else, Eathen" Simmon's voice rose in his eagerness to make the man understand their quandary. "These people got spies everywhere. The one they're not gonna suspect is you, since you're a Legislator and expected to spend a lotta time there anyway. Hell, there for a while, you were spendin' almost all your time in Helena."

"I didn't realize my business was of such interest." He walked over to the window, his back ramrod straight, as he waited for the man to continue.

"Any man as rich as you will always be of interest, Eathen," Simmons laughed, the laughter sounding forced even to him. "You know that."

Eathen turned, glaring through the smoke at the nervous man watching him. "If you gotta point, I would suggest you make it."

"We need your help, Eathen." The man's face paled, as he tried to keep his voice even. "Don't make us force you to give it."

"Go on. I'm listenin'," Eathen seated himself on the edge of his desk.

Knowing the chance he took in angering a man as powerful as Eathen Thornton, Simmons searched his mind for the right way to say what he needed to. "We know about the son you keep hidden in Helena." Simmons hunched his shoulders in defeat. "We would rather not use this information, Eathen," his voice rose as he tried to inject as much bravado into the warning as his small stature and quivering continence would allow, "but if we need to we will."

"Are you sure you wanna to do that?" Eathen asked, his quiet voice sounding lethal to the edgy man watching him.

"No, Eathen, I don't want to do that." He lifted the bottle of whiskey in a shaky hand, slouching the liquor onto the desk as he tried to pour himself a much-needed drink, "But I gotta job to do. If I don't use all the means at my disposal, the government'll pull me off the case and assign it to someone else." He withdrew a starched handkerchief from his back suit pocket to start moping the spilled whiskey.

"My wife's been through a lot her of late." Eathen rubbed the back of his neck. "She don't need somethin' like this added to her problems."

"Then let's hope she never has to learn about it." Simmons heaved a long sigh, gauging the change in Eathen's tone.

"For your sake and the sake of anyone else involved," Eathen pinned him with a steely gaze, "you better pray she don't."

"As much as I hate to bring it up," he tried to control his harsh breathing, "there is one thing more we need to discuss."

"Let's hear it."

"I understand your wife and foreman went to pay Hardiman a visit a while back. I guess she accused him plain out of sellin' reservation beef."

"This is the first I've heard about it." Eathen said, visibly shaken. "I don't doubt it's true, knowin' my wife. Course," Eathen felt his anger rising to new heights as the face of his foreman shot into his mind. "I thought my foreman had more sense than to let her get involved in somethin' as dangerous as this."

"We can't afford to tip our hand," Simmons said, relieved to have Eathen's wrath directed at someone other than himself. "Not this late in the game. By her goin' out there and lettin' Hardiman know she suspects him," he declared, once more in control of the situation, "could blow this whole thing wide open."

"Don't worry. I'll talk to her."

"Then, I guess I've said all I came to say."

"If things work out the way you're plannin' this winter, the Blackfeet won't haveta worry 'bout goin' hungry."

"Does that really matter to you, Eathen?" Simmons turned to watch his reaction.

"Just money-wise." Eathen met his gaze. "Now that Charlotte has wind of what's goin' on, she won't rest until I send up more beef. The Blackfeet are a concern to me when there's money to be made. It ain't my place to feed em."

"I'm sure if need be, the government'll see to it you're compensated for any cattle sent to the agency."

"You're goddamn right they will. Problem is, my wife'll want them supplied now. All I'd be doin' is givin' Hardiman more beef to sell."

"I don't think he's that stupid, but it could be just the ticket we're lookin' for to make him show his hand."

"Then you best get your men situated in Keyl as soon as possible. I ain't about to go under for a bunch of worthless freeloaders."

"Too bad we couldn't talk Wolfer into takin' on the job as Indian Agent." Simmons picked up his hat. "If we could, all our problems'd be over."

"You'd be waistin' your time. Wolfer's a free spirit. He wouldn't settle for a permanent job. I offered him a job here on the ranch years ago. He just laughed and said, "Thanks, but no thanks."

"Must be the Indian in him," Simmons chuckled, walking out the door.

Alone, with Simmon's knowledge of his life in Helena running through his mind, Eathen didn't hear Charlotte enter the room until he glanced up to see her standing in the doorway watching him.

"Guess he told you about Jed's and my visit to the reservation," she murmured.

"Yeah, he told me. It seems like every time I turn around here of late, I hear about one more thing you've done to undermine me."

"Is that what you think I'm doin', Eathen?" She walked the rest of the way into the room.

His brows lifted as she seated herself in one of the chairs. "If you ain't, you're doin' a damn good imitation."

"Maybe it woulda been better if you'd stayed in Helena."

"I'm beginnin' to think you're right, Charlotte." He laced his fingers behind his head, pulled upward, trying to relieve the tense muscles in his neck.

"I guess forty-nine years of marriage don't mean much anymore." She drummed her fingers on the arm of the chair.

"You're the one who suggested I stay away." Eathen busied himself with clearing off his desk, trying to blot out the thoughts racing like a ricocheted bullet through his head.

At his cold tone she drew herself up straighter in her chair. "I've closed my eyes to the things you've put me through for a lotta years, Eathen. But no more." Her hands tightened on the chair trying to still her trembling. "I always told myself there had to be a streak of decency in you deep down. I don't care to search for it anymore."

"I always came back, Charlotte." Eathen turned sideways in the chair, trying to read what could be bringing all this on. Afraid, he might already know.

"Yes, but just when it suited you. The people of this county are moral, Christian people, Eathen. They couldn't wait to let me know what kindda man my husband is."

"Christians!" Eathen scoffed. "Those pious hypocrites wouldn't know a Christian act if it bit'm in the ass! Men have needs, Charlotte. Sometimes those needs can't always be satisfied at home," he growled, keeping his face turned away.

"Did you ever stop to think," she smacked her fist down hard on the arm of her chair, "women have needs too?"

"Your need for me ended a long time ago. We both know that. I'm gettin' old, woman!" he rolled his shoulders as the tension in his body mounted. "I don't have time to sit back and wait for life to come to me!"

"Does that give you the right to destroy my life in the process?" Charlotte wiped a hand across her eyes.

"I ain't no different now than I was almost eighteen years ago. Why are you makin' such a big deal about it all of a sudden?" Jerking open a desk drawer he pulled out the bottle of whiskey.

"Do you realize what you just said?" She walked over to stand beside him.

"Yeah, I said I ain't no different now than I was years ago." He unscrewed the cap, reached for a glass.

"No, Eathen. You said you ain' no different now than you was almost eighteen years ago." Charlotte leaned on the desk. "It's been close to eighteen years since we lost Jessie."

With the glass poised halfway to his mouth, he looked at her. Unable to believe so many years could have gone by when the wound in his heart still felt so fresh. Without a word he pushed the desk chair out of his way. But as he started to walk towards the door, Charlotte's next words stopped him.

"Why can't you admit how much Jessie's death has changed you?"

As he turned to face her, the anguish in his face almost made Charlotte reach out to him but she forced herself to remain still.

"Jessie's diein' ain't what destroyed me, woman. I died long before she did," Eathen laughed a bitter laugh. "I just ain't had the good grace to lay down yet."

Chapter Twenty-Six

Charlotte was sitting at the table finishing her coffee when the sound of a car door slamming out front brought her to her feet. "See who that is, Hattie and if it's Doctor Prichard, he can see Tia in the parlor. I'm in no mood to listen to any of his lectures today."

"Is Doctor Prichard giving you a hard time, Gram?" Tia dabbed a napkin at the corner of her mouth.

"No more'n usual. He wants me to come in for a checkup. Just wants to run my bill up's what it amounts to."

"You gots comp'ny, Miss Charlotte," Hattie glanced out the window. "Ah'll put de coffee-pot on."

"Well, who the hell is it?"

"It's me, Charlotte." replied a cheerful Sarah McKennah.

"Good God Almighty! Does Frank know you're out?" Charlotte grinned, pushing the chair beside hers back from the table.

"He had some business in town today, so I just made up my mind I was goin' visitin'. I don't think him and Jeremy were outta sight fore I jumped in the car and scooted over here. Thought you might enjoy some fresh baked Cherry Pie. Be careful," She set a large pie down on the table. "It's still hot."

"Tia," Charlotte tapped her granddaughter on the arm, "you ain't tasted pastry 'til you've tried some of Sarah's. This woman takes blue ribbons like nothin' you ever saw." She glanced in fondness at her friend.

"I must admit," Sarah seated herself at the table, "I do enjoy enterin' things at the fair. It gets me outta the house and Frank's always so proud when I win."

"As well he should be," Charlotte delivered with a fierceness echoing in her voice.

Tia had been sitting back listening to the exchange between her grandmother and Sarah McKennah. Her heart went out to this frail woman who was, so obviously, hurting. The memories Tia had of the destruction of the Indian camp helped to strengthen her total hatred of Frank McKennah.

"Tia," Charlotte nudged her, "Sarah asked you a question."

"I'm sorry, Mrs. McKennah." Tia turned, giving Sarah her full attention. "I guess I drifted elsewhere. What did you say?"

"That's all right, dear." Sarah flashed her a heart-warming smile. "I wondered how you're feelin'."

"I'm feeling much better. Thank you."

"Effen you ast me," Hattie scored the pie into four large pieces, then slid the end of the knife underneath one wedge. With a finger, holding the slice in place on the point, she transported the tempting dessert, all in one piece, onto one of the small plates she had ready and waiting on the table beside her. "Ah think you needs ter gits outta dis house fer aw'ile. It ain' right fer a chile yo' age ter bes cooped up wid two ole womens day affer day."

"Speak for yourself, Hattie." Charlotte shot her a sour glance. "But, since you brought it up, it ain't a bad idea. I'm sure Jed would be more'n happy to take you out to supper at one of them fancy restaurants over in Cut Bank." Charlotte chuckled, winking at Sarah.

"Please! Don't either of you ask Jed to take me anywhere!" she pleaded.

"Of course we won't, if you don't wanta go," Charlotte told her. "I just figured it'd be somethin' to do 'sides sittin' here bein' bored."

"Effen y'all want ter knows whut ah thinks," Hattie pushed her fork down on the last moist piece of crust on her plate. "Ah thinks whut bes needed hyah is a pahty. Wid eve'body in de county invited."

"Oh, Hattie, I think that's a wonderful idea!" Sara squealed. "Make it a real dress up affair!"

"For once, I think you got somethin', Hattie. Do you feel up to bein' around a bunch of boisterous cowboys and gigglin' women?" Charlotte took a bite of pie, rolling her eyes in appreciation.

In her heart she knew she would rather decline, but as her gaze fell on Sarah, whose sad brown eyes beseeched her, Tia concurred.

"Good! Now, all I haveta do's convince Eathen!" Charlotte stood, as she heard the slamming of the front door. "Hattie," she fixed the woman, gazing with longing at her empty plate, with a warning look, "I expect my pie to still be here when I get back."

Eathen had already made it half-way up the stairs when Charlotte called out to him.

"Eathen, do you have a moment?" she asked, her voice taking on a serious tone, "There's somethin' I wanna discuss with you."

Retracing his steps, he walked into his den. Closing the door with a quiet click behind them, Charlotte turned to find her husband watching her, an anxious look on his face. She noted the slight tremble in his hand as he poured them both a drink.

"What is it, Charlotte?" His voice sounded on edge, even to him.

"Eathen, is somethin' wrong?" She took a step toward him. "You seem upset."

"Do I have somethin' to be upset about, Charlotte?" He set the decanter back down with unnecessary force. "You asked to talk to me. Remember?"

"Have we grown so far apart we can't have an innocent conversation?" Charlotte murmured, stung by his callus tone.

"I have things to do, Charlotte. If you got somethin' to say, just say it, for Christ's sake."

"All right, Eathen, I will!" Charlotte's own voice grew cold. "What would you say to our thrown' a party? Before long the snow's gonna be here and everyone'll be shut in for the winter." She shrugged her frail shoulders. "I just thought it'd be fun to get together with our friends while we still can."

"That's it?" He stared at her in amazement. "That's what you wanted to talk to me about?"

As Charlotte nodded, Eathen could feel his taut muscles begin to relax. In a flood of relief he laughed. "Hell yes, you can throw a party, woman! I'll get hold of Wolfer, tell him to bring a fresh supply of whiskey down outta Canada right away and we'll throw a party the likes of which this county ain't seen in years."

"Thank you, Eathen." Charlotte patted her husband's hand as it lay on her shoulder. "This old house could do with some laughter, and it'll do Tia a world of good to hear it."

The moment she mentioned Tia's name she realized her mistake. The laughter disappeared from his face as he withdrew his hand. "I'm not doin' it for her, Charlotte."

"I know that, Eathen." Her heart constricted. "It's just that, with Tia I can reach out and hold a small part of Jessie. Please don't begrudge me that." She covered her mouth swallowing a sob.

Standing across the room, Eathen stared at the woman who had shared the better part of his life. And as much as he fought against it, the face of the woman who waited for him in Helena crept into his thoughts. Almost without realizing it, his mind slipped back to the first time he had seen her, almost sixteen years ago.

He had been in Helena working with the Legislature on a new law Montana hoped to get passed, giving the state complete control over the mineral rights. One of the legislators, a man by the name of Terrance Martin, invited him to a dinner one evening in celebration of his daughter Pamela Ann's thirty-first birthday. Eathen found himself taking an instant liking to the beautiful young woman. She had a way of looking at him that made him feel young again. Before either of them knew what had happened they found themselves in love. Eathen tried many times to end the affair, but within weeks of his return to the ranch and Charlotte, the memory of a green-eyed, raven-haired woman with the whitest skin he had ever seen, called him back. When she told him she carried their child, Eathen finally admitted to himself, he had lost the battle to put her aside. As much as he hated to deceive Charlotte, he could not bring himself to give up the one person who made him feel as though life decided to give him another chance. After the birth of their son, Eathen bought a house in Helena for his new family. With all his heart he wanted nothing more than to give his son his rightful name, but even he didn't feel that brave. Pamela Ann never complained about being hidden away. She kept their house clean and inviting and waited to greet him every night he came home. With Pamela Ann in his life, he no longer had any desire for the nightlife he had always enjoyed before. She and their son became the most important people in his life and they made his life complete. Still, he couldn't bring himself to leave Charlotte. She couldn't be blamed for the double life he had chosen. All he could hope is that Charlotte never learned of Pamela Ann, or their son Charles Eathen, who now shared his world in Helena.

As he stood looking at the woman who still reached out to him, after all he had put her through, his mind raced with the knowledge he had fallen out of love with her. His life now centered around the woman he cherished, and their son, who so resembled Jessie it made his heart ache to leave him.

"You got your party, Charlotte. I may not be here to enjoy it with you, but I'll see to it that it'll be one to remember."

With the party a mere two days off, Charlotte made up her mind the old house would be cleaned from top to bottom. A task Hattie did not feel agreeable to.

"Ah doan knows how you specs us ter gits dis house ready fer a pahty in jes' two days." She looked around the disassembled room. "Sides dat, wid all de people you gots invited, it jes' gwine ter gits messed up agin anyways."

"If you'd do more cleanin' and less bitchin' we'd be through," Charlotte blew a damp strand of hair out of her face. "Did you get the silver polished like I asked you?"

"Ah ain' even had times ter wash up de breakfast dishes let alone git ter de silverwares." Her eyes flashed with anger on her behalf.

"Gram, I can polish the silver," Tia spoke up. "I'm feeling much better, and if I can attend a party I can very well do something to get ready for it."

"I guess you could do that," Charlotte looked around the untidy room. "Now I know why we ain't had a party here in so long. It takes so damn long to get ready for it."

"What the hell's goin' on here?" Eathen growled, standing in the doorway.

"It's called cleanin', Eathen. We can't give a party in a house that ain't ready," Charlotte said.

"No one gives a damn about the house. They're just concerned with how much free liquor and food they can get."

"I can't argue with you there, Eathen. Still, I won't be comfortable until everything's just right."

"Then, get on the phone and get Jed's ass up here with some of the hands. I don't want you movin' this heavy furniture."

"How sweet of you to concern yourself, Eathen." She patted his cheek as she walked past him. "I don't know why I didn't think of it."

"While you're at it, why don't you call Sarah and some of the other women to come over and lend a hand? Wouldn't hurt any of them to pitch in for once." As he passed the dining room he noticed Tia seated at the table. "What the hell's she doin' down here?" He swung his head in Tia's direction. "I thought the idea is to get her well so she can leave."

"That's enough, Eathen," Charlotte told him. "Tia's well enough to be downstairs. She offered to help and I appreciate it."

"I suppose you're gonna let her attend the party, too." He threw up his hands in disgust. "Might as well let everyone in on the family secrets! Right?"

"I'm not ashamed of my granddaughter. Besides, she's already attended the spring dance, so she's acquainted with everyone who'll be here anyway. What's one more party gonna hurt?"

"Is there no goddamn limit to what you'll do to embarrass me?" He stood, his legs spread wide, glaring at her.

"Tia's a beautiful girl. You don't have any reason to be ashamed of her." She picked up her dust rag. "Now if you don't mind we got work to do."

For a moment, Eathen remained standing, then shaking his head he continued on his way through the room.

"Maybe I should go back upstairs, Gram. I'm sorry." Tia bit her lip in an effort to keep from crying. "I didn't think he would be coming in this early."

"You stay right where you are." Charlotte shook a finger at her. "That silver ain't gonna polish itself and it needs to be done. Just ignore your grandfather. I do!"

"Ah doan know why she puts up wid his bad seff." Hattie shook her linen-wrapped head in amazement.

"It's plain to see why, Hattie. She loves him."

"He doan deserves it." Hattie cocked her head to the side in her anger, "Ah knows dis ain' any of mah bizness, but yo' comin' hyah ain' de reason he treats her lak he does. Mist Eathen ain' been de same since he found out yo' ma wuz spectin' you."

"You're right, Hattie, we shouldn't be discussing my grandparents behind their back. I realize you are telling me these things to make me feel better, but their problems are better left alone." Tia turned back to the table, then as a thought flashed through her mind, she turned back to Hattie. "There is something I would like to know about though."

"Whut's dat, chile?" Hattie leaned closer.

"Why did they feel the need to send my mother away, when she needed them so much?"

"It ain' up ter me ter tells you 'bout dat, chile. Dat bes Miss Charlotte's place." Hattie busied herself with wiping down the china closet.

"Time you got busy doin' up the dishes, Hattie," Charlotte walked into the room.

As Hattie turned away, Tia began removing the sliver from its velvet-lined case to lay it down on the table. "Please don't be harsh with her, Gram. I asked her about my mother. She didn't tell me anything."

"What goes on between your grandfather and me is our business. I won't tolerate idle gossip." She ran a damp cloth across the inside of the silver case.

"I don't mean to create problems while I'm here, Gram, but I want to know about my parents. If someone is willing to help me, I won't hesitate to ask."

"I can't fault you for that, Tia. You're strong-willed just like your mother was." Charlotte heaved a deep sigh. "But, I'd appreciate your not makin' any more trouble for me just now. I got more'n I can handle already."

"All right, Gram. You have my word. I won't create problems, but I want your word on something too."

"What is it, Tia?" She turned toward her.

"I want your word that before I leave here, you'll tell me about my father."

"All I can do is give you my word that I'll do the best I can 'bout the matter. Now, Jed and some of the hands'll be here in a moment to help with movin' the furniture, so I suggest you keep yourself out here at the table outta the way." Charlotte pushed her down in the nearest chair. "Jed has a hard time concentratin' on what needs to be done when you're around." Charlotte chuckled.

On impulse Tia reached out, hugging her grandmother close, "I love you, Gram."

"I love you too, Tia," Charlotte returned her granddaughter's show of affection. "Now be a good girl and get the hell outta the way!"

"Yoo hoo! Charlotte!" called Sarah McKennah. "We've come to help!"

"Who's we?" Charlotte breathed, turning her attention to the new arrivals.

"Thought you could use an extra hand, Miss Charlotte," Jeremy McKennah grinned, ushering his grandmother through the door.

"When I mentioned I wanted to come over and help you get the house ready for the party, Jeremy insisted on comin' along." Sarah patted her grandson's face. "He's such a dear boy."

"You must be proud!" Charlotte eyed the young man standing before her.

"Miss Tia." Jeremy smiled, walking across the room to drop a smart bow. "I hoped I'd see you. It's plain to see you've recovered quite nicely."

"Thank you, Jeremy." Tia pulled her hand from his, feeling the same revulsion she had felt when he had kissed her hand at the dance. "I'm feeling much better.""

"Well. Well." Jed hung his work-worn Stetson on the coat rack. "First time I've known you to lend a helpin' hand, McKennah."

"I try'n make it a point to be where I'm needed." Jeremy stood with a possessive closeness to Tia's chair.

"That case there's no need to wait around." Jed kept a well-placed smile on his face, "I'll be glad to give Miss Sarah a ride home when we're through."

"Wouldn't think of puttin' you out, Stanford. Jeremy turned his attention to Charlotte, "What can I do to help?"

"You can help the men move all this outside onto the porch," she threw out a hand, encompassing all the heavy furniture. "God willin', it won't rain 'til we're through in here."

"That's all right, Miss Charlotte." Jed picked up a chair to haul it outside. "The boys and me can handle it. We wouldn't want Jeremy to risk gettin' a blister on them lily white hands of his."

"Why thank you, Stanford, that's right thoughtful of you." He pulled a chair up close to the one Tia occupied. "Guess since I'm not needed, I'll just sit here and keep Miss Tia company."

Knowing in what direction all this would end up, Charlotte stepped between the two combatants. "That's enough outta you two," she told them. "If I'd wanted a cock fight, I woulda ordered one. Now, get busy haulin' this furniture outside."

***

Hattie placed a large punch bowl filled with cider in the center of a long, linen-draped table. "Doan look lak Mist' Eathen's gwine ter meks it back in time, do it?"

"I didn't really think he would," Charlotte murmured, her blue eyes watching the front door. "By stayin' away, he won't haveta watch his neighbors drinkin' his liquor and enjoyin' themselves at his expense.

"Effen he bes worrit 'bout dat, why'd he agrees ter a pahty in de fust place?" She cut thin slices of a large red apple into the bowl.

"To humor me, I guess. Tell you the truth, I think his takin' this trip to Helena, at the last minute's, just another excuse to be outta the house."

"Den ah twouldn't lets it bodder me effen ah waz you." She bent her head close to Charlotte's. "We wuked extry hard roun' hyah a-gittin' eve'thing ready. We's gwine ter enjoys it."

"You're right, Hattie, we should." Charlotte looked around the crowded room, noting the gleaming hardwood floor skirting the large, Spanish-print rug, she herself had helped to beat the dust out of. The scent of Lilacs setting in large vases on the mantel mixed with the smells of wood polish drifted over to her. Charlotte smiled, taking pride in her home. "I thought Jed'd be here by now. Never knew him to stay away from a chance to dance the night away. 'Specially, now that Tia's here."

"Well, dat McKennah boy sho ain' a-wastin' no time," Hattie nodded.

Following her line of vision, Charlotte frowned as she saw the young man in question waltzing her granddaughter around the crowded parlor.

"I didn't even see him come in." Charlotte brushed flour from the sides of Hattie's black satin dress, hoping she wouldn't find more. "If he's here Sarah and Frank can't be far behind."

"Yo' right. Hyah come Miss Sarah," Hattie stretched her neck, trying to see over the crowd of people. "Ah doan sees Mist' Frank though."

"Charlotte, just look at this turnout." Sarah reached out taking hold of Charlotte's hand. "And everyone looks beautiful," she said watching the women dressed in soft summer dresses being swung around to the beat of the music by men slicked up and dressed in their finest for the occasion.

"And look at you," she said as Sarah twirled showing off her new dress of pale pink satin. "Where's Frank?"

"Believe it or not, Frank couldn't come tonight." She touched a hand to her upswept hairdo. "He started ailin' earlier this afternoon. Said he better not try'n make it."

"That's a first!" Charlotte checked to make sure her white silk blouse remained tucked into the waistband of her black velvet skirt. "With both Eathen and Frank gone, this party could turn out to be a happy occasion after all," she quipped, straightening her black, bolero jacket.

"It might at that!" Sarah gave Charlotte a brief hug. Dropping her voice to a conspiratory whisper, she directed Charlotte's attention across the room. "Looks like Jeremy's enjoyin' hisself. Wouldn't it be somethin' if him and Tia took to each other?"

"Sarah," she looked up at the woman envisioning her granddaughter's life, "if Tia took a likin' to Jeremy, I gotta admit, that'd do it for me!" Charlotte shook her head in amazement.

As the song drew to a close, Jeremy twirled her around one more time. The movement giving him a nice view of the slender calves of her legs as her full-flowing, white rayon dress whirled around her.

"Thank you, Jeremy." Tia stepped from McKennah's embrace. "I'm going to get something to drink. I noticed Gram talking with your grandmother by the buffet. I think this would be a good time to join them."

"That's a good idea, Tia." He tucked her small hand in the crook of his arm. "I'll join you."

"I thought Jed would be here by now." She looked around the crowded room as one hand toyed with the small set of pearls encircling her throat. "I wonder what could be keeping him?"

"I swear, your grandparents got to be the exception to treat the hired help like they do." Jeremy smoothed his thick, curly hair, turning his head this way and that as he caught his reflection in the large mirror hanging above the buffet table. "You sure wouldn't find a McKennah sharin' an evenin' with the stable hands."

"Gram and Grandfather Eathen don't think they're better than others, Jeremy." Her soft voice took on an angry tone. "Everyone on this ranch does a good job. My grandparents appreciate their worth." She pulled away.

"I didn't mean to offend you, Tia," Jeremy became contrite. "I just meant, Stanford needs to know his place."

"I know what you meant, Jeremy," she said, her anger becoming sharper. "Jed is one of the nicest people I know, and I looked forward to his being here tonight. I'm sure Gram did too."

"Come on now," Jeremy ran a light hand down her arm, refusing to be put off. "Let's not let someone as insignificant as a mere foreman ruin our evenin.'"

"I think it's too late for that, Jeremy." Tia replied, before walking away.

As he watched her disappear into the crowd, McKennah could feel his anger, at her refusal to be brought around, spin out of control. Walking behind the well-stocked bar, he grabbed a full bottle of whiskey.

Placing it beneath his suit coat, he continued on his way through the swinging kitchen door. At the sight of a young black girl, Charlotte had hired to help out for the evening, his cold blue eyes took on an unholy light.

"Vada Lee," his usual high-pitched voice, deepened, "I sure didn't expect to find you here tonight," he grinned, pulling her up tight against him. "I got a feelin' my luck just changed for the better."

"Mist' Jeremy, please." Vada Lee pushed against his strong chest, turning away as he brought his face close to hers. "You knows my maw'd whup me good effen she was ter comes in hyah an' ketch us."

"Then, let's go where she won't find us," McKennah pulled her out the back door.

Once away from the house, he picked her up in his arms and after a quick glance around moved off into the night.

"Mist' Jeremy, I kain do dis." She began to struggle against him. "Sumbody'll come lookin' fer me."

"You just let me worry about that," he panted, standing her on her feet, pulling her thin dress up and over her head.

As the cool air touched her bare skin she shivered. "Ah doan wanter. I wanter gos back inside," She started to cry bending down to pick up her dress.

His hands shot out, grabbing her own and curling his fingers over their immature slimness. "You don't mean that, Vada Lee. Why, I could have my pick of any one of those girls inside," he nodded toward the gaily lit house, "but you see where I'm at. Don't you? I'm here with you." His labored breath bathed her sensitive nose in a hot, sour odor. "Now, stop pretendin' you don't want it. You're wastin' time."

"Ah ain' pretendin'! Ah doan wanter bes hyah."

Releasing her for a moment, he reached into his suit pocket, withdrawing the bottle of whiskey he had stolen from the bar and unscrewed the cap. "Take a drink of this," he held the bottle up to her mouth, "It'll warm ya."

"No!" she slapped the bottle away. "Lets go of mah dress. Ah's goin' back inside!"

Bringing the bottle up to his own mouth, McKennah drank long and deep. As he screwed back on the cap he stood looking at the young girl shaking and shivering in the cool night air. "I didn't want it to have to be this way, Vada Lee." He tossed the bottle onto the grass. "I didn't bring you all the way out here just to let you go, though."

"Doan hu't me, Mist' Jeremy," she pleaded with him, wrapping her small arms around herself. "Jes' lets me gos! Ah woan tells nobody. Honest ah woan!" she cried, backing away.

"Oh, I know you won't, Vada Lee." Jeremy wiped a hand across his mouth as he moved towards the frightened girl. "Ain't no one gonna know 'bout you bein' anywhere near me this night. And I'll give you fair warnin'," Jeremy said, enjoying the terror in her wide dark eyes, "If you scream I'll kill you. All you have to do is be a good girl and share some of this good whiskey with me and let me cuddle you a little, then I'll let you go."

The girl watched him almost afraid to breathe as McKennah unbuttoned his pants. Knowing she needed to get away from him she turned to run. Jeremy grabbed her by the hair and slung her to the ground. Kneeling over her he drew back his hand to deliver a vicious slap across her face. The small girl went limp, all the fight gone from her now as she gazed up at the harsh-breathing man above her.

Without any thought to the young girl lying spread-eagled beneath him, he lunged, invading where no man had ever been before. The sharp scream bubbling up from her throat was silenced as he clamped his hot mouth over hers.

She thought he would never be finished as she lay on the hard ground beneath the rutting animal driving himself again and again into her tortured body. At last she felt him slump forward, then lay still.

Rolling from the young girl trying to control her crying, McKennah rose to his feet to rearrange his clothing. When he felt satisfied his appearance showed none of the dalliance he had been entertaining himself with, he looked down at her, a wide grin splitting the corners of his thin mouth.

"You need to get up and dress yourself, Vada Lee. Ain't your mama ever told you that's a good way to catch your death?"

Staggering to her feet, she stood still ignoring the blood running down her legs in a steady stream. In silence, she stooped to pick up her dress. Steeling herself against the pain she pulled the dress down over her throbbing thighs, brushing her shaking hands down the sides in a vain attempt to lengthen its meagerness with the sound of McKennah's laughter ringing in her ears. At that moment something snapped inside her mind and a strange coldness crept over her. With her dark eyes flashing fire she turned on him.

"You think yo' gwine ter gits away wid whut you done ter me. Well you ain! Jes' as soon as ah gits inside, ah's gwine ter tells eve'body whut you did ter me!" her young voice, devoid now of its fury, dropped to a low whisper. "Yo' nuthin' but filthy w'ite trash! Nuthin' but filthy w'ite trash."

As she turned to run, McKennah reached out grabbing the back of her dress to yank her back to him. She had but a moment's glimpse of madness before his fist began raining their destructive blows on her face and head. When at last he allowed her small broken body to slip to the ground, twelve-year-old Vada Lee Coals was beyond feeling anything, anymore.

Chapter Twenty-Seven

Keeping well-hidden back amongst the trees, the men watched and waited, as the lengthening shadows of night grew ever darker.

"I hope to hell we didn't miss a great party to wait out here all night for nothin," Jed growled.

"Wolfer said tonight's the night. I trust him to know what's goin' on," Eathen replied.

"I can't believe Hardiman's this fuckin' greedy." Jed loosened his feet from the stirrups, stretching his legs out straight. "Hell, it's just been…what…a few weeks since we sent them cattle up here?"

"If Hardiman had any sense, he wouldn't be involved in this shit in the first place. Which calls to mind somethin' I been meanin' to discuss with you." Eathen stared over at him. "I understand you took Charlotte with you when you came up here a while back. What the hell were you thinkin' to pull somethin' that stupid? You knew we already suspected him."

Turning in the saddle Jed stared into the inky darkness. "Yeah, I knew, but you gotta remember, this is your wife we're talkin' about. When she gets somethin' in her head, there's no talkin' her out of it. Believe me, I tried."

"You gotta point, still…."

The sentence went unfinished as Jed cautioned him to silence.

"Somebody's comin."

"Thornton?" someone called out in a low voice.

"Yeah, over here," Eathen replied.

Within moments, three riders rode up beside them, the sounds of creaking leather echoing in the still darkness.

"We started thinkin' you had decided not to show," Eathen said.

"I had to wait for Pehta. He thought it best we wait 'til dark, 'fore tryin' to leave," Wolfer told him.

"I brought twenty of the hands. Figured that'd be enough. How many you think'll be comin'?"

"No more'n ten or fifteen, and about five trucks," Simmons spoke up. "I suggest we let'm get the cattle loaded and start to drive off, fore we make our move. That way, we got our proof."

"All right, here's the plan," Eathen delivered. "There's to be no shootin' less they leave us no choice. The government wants these men alive. 'Specially Hardiman."

"Keep in mind, the worst thing you could do for any of them is to let them spend about ten hard years in the federal prison. Killin' them would just put'm outta our misery and theirs," Simmons cautioned.

"Hardiman deserves to die," Pehta said in a clear voice. "He' is a white man and he will be judged by a white man. If we do not kill him, he will go free."

"What happens to Hardiman or any of the rest of'm, ain't no concern of yours," Eathen growled. "Wolfer! You see to it he keeps a cool head, or you'll answer to me when this is all over."

"I don't like threats, Eathen. From you or anyone else," Wolfer breathed, anger at Eathen's treatment of Pehta and himself, apparent in his cold voice. "I came out here at the government's request not yours. Pehta's gotta right to be pissed off at Hardiman. He's done nothin' but treat him and his people like shit for years."

"I ain't arguin' that. I'm sayin' we don't need no hotheaded Indian 'round when trouble starts! Goddamn it!"

"Quiet, all of you! Here they come!" Simmons ordered.

Five sets of headlights shown through the trees. Caught in the glaring beams, the nervous cattle moved around the small pen, bawling their fear and calling out to each other as the trucks moved closer.

Breaks left over-long without repair, squawked in protest as the old trucks groaned to a stop. Loud creaking could be heard as the men in the trucks pushed against rusted hinges.

"That's good. Now, I want you to pull up, then back it almost even with the pen," one of the men called out. "Right where you see this lantern's where you'll stop."

"Rigby," another man spoke up, "get over here and get these lanterns lit."

"You need to keep your voices down," Hardiman whispered looking around. "Ain't no tellin' who could be roamin' 'round out here."

"Relax, Hardiman," Rigby pushed his voice low in his throat, curling his fingers and creeping forward with his hands held high. "Ain't nobody out here 'ceptin' us cattle rustlers."

"You never can tell." Hardiman withdrew a plug of tobacco from his coat pocket. "The way them goddamn heathens sneak about," he bit off a large plug, "one could be right under your feet, and you wouldn't know it 'til ya tripped over the son-of-a-bitch."

"You needen worry 'bout that." Rigby broke off a piece of the sticky tobacco before Hardiman had a chance to put it back in his pocket. "Hell you'd smell'm, 'fore they got fifty feet from you."

"I don't like this. Somethin' just don't feel right." Hardiman wagged a finger in the air. "I still think we should wait. Thornton'll be checkin' to make sure everythin's all right up here. What the hell am I supposed to tell him?"

"Same thing you told him every other time, you simple fucker," Rigby wiped a stream of brown juice from his chin with the back of his hand. "Thornton don't give a shit 'bout these people. All he cares about's the money he collects every time the government needs more beef."

"I don't care what you say, Rigby," Hardiman pulled the collar of his old, wool coat up higher around his neck, "somethin' don't feel right. I still think we shoulda waited, like I wanted to."

"The boss said we move'm tonight. That's good enough for me."

"Ain't he comin?" Hardiman's voice roughened with anger. "Or's he plannin' on leavin' me here to handle all this shit?"

"He'll be along," Rigby turned up the wick in a large lantern, snickering to himself, as a loud "whoof" followed the lighting of the fuel oil making Hardiman jump. Reaching out he lifted another lantern down off the truck. "Hell, this whole cattle stealin' business was his idea in the first place. He knows Uncle Sam's never in any hurry to pay for what he gets. So, the way he's got it figured," he turned up the wick, lit the lantern, "if the government keeps a runnin' tab on Thornton beef, with a few more heads goin' out and nothin' comin' in, Thornton'll go under. He wants to be here to watch the decline."

"Yeah, well just so I don't decline along with him, I best be gettin' my money." He stuffed his gloved hands into his pockets. "After tonight, I'm outta here. Thornton ain't a man I wanna tangle with. The boss can enjoy that pleasure all by hisself."

"You ain't plannin' on leavin' just when the end's in sight, are ya,

Hardiman?" breathed a deep male voice.

Spinning around, the Indian agent looked up into the laughing face of Frank McKennah.

"You're goddamn right I am." Hardiman pulled a soiled handkerchief from inside his coat, and despite the frigid temperature wiped the sweat beading in small pools across his forehead. "Thornton ain't done nothin' for me to try'n ruin him. If you gotta burr in your ass for him, that's between you and him. I ain't gotta fuckin' thing in this, McKennah. All I want's the money I got comin'."

"Don't worry, Hardiman. You'll get what's comin' to you," McKennah said. Turning his attention to the waiting men, he swung his arm in a wide circle. "Let's load'm up!"

"That two-faced son-of-a-bitch!" Eathen growled. "It's gonna be a pleasure puttin' that bastard away."

"Just stand easy," Simmons cautioned him. "We're almost ready to make our move."

"In all the years I've known that worthless piece of shit, I never figured him to do somethin' like this."

"Jealousy can make a man do a lotta things," Jed spoke up, kneeing his horse forward.

"His wife's Charlotte's best friend," Eathen told Simmons "I sure don't look forward to tellin' her about this."

"They're loaded. Let's get ready. Besides Hardiman and McKennah, my three men are the ones ridin' horses," Simmons told them. "Wait 'til they ride off to the side, 'fore we show ourselves."

"Pass the word we're fixin' to move out," Eathen told Jed.

As the loaded trucks roared to life, Eathen and his riders moved from cover.

"You can stop right there, boys," Simmons called out to the surprised men. "It's all over."

"What the hell...," McKennah wheeled his horse, as he saw himself and the others being surrounded.

"Might as well give it up, Frank," Eathen advised in a calm voice, riding towards him. "You ain't goin' nowhere."

"Fuck you, Thornton!" Frank yelled, kicking his horse forward. "You ain't man enough to take me!"

When McKennah drew even with him, Eathen leaped from the saddle knocking a surprised McKennah to the ground. Tumbling over each other, the men rolled out of the way of their skittish mounts.

Yanking McKennah to his feet, Eathen drew back smashing one large fist into the snarling man's face. "You son-of-a-bitch!" he panted, grabbing him up by the back of his shirt to haul him to his feet. "After all I did for you! Feedin' your family through hard winters, then you'd dare do this to me? I oughta kill you!"

Kicking out, McKennah landed a heavy boot square in the middle of the other man's stomach. Doubling forward, Eathen fell to the ground, unable to get up.

"You ain't gonna kill nobody! You arrogant son-of-a-bitch! But I am!" Frank snarled, drawing his gun. But before he could pull the trigger, a shot rang out slamming him to the ground.

All eyes turned, as Pehta dismounted to walk forward a smoking rifle still in his hand. Looking down at the man lying unmoving on the cold ground, Pehta declared, "No more will you starve our people for your own greed. Never again, will you boast of the lives you took all those many years ago. The spirits of my people are waiting, white man. Go to them, now."

Moving the old Indian out of the way, Jed knelt down to check the seriousness of McKennah's wound. Rising to his feet he shook his head. "He's dead. Couple of you boys tie him on his horse, so we can take him home."

Staggering to his feet, Eathen stood looking at the man who had tried his best to destroy him. With a low growl, he told him. "You got off easy, Frank. Deer Lodge woulda loved you."

"Thornton!" A wheezing Hardiman hastened to stand beside Eathen. "You gotta listen! None of this was my idea!" He tugged on Eathen's coat. "I told all of them just leave me outta this! But they wouldn't listen!" His small eyes rolled with terror. "You gotta help me, Thornton!"

Shrugging the whining man's hand from his arm, Eathen turned on him. "Get away from me, you gutless bastard! At least be man enough to admit your involvement in all this!"

"But...but... I didn't do anything, Thornton," he cried in his behalf, as the government men led him away.

Eathen lifted his foot into the stirrup and pulling himself into the saddle turned his attention to where Jed, already mounted and waiting, watched him. "Let's get the hell outta here." He smacked his horse with the reins. As Jed fell in beside him, Eathen watched as Simmons mounted then reached out, taking the reins of McKennah's horse to lead him away.

***

"I still can't believe it," Charlotte murmured, shaking her head.

"The more I think about it, I don't find it all that hard to understand. The two good ones in that whole family is Little Frank and Sarah. How's she holdin' up?" Eathen asked.

"I don't know," Charlotte shrugged her shoulders. "I didn't get to talk to her. When I called earlier, Jeremy said she was restin'. I told him I'd try again later."

"Looks like Sheriff Wilks out front," Eathen glanced out the window. "I'll go see what he's found out. Goddamn!" He strolled to the door. "What a night!"

"Mornin', Eathen." Wilks walked up the front porch steps.

"Wilks," Eathen said, "any news yet 'bout last night?"

"Not a hellva lot, he dropped down in the swing, "No one at the party remembers seein' her leave with anybody. It's too bad," He pulled a plug of tobacco from his shirt pocket, stuffing a large wad in his mouth. "Whoever the son-of-a-bitch is that raped and killed her needs to be caught. We don't need someone like that runnin' round the county."

Eathen settled himself against the porch banister. "You'd think with somethin' that vicious, the one who done it'd be scared up. I knew that little girl. She wouldn't give in without a fight."

"I don't know what this county's comin' to, Eathen." He worked the plug of tobacco to the side of his jaw. "We ain't hadda funeral around here in over three years. Now we got two of'm to attend."

"Maybe you do. I got one," Eathen removed a cigar from his vest pocket, "Fanny Coals is a good woman. I'll see to it her little girl's laid to rest proper." He bit off the end of the cigar, spit it over the banister. "As for McKennah!" Eathen brought a lit match to the tip of the cigar, puffed for a moment, then blew a stream of smoke into the air. "That son-of-a-bitch could rot out on the prairie for all I give a shit."

"How's Miss Charlotte takin' it?"

"Not very good. She never liked Frank any more'n I did, but she cares an awful lot for Sarah."

"Well, I best get back to work." He stood up from the swing. "Some government men are comin' by later this afternoon to take Hardiman and that bunch off my hands. Guess my deputy put the fear of God in Hardiman."

"Oh? How's that?"

248

"He told him there are about eighteen Blackfeet incarcerated up at Deer Lodge, and what he could expect when he got there." Wilks laughed, his big belly shaking beneath his shirt. "That poor little bastard got so scared," he hawked a wad of spit over the banister, drew a hand across his mouth, "he pissed his pants standin' right there in his cell."

"He ain't got no one to blame but himself." Eathen knocked the fireball from his cigar. "Thievin' little fuck!"

"I'll keep you posted on Vada Lee's murder," Wilks stepped off the porch. "Ain't a person in the county'll be safe 'til we catch him."

"It just makes me sick to think what that poor child went through." Charlotte filled Eathen's cup, setting the coffeepot down on the potholder. "And right here on our own property, no less."

"Ah kain unnerstan' why nobody heared nuthin." Hattie stirred a spoon of sugar into her coffee.

"We had music playin' pretty loud and people laughin' and havin' a good time." Charlotte pushed the creamer towards Eathen. "I guess we coulda missed it if she called out for help."

"Where did you last see her?" Eathen asked.

"I think in the kitchen, slicin' up more meat for the buffet table. Sarah and I visited in the dining room. She kept goin' on 'bout how well Tia and Jeremy seemed to be gettin' along."

"Jeremy came last night?" Eathen set the cream pitcher back down on the table.

"Yeah, him and Sarah came together." Charlotte sipped from her cup. "He disappeared before the party ended, 'cause Tom hadda give her a ride home."

"Did he look drunk?"

"I didn't get close to him." She glanced toward Hattie, who shrugged her shoulders. "The first I even knew about him bein' here is when I saw him dancin' with Tia. That's right after him and Sarah showed up. I never even gotta chance to speak to him."

"What about you, Hattie. Did you see Vada Lee?"

"Las' time ah seed her wuz w'en ah's inda kitchen a-fixin' up de cider bowl."

"What time you plannin' on goin' to see Sarah today?" Eathen cupped both hands around his cup, his elbows relaxing on the table.

"Later this afternoon, why?" Charlotte looked at him.

"Thought I'd ride along with you. I'm sure she could use some friends right 'bout now."

"That's very thoughtful of you, Eathen," Charlotte leaned her white head against his arm.

"Do me a favor though. Okay? Don't let her know I'm comin. That mess with Frank's bound to make her shy away from anyone but you right now, so just let my comin' along be a surprise."

"All right, Eathen. Whatever you say."

***

Later that day, a surprised Jeremy McKennah opened the door to Eathen and Charlotte's knock.

"Jeremy, we've come to pay our respects to your grandmother. Is she up?" Eathen asked, ushering Charlotte through the door.

"Yeah, she's in the parlor. If you'll wait a minute, I'll tell her you're here."

"That's all right, Jeremy," Eathen moved Charlotte ahead of him. "We know the way."

As Jeremy started walking towards the door, Eathen stopped him. "I think it'd be better if you joined us, Jeremy. I'm sure your grandmother could use your strength right now."

Shoving both hands deep into the pockets of his jeans, he followed them to where his grandmother sat in silence, staring out the window. As she felt someone put their arms around her, she looked up into the saddened eyes of her best friend.

"Oh, Charlotte!" she moaned. "Whatever am I gonna do without my poor, poor Frank?"

"I'll help you, Sarah. We'll get through this together." She gathered the frail woman close. "I promise."

"That horrible little man musta had somethin' powerful on Frank to make him get involved in something that awful." she blew her nose into the lace-trimmed handkerchief Charlotte handed to her.

"I'm sure you're right, Sarah." Charlotte rubbed a soothing hand up and down Sarah's back. "Hardiman was a terrible man."

"If there's a God in heaven, and I know there is," she sat up straight in her chair, "Hardiman and those men will get what's comin' to them, Especially the one who shot my poor Frank!" Sarah wailed her misery.

"Good thing you weren't involved in that mess last night, Jeremy," Eathen spoke up. "I'm referrin' to the reservation incident."

"No," Jeremy shook his head in denial, "you wouldn't catch me bein' involved in somethin' like that."

"Close as you and ole Frank were I'da thought you mighta heard him mention somethin' about it."

"Naw, he never said anything to me," Jeremy cast a worried glance at his grandmother.

"That was a terrible thing that happened out at our place last night." Eathen's voice rose. "First Frank, now Vada Lee."

"Eathen," Charlotte glanced up from where she sat on the Ottoman in front of Sarah's chair, "I don't think this is a good time to go into all that."

"Go into what?" Sarah asked, dabbing at her swollen eyes.

Ignoring Charlotte's stern glare, Eathen replied, "The little girl Charlotte hired to help out with the party was murdered last night. One of the hands found her this mornin' layin' out near the orchard."

"Oh, my Lord!" Sarah cried, her grief over Frank forgotten for the moment.

"Yeah, whoever did it, is one sick son-of-a-bitch," Eathen eyed the nervous young man watching him.

"Do they have any idea who it might be?" Sarah whispered.

"Not yet. Seems no one heard anything," Eathen laid one leg over his knee. "Charlotte tells me you left the party early," he glanced toward Jeremy. "You didn't by chance hear or see anything did you?"

"Me? No!" Jeremy stammered.

"Jeremy told me he came home early to check on his granddad," Sarah murmured. "The way it turned out, he needen have bothered."

Gathering the now, sobbing woman into her arms, Charlotte declared in a stern voice. "That's enough talk about Vada Lee. I feel bad about what happened to her too, but right now Sarah has enough problems."

Walking across the room, Jeremy knelt down in front of his grandmother. "Let me take her, Miss Charlotte," He pulled the wailing woman against his chest. "I'd be much obliged if you'd go tell Lilah to fix her a strong cup of tea. It wouldn't hurt to put a little whiskey in it too."

"Of course I will, Jeremy. I'll be right back." Charlotte patted Sarah's hand as she left to find the McKennah's housekeeper.

"I don't think there's any reason for you to hang around, Eathen. I'll be glad to give Miss Charlotte a ride home later," Jeremy said, without raising his eyes.

"You're right, there ain't. I think I got what I came for," Eathen gazed at the ugly bruises discoloring Jeremy's knuckles. At the door he turned to find the young man glaring at him. "I'll be back later for my wife. I wouldn't wanna put you out in your hour of grief."

Chapter Twenty-Eight

For weeks the death of Vada Lee and Frank McKennah remained the lead topic in the Thornton household. Although Eathen had forbidden his wife to go to the McKennah ranch, Charlotte refused to be intimidated. She and Tia spent so much time with Frank's widow Jed began to be concerned.

Rapping on the back door, Jed waited for Hattie to answer. When she didn't, he let himself in. He had just finished pouring a cup of coffee when Hattie walked into the kitchen.

"Mornin', Hattie. Miss Charlotte up yet?"

"Up an gwan. Her an Miss Tia done lef' 'bout an hour a go. Says dey wuz gwine ter spends de day wid Miss Sarah agin." She placed her hands on her wide hips. "Ah thinks in de las' three weeks dey's been hyah two days, an dem ain' been in a row. But she doan lissen w'en ah tells her she bes over doin' it. "She slammed a large skillet on top of the stove. "All Miss Sarah has ter do is calls an tells her she bes feelin' po'ly and dey's off agin'." Hattie scraped Charlotte's unfinished plate of food into a large bowl used to collect scraps for the dogs.

"Did they give you any idea what time they'd be home?" He withdrew a jar of fresh milk from the icebox and unscrewed the lid.

"Says dey'd bes hyah fer supper," Hattie took the jar of milk away from him and setting it on the table began skimming off the cream. "Dat means Miss Charlotte woan bes gittin' her nap agin." She spooned some of the cream into a small creamer she had waiting nearby. "De way dat Miss Sarah runs off at de mouth, a body couldn't rest effen da'd a mine ter."

"Somethin's gonna haveta be done. She won't listen to Eathen." Jed poured cream into his coffee. "I've a good mind to call Doc Prichard out here to order her to start takin' it easy."

"Woan do no good." Hattie recapped the milk and set it back in the icebox. "He awready tole her ter comes in 'bout dem chest pains she's been-a-havin'." She pushed the sugar bowl towards him. "Miss Charlotte, she jes' keeps a-putin' it off."

"What the hell you talkin' 'bout?" Jed stirred a heaping spoonful of sugar into his coffee. "She never said anything to anybody 'bout havin' chest pains."

"Dat's kase she doan wants nobody ter knows 'bout it. Onlyest reason de doctah tole me is sos ah kin keeps an eye on her," Hattie hastened to explain.

"Seems to me, you gotta poor way of goin' 'bout it," Jed growled, emptying the cup of coffee in three loud gulps, before turning on his heel and stomping out the back door. A few minutes later she heard a truck roar to life, then the high-pitched squeal of the tires as Jed drove off in the direction of the McKennah ranch.

***

"I wish this blasted rain'd let up," Sarah whined, dropping the curtain back in place. "Seems like even the heavens are sad about my poor Frank's passin'."

"I doubt that," Charlotte murmured to Tia. "If anything, they're lockin' the gates and barrin' the doors to keep him down where he belongs."

"Did you say something, Charlotte?" Sarah turned to look at her.

"No, just agreein' bout the rain, Charlotte lied. "We've sure had more'n our share of it."

A small feminine squeal followed by husky laughter filled the air as the kitchen door swung open, and Lilah walked into the room carrying a heavy-laden tray.

"Just put it down on the coffee table, Lilah," Sarah directed her. "We'll serve ourselves, thank you." As Lilah set the tray down, Sarah asked. "Have you seen Jeremy this mornin'?"

Without lifting her eyes, the young girl nodded. "Yes, ma'am. He's havin' coffee in the kitchen."

"Would you tell him I'd like to see him, please?"

"Yes, ma'am."

"My grandson's such a kidder." She smiled over at Tia. "He's got so much of his granddad's personality, it's astoundin'."

As the kitchen door remained closed, Sarah stood up. "I'll be right back. Go ahead and help yourselves to the coffee."

Leaning forward, Charlotte lifted the heavy pot. "If she had any sense, she'd get that idiot gelded fore he ruins half the county.

Within a few moments of Sarah's disappearance, Jeremy swaggered into the room. "If I'd known you were here, Tia, I'd been out a lot sooner." He strolled over to her. "Sure would like to know what it is, keeps drawin' you back day after day."

"You can bet your ass it ain't you, McKennah," Jed's deep voice replied from the doorway.

"You got some business here, Stanford?" Jeremy's eyes snapped open wide as he turned in the direction of the door, "I sure don't recall anyone invitin' you."

"You're damn right I do. You two get your things together." Jed jabbed a thumb towards the coat-rack. "We're goin' home."

After making hasty apologies to a gaping Sarah, Charlotte hurried outside, followed by a grinning Tia. Walking to the driver's side of the truck, Charlotte let loose on her young foreman.

"Just who in the hell do you think you are, Jed Stanford, to be givin' me orders? You seem to forget," she poked a finger against her chest, "I'm the boss here, not you. I've a good mind to…"

She never finished as Jed threw open the door and without a word, hauled a still, fussing Charlotte inside.

"Go on, Tia. I'll meet you at back at the ranch," he yelled over the angry curses of his employer.

"I have never been so humiliated in my entire life, Jed! Have you lost all your senses?" Charlotte glared at the smiling young man seated beside her.

"Quite the contrary, Miss Charlotte. If you won't take care of yourself somebody has to."

"Where'n the hell are you goin'?" Charlotte asked, turning in her seat. "You just missed the turn!"

"I'm takin' you to see Doc Prichard." He glanced over at her. "I understand he's been after you to come in about those chest pains you been havin'."

"Hattie!"

"Don't go blamin' her. I already chewed her out."

"Did you see Eathen before you left?"

"I think he was in the den, I don't know. I'm surprised he didn't come after you himself the way he feels about Jeremy."

"Eathen has no proof that boy's responsible for what happened to Vada Lee. I don't have any great likin' for Jeremy either, but I ain't gonna accuse him of murder 'til I know what I'm talkin' about."

"Eathen's convinced Jeremy did it." Jed slowed the truck to a safer speed as the road became rutted, causing the truck to bounce and Charlotte to hold onto the door handle. "That's one reason he don't want you goin' over there."

"What's the other?" She stared out the window.

"He feels the same as everyone else; you need to start takin' it easier." He shifted to a higher gear as they drove onto the main road. "I don't think he's outta line to tell you to stay away from the McKennahs."

"Sarah McKennah's my best friend!" Charlotte inhaled a deep breath, fanning herself with her hand. "I'm not about to abandon her in her hour of grief, just because my husband has some fool notion Jeremy McKennah's responsible for that little girl's death."

"Simmer down," he told her, worry for her making his voice sharper than he intended, "you're gettin' yourself all upset. I swear to Christ! When this year's up, I'm puttin' in for a raise!" He chanced a quick glance at her face. "With all the shit I gotta put up with, I deserve it!"

"Nobody asked you to stick your nose in," Charlotte told him. The corners of her mouth lifting in spite of herself.

"No, they didn't." He turned to look at her more fully, all the anger gone now from his voice, "But if Eathen is on to somethin', I ain't about to sit by while you and Tia put yourselves in needless danger."

"Lord help us if Eathen's right," she sighed. "'Cause if he is, God better get ready for 'nother one 'cause this'll kill Sarah for sure!"

"Sarah McKennah ain't the one I'm worried about right now," Jed turned the truck onto the street where Doctor Prichard had his office.

"I guess I might as well get this over with." Charlotte blew out a long breath as Jed drew up in front of the office.

"I'll wait out here," he told her turning off the key. "But, rest assured, I'm gonna question him about what he finds, so it won't do you no good to lie."

"With any luck I won't be long, Jed." She patted his arm.

As Charlotte disappeared inside the small building, Jed felt a cold chill pass over him. "I hope to God she ain't waited too long," he whispered.

***

The sharp jingle of the telephone echoed throughout the early morning hour. It's incessant code of one long and two short rings demanded to be acknowledged.

Still half asleep, Hattie picked up the receiver. "Hello?"

"Yes! May I speak to Eathen Thornton, please?" said a female voice on the other extension.

"Who bes callin?"

"It's not important who this is! Get him to the phone!"

"Who is it, Hattie?" Charlotte asked, coming to stand beside her.

"She woan say." Hattie held one hand over the mouthpiece. "It bes fer Mist' Eathen."

"Give me the phone." Charlotte held out her hand.

"Should ah go calls him?" Hattie handed her the phone.

"Just wait a moment." Charlotte held up her hand, "Who is this?" Charlotte demanded of the person on the other line.

"This is Mrs. Terrance Martin, of Helena. I'm trying to reach Eathen Thornton. Is he there?" The woman cried. "This is of the utmost importance."

"Hold on a minute." Charlotte pressed the phone against her chest, "Go call Eathen!"

"My housekeeper's gone to call him." She spoke into the phone again. "He'll be here in a minute."

"Thank God!" The woman on the other end breathed a sigh of relief. "I didn't want to bother you with this, Mrs. Thornton. Especially, since you've been so understanding about all this. But, I have no choice."

"What's happened?" Charlotte tried to make sense of what the woman was talking about.

"It's Pamela Ann! She's had an accident." The woman rushed to explain, "She keeps calling for Eathen! He's got to get here! Oh God! I don't know what I'll do if she dies!"

"All right, just calm down." Charlotte tried to soothe her. "He'll be here in a minute."

"She had Charles with her." She continued in the same hysterical tone. "Thank God he didn't get hurt, but he needs his father to be here!"

"What the hell's goin' on?" Eathen growled, reaching for the phone, "It's three o'clock in the goddamn mornin'!"

As if in a daze, Charlotte handed the phone to her husband of forty-nine years, before pain and darkness swallowed up everything else around her.

Charlotte swirled in and out of consciousness as she tried to hold on to reality. The weight had lifted from her chest but the pain continued to make itself known, sliding down her arm in a throbbing ache. As if in a dream she caught glimpses of people she knew but they kept whirling away when she tried to speak. When she came to, Eathen sat beside the bed, his head cradled in his hands.

"Eathen," she murmured trying to take hold of his arm, but her hand would not obey her command.

"I'm here, Charlotte. Just lay quiet," he grasped her frail hand.

"What happened?" She gazed around her. "I feel so weak."

"You've had a heart-attack," Eathen told her. "Doc Prichard's downstairs. He said to call him the moment you awoke." He pushed his chair back from the bed.

"No," she whispered, clinging to his hand. "I want to know…that woman said… you have a son."

"Charlotte, you need to stay quiet. Please! I'm gonna go get the doctor." He pulled away from her.

"Eathen, tell me about Charles," she panted. "Does he look…anything like our Jessie?"

It was on the tip of his tongue to tell her it was all a bad mistake, but as he looked at her all thought of lying flew right out of his mind. Seating himself by her side, he told her what she wanted to know.

"All right, I'll tell you everything." He curled his hand over hers. "Let me get it all out without any interruptions or I'll never be able to finish."

Nodding, she waited.

"About sixteen years ago, I met a woman in Helena by the name of Pamela Ann Martin. It was the night of her thirty-first birthday. I never meant to fall in love with her. It…just happened." He could feel the hand in his grow colder. "Every time I came back to the ranch I promised myself it was over, but I kept goin' back." Drawing a deep breath, he held it for a moment then released it from his lungs as he felt tears slip down his face. "Then she told me she was gonna have my baby. Charlotte, it was like…life had givin' me a second chance," he gulped not looking at her. "I didn't wanna hurt you, but I couldn't leave her either. When Charles was born, it seemed as if God had given me back my Jessie. He looks so much like her, Charlotte…." his voice trailed off.

Charlotte lay still, watching the tears running down his face as he told her about the two people he loved most in this world, and all she could do is stare at him. Forcing breath into her lungs, she whispered.

"Eathen, lean down here a second." When he did she drew back, and with all the strength her frail body could summon, slapped him across the face. "I want you to pack your bags...and get...the hell...outta my house! I'll leave word, that when I'm dead...you can have it all. Until then, I never wanna look at your lyin' face again!"

"Is that all you have to say to me?" He drew back staring at her, his face drained of color. "After I laid my soul at your feet?"

"No, Eathen." She struggled to breathe, "There is one more thing...you can do...for me...before you leave."

"What is it?" he asked.

"You can send...my granddaughter to me. It's time she learned...about her father."

"Are you plannin' to tell her everything?" He watched her, his blue eyes narrowed to mere slits.

"You're damn right I am,"

For a long moment he continued to watch her. Then he walked to the door. Without turning, he declared. "Goodbye, Charlotte."

She lay in the big bed she had shared with her husband for over half of her life and she waited for the pain of his walking away to begin. Oddly, all she felt was freedom.

"If he'd had the balls to tell me about this years ago, we coulda both lived a half-ass decent life," she laughed surprising herself.

***

At the quiet tapping on her bedroom door, Tia reached out switching on her small bedside lamp.

"Who is it?" she called out.

"It's your grandfather." Came her shocking answer. Snatching a robe lying across the foot of her bed she slipped it on over her nightgown as she ran to open the door.

"Has something happened to Gram?"

"She wants to talk to you." His voice, as he talked to her, sounded cold and impersonal. "She's waitin' in her room." Without a backward glance he walked away.

Padding barefoot down the long hall, Tia came to stand outside Charlotte's door.

"Gram," she called out.

"Come in, child," Charlotte murmured.

The room was dark except for the small lamp beside Charlotte's bed. Seeing her grandmother propped back among the pillows, Tia walked the rest of the way into the room.

Patting a place beside her on the bed, Charlotte beckoned her forward. "Come here, Tia. I wanna talk to you."

As Tia sat on the side of the bed, Charlotte smiled. "You're gonna know all about it anyway, so I might just as well get it over with. Your grandfather informed me a little while ago that he's found someone else. I guess it's been goin' on for quite some time."

"I'm so sorry, Gram." Tia reached for her hand. "He must have hurt you terribly."

"You know," a surprised look came over her face, "the biggest emotion I feel right now is freedom. And, even, a little stronger. I wish he'd told me about this when it happened. The two of us would have been a lot happier if he had, 'stead of fightin' all these long years."

"I felt very surprised when he came to my room to tell me you wanted to talk to me." Tia gave Charlotte's hand a light squeeze. "I feared something had happened to you."

"Somethin' did happen to me," she laughed, then drew in her breath at the pain in her chest, "I had a damn heart-attack when I found out your grandfather's gotta a son in Helena."

"Oh no!" Tia's small hand went to her throat.

"Oh yes!" Charlotte nodded. "His name's Charles." Charlotte looked thoughtful for a moment. "I never did find out how old the little bastard is. I got so mad, I sent Eathen away before he could tell me. It don't make no difference." Her head lolled back on the pillow. "The fact remains, Eathen's been livin' a double life."

"I don't know what to say."

"I know what to say, Tia." Charlotte gazed at her granddaughter. "And it's somethin' I shoulda said years ago. You came out here to find out about your father. I had Eathen send you to me so you could finally do that."

Tia could feel her heart pump in her chest. At last she would learn about the man she had been searching for all her young life. Leaning forward, she waited.

"My Jessie was a beautiful girl, with fiery red hair and dancin' blue eyes." Her own eyes closed as she brought forth the images to her tired mind. "Boys all but tripped over themselves tryin' to please her, but there was never anyone special until the year she turned sixteen.

"An Indian off the reservation, by the name of Two Spirits, came to the ranch one mornin' lookin' for work." Charlotte tugged Tia up beside her on the large bed. "Eathen had all he could handle tryin' to break a new string of wild horses just rounded up. The Indian told Eathen he could take a lot of the work off his hands, that he was good at handlin' horses. Never one to turn anyone away, your grandfather gave him a job. True to his word, the boy soon proved his worth.

Now," she heaved a long sigh, "at that time there still remained a lotta hatred toward the Indians, but no matter how much the other hands teased or made fun of him, Two Spirits kept right on workin'. One of the men nicknamed him, Johnny Two Spirits. Said, if he was gonna have a white man's job, he needed a white man's name to go with it."

"Hand me some tissue, Tia," she asked. Taking the tissue she wiped spittle from the side of her mouth. "I musta hit my mouth when I fell. It feels numb."

"Anyway," she leaned her head back on the pillow, "I don't know why I didn't notice when things began to change with Jessie. I should have. Boys would come to the ranch askin' for her, but she no longer wanted anything to do with them. It got so every time I needed her for somethin' she was nowhere to be found.

One day one of Eathen's friends came by lookin' for him. I went out to the corrals, where I thought he'd be, to let him know he had company. There, pretty as could be, sat Jessie.

She didn't hear me walk up, and as I watched her, I saw she was starin' at somethin'. Followin' her line of vision, I soon saw what had her so impressed. She was watchin' that young Indian." She rubbed a light hand across her chest. "For the first time I took a really good look at him. What I saw, I'm ashamed to admit, I didn't like. He had to be the most handsome man I had ever seen. Tall and lean and not an ounce of fat on his muscular body anywhere. But his eyes is what struck me the most. They was almond shaped, just like yours and so black they looked like big chunks of coal."

Without realizing it, Tia raised her hands to her own eyes.

"His hair," Charlotte continued, "hung all the way down his back. Not coarse, but... almost like fine satin. As I stood there, I saw somethin' pass between them.

I called Jessie over. Tellin' her to get herself in the house and not to come back 'til we'd had a chance to talk. I couldn't pinpoint why that look...scared me like it did. When I went back to the house, I told Jessie not to be makin eyes at him. That if she did, I talk her daddy into lettin' him go.

Come to find out, I'd already waited too long. Jessie was carryin' his child."

The light in Tia's eyes, as she took in her grandmother's words, could not be hidden. The Holy Ones had given her spirit to an Indian to be reborn into this life.

"Please don't stop now, Gram. I want to hear everything."

Nodding, Charlotte glanced at her.

"When Eathen found out, I thought he would die." The pain in her chest worsened, but she wouldn't stop talking. "Jessie was his world. The one person who could do no wrong." She pulled the neckline of her nightgown away from her throat. "He couldn't see her havin' the same wants and needs like the rest of us.

Every hope, every dream we ever had for her was destroyed in one thoughtless move." Charlotte raised the hand holding the tissue to her face, moping away the clammy perspiration clinging to her skin. "There's no way she could have stayed with us and given birth to that baby. Not in Montana."

Tia got off the bed, to wet a washrag in the small pan setting on a table across the room. Wringing as much water as she could from the cloth, she walked back to the bed. With a gentle hand she bathed her grandmother's face.

"Just fold it and lay it over my forehead, Tia." She patted the small hand. When she felt sure her voice would not fail her, she proceeded to tell Tia more about her mother.

"We talked it over and decided to send her back east to have her baby, away from the prejudice and hatred. We never even told John and Martha who had fathered you. But come to find out, Jessie did." Her breath became more labored. "We felt we'd done the right thing by her. God in his heaven knows we never meant to hurt her, but we couldn't have been more wrong."

Tia reached up to turn the washcloth over, surprised at the warmth clinging to the cloth.

"Jessie fought us every step of the way." Charlotte said, as though talking to herself. "She even threatened to tell everyone in the county she carried Two Spirits' baby, in hopes we wouldn't send her away. I can see that night just like it was yesterday," Charlotte declared.

"Gram, that's enough. You're not well. I'll come back later in the day, after you've had some rest."

"No!" Charlotte grabbed her hand. "We might not have time later. I have to finish this,"

Reaching behind her grandmother, Tia pulled her pillows up higher.

"She stood right in the middle of the parlor, screamin' out her fury at the two people who loved her more'n anyone else in this whole wide world!

Hattie came runnin' into the room to see what was goin' on. Jessie kept screamin' how we all hated her except Two Spirits. And that if we didn't let her go back to him she'd tell everyone whose baby she carried.

Eathen was in a fury. Before any of us knew what had happened he reached out, slappin' Jessie to the floor. I started to go to her, but Hattie held me back. As if in a daze, I saw Eathen standin' over her, shakin' his fist, and yellin'", 'You ain't goin' anywhere, little girl. If I have to lock you up to see to it, I will! That red bastard will never put his filthy hands on another white girl either! I can promise you that!'

Charlotte's breath had become more shallow, but she refused to stop the words pushing their way out of her mouth as if they had a will of their own.

"Then he was jerkin' Jessie to her feet and shovin' her up the stairs. I heard her door slam and Eathen yellin' at her not to try goin' out the window, that all she would accomplish was breakin' her neck. When he came back down, I watched him strap on his gun.

I tried to reason with him," she dabbed at the spittle sliding down the side of her mouth, "but it was like he couldn't hear me. I had never seen him like that. As he slammed outta the house I could hear Jessie screamin' overhead, like a wounded animal."

For a long moment she became quiet, then with a slight shake of her head, she began again. "He never told me what he did to Two Spirits." She touched the tissue to her mouth again, "I never asked. I didn't need to. After that, Jessie was like a different person. She no longer fought us about goin' back east. She never voiced her opinion one way or the other. We felt, given enough time, she'd be all right.

The mornin' after she gave birth to you, your mother took her own life. When the wire came tellin' us what she'd done, I thought my life was over. I blamed myself." The tears ran unchecked down her face. "For a while, so did Eathen, although he never at any time said it out loud.

He refused to go back East with me for Jessie's funeral. Said he could never bring hisself to look upon no half-breed baby what killed his little girl. So every year, I made the long trip back east alone to see you."

Tia could feel the hot tears rolling down her face. She left them to fall.

"When I got your wire, tellin' me you was on your way, I was scared to death. I didn't have any idea what your grandfather might do." She ran a light hand down the side of Tia's face. "But I'll tell you somethin', Tia, your comin' out here, at this time, is the best thing you coulda done." Charlotte smiled through her tears. "Because…if I didn't have you here for me tonight, I'd just…plain…out…give up."

"So," Tia swallowed, "what you're telling me, is my father is dead," Tia whispered.

"Yes, Tia," Charlotte murmured, "I'm afraid he is."

Chapter Twenty-Nine

She could think of just one person she wanted to see right then, and she made up her mind to get word to him before the day ended. Waiting until she knew he would be up, Tia walked outside to look for Jed. She saw him almost at once down by the corrals. Without stopping to think, she made her way towards him.

"Good morning, Jed."

"You're up bright and early." He walked over to her leading a large buckskin. "What's goin' on?"

"Everything. I need to talk to you about something."

"I'll always listen," Jed told her, delivering a gentle slap on the side of the horse's neck to calm his skittish prancing.

"I don't know where to begin," She worried her lower lip with her teeth. "So much has happened in the last few hours, I feel as though I've lived a lifetime."

"Your late night visitor ain't back is he?" Jed's brows knitted with concern.

"No," she smiled shaking her head, "that's all been resolved."

"Then what is it?" Jed touched her arm.

"Grandfather Eathen told Gram he's in love with another woman. And...to make matters even worse, he has a son by this woman."

"She told you all this?" Jed stared at her in disbelief. "Christ almighty. That poor woman!"

"My grandfather came to my room in the middle of the night to tell me she wanted to talk to me. After she told me all that he had been up to, she told me about my father."

"You know where he is?" He turned in the direction of the tack room.

"I think so, but I need you to do me a big favor, Jed, if you would. I want you to get hold of Wolfer and tell him I'd like to talk to him."

"I think I can handle that." Jed threw a dark red blanket over the horse's broad back. "How's Miss Charlotte takin' all this?"

"Believe it or not," Tia took hold of the horse's bridle, calming him as he began to prance around, "I'd say she's handling it quite well."

"That's good to hear," he called back over his shoulder as he walked into the tack room. "With her health, bein' what it is, this little piece of news coulda done her in."

"That could still happen, Jed. I guess the way it all started, is with some woman calling to talk to my grandfather." Tia lowered her voice as Jed walked back over to her. "She told Gram about the boy. The news shocked her so much, it brought on a heart-attack."

"She learned about this over the phone?" He stooped to pick up the heavy saddle he had waiting nearby. "Everyone in the county knows about it by now. A party-line's the best source in the world for learnin' gossip." He heaved the saddle onto the horse's back. "Where's Eathen now?"

"Gone back to his other family, I guess." She rubbed her hands briskly up and down her arms as the cool morning air touched her. "Hattie said he passed her early this morning carrying two suitcases. This may sound cold, Jed, but maybe it's for the best. He hardly ever had a kind word to say to Gram."

"He may be your grandfather, Tia," he cinched the saddle up tight, "but in my book, Eathen Thornton's one selfish son-of-a-bitch!"

"He's more than that, Jed." she told him walking away. "Believe me."

***

Two days had passed since she had talked to Jed, and still she had not had any word from Wolfer. Finally she took matters into her own hands and saddled up the big paint. She had an idea where she needed to go and so it seemed so did the horse as he picked his way through the tall bunch grass leading to the lake. Sitting atop his back, she stared out over the calm waters, as the memories of a distant past filled her mind. Then she saw them. Two riders made their way towards her. Dismounting she waited for them to reach her.

Dismounting, Pehta gathered her into his frail arms holding her close against his chest.

The years slipped away as she looked into the face of Appearing Wolf's brother.

"Now," he whispered, holding her at arm's length to peer into her lovely face, "you remember."

"Yes, Pehta," she nodded, tears sliding down her face. "Now I remember. I'm so sorry," Tia ran a gentle hand down his weathered cheek, "I hurt you by my fear of what I could not know."

"When I returned to our camp that morning long ago, I found all of our people dead. My heart cried with the knowledge I could do nothing. As I walked through the camp, everywhere I looked I saw what had been done to our loved ones." His breath deepened as he fought to get his words past the lump growing in his throat. "When I found your body lying a short distance away from my brother's, I knew your spirits had not walked your paths to the Holy Ones." His small shoulders trembled with anguish.

With gentle arms she rocked him until all the pain in his aged and wasted body had been stilled. Only then did she move away. When she glanced up, she saw the sad eyes of Wolfer watching her.

"I knew I'd find you here." She held out her hand to him. "Thank you for bringing him to me."

"When Pehta told me we must come here to meet you, I almost doubted him." He clasped her small hand in his, then without a word, he pulled her into his arms in a tight hug. "Even after all these years of livin' around the Blackfeet, I still find it strange."

"I know that my father was an Indian named Two Spirits. Gram told me all about him."

"Yes," Wolfer turned away to tie his horse's reins to a low-hanging branch. "I knew your father well," he looked over at her. "Did she also tell you what happened to him?"

"She thinks my grandfather killed him. Is she right?"

With a slight nod, he confirmed her worst fears. "If you'd like, I can show you where I buried him."

"Are you sure my grandfather is the one who killed him? Maybe he had someone else do it," She hoped against hope that would be the case.

"No, Tia. I rode up right after it happened." Wolfer removed his hat, running one hand through his thick gray hair. "I don't think Eathen knew about my being there. After he left, I brought your father's body back here and buried him. His grave's over there," he pointed, "near that big pine."

As though her feet had a will of their own, Tia proceeded to walk forward. When she reached the area she knelt down to sit beside his grave.

"You never put a marker on his grave?" She looked up at Wolfer.

"No. I feared it might be desecrated."

"All these years I've been searching for someone who was already gone."

"His body is gone, Tia. His spirit still roams this land," Pehta explained. "The white man has been able to control the Indian's body, but they could never control his spirit."

"I would like to think my mother rested here with him. But she is buried in a cemetery in Boston, many miles away."

"Tia, it is the body that is limited. The spirit can go anywhere." He waved his frail arms in a wide circle. "If their love remained strong, then she is here where she found love and peace."

"If that is true," she looked up at him, "then my search to find them has not been in vain."

"The spirits guided your steps to this place, Tia. My brother has waited many years for you to return." Pehta pulled her to her feet, "His search has not been in vain, either."

As she walked away, a slight breeze ruffled her hair, while all else around her remained still. Looking to where Pehta stood, watching her, she smiled. "Now, my heart is at peace."

"What will you do now, Tia?" Wolfer matched his steps with hers.

"I'm going to stay and help my grandmother. She needs me very much now that my grandfather is no longer here."

"Then she has learned of his other family who lives with him in Helena."

"Yes, she knows, Wolfer. I think she will be able to handle his going away though."

"Miss Charlotte's a good woman. Eathen didn't know what he had in her."

"I wonder if he ever loved her at all. If he did, he couldn't have hurt her like this."

"Your grandfather could never accept the fact Jessie had grown into a woman with a woman's feelin's. He tried to keep her a little girl. When she rebelled," Wolfer shrugged his shoulders, "he couldn't live with that and I think that is when he started to change toward your grandmother."

"How did you get so wise, Wolfer?" She laughed for the first time that day.

"I guess it comes with age, Tia." He laughed with her. "That, and livin' with a Blackfeet Indian for a pa."

"I'm glad to see your life turned out happy, Pehta. I hope we can be together again real soon," she told him, slipping her arm around his thin waist.

"That is one thing I can promise you, Tia. Before the snow falls, we will be together."

Chapter Thirty

Riding into the yard, Tia spied Jed striding towards her. Dismounting, she handed him the rains.

"Is something wrong, Jed?" she asked.

"You're damn right somethin's wrong," he growled. "It ain't been but a couple months since that son-of-a-bitch you're ridin' almost killed you! Now, here you are takin' him out again!"

"That could have happened with any horse, Jed. He can't be blamed for that." She tried to walk past him.

"You don't know that." He grabbed her by the shoulders, "Your grandmother has enough to worry 'bout without you givin' her more."

"You're making too much of this," Tia told him, trying to loosen his hold on her. "Besides, Gram has no way of knowing what horse I took riding."

"Yes she does. While I was up at the house talkin' with her, Tom came to tell me about seein' you ride off."

"Listen, Jed," she jerked away from him, "I appreciate your concern, but I'm not a child. I can make my own decisions, thank you." She turned to walk away.

"Wait a minute, Tia." Jed placed a rough hand on her shoulder.

For a moment she stood glaring at him. Then seeing the worry in his light gray eyes, she declared, "All right, Jed. If it will make you feel better, I won't ride him anymore."

"I know it ain't my place to dictate what you do around here." He brushed a strand of her long silky hair back over her shoulder. "I just want you to be safe."

"Apology accepted." She smiled up at him as she laced her small arm through his.

"I still ain't hadda chance to get hold of Wolfer yet." The tautness in the back of his neck easing somewhat. "Guess he's off somewhere."

"There's no need to now. I ran into him and Pehta while out riding. I found out everything I wanted to know. Wolfer has been here a long time. He knows pretty much what goes on around the county."

"Yeah, he does," Jed handed her ahead of him up the porch steps, enjoying the way her riding pants formed the outline of her small bottom. "He's the one I thought might be able to help you find your pa."

"I'm no longer worried about that, Jed." Tia stretched her arms over her head, at the same time arching her back in an attempt to relieve her knotted muscles, "I've decided to put the past behind me. From now on, I'm going to look to the future."

"Sounds like a wise decision to me." He leaned back against the banister.

Without waning a shot rang out, almost hitting Tia. Jed shoved her down on the porch. Drawing his gun, he tried to see where the shot had come from.

"What in the world is going on, Jed?!" Tia cried, lifting her head from the floor of the porch.

"Stay down!" he ordered her. "Somebody just took a pot shot at us from those trees over there!"

"Who the hell's shootin', Jed!?" Tom yelled, running forward, his own gun drawn and ready.

"It came from the tree line. Soon as I get Tia in the house, we'll go take a look."

Pulling the frightened girl to her feet, Jed ran with her through the front door.

"Whut in de worl's gwine on, Mist' Jed?" Hattie stood in the hallway staring at them, her dark eyes wide with alarm. "Ah heer sumbody a-shootin!"

"Somebody almost shot Tia." He headed towards Eathen's den. Opening the glass door on the gun-cabinet, he withdrew one of Eathen's rifles. Filling his pockets full of ammunition, he hurried back out to where a nervous Tia and Hattie waited for him. "You two stay in the house. The boys and me are gonna try and find out what's goin' on."

"Let's git upstairs, chile, whar we'll bes safe." Hattie pulled her along after her.

Keeping low, Jed and some of the hands made their way toward the trees.

"See anything, Tom?" Jed breathed.

"Not yet. Why in the hell would someone take a shot at you?"

"They didn't want me, they wanted Tia."

"What the hell would someone wanta shoot her for? That don't make no sense."

"It does when you stop and think 'bout the fact we have a deranged killer runnin' loose around here now. Vada Lee was just a kid. It takes a sick son-of-a-bitch to do what he did!"

"Oh shit!" Tom rubbed his stubbled chin. "I forgot 'bout that."

"Eathen's gotta idea who did it."

"Who?" Tom growled.

"He thinks it was Jeremy McKennah."

"What the hell gave him that idea?"

"He told me he saw bruises across Jeremy's knuckles the mornin' after the murder," Jed told him, his alert eyes continuing to scan the trees. "I went with Wilks to help him get Vada Lee's body ready for transport. Her face had been beat so bad you almost couldn't recognize her. Whoever did it, had to be carryin' some marks on him."

"Why the hell didn't Wilks pick him up?"

"No proof." He raised his arm, signaling the hands to come forward out of the trees. "Then too," he hunkered back down beside Tom in the tall grass, "I think he wanted to protect Miss Sarah, 'cause of Frank."

"That woman's had more'n her share of grief," Tom declared, never taking his eyes from the trees. "I think she's better off, though. I never cared much for McKennah."

"I didn't either. And I sure as hell don't cotton to the idea of her and Lilah bein' alone in that house with a killer."

"Looks like he's gone now." Tom stood up as he saw the hands walking out of the trees. "I guess you'll be wantin' some of the boys to stand guard around the house tonight. Am I right?"

"No. I want someone on guard soon as you get back to the bunkhouse. It makes my scalp crawl to think how close Tia came to diein' just now. If he'd caught her out ridin', she'd be dead."

"I think it'd be a good idea if you started sleepin' in the house. Now that Eathen's hauled ass, them women need protectin'."

"I already thought of that." He laid the rifle over his shoulder holding onto the butt. "Since Doc Prichard's ordered Miss Charlotte to bed, she won't know I'm there. The less she knows, the better."

"Do *you* think it's McKennah?" Tom squinted over at him.

"I don't know, Tom, but I sure as hell intend to find out."

***

"Supper'll bes ready soon as ah gits Miss Charlotte's fixed," Hattie told the two young people sitting at the table.

"I'll take it up to her, Hattie," Tia said.

"Awright, ah'd 'preciates it. Ah been up an down dem stairs til' ah's 'bout daid on mah feet." She handed Tia the heavy-laden tray.

"Why don't you and Jed go ahead, while everything is hot," Tia suggested. "I want to stay with Gram while she eats."

"Effen you's sho you doan mines." She set a large bowl of whipped potatoes on the table. "Ah is a lil hongry."

"I'll carry that up for you, Tia." Jed got to his feet to lift the tray from her hands. "It looks pretty heavy."

"Thank you, Jed. It is a little more than I expected."

"I want you to know you have nothin' to worry about," he told her, as they climbed the stairs. "I'm gonna be sleepin' on the couch in the parlor til we find out what all that was about today. Just don't let Miss Charlotte know what's goin' on."

"No, she doesn't need any more excitement. I'm so worried about her, Jed."

"Yeah, me too. Eathen tellin' her everything right now sure as hell didn't help matters."

"Hi, Gram," Tia greeted her with a smile, pushing open the bedroom door. "We brought you some nourishment."

"I hope you're plannin' on sharin' it," Charlotte murmured. "Knowin' Hattie, she made enough."

"I plan on sitting right here with you."

"Ain't this a hell of a note, Jed?" she asked, as he placed the tray across her lap. "I'm as weak as a three-day-old kitten."

"This'll help you get some strength back," he told her.

"Anyone heard from Eathen, since he slunk outta here in the middle of the night?" She moved the tray to a more stable position across her lap.

"I didn't take any calls," Tia told her. "But I'll ask Hattie as soon as I go back downstairs."

"It ain't important." Charlotte poo pooed the idea away. "I just thought he might have the decency to wanna know how I'm doin'."

"If you lovely ladies'll excuse me," Jed tried to keep the anger out of his voice at Eathen's coldness, "I better go. You take care, Miss

Charlotte. I'll check back a little later." Jed closed the door behind him.

"That's a fine young man right there, Tia." She gestured with her fork. "He'll make some girl a real good husband."

"I couldn't agree more." Tia propped Charlotte up higher in the bed.

As Tia tried to eat, she watched her grandmother pushing the food around on her plate, until at last, she laid her fork down on the tray.

"I appreciate your tryin', Tia, but I can't eat. I got too many worries 'runnin' round in my head."

"Like what, Gram?" Tia laid her own fork across her plate.

"Like what's gonna happen to you if I don't make it. I had thought to leave everything to you after your granddad and I passed on, but he shot the hell outta that idea, didn't he?"

"In the first place, you aren't going anywhere for a long time, and in the second, I know now I'm going to be just fine."

"I hope so, Tia," Charlotte cried, unable to hold the tears back any longer.

Moving from her chair, Tia removed the tray placing it in her vacated chair and gathered the sobbing woman into her arms.

"It's going to all work out, Gram." She smoothed the white hair back from Charlotte's damp forehead. "You just have to trust."

"I've always been so strong...and now...I can't even get outta this bed. Oh, God! Everythin's fallin' apart."

"Would it make you feel better if I called Grandfather Eathen and asked him to come back?"

"No. Don't do that." Charlotte shook her head. "Please, don't do that. He's with the ones he loves now. We'll leave him alone."

"All right, Gram, whatever you say."

"Pull these pillows out from behind me, please. I think I better lie down for a while."

Turning she reached out for the pillows an uneasy feeling passing over her. It's icy touch making her shiver.

"I know what I can do to help you relax. I remember, you always enjoyed having me brush your hair. Would you like that?" Tia asked, her calm words belying the cold hand of fear clutching her.

"Yes, Tia. I think that would be real nice." Charlotte labored to breathe.

Going to the vanity table, she found an ivory-handled brush. As she picked it up, she caught Charlotte's reflection in the mirror. The stark pain showing on the woman's face made Tia's heart race. Forcing herself to move, she returned to her grandmother.

"Wherever did you find such a beautiful brush? It must have cost a fortune."

"Your grandfather gave it to me for our thirty-third wedding anniversary." She struggled to speak. "Now I know why."

Shaking out the heavy braid of white hair, Tia pulled the brush through the long tresses. As she sat there in the lengthening shadows by Charlotte's side, she could hear the dull ticking of the clock. Its incessant rhythm whispered a subtle warning.

Charlotte heaved a long sigh, then lay quiet.

"Gram," Tia stopped brushing Charlotte's hair. "Gram?" she cried louder this time.

As Charlotte lay unmoving, even after Tia gave her a gentle shake, Tia burst into tears. "Oh god. No!"

Moving off the bed she headed for the door. But as her hand touched the knob she turned, retracing her steps. Bending down she placed a gentle kiss on Charlotte's forehead. Then closed the unseeing eyes.

"I love you, Gram," Tia told her.

Walking downstairs, Tia could hear the happy voices of Jed and Hattie coming from the dining room. When she got to the doorway she stopped, unable to move.

Looking up, Jed saw her standing there, her face stricken with pain.

"Tia, what is it?" he asked, pushing back his chair.

"It's Gram." She burst into tears.

"Oh, mah Lawd!" Hattie cried cupping a hand over her mouth.

Taking the stairs two at a time, Jed ran to Charlotte's room followed by a wheezing Hattie.

Tia dropped her face in her hands as a long, high-pitched wail echoed through the house.

Chapter Thirty-One

Passing by the parlor door, Doctor Prichard spied Tia sitting alone. Going over to her, he laid a gentle hand on her shoulder.

"Tia, are you all right?"

At her slight nod, he pulled a chair over beside her.

"I had to give Hattie a sedative. She should sleep through the night. I can do the same for you."

"No, I'll be fine. I just want to sit here for a while."

Ignoring her request to be alone, he leaned forward. "Tia, I know you and your grandmother weren't together all that long, but I could see the closeness between you. These next couple of days are gonna be pretty rough, what with the funeral and all. I want you to know if you need me, I'll be here for you. I thought a lot of Miss Charlotte. Hell, I've known her forever it seems."

At the catch in his voice, Tia looked up to see tears falling unchecked down his face. Without a word she gathered him into her arms.

"It's all right if you cry, Doctor Prichard," she told him rocking him in a gentle sway, "she would have cried for you."

When at last he felt some control returning, he wiped his eyes, then blew his nose into a big red handkerchief he stuffed back into his suit pocket.

"I came in here to tend to your needs, and you ended up doin' all the comfortin'. Thank you, Tia, I'm really gonna miss that ole gal." He cupped a hand over his eyes. "She's the one person I knew who said just what she thought." The corners of his mouth lifted. "Even when she would be chewin' you out, you still had to respect her for havin' the gumption to do it." He pushed himself to his feet. "I'm thankful for one thing though," Prichard drew a shaky hand over his mouth, "I didn't have to stand by helpless and watch her suffer. She went quick in the company of someone she loved very much. That had to make it easier."

"Yes, Doctor Prichard," Tia nodded in agreement, "I truly believe, at long last, she's at peace."

***

A light sprinkle of rain continued to fall as Charlotte's neighbors followed behind the old black hearse making its way towards the Cut Bank cemetery. Just as they had attended the many dances and barbecues given throughout the years, everyone in the county was there. Except this time, they had come to say goodbye to a lady most of them felt great admiration for.

Seeing the black car pass beneath the big cemetery sign hanging high overhead, Jed felt his nerves react. Stopping a short distance behind the hearse he switched off the motor.

In the quiet of the closed car Jed could hear the soft cries of Tia and Hattie. Without a word he pulled Tia into his arms. "We gotta go now. I'll be with you every step of the way, so if you need to, you just lean on me. That goes for you too, Hattie."

Nodding, Tia hastened to dry her eyes. "I'll be all right, Jed."

Walking around the car, he opened the doors for the women. Taking a firm grip on Tia's hand Jed helped her out of the car. When she stood before him he reached out a hand for Hattie, then with a supportive smile walked with both women towards the gravesite.

She had chosen to dress all in black. The long veil falling over her face helped to hide the sad dark eyes peering out over the gathering crowd. "I wish my mother and father could have come," Tia said.

"I'm sure they would have if your pa had'n taken sick." Jed felt his stomach tighten as he watched the small casket being carried forward to be placed atop the fake greenery laid across the opened grave.

Her breath caught on a sob, as Tia remembered something she had said many years ago in another lifetime. *"Even the heavens will be crying over what I am being forced to do this day."*

That event in her life had turned out well, but how could she hope to get through this? She was losing everyone she held dear, including Appearing Wolf. If her grandfather made her leave as she felt sure he would, she knew he too would be gone from her. Trying to quiet her rushing thoughts, she watched the many mourners who had come to pay their respects.

"Are you all right?" Jed leaned his head close to hers.

"Yes," she said, then drew in her breath as she felt someone step up beside her.

Eathen stood his hands folded in front of him, his swollen blue eyes never leaving the pale, lavender coffin holding the body of the woman he had wronged. Without thinking, Tia reached out, taking his cold hand in hers. With a loud sob, he gathered her small body into his arms. As he held her, they heard the eulogy begin.

"We are gathered here today to pay homage to our dear departed sister in faith, Charlotte Vanessa Thornton born July twenty-eighth, in the year of our Lord eighteen and fifty-five. She took for her husband, Eathen Charles Thornton. The Lord blessed this union with a daughter, Jessie Victoria. But as the Lord giveth, He can also taketh away. Jessie returned to our Heavenly Father in the year of our Lord, nineteen and three." He stood for a moment looking out over the many people who had braved the inclement weather to be there. "All of us here will miss Charlotte, who was a fine lady and a credit to our community. I personally remember a time a few years back. There was a family living here in dire need of food and clothing." The reverend smiled and taking a handkerchief from his back pocket mopped his eyes before continuing. "I stopped by the Thornton ranch right after church and as I walked up the steps, Charlotte came outside to meet me. Now, I ain't throwin' any stones when I say this, but the first words outta Charlotte's mouth, were to tell me I'd be wastin' my breath to try and get her to come to church. I said, although I'd love to have her join our church, that wasn't why I had stopped by." He chuckled as he remembered the doubting look crossing Charlotte's face. "When I told her the reason for my bein' there, she took my hand. She said, 'In that case, come on in the house.' She sat me down at her table and served me coffee and cake just like I was a friend of hers. To make a long story short, by the time I left, I had Charlotte's promise the family in need would be taken care of. She kept that promise and I never forgot her for that." He nodded to the man standing closest to the casket who lifted the top half up and back. "As we look now upon the face of our sister, I would like us now to ask our Heavenly Father to receive Charlotte into his holy kingdom, after which time, we will give to Charlotte, our last good-byes on this earth," Reverend Jordon declared.

Keeping a firm hand on both Tia and Eathen, Jed led the three of them forward to stand before Charlotte's opened casket. Dressed in a pale green suit, with her white hair braided and pined atop her head, Charlotte seemed to be enjoying a rest.

As Eathen brushed one large hand down the side of her face, they heard his breath catch.

"I know our last moments together were filled with bitterness, but…Charlotte…with all my heart…I'm askin' for your forgiveness," Eathen sobbed, his large shoulders shaking.

As he started to weave, Tom rushed forward. Placing Eathen between them, Jed and Tom walked back to the car, followed by Tia and Hattie. After helping the overwrought man into the back seat, Jed closed the door. In silence they all bowed their heads, as Reverend Jordon concluded the interment.

All through the long, rain-filled day, Tia helped Hattie serve the many people who had followed them back to the house. As evening drew near, and the last of the mourners had taken their leave, Tia fixed a small plate of food to take up to Eathen. He had gone up to his room as soon as they arrived back at the ranch.

Standing outside the closed bedroom door, she started to knock then withdrew her hand as the sounds of weeping came to her from the other side. Not wanting to intrude on such an intimate moment, she turned away.

"Is he all right?" Jed asked, coming down the hall.

"I'm not sure." She motioned him forward.

Jed listened for a moment then pulled Tia back down the hall after him.

"I think he'll be all right. It's when a person tries to keep the grief locked inside the trouble starts." He draped an arm around her shoulders. "I wouldn't put too much stock in what happened out at the cemetery though. He might of been willin', right at that moment, to lean on anyone. So, don't get your hopes up."

"I think you're wrong, Jed. I can't explain why I feel the way I do, so please don't ask me."

"I hope you're not lettin' yourself in for more heartache," he said, as they walked downstairs.

"Hattie," Tia halted her, as she watched her carry yet another stack of dishes to the kitchen, "why don't you leave the cleanup until later? Neither one of us is in any mood to do it now."

"Ah doan mine," she placed the dishes in the sink, "it'll keeps mah hands busy. Miss Tia," she turned around, "wuz you able ter talks ter Mist' Eathen?"

"No. I thought it best to leave him alone."

"Awright den," she pumped cold water into a large dishpan, "but effen he does gits hongry ah'll keeps his food wahmin' in de oven fer him."

"Thank you, Hattie."

"Dis ole house woan bes de same widout Miss Charlotte hyah ter talks ter." She lifted the teakettle from the stove. "Ah doan knows whut's gwine ter happens ter dis fambly anymo'." Hattie poured hot water into the dish pan, "Miss Charlotte wuz de only one dat could holds it tergither."

"I can still feel her presence." Tia slipped her arms around Hattie's waist, laying her head against her broad back. "I've often heard a spirit will linger on for a while in a place where they felt happy. I know Gram had a lot of heartache in this house. But, Hattie, there had to have been a lot of good times too."

"Der wuz," she nodded her linen-wrapped head in agreement. "Ah knows dar wuz, b' kase ah wuz a part of it. Miss Charlotte, she never treated me lak ah wuz jes' de hired he'p," she murmured, her soapy hands stilled as she recalled the happy moments. "Ah's sho glad you come w'en you did, chile."

"When I think of all the times I wanted to come to Montana and didn't, I could cry. All those years we could have had together, instead of the few weeks every year that she came to Boston to see me. I'm glad I didn't give Mother and Father a chance to talk me out of it this time."

"Maybe de time wuzn' right til now."

"That could be. She told me how frightened she felt when I showed up without any warning. She feared how my grandfather would feel about seeing me. But I'll tell you, Hattie, no matter how this all turns out, now that Grandfather Eathen is back, I'll never regret coming."

"Ah'm glads ter hear dat, chile."

"Hattie," Tia said, then waited for the woman to turn around to face her, "I don't want you to worry about anything. If it turns out you aren't welcome here anymore, then you will come back to Boston with me."

"Lawd, Miss Tia," her dark eyes went wide with worry, "ah never even gived dat a thought." She looked around the large kitchen. "Dis ole house's been mah home fer forty-one y'ars. Ah jes' kain leaves hyah. Mist' Eathen'd never does dat ter ole Hattie," she cried, her big shoulders shaking. "Ah jes' knows he twouldn'."

"Hattie," Tia pulled her apron away from her face, "I am sure you're right. Come on now, dry your eyes." She handed her a clean dishtowel, then drew back as Hattie proceeded to blow her nose into the towel. "I want you to put all this from your mind."

Hattie lifted her apron to her eyes wiping them dry. "Ah sho hopes you bes right, Miss Tia. Lawd knows Ah do."

Tia took the soiled dishrag from Hattie's hands. Going through the door onto the screened-in back porch, she draped the dishrag over the washtub.

"Tia," Jed said, standing in the doorway, "could l talk to you a moment?"

"Of course, Jed. Let's go into the parlor."

As the two young people walked away, Hattie watched them shaking her head with sadness.

Seating herself in the chair nearest the hearth, Tia waited for Jed to tell her what he wanted to talk with her about.

"This might not be the right time to talk about this, Tia." He sat down on the edge of a chair near to the one she had chosen, then got to his feet, unable to stay still. "But now that Eathen's here, we might not have any time."

Steeling herself for what she felt sure he wanted to say, Tia gazed at the nervous young man standing before her.

"Have you given any thought to what you'll do if Eathen tells you he don't want you here now?"

"I haven't thought of anything else, Jed. I guess I'll pack up and go back to Boston."

"Could I make a suggestion? He tugged the tie from around his neck.

With a slight nod she waited.

"I know I'm just a foreman and don't make much money, but I been savin' up to buy a piece of land not too far from here." He dropped the wadded up tie on the chair. "I've always been handy with a hammer and nails. I'm sure I could turn out a fair cabin..." his voice trailed off, as Tia left her chair.

"I appreciate what you're trying to do, Jed. Your wanting to take care of me, now that you think I may not have any place else to go, is very thoughtful. But, I can't let you do that. You have too much to offer a girl. Staying with someone you're not in love with, wouldn't be fair." She winced as she saw the pain in his eyes at her words.

As he stood there, Jed felt his heart twist inside his chest as though a giant hand had reached inside to rip it from his body. All he could see was her back. It seemed to blot out everything else in his world as he watched her walk out of his life.

***

Dressed in one of Charlotte's old flannel nightgowns and robe, with her tiny feet encased with slippers, Tia sat curled up in a big, over-stuffed chair. The flames in the hearth flickered, warming her in the dark stillness. As she sat there alone in the quiet room, her thoughts reflected on all that had happened since she had come to Montana.

She could see her grandmother's face as she waved her forward that early morning after she stepped off the train in Cut Bank. In spite of herself, she had to laugh at the sight in her mind's eye of Jed hauling the gruff cowboy, who had insulted her, off his horse to send him sprawling into the muddy street. Then she pictured Jed as he looked that evening after her grandmother was laid to rest, his handsome face alive with feeling offering to take care of her, and her laughter faded. So many memories, she thought. Had it really been less than five months since she came? So much had happened in that short span of time. An entire lifetime.

Appearing Wolf came stealing into her thoughts as she sat there. She remembered the pain in his ebony eyes when she did not recognize him the first time he had made his presence known to her. And the way her heart had filled with fear the night she awakened to find him standing at the foot of her bed. How she wished they could have remained in the past with their people safe and alive, and their son growing up surrounded by their love. She missed him so very much. No matter how long it took for her to return to him, she knew she would never love another.

"Tia," startled she looked up, surprised to see her grandfather standing beside her, "I don't mean to disturb you, but I think the time has come for us to talk." He pulled a chair up beside hers. She heard him emit a warm laugh. "I remember when Charlotte would wear that old gown and robe. She said it kept her bones warm."

"I hope you don't mind my wearing it. It still carries a faint smell of her perfume." She lifted her arm to her face, inhaling the sweet scent. "I guess it made me feel closer to her somehow."

"No, I don't mind." Eathen ran a light hand over the sleeve. "I think that's the reason I've been spendin' so much time in our room since I returned. That's where I feel the closest to her."

"I feared you might be staying away because you didn't want to see

283

me." Tia looked over at him.

"I won't lie to you, young lady," his dark blue eyes gazed at her, "that's part of it. But if I've come to realize one thing in all my years of livin' on this earth, it's the realization that you can't hide from the truth."

"Yes," she agreed, shocked at how much he had aged in the last few days, "yet we all try."

"If you were directin' that statement at me," Eathen said, his voice devoid of any anger, "I don't deny it, Tia."

"No, it wasn't directed at you, Grandfather Eathen," she told him, her own voice filled with understanding, "I meant that we all tend to delude ourselves at one time or another."

"Little girl," he leaned forward in his chair, "I been runnin' from the truth for damn near eighteen years! And I'll tell you, it's damn near ruined my life. I can't change what I've done in the past. That's a given! All I can do is try'n make amends for the mistakes I've made these many years. If you'll let me," he offered his hand to her, "I'd like to start with you."

She sat still trying to calm herself. Then she looked him straight in his eyes.

"I wish I could say all is forgiven, but I can't. Not until you tell me what happened to my father."

"Just like your grandmother, you don't mince words," he gazed at her, with something akin to respect. "All right, Tia, you asked me somethin' you gotta right to know." He left her to move over to the hearth. "But bear with me 'cause I don't know if I even know the answer to that question myself."

Striking a match against the dark red bricks, he held the flame to the tip of a long cheroot held between his fingers, drawing on the end for a moment before throwing the burnt match into the fire. Through the gray blue smoke he watched her. As though he had made a decision, he declared.

"Other than losin' your mother, and layin' your grandmother to rest, this is gonna be the hardest thing I've ever had to do."

"I'm sure it will be almost as difficult to hear." Tia tucked her long legs beneath her in the chair.

"Right now," he told her, "I'd be glad to trade you."

"Gram already told me everything concerning my mother, the night you found out she carried me. She could only tell me what she suspected about my father."

"And what did she tell you?" He held his breath waiting for her answer.

"She believes you killed him." Tia faced him unafraid.

Without flinching he breathed. "She's right, Tia, I did."

"Why?" Tia's legs hit the floor. "You didn't have to do that. He was my father!"

"He was the man who had soiled my little girl!" Eathen matched her in her anger.

"They loved each other!" Tia screamed, coming all the way to her feet.

"Love had nothin' to do with it!" He turned his back to her. "He used that to put his filthy hands on a white girl! Jessie is all I had!" Eathen whirled to face her. "The one person in this whole goddamn world who truly loved me!"

"Gram loved you! And I saw where it got her! You didn't only kill my father!" Tia glared at him. "You killed her too!"

"That's not true!" The fight drained from him. "I gave her all that money could buy! She never wanted for anything!." In desperation his rage rekindled itself, "Not...one...goddamn...thing!"

"*You* are all she ever wanted! Tia walked over to stand before him. "But you couldn't give her that!" She balled her fists on her slim hips. "The family you have in Helena is all you care about!"

"She didn't miss a lick, did she?" Eathen stood gaping at her.

"She had to share that burden with someone!" Tia's dark brown eyes flashed fire. "I am the one who stayed with her while she died. The last thing she talked about is the ivory-handled brush you gave her for her thirty-third wedding anniversary."

"What did she say?" He clamped down hard on the cigar.

"She said, 'now I know why he gave it to me.' I don't understand the meaning of that, but I'm sure you do."

With a slight nod he turned away, but not before she saw tears running down his face. "Just before our anniversary is when I met Pamela Ann, the mother of my son. She musta thought that's the reason I gave her such an extravagant gift."

"Isn't it?" Tia's voice sounded cold.

"No!" He drew a hand across his face. "When I saw it there in the store, I remembered how much she had admired one just like it when we still lived in Boston, a few days after our weddin'. Back then, all I had is this land. He spread his hands wide. "It takes time for investments to pay off. Time, luck, and nerves of steel to gamble everything on gut instinct," he said almost to himself, then shaking his head, continued. "I remember how her beautiful blue eyes lit up when she took it outta the box." His shoulders slumped. "Now…you're tellin' me I destroyed that memory too. On her death bed."

Tia fought to hold onto her angry feelings, telling herself, because of him her parents had been taken from her, but it didn't do any good. She had been raised on forgiveness. The coldness in her heart melted. "I'm sorry, Grandfather Eathen." she wiped the tears from her face. "I shouldn't have told you."

Shocked at the look of warmth on her face, after the terrible way he had treated her all her life, Eathen gazed at her in utter amazement. "Tia, I don't know if you'll believe me or not, but you couldn't tell me anything, I ain't already told myself a million times."

"I still don't understand why you killed my father, but I do know you're sorry for hurting Gram."

"I killed your father in a fit of rage, Tia," he said, as though realizing it himself for the first time. "And nobody coulda made me believe I'd ever regret it. But I know now I'm the one who destroyed my Jessie." He gulped a sob, dropping his face in his hands. "Not you…not your grandmother…me."

"We all make mistakes, Grandfather Eathen. When we realize those mistakes, is when we can begin to heal from them."

"Do you think you could ever forgive me, Tia?" He pulled a handkerchief from his back pocket. "Not just for what I did to Jessie and your father." He mopped his face, then blew his nose. "But also for the way I treated you?"

Without a word she walked over to him and standing on her tiptoes placed a soft kiss on his stubbled cheek.

Before she could move away, he reached out hugging her small body close to him.

"You don't need to worry 'bout goin' back to Boston, Tia. You gotta home here just as long as you wanna stay."

In an instant, the sound of soft laughter echoed throughout the quiet house.

Chapter Thirty-Two

"Jed, hold up there," Eathen ordered, walking towards the mounted ranch-hands. "I need to talk to you."

Kneeing his horse a short distance away from the waiting men, Jed gazed down at him. "You needen concern yourself, Eathen." He pulled up on the reins of the skittish horse. "I'm just a foreman. Your granddaughter put me in my place."

Squinting up at the young man still seated in the saddle, Eathen growled, "I don't have the first goddamn clue what you're talkin' 'bout. What I wanna know about is someone tryin' to hurt Tia. We'll get into the other later." Eathen held Jed's stare a moment longer.

"Yeah, I'm sure we will," Jed breathed, turning his full attention on the man watching him. "I'd been in the house talkin' to Miss Charlotte when Tom came in to tell me Tia had taken off on that big paint. The one that damn near killed her. I'd headed out to go lookin' for her when she rode in." He rubbed the horse on the side of his neck to quiet him as he began to prance eager to be gone. "We'd been standin' on the porch talkin' when a shot rang out that damn near hit Tia, I got her inside as fast as I could, then me and Tom went lookin'. By then, whoever shot at her had already gone. So, I posted some of the hands to stand guard around the house for the night and I slept inside."

"Which brings us to the part about my granddaughter puttin' you in your place." Eathen glared up at him. "If you tried anything with her," he shook a finger at Jed, "I'll personally beat you within an inch of your life!"

"All I did to your to your granddaughter," Jed growled, "is offer her a life with me, as my wife. 'Fore you gotta chance to kick her to the road!"

"Just goes to show how goddamn wrong you were, don't it?" Eathen held his gaze steady. "Tia's my granddaughter. She ain't goin' nowhere. And you," Eathen slapped the horse on the hindquarters, "have had your first and last warnin' to stay away from her."

"You ain't got no worries there, Eathen." Jed pulled the prancing horse back around. "She made it damn clear she ain't interested."

"Then I guess you still gotta job as foreman." Eathen turned on his heel to leave then halted as he spied Wolfer riding towards him. When the man drew even with him, Eathen declared, "Come on up to the house, I wanna talk to you about somethin'."

Wolfer had just sat down when Eathen walked behind his desk. "I gotta blank check right here, right now! All you gotta do is name your price!" Eathen slapped a checkbook down on the heavy oak top.

"Who do I haveta kill?" Wolfer grinned, propping one leg atop of his knee.

"Jeremy McKennah." Eathen delivered the tone of his voice, leaving no doubt as to the seriousness of the situation.

"What's happened?" Wolfer dropped his leg to the floor, leaning forward in his chair.

"Somebody took a shot at my granddaughter the other day. I think it could have been McKennah. He's the one who murdered Vada Lee. I'm willin' to put money on it! Now he's out to get Tia." Eathen rubbed a rough hand across his stubbled chin. "The one thing I don't understand is why."

"Have you talked to Tia about this?" He withdrew a rolled cigarette from his shirt pocket. "Maybe in his mind she gave him a reason."

"I guess it wouldn't hurt. Although with a sick son-of-a-bitch like that, he don't need a reason." Eathen shoved an ashtray across the desk.

"I'd see what I could find out, 'fore we go off half-cocked and do somethin' we'll regret."

"Shit!" Eathen gave him a sideways glance. "Killin' McKennah wouldn't cause me any regrets! But you're right. I'll have a talk with her."

"She's quite a girl." Wolfer struck a match, holding it to the tip of his cigarette. "You're real lucky to have her."

"I'm finally beginnin' to see that, Wolfer." He grinned, as he saw the shocked look on the man's face. "I've wasted a lotta years tryin' to run from life, when all I had to do is stand still and enjoy it." Eathen withdrew a bottle of whiskey from the side drawer of the desk. "I guess we never get too old to learn, huh?"

"I guess not," Wolfer took the glass of whiskey Eathen held out to him.

"If it turns out I'm right, about Jeremy, the money'll still be here."

"If it turns out you're right," Wolfer emptied his glass in one swallow, "you won't haveta pay me."

Wolfer had almost reached the door when he heard Tia call out to him. Coming down the stairs, she greeted him. "You weren't going to leave without seeing me. Were you?"

"I'm glad now I didn't." He smiled, taking her small hands in his.

"Come on," she told him. "I'll walk out with you."

Grabbing his hat from the coat rack, he followed the laughing young girl outside.

"How is Pehta?" She linked her arm with his. "Have you seen him lately?"

"Not since the day the three of us spent together." Wolfer patted the hand on his arm. "He was very glad to see you. You're all he could talk about after we left."

"One day soon you'll have to come over, and we'll go visit him."

"He'd like that, Tia." Wolfer stepped into the saddle. Touching a light hand to the brim of his hat, he rode away.

"That's one hellva man right there," Eathen said.

"Yes," Tia agreed, "I like him a lot."

Wrapping a strong arm around her waist, Eathen walked with her towards the house, when he stopped and looked up at the sky. "Look at that," he pointed. Following his gaze, she saw a long line of geese their honking cries echoing through the still afternoon. "The snow ain't far behind now," he wagged his broad head at the thought, "funny how the animals and wildlife always seem to know, ain't it?"

Tia slipped her own arm around his thick waist above his wide belt buckle, smiling, as she nodded her agreement.

"Let's set down here a moment." He dropped down on the front porch step.

When she sat beside him, he pulled a long slender pipe from his pocket to tap it against the banister.

"Will this bother you?"

"Not at all," she grinned. "I like the smell of a pipe."

"Tia, how well do you know Jeremy McKennah?"

"Not very well" Her brows lifted at his question. "I try to avoid him when I can."

"Oh? Why's that?"

"He makes me uneasy." She smoothed out her long skirt. "That and I could never abide those who think they're better than others. The night of Gram's party he made a snide remark about Jed's being invited." She wrinkled her nose at the memory. "I let him know I didn't appreciate it."

"What did McKennah have to say to that?"

"I didn't give him time to react. I just walked away from him." Tia drew back, looking up at her grandfather. "Come to think of it, I didn't see him anymore after that."

"You didn't happen to notice if he went to the kitchen did you?"

"No. I just wanted to get away from him."

"I'm glad to hear that, Tia." He clamped the pipe between his teeth. "He ain't a person I'd want you to keep company with."

"Gram felt the same way. She always made sure she stayed nearby when we visited with Sarah."

"I don't like to scare you, Tia, but I think Jeremy McKennah's the one who killed Vada Lee. I also think he mighta been involved in that shootin' incident the other day."

"Why would Jeremy want to harm me?" She lifted a nervous hand to toy with the buttons on her shirt. "I've never done anything to bring on such feelings."

"When you're dealin' with a sick mind, there don't have to be a reason. If you walked away from him in front of a crowd of people, that could be enough."

"What am I going to do?" She pulled her wind-blown hair out of her eyes. "If you're right, that means I can't even go riding anymore."

"No, Tia. You are not to leave this ranch until this is all over!" His voice deepened with authority.

At the look on her face, he laughed. "I sound like a grandfather. Don't I?"

She leaned her head against his shoulder. "At long last."

"Amen to that!" He returned her affection.

"What are we going to do about this problem, Grandfather Eathen?" she asked, in all seriousness.

"That's somethin' you don't need to worry your pretty head about, Tia. Everythin's bein' taken care of. All you have to concern yourself with is what you want to do with the rest of your life."

"I really haven't given it much thought. I do know I don't want to return to Boston. Even though it will hurt my mother and father very much when I tell them. My life is here, now. I don't want to live anywhere else."

"Even knowin', that someday soon, I'll be bringin' Pamela Ann and Charles here to live?"

The thought of another woman living in her grandmother's house, and sharing a life her grandmother had yearned for all these many years, filled Tia with a deep sense of loyalty to her grandmother's memory. But as she sat there trying to reason out what she should do, the thought of another woman and child going through the same pain she and her grandmother had suffered left her with but one choice to make. The time had come to let by-gones be just that. "You have to live your life in your own way, Grandfather Eathen. Just as I have to live mine," she told him.

Tia knew Jed went out of his way to avoid her now and it made her heart ache to lose the closeness between them. Standing alone on the back porch, she could hear him talking and laughing with the other hands. Had he not made his feelings known to her, they could still be enjoying the friendship that had made her days on the ranch so much easier.

Unwilling to accept Jed's stubbornness, she began making her way to the bunkhouse when she spied Wolfer riding towards her.

"What a lovely surprise," she said, shading her eyes from the sun as he dismounted.

Wolfer took her small hands in both of his. "It's always a pleasure to see you, Tia."

"Grandfather Eathen is in the house. Come on, I'll go with you."

"I didn't come out here to see your grandfather, Tia." He held onto her hands. "I came to see you."

At her questioning look, he replied.

"Pehta asked me to stop by. He wants you to come see him. He didn't think Eathen would look upon his comin' here with a kind eye after what happened with Frank McKennah. I thought we could all meet down by the lake, like we did last time."

"When?"

"He's waitin' for you now."

"Hey, Wolfer," Eathen called out. "What the hell brings you all the way out here again?"

"I came by to see if Tia would like to go ridin' with me. Stayin' cooped up on this ranch day after day's got to be wearin' a little thin."

"I don't think that's a good idea, Wolfer." Eathen pulled Tia against his side. "I'd prefer her to stay close until whoever took a shot at her the other day's caught. I know you think you can protect her," he held up a hand as Wolfer started to speak, "but I'd feel a lot better if she stayed here."

"I can't fault you for that, Eathen," Wolfer said, turning to leave.

"You don't haveta leave," Eathen slapped him on the back. "Come on inside, I got something I need to discuss with you anyway."

"I guess I can stay for a few minutes. I'm sorry, Tia. Your grandfather's just doin' what he feels is best for you. There'll be other days."

Nodding, she walked away.

Seated before the crackling fire, Eathen rolled his glass of bourbon back and forth between his hands. Almost to himself, he declared, "I told Tia I planned on bringin' Pamela Ann and Charles here to the ranch to live."

"What was her reaction to that?" Wolfer took a long swallow of his drink.

"She seemed to have no problem with it." He shrugged his shoulders. "I wasted a lotta years with that girl. She's one in a million."

"With all she's been through, she still has time to think of others." He held up his glass in a salute. "That's rare in someone her age."

"Yeah, it is," Eathen agreed. "John and Martha done one helluva job in raisin' her. I'll give them that."

"I'm gonna tell you somethin' I doubt you're gonna approve of. The real reason I came out here today, is to ask Tia to go with me to meet someone she's become very fond of."

"Who's that?" Eathen shot a wary glance across the desk.

"Pehta."

"I didn't even know that she knew him." Eathen's chair creaked as he leaned forward.

"She met him the day Jed took her to the reservation to pick up those horses you bought off Hardiman. Then again, the day he came here to the ranch with Black Elk about the two cows some of their men stole from you."

"I never heard anything about it, but I have just myself to blame for that. People couldn't tell me somethin' if I was never here to tell."

"She really would like to go see him. I'd make sure nothin' happened to her."

"Why didn't you just bring him here?"

"He thought it'd be better to see her away from the ranch," he glanced at Eathen over the top of his glass. "He thinks you might still be upset over his killin' McKennah."

"Goddamn it! I couldn't give a shit less about McKennah," Eathen growled. "He shoulda known he could come here. Where the hell is he?"

"He's waitin'," down by the lake," Wolfer told him.

***

She could not believe how easy it had been to coax the horse away from the others. It was almost as if he had been waiting for her.

"Grandfather Eathen will be furious when he finds me gone, but I can't disappoint Pehta, Shadow Dancer," she told the big paint, as they made their way towards the lake. As if in answer, he threw up his head, snorting , his silky black mane shimmering in the crisp afternoon sunlight.

Riding through the familiar surroundings, the memories of those long-ago days raced through her mind. She could see the happy faces of her people, hear their joyful laughter. Her heart ached for their closeness again.

The spirit of her mother came to her. Sitting her horse, Tia waited.

"My daughter, my eyes have ached to look upon your smiling face again. You do not belong in the white world, Tia. Your place is here, amongst your people," Jolisha whispered.

Through the mist, Tia could see the Blackfeet camp as it had been before the massacre. Her loved ones gathered there, watching and waiting. Then before her eyes they began to fade, until she could no longer see them. With a sob, she kneed her horse forward once more.

Up ahead, in the tall bunch grass, she saw a movement.

A shot rang out, pulling Eathen from his chair.

"Now, what the hell's goin' on?" Eathen growled, glancing out the window.

"Your guess is as good as mine, but I intend to find out!" Wolfer said, already heading out of the room.

"Mist' Eathen, sumbody's shootin'! Hattie called out running from the kitchen. "It gittin' so a pusson ain' safe in dey's own house."

"Where's Tia?!" Eathen asked her.

"Ah thought she wuz hyah wid y'all."

"No, hell, she ain't with me goddamn it! He strode to the gun cabinet. Opening the glass door, he lifted out one of the weapons,

293

levering a shell into the chamber on his way to the door.

"Get upstairs and see if she's there," Eathen ordered over his shoulder. "If she is, holler to me out the window."

"All's dis 'citement's gwine ter puts me right alongside Miss Charlotte!" Hattie grumbled making her way up the stairs.

Finding Tia's room empty, she sat down on the bed, wringing her hands in a worried manner. "Lawd Jesus! Gives me strent!" she cried rolling her big dark eyes heavenward.

Eathen had almost reached the bunkhouse when another shot rang out. The twanging sound of a bullet meeting metal echoed through the stillness. With a roar of anger, he came around the corner just as Billie took aim on another can.

"You drop that fuckin' hammer," he raised a shotgun to his shoulder, "I swear to Christ, I'll shoot you where you stand," Eathen vowed.

Lowering the rifle a gaping Billie looked to where Eathen stood glaring at him. "We's just doin' ah little target shootin, Mr. Eathen," he stammered. "We ain't destroyin' nothin'."

"Just my goddamn sanity's all!" Eathen snarled.

"Where the hell's your brains, Stanford?" He turned his attention on Jed. "A few days ago somebody took a shot at my granddaughter! Now here you are, out here bouncin' goddamn cans off a post. You either get your shit together, or get the hell off my property!"

Unable to argue, Jed turned away.

"Now where in the hell's Wolfcr?" Eathen swung around, eyeing the men standing with their heads lowered. "He came out here ahead of me to see what the hell's goin' on."

"He rode out a few minutes ago." Tom pointed a thumb in the direction of the path leading away from the ranch. "He asked why the big Paint wasn't in the corral and when none of us could tell him he mounted up and left."

"There ain't a fence in Montana could hold that big son-of-a-bitch when he takes a notion to go," Jed growled. "If I didn't know better, I'd think he belonged to the devil hisself. It'd suit me just fine if he stayed gone."

"Ain't that the one Tia always rides when she takes off on her own?" Eathen asked.

"Yeah," Jed nodded, "but she didn't take him this time, or one of us woulda seen her."

"Don't be too goddamn sure," Eathen snapped. "Saddle up my horse."

A cold hand of fear clutched Jed's heart as he made his way toward the corrals. "Hold up a minute, Eathen."

Without breaking stride, Eathen called back over his shoulder, "You better hope to hell she's all right, Stanford."

"I thought she was inside with you," Jed growled, hastening his steps. "There's no goddamn way she coulda got past all of us, without one of us seein' her."

"Well she did!" Eathen stepped up on the corral fence. "She ain't in the house. Hurry up with that horse, damn it!" he yelled at the hand busy cinching up the saddle. "Wolfer said Pehta was waitin' for her down by the lake." He struck a match on the fence then held it to the tip of his cigar. "It'd be my bet that's where we'll find her."

"Of all the foolhardy goddamn things to do." He punched the fence bruising his knuckles. "Ken," he yelled to the man leading Eathen's horse toward the corrals, "your horse is already saddled, so I'm takin' him to find Tia."

"All right, Jed! Go get him!" Ken called back.

"That granddaughter of yours needs to be upended and a hand laid across her little ass!" Jed breathed.

"Rest assured, Stanford," Eathen told him, snatching up the reins Ken held out to him, "it won't be your hand!"

Without waiting, Jed stomped off to where Ken's horse stood tied to the fence. Stepping into the saddle he slapped the reins against the horse's side, to send him racing toward the lake. Praying all the while they weren't too late.

Chapter Thirty-Three

"Pehta, wait!" Tia called out, as she glimpsed a horse disappearing amongst the trees.

At the sound, the rider turned back, waiting.

Dismounting, Tia began walking toward the trees when a slight movement in the tall bunch grass caught her eye. Running forward, her heart leaped in her throat as she saw Pehta crawling through the grass.

"Pehta, my god, what happened!?" She knelt beside the wounded man.

"Tia! You must go!" He tried to reach out to her, but his hand fell back to the ground. "You are in danger here!" Pehta's breath labored in his chest.

"I can't leave you," she whimpered, staring at the bright blood staining his shirt. "Who did this?"

"Jeremy McKennah," he murmured. "He's up there in those trees."

"Do you think you can stand? We need to both get out of here."

"Don't wait for me, just go!"

"I can't!" she screamed. "You have to help me! Oh please! Get up!"

Shaking his head, he tried to speak but a pinkish foam bubbling up from his throat made any words he might have spoken impossible.

"Noooo!" she wailed, pulling him to a sitting position, only to have him slump back to the ground when she tried to lift him. With her heart pounding in her chest she looked around for Shadow Dancer, but to her horror she saw he no longer stood where she had left him.

"Oh, god!" she sobbed, dropping down beside the dying man once more. "I don't know what to do, Pehta!"

With sadness he grasped her hand.

"Maybe Grandfather Eathen will realize I'm gone, and come after me," Tia told him, knowing, even as she said it, no one would be able to get to them in time. As if in a daze she looked up to see a rider coming towards them. When he drew closer, she could see the grinning face of Jeremy McKennah watching her.

"Nice of you to call out, Tia," he told her, dismounting. "I was already on my way back to the ranch when I heard your sweet voice."

"Why did you do this, Jeremy? Why?" She choked out the words.

"I did it for my granddaddy, Tia. I couldn't let this red nigger live after he went and killed my granddaddy," he hunkered down beside her. "I'm a McKennah. Why, I wouldn't be able to hold my head up around here if I didn't revenge ole Frank's murder."

"And Vada Lee?" Tia crawled to her feet. "She was just a little girl. What could she have done to deserve what you did to her?"

"That little pickaninny? She shoulda been glad I even wasted my time on her." He pulled a rolled cigarette from his shirt pocket. "And after I busted her, do you know what she did?" He stuck the cigarette all the way in his mouth then pulled it out real slow, leering at Tia. "She threatened to tell everyone. Do you think I wanted it known, I hadda settle for a stinkin' nigger? There are just too many people runnin' 'round, who don't know their place." He laughed, as his hand shot out to jerk her up against him.

"You're sick, Jeremy." Tia pushed against his chest. "Can't you see that?"

"Yep, just too many people who don't know their place," he repeated, as if she had not spoken.

"You are the one who shot at me!" she said, as he began dragging her towards his horse. "Aren't you, Jeremy?"

"You're trash, Tia. I could overlook the fact, but when you walked away from me the night of the party in front of all my neighbors like you was better'n me, I couldn't overlook that," he grinned cupping her face and dragging her mouth to his.

As she felt his tongue slide into her mouth she bit down with all her might.

"You little bitch!" He slapped her away from him.

"You'll never get away with this. Grandfather Eathen knows where I am." She rubbed her bruised cheek. "If I'm not back soon, he'll come looking for me."

"He'll come lookin', but he won't find you." Jeremy grabbed her breasts hard, laughing when she screamed out in pain. "I got plans for you, bitch. You got any idea how much some of the men up in these mountains'd be willin' to pay for a nice little piece like you to keep them warm through the long winter?"

"You wouldn't dare try something like that." Tia stumbled to the ground as he shoved her away from him.

"Oh, but I would, Tia. At first I had planned on killin' you. It was pure luck I missed. With Granddaddy gone, I gotta look out for myself." Jeremy flicked the half-smoked cigarette into the air. "Now that we ain't got the cattle business to fall back on, things are startin' to get a little tight."

"Frank McKennah got just what he deserved!" Tia screamed at him. "I'm glad Pehta killed him!"

In an instant, his hand shot out to deliver a vicious slap across her mouth. "You filthy red trash! You ain't even fit to speak his name!"

An idea crept across her mind that seemed to push all the fear she had been feeling, as she looked into the craze-filled eyes of Jeremy McKennah, deep inside. Wiping the blood from her mouth, she smiled.

"Don't you know where you are, Jeremy?"

"Yeah, I know where I am, you stupid bitch," he breathed. "I'm standin' here with the stench of a dead red skin burnin' my nostrils so bad it turns my guts. Let's go before I get sick," he snarled, reaching for her.

Backing out of his reach, she laughed. "Oh believe me, Jeremy, you're going to be much more than sick. You're going to dead."

"That slap musta knocked you senseless. No one's gonna touch me."

"Didn't your grandfather ever tell you what happened here?" She continued to taunt him. "Didn't he tell you how he led a bunch of the ranchers here to slaughter my people?"

"Your people?" Surprise flitted across his face. "What the hell you talkin' 'bout?"

"The Kainah Blackfeet who lived near this lake were my people, Jeremy. Your grandfather led the raid that killed us. I am one of those he murdered." She advanced in a steady movement towards him. "The same blood that ran in his veins also runs in yours. We have waited many years for you to return to us, Jeremy. At long last our waiting is over."

Now it was Jeremy's turn to back away. "You're crazy," he stammered. "All that talk 'bout this place bein' haunted, are just stupid legends!"

"No, Jeremy," she shook her head, "they are true."

He drew his gun as a cold chill crept down his back.

Noting the way his hand trembled, she lowered her voice. "See, you can feel their icy touch."

"Shut up! Just shut up!" Jeremy muttered, looking around the quiet lake. "I can't concentrate."

"Do you think they will let you leave, when they have been waiting for almost fifty years for you?" Tia dropped her voice to a whisper. "Why don't you go to them? You have never been brave before, Jeremy. Killing a child and an old man does not take strength." She edged closer to him. "Show my people you can at least be brave in your coming death."

"Get on the horse, now!" He pushed her toward his skittish mount.

A cold sweat of fear slid down her back as Tia placed her foot in the stirrup, then forced herself to step into the saddle, gripping the reins.

McKennah grabbed hold of the saddle-horn just as Tia kicked out knocking the surprised man to the ground.

With her heart pumping fast, Tia rammed her heels into the horse's sides in an urgent attempt to escape McKennah's madness then slumped forward as she felt a burning pain rip through her side. Wrapping one hand in the horse's mane and the other around the saddle-horn she tried to stay atop the frightened animal, who by now was doing his best to unseat her from his back. Unable to hold on any longer, Tia felt herself being thrown through the air before smashing into the hard ground.

Blackness swirled all around her. She could hear someone talking to her, his voice sounding as if it came from a long way off. Then she recognized his voice, as Pehta touched her.

"Do not try to fight what must be, Tia." Pehta crawled to her ignoring his own wounds staining the ground around them. "I have suffered the torments of those who walk in darkness that I was not there for you when the evil ones came to take your life. This time, you will die in the arms of someone who loves you," he vowed, as he gathered her against his frail chest.

Tia felt all her fear pass away, as her blood mingled with the man holding her close. A feeling of contentment embraced her, only to scurry away as she felt Pehta slump forward then lay still. She touched his face her fear mounting out of control. The last sound she heard was that of Jeremy McKennah's laughter before she closed her eyes giving in to the numbing sense of peace enveloping her.

Out of the mists Appearing Wolf walked towards her and holding out his hand called forth the spirits of the two people he loved with all his soul.

***

Jeremy had finished holstering his gun when he saw two riders racing towards him. As Eathen and Jed jumped from their mounts to check on Tia and Pehta, a nervous Jeremy McKennah approached them.

"It was an accident, Eathen. I tried to tell her that son-of-a-bitch is a one-man horse, but she wanted to ride him anyway." He hunched his shoulders. "When he bolted with her I tried to shoot him and hit her instead," Jeremy hastened to explain, a smug self-satisfied smile flitting across his face. "And ole Pehta there," he touched Pehta's still body with the toe of his boot, "hell he was already dead when Tia and me found him. I'm sorry, but there ain't a damn thing anybody can do 'bout it."

A short distance away, as the first snows of winter fell to the ground Wolfer calmly withdrew a Model 97 Mauser from its leather case. Crouching down he braced the rifle-butt tight against his shoulder, breathing the chilling air deep into his lungs. "Bet me, you son-of-a-bitch." Closing one eye he focused his other eye through the powerful sniper scope, sighting the crosshairs on a point directly between McKennah's eyebrows. As his finger tightened on the trigger he released his breath. "BET...ME!"

***

Tia stood with a strange sense of agility as she reached out to accept Appearing Wolf's outstretched hand, then laughed aloud as he pulled her into his arms. The days she had been away from him slipped away unnoticed. She turned, gazing down at her own body lying next to Pehta's on the hard ground, then smiled as Pehta moved to stand beside her.

"We are free, Little Sister. It is time to leave this place." He nodded toward the most brilliant sun she had ever seen.

Hand in hand they walked forward their eyes filled with the beauty of the dazzling light when Tia stopped and looking back, watched as her grandfather and Jed, hats held in reverence against their chests, knelt beside their still bodies. She could see tears falling down their faces. Some force pulled her towards them, and she moved to stand beside them. Placing one hand on each man's shoulder, Tia bent down. "Do not weep for us. Look with your heart and see we are alive and well."

"They cannot hear you, Tia," Appearing Wolf told her. "They are still of the flesh, your spirit has left the body you see before you."

"Appearing Wolf, I cannot leave them like this." She stared up at him at a loss as to what she should do.

"No, Tia." Appearing Wolf walked to her side. "Do not allow your feelings toward those who are still here to hold you to them. Many stay after their spirits have left their bodies and remain earth-bound. You do not want this. I chose to stay to find you. Now it is time to leave," he pleaded with her. "I cannot force you to come with us it must be your own choice." The contours of his face took on a sense of worry.

Tia felt torn. The deep suffering, apparent on her grandfather's face, cutting into her heart. "He needs me!"

"No, Aakiiwa. Your grandfather has a family. I need you. Do not keep us here for I cannot leave you."

"Appearing Wolf, you must!" she pleaded with him.

"If you do not come with me then I will stay here." The determination on his handsome face telling her he meant what he said. Tia drug her steps in Appearing Wolf's direction, then paused, as she heard Jed's words.

"I loved her. If that bothers you, Eathen then you can do what you will but the fact remains I loved her." Jed gulped a sob unashamed of his actions in front of the man kneeling beside him.

"No, I can't blame you for what you couldn't help." Eathen drew a cupped hand across his mouth, and rising to his feet reached down to pull Jed up beside him. "I've always heard a person goes when it's their time. I guess it was Tia's time."

"At least the son-of-a-bitch who killed her didn't live to brag 'bout it." Jed glanced over at Jeremy McKennah's lifeless body. "Guess we better get him on his horse."

"Leave him right where he lays!" Eathen ordered, as he saw Wolfer ride up.

"Eathen, we can't leave the son-of-a-bitch layin' out here." Jed tried to reason with him.

"Yes, hell we can!" Wolfer climbed down off his horse, kicking Mckennah's body over with the toe of his boot, then stopped as his eyes caught sight of Pehta lying dead on the rough ground. Pulling his hat from his head he knelt beside the only father he had ever known. "I know you told me this day would come, but I never thought it'd hit me this hard." As Jed and Eathen discretely walked away, Wolfer ran a trembling hand down one side of Pehta's face wiping away the dirt. "I want to believe all the things you told me about livin' on after the body's gone." He shook his head in an attempt to make himself believe his words. In a rare show of affection, Wolfer kissed the tips of his fingers placing them on Pehta's forehead. "Goodbye, my father." He rose to his feet standing very still for a moment then walked back to where Jeremy McKennah lay. Squatting down he shoved his hand into what had once been a man's skull but was now a shattered mass of bloody pulp, and rocked back on his heels when he found what he sought. "Thought it'd go clear out the back of his head but all's well that ends well." He tossed the eight-millimeter slug into the air to catch it with his other hand.

Stunned, Jed looked at the two men standing beside him. "What the hell'd you do that for?"

"You don't think I'm goin' up for killin' this son-of-a-bitch!" Wolfer eyed the other man in amazement. "How many men around here do you know who carry a 97 Mauser rifle?" As Jed's expression changed from disgust to complete understanding, Wolfer declared. "Exactly."

"I'll go get his horse," Jed declared.

"Yeah, guess you better." Eathen said. "If it weren't for Sarah, I'd say leave him for the coyotes, but she don't deserve that."

"I'm sorry about Tia, Eathen." Wolfer stood looking down at her, drawing a shaky hand through his hair. "I arrived just a little too late to stop him."

"Not your fault." Eathen took out his handkerchief, blew his nose. "I'm sorry 'bout Pehta"

"He knew it was comin."

When Wolfer ignored Eathen's questioning look, Eathen shoved his handkerchief back in his hip pocket. "Yeah, well you might not have stopped him in time to save them," his gaze wandered back to the two people lying in the wind. "But at least he won't be hurtin' anyone else."

"That's for damn sure." Wolfer agreed then drew in his breath. Three people stood together in the tall bunch grass, two he recognized one he didn't as they raised their hands in farewell. Without stopping to think how it would look to the two men standing beside him, Wolfer pulled his hat from his head to wave it in the air as they disappeared from his sight.

Judith Ann McDowell

Chapter Thirty-Four

Unseen by the men lifting Jeremy's body onto his horse, Tia stood watching them, then turned to Appearing Wolf as a thought struck her. "My Husband, why can we not see Jeremy's spirit?"

"The white one's spirit is unclean." A look of disgust passed over his face. "He chose to live his life doing evil. He cannot be with good spirits." He breathed a deep sigh of relief. "He will be reborn into this life again; if he does not change he will walk in darkness until he does."

"Appearing Wolf I do not wish to stay here any longer. I want to go home."

"Then we shall, Little One." Appearing Wolf smiled down at her upraised face.

Linking their arms together the three of them walked without a backward glance into the brilliant light. As they emerged on the other side Tia could not believe what she was seeing. The camp of her people lay before her. It resembled the old camp so much Tia doubted its existence.

"Am I really seeing this?" she cried in amazement.

"Yes, Tia," Pehta said. "Here we choose how we want to live."

Appearing Wolf left her side moving quickly to where a young boy stood watching them. Picking the child up in his arms, Appearing Wolf hugged his small body close.

Pehta kept his eyes on Tia to see her expression.

"Who is the child Appearing Wolf holds in his arms?" She turned to the man by her side.

"Come, Tia, I will let your husband introduce you."

The boy wiggled in the arms of the man who held him. Lowering him to the ground Appearing Wolf stood silent as the child ran up to Tia throwing his small arms around her legs.

Laughing aloud Tia bent down scooping the little boy into her arms.

"I have missed you, my mother," he told her, smothering her face with childish kisses.

Tia drew back at his words, in her confusion she looked to Appearing Wolf. "How can this be, my husband?"

"The spirit of the son you carried in your body was not destroyed at the time of your death. Only the shell that houses the spirit can die. The spirit lives on. Say hello to your son, Aakiiwa."

The tears came streaming down her face as she held onto the child filling her heart with his love.

Tia turned around to see her mother and father standing a short distance away, holding out their arms to her. Her steps hastened to them.

"At last you are back with us," Jolisha murmured into Tia's hair as she embraced her.

"We have missed you, my daughter," Spotted Owl told her, his face aglow with his love for her.

"Tawna, Keelah, all of our people are here," Tia's voice spoke of her awe as she gazed at the many faces smiling at her.

A beautiful red haired woman stood watching this great show of affection. Beside her stood two people Tia had never seen before but whom she instantly recognized. She moved to where they stood waiting for her. "Gram," she took Charlotte's small hands in hers. "You're young again, and just as beautiful as I remember."

"Tia, at long last I can introduce you to your father and at the same time let you see the woman you never knew."

Without saying a word Tia hastened her steps to the outstretched arms waiting to embrace her.

"We're glad to have you home, Tia," Jessie said, snuggling her child close to her.

With much love, Two Spirits kissed the side of her face. "Now we will never be apart again, my daughter."

Much later after everyone had welcomed her back home, Tia and Appearing Wolf wondered away to be by themselves.

"Why are you so quiet, Aakiiwa?" Appearing Wolf asked her.

"I am trying to understand how you could have given all of this up to stay behind. Did you not know what waited for you here?"

"No, Tia .I had not passed into the light. I knew I had to find you. You were my bridge to the sun. I did not wish to be here without you."

"But, Appearing Wolf, you could have been here with our son and all of our people."

"Tia you are my heart." He took her face in his hands to kiss her. "Without you, my spirit had no reason to live."

Tia laid her head on Appearing Wolf's chest secure in the arms wrapped around her. "Our people look so healthy and happy here. Even Pehta is young again. How can this be?"

"Everyone is young and healthy here, Tia. Our spirits are free. Only the body ages and falls prey to disease and harm."

"If only people knew that there is no death all their fears would be gone and they could spend their lives happy."

"But there is death, Tia, death of the body. It is the soul that lives forever."

"If we could tell them what they have waiting for them it would make everything so much easier."

"We cannot do this. If they knew then they would not strive to perfect their souls and that is why we live many lives." Appearing Wolf kissed the tip of her nose.

"I never wish to live another life. I want to stay here forever safe with the love of our son and all our people surrounding us." She snuggled closer in his arms.

Slipping an arm around her waist he walked back to camp with her. Secure in the knowledge that now he would never lose her, and confident that, here in the valley of the sun, death was not the end, but the beginning.

About the Author

Judith Ann McDowell is a novelist with four finished books. When not working on a manuscript, Judith along with her husband like to travel to different cities such as New Orleans to talk with people about voodoo and to talk with those who have experienced firsthand, true hauntings.

Judith is the mother of four grown sons Guy and David and Rhett and Nick and lives in the Pacific Northwest with her husband Darrell and their two Pekingese Chi and Tai and three cats Isis and Lacy and Keefer.

Judith is at present working on her next novel.